CW01424723

THE PUBLISHER'S TALE

Or

· THE TUSITALA

By

Terence F. Moss

*Dedicated to friends
no longer with us.*

Other works by the author.

Angels and Kings (Musical)
Sole Traders (Musical)
The Inglish Civil War (pilot TV Comedy)
Closing Time (pilot TV Comedy)
Dave (pilot TV Comedy)
The prospect of Redemption 2011
The Killing Plan 2013

Contacts.
Terence F. Moss can be contacted at
WWW.ANGELSANDKINGS.CO.UK
THE-KILLING-PLAN@OUTLOOK.COM
Terence F. Moss on Facebook

`

Table of Contents

"He walks there quietly at your side or in your shadow and you don't care to even give him a second glance... and then one day he suddenly clears his throat and you are startled by his presence..."

2nd
TITLE
PAGE

Mesopotamia 1915

Am I dead?
Why do you ask?
I am not sure.
So how will you know for certain, if I answer
…I could tell you a lie?

I will trust you.
But if you would trust me, why not trust yourself?
Because I do not know for certain, that I am alive.
You could lie to yourself.
I could, but that is why I am asking you.
Why?
I need to be sure.
But can you be sure of anything?

Can I ask you another question?
Of course.
Are you dead?
Not dead, not as you would understand.
So what is your name?
My name; Ah well my name it means nothing,
for it comes in many tongues and on many
tides and is infinite.

Why do you talk in riddles?
Because all life is a riddle, have you not yet realised   that?
Am I dead?

It was a cold grey early Sunday morning and the overnight bombing of the allied trenches and the pitiless area of no-man's land in between the furrows of hopelessness and despair had been particularly intensive. The Turks intention was to comprehensively demoralise the English long before they had prepared for their next advance and they were succeeding in their objective.

The Turkish intelligence reports indicated the English were intending to make a major push forward that morning. So they had taken advantage of the heavy overnight rain to ensure the patch of barren wasteland that existed between them; the ground that was being so bitterly fought over; was as inhospitable as possible for the next assault.

The earth had been turned into a raging quagmire of mud and the dismembered parts of unrecovered decaying bodies from previous failed assaults. The greyed eyes that now gazed with bewilderment to heaven, left for the crows to peck out - the remains of the bodies, for the rats and foxes to ravage for they too must also hope to survive.

The darkened swamp of human detritus was eighteen inches deep in places and that alone would severely impede any movement towards the enemy position. The malodorous foetid stench of degeneration was always there in the air, the bittersweet aroma of death that would always linger in your memory, the essence trapped deep within the nasal passages for a lifetime, if you were destined to have a lifetime to expect.

Creeping stealthily over the sides of trenches and rolling along the walkways, the mist of putrefaction would have deterred any sane person from venturing one yard further into this cesspit of hell, this fiery furnace of gases, flames, disorder, chaos and noise… the sound of failure and death. If the fetor, the sulphurous anal halitosis of decay did not make you wretch, then the thought of certain death, which could be, only a few moments away certainly would. Worse still, the ever-present threat of partial dismemberment, the final insult that you should linger on, to survive to tell the tale of how you had ceased to be that which you once were. That boy, that bloodied perfect body delivered from your mother's womb in a moment of

EXULTATION

sublime ecstasy held high in praise to a God, now transformed by another perfect body into something that you could never, in your maddest hallucinations, your worst nightmares ever have imagined.

FAILURE

The visions and memories gently torment your mind as you crawl back through the detritus of death, with maybe only one leg or one arm - the batsman who once scored a tireless century cheered on by team, by friends, and by lover - never again. His talent won the day, but never more. NO The Cambridge blue no longer able to pull an oar as before, one arm now a withered blackened stump. No longer trailing fingers in the Cam. JUST EMPTY SLEEVES.

THE SOLDIER

HOLDS ONTO

Although hopelessly dying, he still has a vague belief that if he could make it to the safety of his own furrow, that place he had left only a few minutes earlier, then he might live, but he probably wouldn't. What the Turks could not finish; the exigencies of a prolific choice of possible injuries, the dearth of medical personal, facilities and medicine most certainly would.

OF RESPITE OR SAFETY

SOMY ENEMY

With the Turks holding the slightly higher ground, the blood soaked rain that refused to mix any further with the waterlogged mud slowly ran back into the potholes and into the English trenches, trickling down the sides of the mud and sandbag walls, darkened umber rivulets of life.

The assignment today was an impossible manoeuvre, uphill, bad ground, barbed wire, heavily fortified, and outgunned. The expectation of success was extremely low if at all - the probability of survival past the first five minutes virtually none existent. However, their instructions were explicit, unambiguous, clear, and precise without any room for discretion.

SO ELEQUENTLY

"We must take the trench at any cost; this could be a turning point in the war." This was the order cracked out by the sergeants,' who had been briefed by their captains.

"This could be the battle that sees the beginning of the end of this conflict," barked the captains and majors, oblivious to the madness of the generals. But there would be no end to this conflict for many years, just the end of

MORE LIVES,

thousands of lives squandered on a foreign land. Fodder for
the foxes, eyes for the crows.

INFANTRY

The English guns stopped pounding the Turkish
position at five minutes to eight; even the English were not
stupid enough to bomb their own soldiers. A pallid misty
cloud crept slowly over the field of play between the lines.
The protocols of engagement appeared to indicate that
surprise was extremely bad form and definitely "not
cricket".

The English had effectively given the Turks a very
decent five-minute warning. Time enough to prepare
themselves for another easy slaughter of the virgin soldiers.

The whistle blew and the officers and soldiers climbed
up the short ladders to crawl over the top of the trenches
and ready themselves to stand up and charge forward…
screaming, shouting, bayonets fixed, ready for the battle to
commence.

guns

Captain Phillips led his platoon of thirty men out of the
trench with his Webley pistol held firmly in his hand.
Sergeant Drew ran swiftly, ever diligently by his side
encouraging the men to keep in a straight line. The flames
of hell leapt out from the Turkish lines decimating half the
platoon within seconds. Shooting fish in a barrel does not
even come close to describe the killing.

The grim reaper rode merrily amongst them waving his
sword and laughing, laughing at the idiocy of it all, the
takings today would be good and his thirst would be
quenched in full. He had no need to make any further calls
for a while, at least not until his thirst returned.

Artillery shells landed everywhere separating men from
their extremities, heads disappeared, men disappeared,
vaporised by the heat and shrapnel of exploding shells.
Captain Phillips was still in front when the ratchet of
machine gun fire severed his leg… he stood precariously
for a few moments, a solitary dazed figure on a single
spindle and then fell. The machine guns swept the ground
around him again throwing up large clusters of mud and
water, but he was lost in the mud, and they could not find
him. Two soldiers ran towards to where he fell, but another

HE   THE PLACE?   HAD FALLEN
THE SPOT

shell landed close by and they were gone in an instant a red mist slowly descending to earth was all that remained.

Sergeant Drew had been drawn to the left of his position in order to avoid a large bomb crater, but seeing Phillips fall to his right he turned and made his way back around the crater to where his Captain had fallen. The machine guns followed his path as he ran, raking the ground with their dancing pirouettes of death, close, but not close enough to do any harm. Drew defied them to do their worst and after a few minutes arrived back at the place, where Phillips had fallen, now lying face down in the mud. Turning him over, Drew could see that he was still alive although seriously wounded. BUT POSITION

The machine gunners mercilessly continued to fire on Drew, seemingly concerned that one man endeavouring to save another man's life might be a serious danger to them or might even change the outcome of the day. No time for honourable intentions, mercy, or compassion, that would be left for another day. JEOPARDISE MIGHT END

For whatever reason the gunners could not find their mark that day and Drew, seemingly impervious to all the carnal butchery being played out around him, slowly dragged Captain Phillips backwards towards the bomb crater he had just passed and they both fell into the relative safety of being below ground level. Drew carefully looked over the edge of the crater to see how his men were fairing, unsure as to whether he should resume his position as platoon leader or endeavour to try to save the life of Captain Phillips. But they were all gone, a half dozen had made it to the barbed wire defence, but had been shot to pieces and hung like unloved rag dolls on a line. NOW SLOWLY

The battle raged on above, but he knew he could do no more. Drew slipped back into the crater and looked across at Captain Phillips who was unconscious and still bleeding badly from where his leg had once been. He took off his belt and tunic and using his bayonet ripped the tunic in half. He slipped this over the tattered remains of Captain Phillips's leg just above the knee and wrapped it around his thigh. He then tied his belt tightly round the thigh to staunch the bleeding. It was at this moment that he became

SEVERED

aware of somebody else in the crater. He turned quickly to see an elegant man shrouded in a grey cloak, sitting on the other side of the pothole. Was this the reaper thought Drew gazing at the man, he looked up to the sky expecting death at any moment, but there was nothing. He reached for his Captains pistol and pointed it at the figure.

'Who the hell are you,' demanded Drew?

The figure seemed unconcerned by the battle raging above and even less so about the pistol now facing him. *POINTED AT HIS FACE*

'I am intrigued by your wanton disregard for your own safety and your heroism,' he replied, 'I thought you might require my services.'

'Who are you,' repeated Drew, 'are you a doctor?'

'I am many things, the darkness in your soul, the fear you cannot hide, the you, that you would rather never know. I am your revenge and your strength to smite your enemy and those who have betrayed you.'

'I have no time for your riddles,' shouted Drew, 'tell me who you are or I will shoot you where you stand.'

'I am sitting,' replied the man instantly, looking at Drew with a curious expression.

Drew, stunned by the man's ill-timed flippancy replied... 'Sitting, standing it makes no difference, tell me who you are or...?'

The man smiled. 'I am your friend and I choose my friends very carefully. My name is Mephisto.'

Mephisto? What kind of name is that? Are you a fucking Turk?

'No I am not.' replied the man indignantly, 'Mephisto is the name I travel under. I am a man of the world, a man of many names, but not from any country.'

'You talk in conundrums and puzzles and you make no sense. But if you are a friend then you will help me to carry Captain Phillips back to our lines,' pleaded Drew.

'I will help you my friend in good time,' replied Mephisto. *ALL*

'There is no time, he is dying,' exclaimed Drew who was now becoming frustrated at the strangers apparent inability to fully comprehend the magnitude of Captains Phillips wounds.

'He will not die,' replied Mephisto.

'What?' exclaimed Drew astounded by the man's arrogant declaration?

'I told you, he will not die, whatever the outcome of our discussion he will not die today or any day for that matter, not from this wound anyway. He will die eventually of course, as we all must, but not for many years.'

Drew felt a power begin to engulf his body, a sense of immense wellbeing, something he had briefly felt when he was much younger, but not since. His immediate fears and concerns for Captain Phillips began to ease. It felt as if he were taking communion and all his sins were being forgiven. He lowered his gun and rendered himself up to this man who called himself Mephisto

'Alright,' said Drew, 'what do you want?'

'Can you feel anything?' asked the man.

'Yes, yes I can,' replied Drew.

'Do you know what that is?' he asked.

'I'm not certain,' Drew replied.

'Yes you are, you know exactly what it is,' replied Mephisto. He smiled and moved his head around in a small circle as if he had a neck ache.

'You tell me, if you know everything, you tell me what it is?' said Drew with challenging belligerence.

'Immortality, that is what you feel right now and that is what I can offer you, immortality.'

'To live forever?' asked Drew.

'Not quite forever, but a very long time, for you that is, but I cannot wait forever.'

Drew wondered want he meant. 'Who are you to tender such a gift?'

'Whoever you want to be,' said Mephisto.

'Only the devil can offer such a prize and as I remember there is always a price to pay.' *SomeOne Always pays THE TILLERMAN COMMAN*

'Of course there is a cost; I want your soul eventually, but not just yet, in a few years, when you are probably finished with it and our contract is concluded. Anyway, no man really wants to live forever, just a little longer than everybody else does. Sufficient time to enable them to satisfy all their essential needs, desires and objectives.

So you will only be trading something in the future that you will have no further use for, for something far more valuable now, oh, and there's one other benefit, that may be of interest.'

'What' said Drew?

'How old are you?' asked Mephisto. *BE ... AGE*

'Twenty five years.' replied Drew, 'why?'

'You shall remain this age, until the bargain is fulfilled.' *THAT MEANT ANYTHING TO ME*

'But I have already lost everything so what good is immortality to me. That would just be one purgatory exchanged for another,' questioned Drew. *KIND OF*

'Not quite,' replied Mephisto, 'I will give you immortality until you have taken back a wife, a daughter and everything that belonged to you, that which the perpetrators of that theft took away. But on the day you take possession of the last of those goods your soul will be mine forever, agreed? *FOR AS LONG AS IT TAKES*

Drew laid back against the mud wall, the crater slowly filling with water and looked across at Captain Phillips moaning quietly as he drifted in and out of consciousness, but he noticed that the bleeding had stopped which was a little unusual in his experience. He looked back at this stranger, but said nothing. *AND CONSIDERED HIS THE PROPOSAL*

'What have you to lose? entreated Mephisto, 'Your life was over anyway, your novel was stolen, all the money that should have been yours has been taken, your wife left you for another man, your daughter died because you were too poor to pay for a doctor and now maybe your friend is going to die, oh and your platoon are all dead...' He popped his head over the side of the pothole, and had a

AND THEY DIED

quick look around, 'except that is for a few mumblers and grumblers and they will be dead soon enough, when they eventually decide it is time to give up.'

'You said he wouldn't die, no matter what.' exclaimed Drew.   *Pointing at Phillips*

'So I did, fair enough, he lives, but you will have to carry him back.'

'How did you know about...' but he stopped, for he now knew who he was talking to, this was no delusion.

'Why me?' asked Drew, 'and why today?'

'I like tragedy, it satisfies a desire,' replied Mephisto, 'it's very much the same as comedy, two sides of the same coin in fact,' he smiled and casually leaned back. 'Life and theatre is all about timing you know and good timing can intrigue and entertain an audience.' He took out a packet of cigarettes and lit two, offering one to Drew, 'and this entertains me.'

Drew took the cigarette. 'You think this is funny?'

'No, not at all. I did not say that... in fact, I think this is a tragedy. I just like to pick my moments for the best dramatic effect.' Mephisto smirked again.

Drew said nothing for maybe ten seconds. He was deliberating over a decision that would change his life forever, but as the man had said; "what did he have to lose?"

'I want him to live!' exclaimed Drew suddenly, pointing at Captain Phillips.

'I have already agreed to that, you can have him as a gift... whether you trade or not.'

'I wouldn't need to trade if we both got back?' queried Drew.

'I didn't say you would both get back alive.'

'Oh!' Said Drew, 'I thought that...'

'You thought wrong. You would carry him back to your lines safely and then at the very last moment just as you thought you had made it and you were slipping safely back into your trench... Bang! Lucky shot right between the eyes and you're dead, bloody sniper.'

'That's outrageously unfair!' exclaimed Drew.

Mephisto laughed. 'Of course it is that is life, have you not worked that one out yet? It is all one big outrageously appalling joke, but then maybe not, who knows?' He laughed again, pulled out a sword from a scabbard, and swished it in the air and the sun began to shine with intense brilliance.

'So here we are, decision time,' said Mephisto who was now eating a banana, something that Drew had only seen once before in his life. Mephisto offered half the banana to Drew, but he declined, more out of disbelief then for any other reason.

'So what do I do?' said Drew, still a little confused, but now succumbing to the offer.

'Nothing much,' replied Mephisto, taking another drag on his cigarette and blowing some smoke rings into the air. 'Just climb out of here and carry your Captain back home. If you haven't declined my offer by the time you get back into your trench you will both arrive safely, but if you say the words "You may never take my soul" between here and there, then you may be shot, I don't know, it depends, but that would have happened anyway and that's nothing to do with me. My partner deals with fate, it's a sort of job share arrangement we have,' he smiled.

Drew sat for a few moments gazing at Mephisto, who was finishing off his banana then turned to pick up his Captain and begin his struggle to pull him over the edge of the crater, but he could not gain purchase on the sodden ground at first and kept slipping back.

'Can you give me a hand?' asked Drew.

Mephisto laughed, 'I have already given you his life what more do you want... you will manage.'

Just at that moment, he somehow seemed to find an inner strength; enough to enable him lift the heavy almost lifeless body out of the pothole. Then he clambered out and half lifting his captain onto his shoulder he pulled him up and began to slowly make his way back to his lines. The machine guns immediately began to rake the ground around him, but once again, they could not find their mark. He made it back to the trench and carefully lowered Captain Phillips down to waiting hands, totally disregarding the bullets landing all around him.

He turned to face the position where the crater was where they had been sitting and as he did so, a shell landed in the crater and there followed an enormous explosion. Drew said nothing and slipped over the sand bags back into the waterlogged trench to the cheers of his fellow warriors.

The devil's supply of souls needs to be constantly replenished for without them he cannot inhabit the earth. Today Gideon had made a trade, but at what cost to his very being, was his very existence now in jeopardy for a fools bargain.

Chapter 1

1984

This story really starts long after it has already begun and finishes somewhere before the end. In fact, the end is actually the beginning in a manner of speaking. It is for you, the reader, to determine where and when it reaches its final destination and from where it could have begun.

Blake Thornton, sitting in his study, leaned back in his slightly tattered, green leather captain's chair and looked at the photograph of his wife Catherine and their two children, Max and Claudia. The antique silver picture frame had been a present from Catherine on his thirty fourth birthday back in 1981 - with the photograph, which she'd, had professionally taken. That had been one of the happiest moments in his life.

'Something to inspire your wearisome days,' She whispered as she gave him the present. 'Something for you to look at every day, and when you do, you will know that I will always be looking over you and no matter what happens I will always love you,' and then she'd gently kissed him. It was a declaration of love unlike anything he had heard before. Then she had grabbed his hands and pulled him to his feet.

'Dance with me Thornton and show me how much you love me,' she had commanded. Blake wasn't a very good dancer and had always been a little shy about it, but with Catherine, it had always felt different. It was as if nothing else mattered in the world, it was just the two of them. Catherine touched the play button on the stereo system and Billy Joel's "All about Soul" started to play and they began to dance together before slowly falling back onto the sofa kissing and caressing each other and eventually making love on the floor. The children were in bed fast asleep.

Blake was surprisingly comforted by Catherine's simple words, he never felt he needed protection, but for some reason on that occasion, he found them strangely reassuring, but how little did he appreciate the prophetic irony of what she had said. Blake loved the photograph and the sentiment because it reminded him of how uncomplicated things had once been before the manuscript for Prospect Road arrived at his office just one year later.

Like most people, he loved to receive presents and enjoyed surprises, but he particularly cherished this photograph for it marked another very special moment in time, a moment that he would never forget. On that day, Catherine had also told him she was pregnant again. It also marked the year he officially took over completely from Reggie Clanford as the owner of Clanford and Fox book publishers and literary agents. A few months later Catherine lost the unborn baby and thinking back, Blake began to wonder if maybe that was when things had begun to change.

After a few moments, his mind wandered back further to 1968 to when he first joined Clanford and Fox as a new manuscript reader and proof editor. He was just twenty-one and fresh out of university having gained a first in English Literature and History. He wasn't sure what he would do with his life and had visions of maybe going into television, even the newspaper business and then quite unexpectedly with serendipitous intervention this job had turned up. He had been having a drink in a Chelsea wine bar with Sean - a friend from university and Sean had mentioned the vacancy at a publishing house. Sean had already been offered a job with another company so he was not going to bother attending the interview, but suggested Blake might want to consider it. It sounded interesting, he was broke, so he telephoned the company, arranged an interview, was offered the job on the spot, and accepted it; little realising just how much that decision would affect the rest of his life.

Blake got on well with Reggie Clanford right from the start. Reggie had taken him under his wing and within a couple of years, he was treating him like the long lost son he had never had. Fortunately, Blake had a natural flair for the business, getting on well with authors, understanding their foibles, idiosyncrasies, eccentricities, whims, whimsies and occasional strange ways. They were invariably secular and yet spiritual in presence and happily inhabited their own existence with the ease of a tortoise permanently ensconced in its shell. Their most highly valued asset invariably being the independence and freedom they had won from mortal interference, and this they had accomplished by writing novels that allowed the reader to temporarily escape from their own humdrum existence, be it only for a few precious hours.

This privacy, Blake would defend to his last breath and writers appreciated this. He had concluded that most writers lived in their own microcosmic world, totally detached from the reality of a normal existence. This was essential if they were to continue creating interesting characters and engaging stories out of their own and beyond the imagination of ordinary people.

To a small extent, they had to be protected from the real world; reality and creativity were never good bedfellows. He would nurture their ideas and ambitions and listen to their problems, but never ingratiate himself or give the appearance of obsequiousness or sycophancy for that would demean and eventually destroy the delicate balance and dynamic of their relationship.

They repaid his empathetic indulgence by remaining steadfastly loyal to the company once they had become more successful. Some of their authors could possibly have sold more books by switching to larger publishers, but writers mostly wrote for something more than just financial gain. This much he clearly understood.

Clanford and Fox had been small book publishers for over a hundred years; the business - originally started by Joshua Clanford and Obadiah Fox back in Edwardian times - had majored in writers of the ilk of Dickens and Conan Doyle, storytellers with a hint of darkness about them. Unfortunately, for Clanford and Fox, none of their authors had achieved quite the same recognition and popularity as Dickens and Doyle, but they had still found commercially viable success with the authors they had published. They had also managed to stay in business to the present day, which in itself was no mean accomplishment in these changing times for publishing industry.

Now it was his business, since Reginald Clanford had actively retired nearly three years ago and handed over the last remnants of control and all the shares one year later when he died in 1981.

Freddy Fox, Reggie's junior partner, and Obadiah Fox's son had died back in 1966 a couple of years before Blake started working there; apparently, he had committed suicide. The one anomaly being that he had left a suicide note which nobody could understand. The note simply said …"For the sins that must be atoned"… it was all very enigmatic and made no sense to Reggie or Freddie's wife Amelia. For some unexplainable reason in his will, Freddy had explicitly left his complete shareholding of twenty five percent of the shares of Clanford and Fox to Reggie, with nothing being left to his wife, so Reggie Clanford now owned all of the shares in the company. However, Reggie feeling a little embarrassed by Freddie's largesse had offered to provide a small provision for Amelia to receive an annual remuneration from the company, sufficient for her needs and this she had gratefully accepted. Reggie could never understand why Freddie had done what he did.

Obviously, not every suicide comes with an explanation, but there is usually some sort of rational that can be applied to such a deliberate act. In Freddy's case, there was nothing apart from the cryptic note. He was happy at work and in his home life and the business was doing well. Reginald had never gone into any detail about the circumstances except to say that they had been the best of friends for many years, never having a cross word then suddenly one day Freddy changed completely and three months later, he was gone.

Blake's mind shot forward to 1982, just over two years ago, when he had been sitting in the same office talking to his assistant Jamie about the schedule of manuscripts they had to read over the long may bank holiday weekend. Fortunately or maybe not, in his job he was able to work at home at any time that was convenient, just doing what he really enjoyed most, which was reading stories. He had probably read the first three chapters of something like twenty five thousand new books over the last sixteen years, and something in the region of nearly three thousand all the way through to the final chapter. This particular book had been brought to his attention by Jamie who had already read the opening chapters. The editorial reading process had changed considerably since the early days when he first started in 1968 and was now a fully established format. One of the four junior book editors would read the opening chapters and then make a decision as to whether it was worthy of a second reading by Jamie or Marcus the two senior editors. If the senior editor considered the first five thousand words had some literary merit they would request a full copy of the book and then read it again.

If it managed to pass through these three reading stages without too many issues then it would be passed to Blake for him to read, with the benefit of the in house editorial comments, for him to make a final decision as to what they would do next.   To ASSIST in MAKNG

This was precisely what happened when Prospect Road, an autobiographical novel written by an Anthony Theodore Clackle arrived at the office in March 1982. The full manuscript had now been read by Jamie and passed to Blake for a final decision.

10 Settle that clause
in this WILL

Prospect Road 1

Chapter One
Written by
Anthony Theodore Clackle
Thomas Drayton's Story

Aged 6.

My name is Thomas Edward Drayton and I was born in the month of July 1947. It was a very hot summer following one of the coldest winters on record. I do not remember being born; neither do I have any recollection of the long hot summer. I was informed of these details later, once I had attained an age when I could understand the relevance.

The first full colour memory of my existence on planet earth was Coronation day 2nd June 1953 a national holiday. I was nearly six years old. No doubt, all the preceding days had been blessed with colour as well, but for me this particular one was very memorable and completely different from all the other days of my life up to that point. It was a little overcast to start - it had rained overnight and left things a little damp, but the temperature had warmed up as the hours passed and it eventually became a truly memorable day. As I can remember, I had a wonderful time.

This was a day full of promise, many promises now looking back... during a period of great excitement, enthusiasm and exuberance. We had been delivered from the carnage of war eight years previously, although I was not actually around at the time, merely a by-product of the continuing celebrations after six years of conflict.

Rationing was still being imposed, but there was also a hint of exhilaration in the air, a sense of expectancy, and a feeling that things would change. No one seemed to know how he or she would change, just that he or she would and it would be "for the better" as everybody kept saying...

It was as if we were all at the beginning of something wonderful, a journey into the unknown. It felt like those last few days of eager anticipation and excitement just before starting out on a holiday. We hadn't arrived yet, but we knew when we did it would be fun and we would enjoy every minute of it. The country had been suffering from all kinds of shortages for many years, but now things were going to be different, better. Fortunately, I did not suffer from many shortages, as I had never been aware of them in the first place. What you had never had you never missed, as they used to say.

Mind you, I don't think we, that is everybody else who lived in prospect Road, suffered that much from government rationing during the war or directly afterwards anyway.

Apparently, I and everybody else had a ubiquitous relation who we all referred to as Uncle Jim, no matter what the familial relationship was. I called him Uncle Jim, my mother called him Uncle Jim, and all the people in the shops called him Uncle Jim - even the old bill called him Uncle Jim. I found it all a little odd and a very confusing at times. Anyway, it turned out that he was known as Uncle Jim by local tradition. This was an epithet decorously granted to anybody who could always be relied upon to turn up with whatever anybody desired, (within reason) be it sugar, butter, nylons, chocolate, coffee, bananas or even petrol. He had been successfully plying his "trade" throughout the war and for some years after. He appeared to be completely unaffected by the vagaries of Mr Hitler's attempts to prevent us from enjoying such luxuries and utterly oblivious to the government's rationing legislation, (whatever that was). Parsimony and frugality were alien words to Uncle Jim, a complete anathema to his open-minded theories on free trade, which he would articulately defend on any night of the week in the Sailors Return public house, on the corner of Prospect Road. Once again, as with so many of my earlier recollections, they are almost all entirely dependent on third hand information passed onto me, much later in my life. But so vividly were they retold that I now feel certain that I must have heard them first hand after all, however inconceivable that may sound.

He carried on his lucrative business of supplying unobtainable merchandise up until 1954, when rationing

25

finished and everything began to become more generally available. After that, I believe he went back on the road, like a wisp of smoke in a gentle breeze, he was suddenly gone, and I never saw him again.

He was a fascinating character, the likes of which I have no doubt turned up all over the country during this period, tinker traders who kept everybody adequately supplied with the simple luxuries of life.

I later learnt that he was of Romany extraction, a fact that was, a little oddly, always greeted with an element of hushed mysticism and mild disdain whenever mentioned in general conversation. I never did manage to work out precisely why it was that this should make any difference to his innate ability to procure these little luxuries or why he was apparently exempt from conscription.

Uncle Jim had been living with my grandmother during the war, apparently as a lodger. My grandfather (Grandad Bob) had been away in North Africa at the time. He was a little unlucky being forty-three years of age at the outbreak of hostilities and had therefore still been subject to the call-up.

During the war and after it had ended, Uncle Jim, somewhat a little ostentatiously, drove around Portsmouth in an old American Pink Cadillac car selling his black market goods from the extremely large boot. I can vaguely remember the pink Cadillac making flying visits to various address's in Prospect Road around about the time of the Coronation. The only reason I remember this is because the lurid colour stood out so vividly in a landscape predominantly of grey (the warships moored at the end of the road and the pavements) brown (rusted corrugated iron everywhere and the mud) black (everything that could be painted seemed to be painted black) and dark green for anything not painted black. Bright colours were definitely a bit of a rarity in those days.

Many years later, I pondered on how Uncle Jim had managed to avoid the long arm of the law for so long when he drove around conducting his business in the most gregariously outrageous car in Portsmouth.

Eventually I came to the conclusion that they too, must also have been grateful recipients of his trading activities and therefore he had effectively become an "untouchable," or at least someone you didn't bother with if you wanted a pineapple for Sunday tea or some fresh coffee. All this of course was apocryphal and undoubtedly very colourfully embellished over time. I was not really aware of him until I was about four or five and by then his luxury goods empire had begun to crumble. AT THE BOYES

This was now a time to rebuild our damaged country and mend our broken lives and we were encouraged to make plans for the future and most of us did one way or another. On coronation day, my mother, Mary Florence Drayton, but known just as Flo (she was always making plans for something or other) dressed me up, with some satin supplied by the nefarious Uncle Jim, to look like Sabu the Elephant boy. I believe he was a Kipling character Sabus immortalised in a very popular film of the same name from Book the late 1930's. My mother covered my body with some sort of peculiar smelling brown stain, which she had concocted from potassium permanganate (she told me this much later in life) and mud as far as I could make out. My life, as I would later learn, would be peppered with unusual and strange experiences relating to potions and mixtures, concoctions and customs. Macbeth's weird sisters had nothing on my mother.*

I can still remember trying to remove the stain from between my toes, weeks after the party had finished. Eventually I had to resort to having a bath... ahhh.

Twenty Years later I clearly remember using this exact same concoction to soak my feet (without the mud this time.) Apparently, it prevented them from smelling so cheesy, a serious problem when trying to attract members of the opposite sex... (This was another suggestion from my mother).

Flo, as most mothers do, played a large part in forming my views on what life would be like and what I could expect. Fortunately, I also inherited her innate ability to think for myself. This would hold me in good stead for the rest of my life. It wouldn't make me rich, but it would make

me happy, very happy for a while. Fortunately, I did not inherit a number of my mother's stranger tendencies, one of which was a peculiar ritual she enacted every Halloween. For some reason, which I could never fathom out then and have still not been able to fathom out now, on this particular night, she always took the opportunity to play games with the devil and the occult. This concerned me greatly. On the night in question a number of my precious toy lead soldiers (Christmas presents) would invariably disappear never to return. Coincidently, during the latter part of the evening my mother would start to heat up a saucepan, which unbeknown to me, had my lead soldiers in it. Once melted she would have the three of us (my sister Lizzie and I) stand around a large basin of cold water and then she would put her hand on one of our heads utter some kind of strange incantation and then drop some of the boiling lead into the water. This would immediately form a very odd shape, which she would retrieve from the water and then carefully view before telling us what out futures would hold. As you can imagine we were both in awe of this quasi-demonic ceremony, which she religiously conducted for many years, until all my soldiers had disappeared.

[handwritten margin note: WAS THIS SOWING SEEDS FOR THE FUTURE.]

[handwritten margin note: HELD FOR UP]

Flo made a turban for me out of green satin, which she carefully wrapped around my head. She completed the ensemble with a sort of Indian shirt and baggy trousers, which she had made from a red satin material - she was a dab hand on the Singer sewing machine, most mothers were just after the war. I must have looked a picture wandering up and down Prospect Road giving the impression of a refugee with serious sartorial issues or possibly a miniature trainee pimp from a Bombay Harem. (Needless to say, I didn't know what a pimp was at that time).

My sister Elizabeth was dressed up as Nell Gwynne and as I recall she didn't have any real oranges, apparently uncle Jim couldn't manage to source any, so she had to make do with some green apples painted orange or possibly, they had been dipped in the same concoction I had been dipped in. And so we spent the whole of that amazing day wondering up and down Prospect road, in and out of *everybody's house eating and drinking whatever treats we were given.*

The whole of the centre of the road was taken up with tables covered in Union Jack paper and there was bunting strung between the houses. That is where there were houses still standing, as directly opposite Number 4 where we lived, the houses numbered 1-3-5-7 had been hit by a bomb and were no more. My Uncle Keith and Auntie Jenny lived at Number 9. Families lived together in little communes in those days, much the same as today in some poorer areas. But the concept of family ties and mutual community commitment was beginning to be eroded by social engineering. Then the houses were terraced, small, intimate and basic, but nevertheless adequate for our needs.

I have never again experienced that same feeling of family togetherness, unity, and community as I did during those early years. There was something satisfying and comforting about living within walking distance of your relations. Something that I believe, is primitive in its concept and although this was palliated with the total absence of privacy I still found it profoundly reassuring and heartening. There was a sense of wellbeing and wholesomeness; even, I suppose, a nod to purity in its most simplistic form. Religion was important in those days. We looked forward to baptisms, christenings, confirmations, and weddings, all the affirmations of life and commitment. These were always very special days and we (Lizzie and I) always went to Church on Sundays. I didn't really know what it was all for - it served as a moral compass giving us direction I suppose, but that simple life lifted my spirits and roused my soul every single day. Something, sadly I do not believe happens quite so much these days. Now there is intensity, tension, and anxiety in almost everything we do. I am not that naïve to believe that rape, murder, robbery, genocide and various other criminalities are any less prevalent today than they were back then, I just didn't notice it.

~~~

On this very special day, the tables were covered in plates of sausage rolls, lemonade, Cherryade, Tizer and crumpets - sandwiches, cakes and blancmange - sweets and even some chocolate. There were probably many other things there as well, I don't remember.

In the latter part of the afternoon, I remember hearing the distant sound of a plaintive trumpet, sounding not unlike the United States cavalry announcing its arrival at the very last minute, just in time to save the day. I had seen this heart wrenching yet exhilarating spectacle regularly on Saturday mornings, when I visited the local fleapit (The Forum cinema.) We watched films about American pioneers looking for a new life and indigenous American Indians protecting their homelands, mercilessly killing each other with gay abandonment.

As the sound grew closer and fuller, I could just make out the distinctive thud of the bass drum banging out the infectious rhythm of life like an enormous heartbeat, the drumbeat growing louder and louder as it approached.

Then suddenly we were confronted with the all inspiring sight of the Salvation Army brass band swinging round the corner at the end of the road and proceeding to march majestically down Prospect road playing their hearts out as they made their way towards us with all the pomp and circumstance befitting this magisterial occasion. The buttons on their uniforms sparkled like diamonds in the afternoon sun and their brass instruments, highly polished and gleaming, flashed out streaks of sunlight, further enhancing this glorious moment.

All the old men - they probably weren't that old, they just seemed that way to me - who had been drinking in the Sailors Return public house on the corner of the road came out of the pub with pints of beer raised in the air and cheered the band as it passed. It was an enormously rousing and uplifting occasion and I felt oddly euphoric about the whole thing, it was something I had not experienced before and seldom since...

They continued marching down to the dockside at the end of the road and for one terrible moment, I thought they were going to walk straight down the slipway and into

Portsmouth harbour, my immediate concern being the terrible effect the mud would have on their shiny boots, but they didn't. Slowly, with sweeping elongation and absolute precision, they turned through ninety degrees into the road and then carefully turned again and began marching back up the other side. Once again, they passed all the bedecked tables and once again, they received a roaring ovation before eventually making their way up to the top of the road where they turned the corner and slowly disappeared into the sunset as they continued their journey to destinations and destinies unknown.

The celebrations went on into the night and I remember Lizzie and me looking out of the bedroom window down at the street below, completely mesmerized by the evening spectacle slowly unfolding before us. We watched as the tables were moved to one side and the adults began dancing the night away to the sounds of Mantovani and the Joe loss band being played on a record player. The streets lights cast an ethereal glow on the proceedings. The sounds of laughter carried on long after we had eventually fallen asleep. I would remember that day for the rest of my life.

Prospect Road 2

Chapter Two
Written by
Anthony Theodore Clackle

The following day was also a holiday, so we, that is Barry, Carol and I went down the slipway at the end of the road to play in the mud for a while......

The sailors on the destroyers and cruisers moored up to the quayside would throw pennies over the side for us to find in the sludge. They always threw more money if Carol was there. Already she had mastered the art of smiling coquettishly at them and her beguiling expression of heartfelt appreciation for the small gifts raining down seemed to work wonders. Her womanly charms already beginning to make an appearance, but not so that I had noticed still being naïve in these matters due to my age.

Barry lived at number fifteen and Carol lived in the next road, but she always came to play with us. I remember when I was about six or seven, I thought I would like to marry Carol because she made such really good mud castles and her mum always gave me a packet of Smith's crisps when I went round to her house for tea. Mind you, the Smith's factory was not that far away and everybody seemed to have a big square tin of Smith's crisps hidden under the stairs! I remember the big blue lorries used to park overnight at the end of the road on another bombsite. Some days we would walk around the other bombsite and postulate on the number of crisps inside the lorries. On some days, you could smell the fat from the factory frying the crisps. In summer, you could even taste the fried potato in the air. They only had one flavour...potato... with or without salt, which came wrapped up in a little blue twirl of waxed paper.

I can remember one very terrifying experience with Carol, well it wasn't exactly with Carol it was more to do with her mum and my mum. It was when we were about

32

seven and pretending to be married. We had gone back to my house one day to play a strictly platonic game of mummies and daddies in my bedroom and decided to get into bed like husbands and wives do. We were all cuddled up and happily chatting away completely oblivious to the sexual connotations of the situation.

We had shared a bed many times before when we were much younger, normally when my mum was going out for the evening and I had stayed at Carol's mum's house overnight. Therefore, it all seemed perfectly innocent to us. All of a sudden, my mum burst in looking horrified. She began shouting and screaming and jumping up and down and frightened us both. I thought she had gone mad. We jumped up out of bed and then my mum started whacking me on the legs with a cane while still shouting at me. I had absolutely no idea what was going on and Carol started crying profusely, totally confused by what was happening. My mother did not let up on the raging and ranting, and then out of nowhere, Carol's mum appeared at the bedroom door and there was even more shouting and screaming and jumping up and down and then more whacking with the cane. Carol's mum started beating Carol's legs until they were covered in wheals and welts and we both collapsed on the floor crying our eyes out, without a clue as to why we were being beaten. Eventually Carol was marched off home by her mother and I stayed in my room for days, except for when it was time for food or I wanted to go to the toilet. Ten years later, I began to understand what had gone through both our mother's minds. A classic example of childhood innocence being cruelly crushed and lost forever because of a simple misunderstanding and the seriously flawed and hypocritical morality of our parents. They had judged us by their own corrupt standards, a valuable lesson that I would remember for the rest of my life.

...anyway, the tide was coming in so we started to make our way back up the slipway to the road and went to play on to the bombsite where number 1,3,5,7, Prospect Road had once stood. All the bricks had now been taken away leaving lots of pieces of wood, complete doors, corrugated

iron sheets, odd bits of metal (probably bits of a bomb with my luck) and deep trenches everywhere - which had been used for dumping all sorts of unpleasant and unspeakable things over the years. This in turn had created an unusual mystifyingly musty pong, which I will never forget. The smell was always much worse in winter when the earth was very wet. Years later, I would think back to those trenches and wonder how they compared to the trenches in the First World War! Occasionally, as I grew older, I would catch a whiff of something very similar and immediately be transported back to my childhood years and to the bombsite and our underground kingdom.

We covered over the top of trenches with the sheets of corrugated iron or old wooden doors and as we were roughly the same height as the depth of the trenches, we could walk around almost invisible from above in our malodorous subterranean village. I do not remember much about what we did in there, but we would spend hours running around pretending to do something. Probably preparing our defence of Prospect Road against the next invasion.

Whenever it was lunchtime or teatime, my mum would stand outside of number 4 and bellow out my name. Invariably I would pop up from our subterranean empire with my head just visible above ground level and wave to her so she knew I had heard her. She always smiled when she saw me I always remember that. I think she loved me quite a lot. I also think everybody in the road (possibly the next road too) probably heard her, she had a very loud voice. I found out just how loud she could be during the bedroom incident with Carol. I thought then that my ears were going to bleed.

During the daytime, my mum always wore one of those flowered housecoats and a scarf on her head. I can still remember that once a week (I think it was on a Friday) she would go through the routine of polishing the front door step with Cardinal red polish. I have absolutely no idea why she used to do this other than the obvious observation that everybody else polished their steps. Some days, while on "duty" standing in our trench and gazing across the road, we would be entertained by the curious sight of a half dozen mothers all on their knees, heads covered in cotton scarves, happily polishing their steps, in perfect synchronisation, while simultaneously conducting various different conversations. This made no sense at all to me. I could only describe it as an extremely surreal setting for a song from a West End stage musical. (ONCE AGAIN THIS IS RETROSPECTIVE) I HAD NO IDEA WHAT A MUSICAL WAS

Some of the windows in the houses were still boarded up, eight years after the war. Occasionally washing lines would be hung out across the road with carpets hanging on them making the place look like a Bagdad market place. The road had been blown to bits in places, a quarter of the houses were gone and yet amongst all this would be this beacon of defiance, this bright shining front doorstep! I didn't know what to make of it then, and I still don't nearly thirty years later. All this seemed a bit of an ironic juxtaposition and yet amongst all the carnage and destruction my mum was polishing some bricks.

I also remember a character known as Bertie Coggins the local rag, bone, and scrap metal merchant at the end of the road with all the stuff he had collected stacked up inside and outside of his junkyard. (He stood out in my memory because everybody thought he was little more than a beggar and then one day he turned up in a brand new dark blue Humber Super Snipe motor car, the best car I had ever seen, which just goes to prove the old northern saying that "where there's muck there's brass." Everybody spoke very highly of Bert (or Bertram as he preferred to be called after purchasing the Humber) but nobody took any notice and we all continued to call him Bert, much to his displeasure.

When I had no money I would go round the houses and collect newspapers and take them to Bert and he would give me a penny a pound in weight. I also collected bear bottles and took them back to the pub to collect the deposit. I think that was about a halfpenny a bottle. All the money I made invariably went over the counter in "Auntie" Maureen's sweet shop, which was just round the corner in Commercial Road. It also sold Woodbine fags and matches. Next door to "Auntie" Maureen's was, and I am not making this up, "Auntie" Doreen's.

Doreen Cover and her husband Jack sold fruit and vegetables. Both Maureen and Doreen (which always made me giggle for some inexplicable puerile reason) were good friends with mum. They would come to all her parties (my mum loved to have a party) and they were always good to me. "Auntie Maureen", (she was not a real Auntie) would always bring me sweets when she came to babysit, so I was always pleased when she was coming round.

MUM TOLD ME

Next door to "Auntie Doreen" was, Eric Dimblebee - Barber & Hairdresser. What had always fascinated me about Mr Dimblebee was that as well as cutting hair he also sold Durex "Johnnies". Oddly, they were invariably stored tantalisingly high up in a glass cabinet right in front of you as you sat in the chair, ostensibly safely, but somewhat ironically out of harm's way.

I knew what they were, more or less or to be more accurate, I knew there was a tenuous link with sex, but I had no idea what that specific purpose was, not until much later in my life. But the strange mysterious connection between barber and condom stuck in my mind for many years. Up to the age of thirteen, I truly believed you could not have sex until you had your haircut. I used to look forward to having my monthly snip, eagerly anticipating that one day something miraculous would happen to me as it often appeared to happen to the other men that came in to Eric's.

'Something for the weekend sir?' That immutable phrase invariably muttered quietly and surreptitiously into the ear of the customer in order not to cause a panic I presumed. I waited patiently for the day when it would be uttered clandestinely into my ear, but it never was. Oh, those wistful days spent in glorious expectation of wondrous things that would happen to me at some point in the very near future, but they didn't, not for a long time, not until I was nearly nineteen.

The next two shops were not there, it was just a large hole and then there was Wilsons the Butcher shop and then The Royal Oak public house on next corner. As I remember, there seemed to be a Brickwoods pub on the corner of every road in Portsmouth. All Brickwoods pubs were ornately tiled outside and inside usually in shiny dark reds, greens and browns. Quite depressing really. Looking back, they were not dissimilar in design to public toilets and they didn't smell much better inside either.

Further along the road was a graveyard with iron railings running parallel with the road. In the middle was a large ornate arched cast iron entrance through which the hearse would bring the newest arrivals. The two large gates must have been about fifteen feet high and were both swung back to allow the cavalcade in for a burial. Quite often, Barry and I would just lean on the railings and watch the proceedings, discussing in some depth the merits of being dead. No school, no having to tidy our bedrooms, no having to be in bed early, no having to eat our greens, no having to wash, the list was endless, but on balance, we unanimously decided we would give it a go anyway, as being dead looked a little bit boring.

I only sort of half understood what was really happening. I remember a few years later I was passing the graveyard one day and noticed all the gravestones has been uplifted and were stacked against the back wall. I wondered whether there was time limit for how long you could stay in the ground and whether the time limit was up for everybody, but that didn't make any sense and some of the plots had only been filled a year or two earlier.

It transpired that the church had sold the graveyard to a petrol company and they were going to build a petrol station on it. The next we knew all the stones had gone and a new petrol filling station with four separate pumps had been built complete with a large canopy over the top and a shop. I often wondered what happened to all the souls of the departed bodies that hadn't had sufficient time to make the final transition. One day in the future, I might find out.

Anyway, back to Prospect Road. Quite often, there were piles of horseshit left in the road from the tradesman's carthorses. Oddly, canny Bertie never bothered to pick up his own horse's shit. He very kindly left it for budding entrepreneurs like me to handle that end of the market. Still I suppose if I had made a success of it, he might have considered taking me on as an apprentice at some later date.

During the summer, especially during the holidays Lizzie and I would collect the horse shit and then go knocking on doors to see if anybody wanted to buy it, to put on their vegetables. Mum used to shout at me if I called it horseshit and told me to call it garden manure or dung. I would wait patiently for the coalman or the milkman to pay the street a visit, and then I would be off.

'We're just going out to collect some horse shit mum,' I would shout endearingly up the stairs as we hurriedly left with bucket and coal shovel in hand. I especially used the shit word - I was very precocious when I was young having become aware of the delicate sensibilities of my mum and her friends - because I loved to hear her shout back in a despairingly hopeless tone 'its dung darling or manure or pooh, but not that word.' She always sounded so disdainful and that only made it worse as we found the pretentious inflection to be even more amusing...

'Yes mummy, we would reply,' and then wander off up the road saying to each other 'It's not horse shit darling it's pooh.' To which Lizzie would reply 'We are off to collect some poo... not shit... poo.'

'Actually manure sounds nicer,' I would say and Elizabeth would reply 'What! nicer than poo or nicer than horseshit.' This would be the tone of the conversation until we became bored.

But of course, Mum knew best as we would eventually come to learn. I didn't realise then that she had plans for much better things for us all.

'Would you like to buy some horse manure, penny a bucket,' we would politely ask when knocking on doors.

'Yes please, they would say. Could you take it round the back alley?'

Lizzie and I would fall about in fits of laughter when a customer told us he was going to put in on his Rhubarb....you know the rest. A year or two later horses were starting to be replaced by electric floats and lorries with petrol engines and the only person left who still used a *horse was the rag and bone man, who I am sure only did this out of a sense of nostalgia and also to help maintain his image of austerity. He didn't want people to think he was doing well, but even he now had his new car for going out on special occasions.* So HE HAD WELL AND TRULY KILLED THAT ILLUSION ~~ANY~~ ILLUS HE WAS TRYING TO CREATE

So our regular supply of merchandise began to literally dry up. Bert, the rag and bone man had become even sharper and had started to collect his own horse's dung and sell it when on his travels, so that supply of stock was slowly coming to an end, but we still used to collect newspapers and sell them to Bert right up to the day we moved away. Apart from Bertie; the milkman, the coalman, and the dustman also had horses, so I was never short of shit for long if I needed to make a few pennies, but they all eventually stopped using ~~horses~~. THEM

The French onion man, who came on a bike, was always a slightly suspect character, because I knew France was a long way away and I could not figure out why he would come all the way from France to England with just a few rings of onions a*round his neck. It just didn't seem viable even to my naïve business brain. I could understand the horse-shit trade of which I was virtually a connoisseur,* MASTER? *knowing it inside out and back to front in a manner of speaking, and that made perfect financial sense, but his didn't. I stayed awake for hours at night worrying about how he managed to make a living with all the costs of going backwards and forwards to France every day. It was a few years later that I found out that "Onion Johnny" had actually been living all the time with "Auntie" Doreen's sister Doris (whose husband was permanently stationed in Hong Kong). Onion Johnny had done a deal with Jack* AND STORED IT IS OTHER EQUIPMENT *(Doreen's husband) to store his onions in Jack's warehouse.* AT DORIS'S *So every day he just went round to the warehouse and picked up more onions to sling round his neck. Put on his silly beret and striped jumper then off he would go for the day. Apparently, he hadn't been back to France since the end of the war. The onions came from a farm in Petersfield. I was learning something new every day.*

FOR SOME REASON EVERYBODY SAID ONION JOHNNY'S ONION'S HAD A MUCH BETTER FLAVOR THAN ENGLISH ONIONS

The Crumpet man came on a bicycle pushing a little trailer in front, but that wasn't much use to me or my horticultural growth enhancement business.

I don't have many recollections of my dad in those days as he was nearly always away during the week working in Andover, Bournemouth or Guildford and many other faraway places I have now forgotten, but I would see him on most weekends. He worked as a window dresser for Hepworths or Burtons the tailors. I can't remember which. Many years later I would reflect back on this somewhat strange and fading occupation and only then, after long conversations with my mother during my early twenties, did I come to understand that he had been rampantly homosexual most of his life and that this particular occupation facilitated his predilection towards younger trainee window dressers of a similar persuasion.

Occasionally he would bring one of the trainee's home to stay with us for a few days. Heaven knows what the sleeping arrangements were, but fortunately, all this was unbeknown to me and of little consequence at the time, being relatively innocent in these matters. The imminently immerging age of open promiscuity would not arrive for another few years in the 1960's. Along with the decriminalisation of homosexuality in 1967. So for now, I remained naïvely ignorant of such things. It would be many years later, after I had learnt the ways of the world that I would fully comprehend the incongruous nature of my father's inclinations and my mother's apparent tacit acceptance of this peculiar ménage et trois. Despite this strange arrangement, my parents always appeared very devoted to each other and remained so until my father's death.

Sadly, a few years later in 1958, my adorable sister Lizzie was killed in a freak car accident. That left a big hole in my world and I missed her terribly not least because she was a very important part of our fertilizer business being the senior partner in charge of stock control (I looked after sales and marketing). I don't think my parents ever really recovered.

I grew a little closer to my father after Lizzie died, but I always knew that he never really got over her premature death, I don't suppose any parent would.

Sometimes I would come in on them sitting together in the lounge holding each other tightly and gently weeping while looking at a photograph they'd had specially made. It was a sort of monochrome with some parts of it hand coloured. They kept it on the sideboard. These were the precious moments I always remembered long after I had forgotten many other things about them. As with most fathers, they tend to be closer to their daughters, and I felt something left him after that fateful day and never came back, but we still got on OK, although I tended to be closer to my mother, as she was always around.

Even after his death, my mother would never have a harsh word said about him in her presence despite his blatantly promiscuous, adulterous and possibly illegal relationships. She would also, up until her own death only two years after his, always staunchly defend him and vehemently condemn anybody who dared to say anything untoward about his "funny way" (as she always put it.) I often wondered whether she really knew what they got up to; such was her empathetic understanding of his inclination.

Whatever memories they had together, only they shared, and they were something that I would probably never fully understand. Every relationship that lasts a lifetime, does so for reasons far beyond normal comprehension. My one regret is that I never really got to know my father until the very end and I think he also had regrets about the time he had not spent with me when I was younger... a father-son relationship that never quite blossomed, due to circumstances beyond his and my control. I suppose this probably happens more often than it should in the busy complicated lives that we all now lead. I occasionally feel sad when I think back to what might have been and I occasionally grieve for the lost opportunity to get to know the man that was my father and the chance to understand what makes somebody what they become. We all start out as one kind of person and slowly, through circumstances, destiny and sometimes luck, we change into a different kind of person. I sometimes wonder what really controls this strange metamorphosis.

My weekdays were taken up much as before with school, but it is a little more serious now as we are having to learn many different subjects in preparation for an important exam which we will take when we are eleven years of age. The outcome of this exam will determine whether we will continue our education at Grammar school and wear a nice uniform or a secondary modern school if we aren't very bright, where we can wear whatever we like. (So I was told)

Evenings were still spent playing marbles and games in the street or maybe playing in the mud (now normally only at weekends) or in the underground kingdom, but this is less and less now as I had grown too tall and have to bend over to walk underneath the corrugated iron. I had been promised a bicycle for Christmas if I was good, so I was doing the best I can.

In 1955, somebody new arrived in my life. Uncle Bruce, my mum's brother. He was in the navy and had been posted to Singapore since the war, but had now been posted home and has started to live with us for a while. As dad is still away a lot, I tend to treat Uncle Bruce more as a father than an uncle. We make battleships together out of Players cigarette packets with guns made out of silver paper and matchsticks. Bruce isn't married (well I've never seen his wife) and as far as I know he isn't homosexual like dad although of course I write this with the benefit of hindsight, which makes me sound far more aware of my surroundings than I actually was at the time. Nevertheless, I believe I can accurately assess the relationships of my peers with some degree of efficacy. Uncle Bruce smoked a lot (RN naval issue) and drinks rum (Old Navy Rum) all the time, but oddly never normally falls over, which cannot be said for some of the men who frequent The Sailors Return at the end of the road. I remember Bruce brought us all presents from Singapore when he last came home. One was a 3D viewer-scope, which looked a bit like a pair of binoculars and into which you put photographic slides, which then allowed you see the sites of China in amazing three dimensional colour. Bruce died suddenly in November 1956. He fell down a hatchway on his ship (which was moored at the bottom of the road conveniently) while still in harbour.

Apparently, he was heavily intoxicated with alcohol (pissed) at the time according to the coroner's report. All a bit of an ignominious end for someone who had courageously battled his way through six years of war and had been sunk twice without a scratch. My mother swore blind he was pushed, but it didn't seem likely, as he was such a likable and amiable person. There is a lesson to be learnt in there somewhere. But I have no idea what it is. My mother harboured her belief of a foul deed to her dying day. ON THE BASIS THAT HE WAS NEVER DRUNK

Somewhat ironically, only a few months earlier, Bruce had a win on the "pools" a sort of weekly lottery based on which football teams scored a draw each Saturday. If you managed to pick eight score drawers that gave you twenty-four points, which was the jackpot. He didn't score twenty four points just twenty three, but it was enough to win him a prize of over £2,000. This was a lot of money in 1956. He immediately gave half to mum who said she would now buy a house in the posher part of Portsmouth. The house in Prospect Road was rented, but for some reason we didn't move straight away in fact we stayed there for another six months, something to do with the lease I think. My mum inherited the balance of the pools win from Bruce. He had not spent a penny of it, so the future was looking very rosy for us all except of course Bruce....
ALL OF US

As dad apparently didn't earn much money, mum had started taking in a lodger. She had the money from Uncle Bruce's Littlewoods Pools win, but that was "sacrosanct", whatever that meant. She would say this whenever anybody mentioned using it, if we were a bit broke. That didn't happen very often as Uncle Bruce used to bring us home lots of things when he wasn't away at sea, but of course, that had come to a sudden end...
then

We normally only had one lodger. They normally only stayed Monday to Friday, so Lizzie and I would move into

mum's bedroom and our room would be rented out. Bruce had his own bedroom. I remember we met some nice people during this period one in particular was Christine (we called her Auntie Christine) We called all the women Auntie, but oddly, all the men were Mister's until we knew them better.

Auntie Christine would remain a family friend for many years. What I learnt many years later changed my perception of many things that happened during this period. Christine was a very attractive woman, I think she was probably about twenty or twenty one and she worked in the corset and brassiere factory in the next road. I remember she came home very tearful one day, something I don't remember adults doing very much. She had a long talk with mum in the front room (we weren't allowed in) and a few days later (she was ill in bed for a few days) she seemed as right as rain again after that. Mum had somehow managed to make her feel better. MUM USED TO HELP LOTS OF GIRLS FEEL BETTER *Anyway, it turned out she had been pregnant and with a little help from my mum, she became un-pregnant. She eventually married a footballer who played for Ipswich Town. My mum had many other friends so life was always a little hectic, but enjoyable. When mum gave us our pocket money (we received this on Saturday morning if we had been good all week), we would trot off to woollies and spend it. So come Sunday I was broke again. Elizabeth somehow used to save some of hers every week. I never understood how she managed that.*

Chapter 2

GRAMMATICIX NOT PERFT
SWITCHLUT ABRUPTL
FROM PAST TO PRESENCE
TENSE

The narrative appeared relatively pedestrian to start, but nevertheless engaging in that nostalgic retrospective way that selective memories can be. The characterisation worked well; it was believable, the people seemed real and the imageries slowly drew you deeper into the story. The dramatic momentum, which is so important at the beginning of any novel, appeared to lack a little drive. But there was one peculiar, slightly unnerving aspect that kept Blake engrossed in the book. One mesmerising dimension that he had never encountered before and that was the uncanny way the story appeared to so accurately diarise and document the precise chronology of his own boyhood memories of growing up in the heavily bomb damaged area Prospect Road near the Portsmouth docks.

Most, but not all the of the character's names were slightly different, but everything else, a little uncomfortably, was exactly as he remembered it. He felt he could reach out and almost touch the people he had once known thirty years ago, but for one reason or another had now lost touch with. It was the tiny details that really unnerved him, the Bert Coggins rag and bone character in Prospect Road he knew as Bernie Collins in real life and he had one eye that always looked upwards and in a different direction to the other and this used to worry Blake. He never knew for sure which eye was looking at him when he was negotiating the sale of newspaper or scrap iron. He also had a very pronounced Glaswegian accent, which at times was almost impossible to understand.

That relatively insignificant detail wasn't in the book, but he knew it was the same person; there could never be two people quite the same as those two. The same could be said for the Uncle Jim character almost identical in every respect except the Uncle John he grew up knowing only had one leg, which explained why he had not been conscripted. The reason he drove an American car was because it was an automatic and he only needed one leg to

45

drive it. British made automatic cars were very rare in those days. He was also a bit of a boxer in his day (when he had two legs) and still taught a bit of boxing some nights in a gym at the end of the road. There was never a more bizarre sight, then to see a man with a metal leg dancing around a boxing ring knocking over younger boxers, who were too afraid to hit him because they thought he might fall over. I never did see him fall over, or be knocked down.

These were all relatively minor details, but it all made a sort of sense. Everything and everybody seemed to make some sort of sense, which to Blake didn't make any sense at all unless...

In the first chapter, the story recalled events and details that he clearly remembered, or as best as the temporal extent of his recollected powers would allow. In the second chapter, however something changed. The story had now began to recall specific details of events and people of which he had no recollection. For a few moments, Blake actually found this oddly reassuring. The book no longer appeared to be that precise or accurate and he was relieved to find that he could happily consign the previous unexplained similarities to serendipitous coincidence and the vagaries of common generalisation, and was therefore of no personal relevance.

However, after re-reading the second chapter again, the characters suddenly began to rise up off the paper and swirl around in osculating circles confusing his eyes and jolting his memory. Some of the details he remembered about Bert Coggins and Uncle Jim, details that were not in the book the first time he read it, suddenly appeared the second time he read it. It was almost as if his remembrance of things past that had been initiated by reading the book, released further tiny details that as far as he was aware were lost forever somewhere deep inside his brain. Somehow, this had activated some sort of trigger mechanism for the book to rewrite the same chapters with the additional details now neatly inserted into the right places in the manuscript.

The vague, flickering, distant light of long forgotten events began to form clear visions in his mind, as the light grew brighter. It was like an old magic lantern show of trembling images cascading across his optical vortex, but slowly the images became real people and they began to speak to him.

It was then that he realised these events must have had happened to him after all... he had simply just forgotten them or had he. It was all slightly confusing.

He flicked back the pages and started to reread the book from the beginning once again before going any further forward, just to make sure he had not just fallen asleep and had dreamt the whole thing. For a moment, he even considered whether he could have written the story himself - such was the attention to detail, which seemed to become more apparent each time he read a line - and then maybe sent it to himself under an assumed name. Many famous writers did this to engender objectivity, but he definitely had not. That was madness and anyway he was not a writer. He had never had any ambitions in that direction. He was perfectly happy reading and publishing other people's stories.

Anthony Theodore Clackle had written this story, it said so on the front page and anyway, he definitely would not have come up with a pseudonym like that, it just wasn't real.

He finished re-reading the first two chapters and turned over the page to start chapter three, but it was blank. He flicked further forward but there were no more words just empty pages with a number at the bottom and the title at the top. This did not make any sense at all. Maybe it was a printing error he thought. He would speak to Jamie tomorrow and see if he had any explanation.

The next day Blake was a little late into the office and did not have the opportunity to mention the missing chapters of Prospect Road to Jamie immediately. A typical Monday morning was happening with all the incumbent chaos that it brought. The mayhem enveloped everybody. Client authors were phoning in to catch up on end of month sales figures. Printers were chasing confirmation on final proofs for production runs, the postman had delivered another enormous batch of parcels containing the sample

More

chapters of books from more hopeful authors for them to read, and then there were the hundred and one other niggley little things that only happen after everybody has had two days off. It was during the weekend, that clients would think about all the queries, the questions they most urgently needed to have an answer to. So first thing on Monday morning, they would phone.

After lunch, the pandemonium had begun to settle down a little and Jamie took the opportunity to pop his head round the door of Blake's office.

'So how did your weekend go,' asked Jamie jovially, but with a wry expression? Alluding conversely to the chaotic last few hours they had just endured.

Blake did not answer straight away, but just smiled. 'OK… but that book you gave me to read… "Prospect Road", I have a question.'

'Yes,' replied Jamie.

'Where's the rest of it?'

'I gave it all to you - the whole book,' replied Jamie sounding a little puzzled, 'have you lost it?'

'No, no I haven't lost it, I have the manuscript and all the pages, it's just the words that are missing,' replied Blake sounding a little indignant and incensed at Jamie's accusation. (he suddenly realised how stupid that sound it

'Missing, what do you mean missing?'

'Missing as in not there, invisible, non-existent. All I have is the first two chapters, the rest of the pages were all blank, apart that is from the page numbers and…'

'Well I don't know what's happened to it... Page numbers,' mused Jamie as an afterthought.

'Yes page number's at the bottom and the book title at the top, but nothing else in between, just fresh air... 'He threw a moronic smile at Jamie, but Jamie maintained his bewildered expression. apart from the book mystery

'Well it was all there when I read it… oh well never mind I'm sure it will turn up. So eh... did you have a nice weekend?' He asked again, but this time with a slightly different inflection, apparently changing the subject.

'Yes,' replied Blake, 'thank you, how was yours?'

'Good, good,' replied Jamie but not sounding overly enthused. He paused for a few moments to get the timing just right, 'couple of bottles of the old Chateau du plonk?' he suggested wryly.

'Oh no, I know what you are thinking,' replied Blake with a grin, suddenly realising where this going. 'Totally pissed the whole weekend and spent it reading blank paper. Well that was not the case. In fact, I hardly touched a drop. I was working very diligently, reading… or not as appears to be the case,' he stopped for a moment, thinking about what he had just said.

'Well I'll check my office,' said Jamie smiling, 'but I'm sure there was only ever one copy and I gave it to you. I'm certain I checked it before I put it with the other books you took, and I wrote my name and the date on first and the last page as per normal.' (This was an old in-house ritual they had inherited and used for many years to ensure that nobody accidently read the same book twice.)

'Fair enough,' replied Blake, 'I'll have a look in my study again when I get home tonight, just to be sure, but… if I haven't got a complete copy you will have to ask Mr….' He gazed skywards for a few moments searching for the authors name…

'Clackle, Theodore Clackle,' confirmed Jamie.

'Yes, interesting name isn't it,' queried Blake enquiringly, 'almost Dickensian. Do you think that's his real name?'

'Could be a "non de plume", I suppose,' replied Jamie with a Monty Pythoness inflection… and another odd expression.

'What did you make of the book?' asked Blake.

'Let me think,' said Jamie pausing for a moment. Now he was the one gazing thoughtfully skywards, 'that was the story about the young boy set just after the last war… grows up to run a small publishing business ironically, bit like you in fact.' He spoke the words very slowly at first as if plucking them out of the air, '…that's why I thought you would find it interesting. A few things happened along the way that kept it interesting. It was more a series of reminiscences than pure fiction to start with; well that's what I thought. But it was well written and it chugged along, unusual plot development as I remember, not something I've encountered before, not in this sort of format anyway. I thought it could do well, retro reads are always popular, could even be the basis for a television series, TV companies were always on the lookout for something new.'

'What actually happens,' asked Blake?

'I just told you,' replied Jamie.

'No, no the specifics, can you remember anything after the second chapter?'

Jamie was obviously a little intrigued by this odd question. 'Second chapter,' repeated Jamie. He looked down at the floor and thought for a few moments, endeavouring to disentangle the unique characteristics of this one particular book from the many others he had read the previous week. But with a rather curious blank expression he looked back up at Blake and peering over the top of his glasses, through his bushy eyebrows he replied, 'I'm sorry, but do you know what, I don't actually remember very much about it at all, apart from the beginning, which is a little odd... I can usually remember the basic story line of most books I've read in the last six months, but...' Jamie was obviously struggling to remember what he could about the book, but try as he may he couldn't bring it to mind, it had simply slipped his memory, which for him was a little unusual.

'That's all we have then, you can't have read the whole book, that would explain everything,' replied Blake.

'But I have, I made some editorial notes as well,' replied Jamie sounding very certain, 'I gave them to you with the book, but they were only about construction, development, pace, readability, composition, sector interest, sales potential, marketing angles, all the usual things. For some reason my mind is just a complete blank on the narrative details...' He sounded genuinely concerned about the apparent sudden loss of ability to recall almost anything relevant about the storyline of the book. A book, which he had only just confirmed, he had found interesting and readable. Not a particularly glowing endorsement.

'Look I'll contact this Clackle guy and get him to send another copy, and this time I'll make a copy, after I've read it again.'

'Fair enough,' replied Blake, 'let me know when...'

'I will don't you worry,' interrupted Jamie, now positively embarrassed by the shortcoming. He left Blake's office closing the door behind him. Blake continued reading some other documents on his desk and thought no more about it.

The following day Jamie popped into Blake's office again...

'That author Theodore Clackle - Prospect Road...we spoke about yesterday...'

'Yes,' replied Blake leaning back in his chair drinking a cup coffee. His mind appeared to be elsewhere.

'Bit of a problem, his file is empty, and the letter that came with the manuscript and our letter to him are missing, so we don't have a telephone number or an address.'

'So we have no way of finding him,' said Blake

'I can ask Susie to see if she can find a number for him in the phone book,' replied Jamie. 'He's bound to turn up somewhere with a name like that, can't be too many Clackle's listed.'

Blake nodded and Jamie left his office.

Chapter 3

July 1982

A few months later in July, Blake was at home for the weekend rummaging about in his study looking for a paper cutting about a new author he had read about when he came across the manuscript of Prospect Road buried under a number of other rejected manuscripts, which he had not, as yet taken back to the office. He suddenly remembered the problems he had encountered with the missing chapters of this particular story and how Jamie had not been able to locate the writer with the unusual name, a name he could not immediately bring to mind. He and Jamie had all but forgotten about the manuscript. This was a shameful oversight. Blake knew, only too well, that as long as he indolently held onto any author's manuscript the author would be rapaciously clinging on to a slender thread of hope. He was shamefully blocking the channel of civilised protocol between author and publisher, the stream of communication on which the flotsam of expectation travelled. The infectious incestuous illusion of possible acceptance, publication, success, and critical acclaim was being perpetrated, precariously supported, and unnecessarily prolonged by his inert, irresponsible tardiness. The emotional and psychological trauma of anticipated recognition still being desperately clung too, until the very moment the customary rejection letter dropped through his or her letter box and is opened and read and thereby instantly extinguishes another dream.

This was the process, which all writers were conditioned too and fully prepared for; the extrema of swift mercy, rather than the protracted agonising death by a thousand cuts. But this time it was being delayed and this was only antagonising the anguish and the pain being surreptitiously and unintentionally metered out to the author.

He must do the honourable thing and do it fast and he would, on Monday. He swept up the scripts and placed them on his desk, in a place of prominence, in order to remind him to take them all back with him to the office, from where he could arrange for them to be immediately dispatched and reunited with their creators. He would pay dearly for this oversight. There was always a final redemption for lethargy from Thoth the God of all writers, but hopefully, not until the afterlife. But then he remembered they could not send Prospect Road back because they did not have an address for the author. In fact, they were not intending to send it back, they just wanted another full copy of the book to read, before making a final decision, but that had proved impossible, as they had been unable to obtain an address to contact the author with the odd name. It all came back to him now.

But if he took it back to the office, at least it would then become Jamie's responsibility, not his anymore, and Thoth might be more lenient, more merciful with him on the day of reckoning when all publishers were brought to account for their shortcomings, tardiness, and oversights.

He stared down at the front cover of Prospect Road, innocuous, inauspicious, and unassuming. Just a simple typed title "**Prospect Road**" in Courier font at nine or maybe ten points if he wasn't mistaken; an unusual font - most fledgling writers typed out their first creations using modern typewriters or even one of the new word processors and they tended to be manufactured with one font - Times New Roman. But, this one had the strike-on appearance of an older conventional typewriter. Underneath the title was the writers name; **Anthony Theodore Clackle**. There was something intimately esoteric about an apparently hand typed manuscript it had the feel, the touch, even the smell of the writer embedded in every page. Sometimes you could even feel the pain the writer had gone through punching every letter, every word, just to get each line down onto the page.

You could sense how they had painstakingly chosen a specific word to use having probably changed it many times, just to get the right message, ambience, mood, and atmosphere just as he or she envisaged it, over to the reader. Sometimes you could even see the stains where tears or drops of sweat had fallen, it was all so very intimate almost visceral in concept this unique relationship between writer and paper and publisher, it was like no other. The writer renders up his soul onto the altar of the empty page, the vehicle that will eventually, permanently convey his message to the reader by way of the magical interaction of black ink and white paper.

Once on a visit to the United States, Blake had been offered the opportunity to read the original Ernest Hemingway manuscript for The Old Man and the Sea. The original hand typed white pages were now buff brown and there were stains where whiskey or beer had been spilled on a part of it. There were also a large number of words crossed out and replaced and whole sentences removed or moved to a different position. The story was only just about readable with all the alterations, stains and various notes and a number of pages had also obviously been screwed up and then flattened back out again for inclusion in the final draft. The whole document was an indictment to the writers struggle to get the perfect story as he saw it and it was only by looking at that manuscript that Blake had really come to realise just what a writer had to go through to produce a finished work. He had found it to be a particularly moving artefact, which truly emanated the soul of Hemingway and the anguish he had gone through to produce it. The memory of that manuscript always stayed with him and he very briefly returned to it almost every time he read a new book.

He felt an odd tingling sensation in his fingers and found himself irresistibly drawn back to Prospect Road. He sat down in his a captain's chair leaned across the desk and picked up the script, looked at the front page for a few moments, turned it over and began to read the story once more.

After a while, he reached the part of the second chapter where Thomas Drayton had been recalling his feelings after his father had died. Thomas had obviously become very attached to him even though they were seldom together.

Blake stopped reading for a few seconds and looked up. His own father, Robert, had passed away only a few years ago, prematurely from a heart attack. He could feel his eyes welling up with emotion and he felt a tear form in the corner of his eye and begin to roll down his cheek. He too just like Thomas Drayton missed his father terribly. He had missed him being away so much while he was growing up and by the time his father had realised just how much Blake missed his presence, it was too late to do anything about. The stories his mother had told him a few years ago about his father's homosexuality had not concerned him unduly as they appeared to relate to a period in his life when he may have been unsure of himself and who he was.

Blake had never experienced quite so much uncertainty and confusion in his life, but he could still, to a small degree empathise with how Thomas Drayton's father must of felt. In a way, the book seemed to explain some of the many questions that had never been satisfactorily explained to Blake about his own father. Questions that he had never really thought about or even had the opportunity to ask

When Blake's daughter, Claudia was born in 1978 his father's first words to Blake were that he could not wait for the day when he would watch her walk down the aisle on Blake's arm. Blake had one younger sister, but tragically, she had died aged nine in a car accident. So, his father had never made that short journey with her. With his death in 1979, he would never see his granddaughter make the journey either. Blake continued reading until he reached the end of Chapter Two. He placed the manuscript back down on his desk still open at the last page he had just read and looked at his signature under the last word which was dated the twenty sixth of March, that was when he had first read it.

He thought carefully about what he had now read a number of times and how the more he read it the more it seemed to be opening up a window, a sort of portal to a parallel universe, one that allowed him to look back at himself as he was. Each time he had reread the first two chapters, they appeared a little longer than before than with what appeared to be considerably more detail. It was as if the Chapters were self-populating themselves with more information from his past with every reading, and this only increased his bewilderment and confusion over what was happening.

He lifted the read pages, which were precariously attached to the blank pages with a green treasury tag, back onto the main stack of pages and stared at the neat pile of paper. For no particular reason he flicked the corner of the pages and then flicked back to the end of Chapter two, just to be clear on how the story had stopped. He turned over the next page, it was blank, and then he turned over another page...

He was half expecting something, but didn't know what exactly, not until he saw the heading....Chapter Three!

Chapter Three! There had never been a chapter Three, he was certain of that much, but there it was as plain as day... he couldn't understand where it had come from. It wasn't there before, of that much he was convinced, but it was there now, but how he wondered. Could this be a joke that Catherine was playing he asked himself, but he quickly discounted that possibility. She knew nothing of the mystery of the missing chapters and she seldom ventured into his study where he worked anyway, except to run the hoover round from time to time or bring him a cup of tea. He turned over the page and the words were there waiting...waiting to be read.

coffee

Prospect Road 3

Chapter Three
Written by
Anthony Theodore Clackle

After Bruce died mum cried for weeks, it was a very sad time. Then mum and dad told us we were moving and a few weeks later, we started packing everything up ready for the lorry that would take us to our new home at Wadham Road in the posher part of town. The house was enormous (compared to Prospect Road that is) and it had a little front garden and a very large back garden with grass, flowers and apple trees. We never had a garden at Prospect road just a backyard with a toilet in a shed and definitely no trees.

I could not believe it at first, the toilet was inside the house in a special room with a white bath that you did not have to hang up in the back yard. (We didn't actually have a backyard anymore). There was also a sink (which I later learnt was actually a "basin" whatever that was and we used to wash our hands in that after going to the toilet. This was all very new to us, as the privy in prospect road did not have one. The toilet also had a seat that you put down afterwards. Mum put an ornament on the seat, which we had to take off every time we used it. I have to admit that from the age of about thirteen, I occasionally peed in the sink, as it was easier than buggering around moving ornaments off the loo.

The bathroom also had a window, through which I could see the garden. Downstairs was even more confusing, we had a front room for special occasions, a sitting room for the evenings, a dining room that led onto a greenhouse (this was actually a "conservatory" so I was informed) and a separate kitchen. The whole house had carpets that fitted each room perfectly. I do not know where they bought these odd shaped carpets from. Much later, this was also explained to me. We still only had three bedrooms upstairs, but mum transformed the front room with a magical thing called a divan, which was a sofa that converted into a bed after a lot of pulling and shoving.

This was to be my room for the next three years. Elizabeth slept with mum during the week and both the other bedrooms were let out to lodgers. One was let out permanently all week to a young married couple Pepper and Auntie Audrey.

I missed playing in the mud and on the bombsite, but we now had a massive park to play in and fortunately, it backed onto the Portsmouth creek, so I still had the opportunity to play in the mud sometimes, but not like the old days. Come November we would buy a hundred banger fireworks for a pound and bury ten tied together in the mud and let them off. It used to make a wonderful explosion and blow mud everywhere. Great fun. It was around this time that mum introduced us to another uncle; this one was Uncle Dennis who used to live about ten minutes away from our new house in another large house.

Dennis lived on his own. He was an old friend of my mum and dad from the war days, so she said, but he was quite a bit older and he was Welsh. I used to visit him quite often because he used to make little bombs out of old fuse wire (the kind they used for setting off dynamite). I presume this was something once again left over from the war. (There was a bit of a theme developing here, but it went no further.) We would diligently undo the tar covering and take all the gunpowder out then put it into something like an old tin, then stick another piece of fuse wire into the tin, and bury it underground. Uncle Dennis would light the fuse and we would both run back to a safe distance behind an apple tree and watch the explosion. These were much more impressive than my feeble attempts with fireworks in the creek. Uncle Dennis had a tortoise called Norman, which he said, was about a hundred years old. This tortoise was enormous about the size of a dustbin lid and it could move really fast. Sometimes we could be lazing in deckchairs in the garden enjoying the sunshine, just talking about nothing in particular and Norman would sneakily start eating my shoes. If I ran away he would quickly follow, he had obviously acquired an insatiable taste for leather. He had also acquired a highly developed sense of survival as no sooner did we start to unpack our bomb making equipment then he would make a hasty retreat into the greenhouse and not return until we had finished messing around.

Uncle Dennis used to work for White and Co a local furniture removal company; in fact, he was the man that helped move us to Wadham road.

Dennis never married and the house he lived in had been the house where his parents had lived and died. I don't think the inside decoration had been ever been changed. He had an old upright piano that I used to try and play, but he played it much better than me and he would sing old war songs at the same time. He was stationed in Egypt during the war "One of Monty's dessert rats" he was proud to tell me on many occasions. He told me loads of stories about his time out in North Africa and how he had befriended the Arabs who were helping our army beat the Germans. That was the first time he had ever seen a camel. On one occasion one spat at him and Dennis said it was the biggest gob of spit he had ever seen. He loved the sun and the desert and I think despite it being wartime he enjoyed his time out there. As with most soldiers I have spoken to since those days, they tend not to want to speak to much about the more unpleasant things that happened, but he did mention one battle he was in at a place called Tobruk where there were hundreds of tanks fighting each other and eventually we won.

Dennis said he lost many friends during that battle. Those were the same sort of games I used to play with my toy soldiers and tanks (until my mum melted them down ~~one night~~ for Halloween). I found it all incredibly exciting not realising there was always another side to war.

It was like being in another world when I went to visit Dennis, a world where nothing had changed. We were fast approaching the 1960's and all the colourful vicissitudes CHECK *that would bring, but he was still happily living in the 1940's. I remember the last time I went to see him was in the late 1970's when I was visiting Portsmouth on business. I had moved away some years before and had lost touch with him. It must have been nearly twenty years since I had last seen him, but he was exactly same as I remember, just a little frailer now. But the house was exactly how I remembered it. He used to sit in his kitchen and watch snooker on a very small black and white television set. I couldn't believe it. I didn't say anything because he seemed quite happy with that very odd situation. But after I left, I popped into a local television shop, bought a small colour television and took it back to him a couple of hours later. I switched the sets over and watched with amazement as his eyes lit up at the realisation that he could now tell which colours the snooker balls were.*

I think it made his day; I hope so as I never saw him again. Mind you, he probably cursed me when he found out the colour television licence was a lot more expensive.

My school years were relatively uneventful, being filled with all the mundanity of education. After leaving school, I went to university then, by chance secured a job in a publishing company.

My life had now started to mean something and then in 1970 I met Kate, the woman who would become my wife, the woman with whom I would spend the rest of my life. We were married in 1974.

I remember one day, just after our second child was born Kate bought me a silver framed photograph of herself and our two children, something that I would treasure always. She told me it was, 'Something to inspire your wearisome days.' She whispered this as she gave me the present. 'Something for you to look at every day, and when you do, you will know that I will always be looking over you and no matter what happens I will always love you.' That was one of the most important days of my life; I felt I had a purpose, a reason for being.

Remember.

CLANFORD

Chapter 4

August 1982

With some trepidation, Blake began to read Chapter Three. It told of Thomas Drayton and his family moving to a nicer part of town and mentioned people of whom he had some distant memories and then it moved onto to the period when Thomas had started to work in a publishing company ~~in London~~ in 1968, the same year that he had joined Cranford and Fox. It continued to recall with unerring and increasingly detailed accuracy the events as they ~~began to~~ HAD HAPPENED TO BLAKE happen. In July 1970 Thomas Drayton, now a book publisher met Kate at a party for a new book release. He would marry her in 1974, which was exactly how Blake had met Catherine and also the same year they were married. No longer were the characters in the book masquerading behind different names. Whatever bizarre plot he had become unwittingly embroiled in, or maybe more accurately entangled with, it was now morphing into reality. All the demarcation lines between the fictional characters and real people, the essential delineation that clearly separated reality from fantasy was now becoming increasing blurred. The details of two existences were now slowly seeping, bleeding into each other like black ink on blotting paper it was edging itself slowly towards territories it had only casually visited before leaving few a marks... but now it was obliterating everything that had once been visible and before long, everything would be overpowered by a dark mendacity.

Anthony Theodore Clackle was now using characters names for the people in his fictional story that Blake actually knew in his real life. For just one split second, he considered whether he was actually going mad, maybe he was suffering from some sort of paranoia or split personality disorder that would make perfect sense he thought. But then he also knew that a genuinely psychotic person was usually schizophrenic and they or either of their one or more personalities would never countenance the remotest possibility that they were mad, so he quickly OR THE EXISTANCE OF ANOTHER PERSONALITY discounted that option. Of course he could be bi-polar, that wonderfully erudite, politically correct euphemism for severe manic depressives that seemed to have surreptitiously crept, under the cover of political correctness, into everyday language and had now become so popular with the middle classes. A hobble stick for suburbia, like a drunk leaning against a lamppost. FOR SUPPORT MORE THAN ILLUMINA)

No, he wasn't depressed either. This was simply the undramatic consequence of a strange synchromeshing of fiction and fact; it was as unassumingly trite and predictably ordinary as that. As soon as he accepted this, everything else would fall into place, but could he.

As he read further, the story told of the birth of two children, Michael and Carol. Blake and Catherine had named their children Max and Claudia. It also mentioned his uncle's tragic death and Reggie Clanford, the owner of the publishing company that Thomas worked for. Blake stopped reading for a moment, took a bottle of bourbon out of his desk drawer and poured out a large glass. He was feeling just as confused now as he was when he first read the opening chapters of the book a few months ago, but now he was beginning to feel uneasy. A peculiar sense of foreboding was beginning to overwhelm him, something that he felt he could not control. Reading the story repeatedly did not alleviate his concerns as he thought it might. He had reasoned that an element of familiarity with the text would weaken the visceral chill of verity and invoke contempt by assimilating the imagery into normalcy, but it had not. He became frustrated and infuriated with himself for not being able to understand or determine precisely what was happening. He came to the end of chapter three on the day that Catherine (Kate) gave Blake (Thomas) the silver framed photograph of her and their two children. That was a very poignant moment for him and as hard as he tried, he could not stop the tears of uncontrollable emotion welling up behind his eyes. That had always been a very private moment for him and Catherine, something that absolutely nobody else on the planet knew the exact circumstances of or the precise words that Catherine had used, and yet here it was, written down verbatim by somebody he had never met, or was ever likely to meet going by his experience to date. His hand began to tremble and the remains of the whiskey in the glass he was holding began to gently quiver as if an earthquake were about to begin, but it didn't and the trembling stopped. There were no more words.

He flicked through the following pages two or three times to make absolutely sure he hadn't missed anything this time and after assuring himself there was no more narrative he scribbled his signature and the date underneath the last typed line and then closed the manuscript.

He sat down for dinner with Catherine and the children at six o'clock and they talked about various things including their eighth wedding anniversary, which was coming up in three weeks' time. They had decided to invite a few friends around for dinner instead of going out. They both preferred the intimacy of quiet dinner parties at home rather than going to a restaurant. After dinner, Catherine put Max and Claudia to bed while Blake cleared the table. He then went upstairs and kissed both of them goodnight. When he returned Catherine had poured him bourbon with ice and placed it on the table next to his chair. He smiled at her.

'Is there a problem,' she asked with a curious look in her eyes

'No why?' he replied sounding a little surprised.

'You just seem…. distant… preoccupied that's all, something seems to be troubling you, I know that much.'

'It's nothing really,' said Blake.

'What is it, you might as well tell me now?' asked Catherine smiling and gently probing his inner thoughts. She knew he never kept any secrets from her for very long. 'I'll get it out of you in the end Thornton.' said Catherine with a tenacious smirk. Blake smiled at her perspicacity. 'I could resort to torture if necessary,' mused Catherine, 'I could sing.' Catherine sang appallingly with absolutely no sense of key, timing or melody and this above all else would almost immediately render Blake helpless with laughter and pleading for mercy.

'Alright, alright, anything but that.' replied Blake.

Catherine playfully poked him in his stomach.

'It's just a book I've been reading, it's…..' he paused not knowing quite how to explain it.

'I read part of it a few months ago and then forgot all about it until earlier today when I came across it again. It was buried in my study under a lot of other stuff so I thought I had better take it back to the office. I didn't think it was that good when I first read it, there were some unusual problems, but for some reason I thought I would read it again before taking it back… it's just that….' he seemed a little distracted.

'It's what,' said Catherine now a little intrigued.

'Well it's a story about a publisher… like me and the circumstances are a little similar to mine - ours, but it's a little odd, there's something about it that's…' he paused, 'not right, it's a little spooky.' He twitched his nose.

'Well, what's it actually about? Is it well written and how does it end and most importantly would it sell?' Asked Catherine in the pragmatic and prosaic manner she always adopted when dealing with any problem to do with a book.

'I don't know what it's about. That is half the problem. Apart from documenting somebody's life story, someone who sounds remarkably like me, us in fact. It doesn't seem to have a central storyline. It's well written, but in a very naïvely engaging way, and as for how it ends, well that's the oddest thing of all,' he paused to take a sip of bourbon.

'Why,' asked Catherine.

'Well it doesn't end, in fact it stopped at chapter two when I first read it, that was the unusual problem, but when I read it again today, and I know you are going to think I'm going mad, but when I read it today there was another chapter which somehow I had missed the first time round.'

Catherine did not say anything immediately, but just thought over what he had said. She waggled her drinks glass at him nonchalantly, he smiled and shook his head indicating that he hadn't been drunk when he read the book and fallen asleep or whatever she was demurely alluding to. He did however begin to wonder about the issue of drinking, as this was now the second occasion in only a few days that somebody had made a passing reference to his bibulousness and how it might be affecting his work, but oddly only when it related to Prospect Road.

Anyway, he didn't think he drank to excess. Probably no more than a half bottle of wine for dinner, maybe one or two brandies during the evening, but not every night, and of course there was the traditional G & T's on Sunday starting at midday. Oh and maybe a bottle of wine on Saturday night if they went out for a meal. Occasionally he had a pint or two at lunchtimes at the office if going out with a client or discussing a book with Jamie over lunch, but apart from that he didn't drink! Then he thought about what he had just thought about.

'Have they read it in the office?' asked Catherine.

'Yes, one of the junior readers read the first two chapters, liked it, and passed it to Jamie who read them and then requested a full manuscript which he also read. Then he passed it to me.

'So you have just been given the wrong copy,' said Catherine. 'It's as simple as that.'

'Well no...,' replied Blake, 'you see we have a system for marking scripts, so we know who has read what. Whoever reads it signs it at the beginning and at the end or wherever they get to, if they don't manage to read it all. Also, we all make notes, which go into a file on each book under review. The copy I have is signed by Jamie, who read the whole story and made detailed notes. He signed it at the beginning and on the last page. We only have one ~~full~~ copy of the full book, but all the pages are blank after chapter three.'

'So how did Jamie read it,' asked Catherine?

'I don't know. He swears he read it cover to cover, said he liked it a lot which is why he passed it to me.'

Catherine said nothing; she was as flummoxed by the conundrum as Blake was. *simply*

'Well it sounds as if someone has, removed all the chapters after the third one.'

'That could make sense, but why then have I still got all the pages numbered and titled and Jamie's signature on the last blank page, and of course that doesn't explain how the third chapter suddenly appeared from nowhere while the manuscript was here in my study.'

Catherine could not answer that one.

'What happened to the first copy you received?'

'I checked that,' replied Blake, 'it's still in the office but there are still only the first two chapters.'

'Let's have an early night and tomorrow I will look at the book for you and we will sort this out,' said Catherine confidently. Blake smiled. He knew there had to be a simple explanation to the whole mystery and hopefully Catherine would come up with it by the time he returned home the next evening. She had the remarkable ability of being able to solve complex problems with her uncomplicated woman's logic and in a small way, this seemed to assuage some of Blake's concerns. He went to bed that night still troubled, but tried not to let it show and even managed to get a good night's sleep.

The next morning they were up early and once the normal routine of breakfast was over Blake went into his study and brought out the manuscript and ceremoniously, but still with some token resistance handed it to Catherine. He was now having some minor reservations about the manuscript, but nothing specific that he could put his finger on apart from the obvious oddity of the missing narrative.

'Prospect Road, see what you think.' He kissed her gently on the lips then kissed Max and Claudia before leaving for the office. It was a journey of over an hour from Godalming into Denmark Street, central London, where his office was. He usually spent the commute time reading, but today he just gazed out of the window wondering…

That evening when Blake arrived back home, Max and Claudia greeted him at the front gate and took hold of his hands as they made their way back towards the house. It was the archetypal cottage, with the white painted fence panels adjacent to the footpath and the neat front lawn and roses round the front door that Catherine had always wanted when they were first married. It had been a good home for them over the last seven years, but now it was far too small with Max and Claudia growing up and soon they would have to move.

He hadn't really looked at the cottage in a while and suddenly realised how transitory everything really was, nothing really lasted forever. It was an odd thought to come into his mind at that particular moment, tinted with an element of paranoia and fragility, not something he was conversant with, but today he had an inkling deep down that what was happening with Prospect Road was somehow having an effect on him and possibly his family. His and their existence and the everyday things he took for granted could so suddenly be overturned by events beyond his control. He was beginning to feel vulnerable and exposed to forces way beyond his normal comprehension and yet he had no reason to do so. He said a small prayer hoping the maybe Catherine had discovered a simple explanation to the riddle that now haunted him, and that everything would suddenly be OK. He also wondered if, maybe, he was becoming a little obsessed, there was no reason for him to feel that way, but then that was the nature of the beast.

'Mummies in the back garden,' said Max as he and Claudia guided Blake around the corner of the house into the rear garden where Catherine was sitting on the hammock swinging gently back and forth. The script lay by her side on the cushion. She got up to kiss Blake and hugged him tightly in a way that he found immediately reassuring and yet he could sense a tiny element of measured inconclusion.

Blake looked over her shoulder and just for a moment, he thought he could see an enormous grey elephant standing quietly in the corner of the garden nibbling on the grass. The Mahout, sitting on its back in a full evening dress with a bowler hat, and drinking a martini didn't help much. And then it was gone. They wandered slowly over to the borders to see the flowers more closely and Blake snapped the head off a dead rose.

'So how was your day?' asked Catherine.

'Same as yesterday, still hectic,' he replied smiling, but sounding less enthusiastic than usual. Obviously, he was wondering what Catherine would have to say about the book. He peered over her shoulder again to see if the elephant had returned, but it appeared to still be hiding.

'Martin rang,' said Catherine, wondering what Blake was looking for, 'asked if we wanted to go for dinner this Friday, I said I would get back to him after we had spoken.'

'That would be good, how is he?' asked Blake, turning back to give Catherine his full attention.

'Fine, he has a new lady friend he wants us to meet. She's a writer and painter, bit of an extrovert from what I can make out.'

'Writer,' he queried, 'oh, well yes that should be fun; he deserves a little excitement in his life again after all that's happened. It's been a long time.' He was alluding to the premature passing of Martins' wife Ruth, some years earlier.

They had been a gregarious and popular couple in the village, heavily involved in an eclectic array of village activity's, but after Ruth had suddenly and quite unexpectedly died in 1980, Martin seemed to slip back into a less adventurous frame of mind slowly withdrawing from social intercourse as so many people do after bereavement.

'Yes, yes it has,' replied Catherine.

'I do hope this isn't a pitch for a publishing deal,' asked Blake a little cynically?

'No its not, I did ask him. She just write's plays and a local Am-dram society puts them on, she even does a bit of acting, but definitely no novels.'

'Oh I see, I apologise for jumping the gun, I was ...' he did not finish what he was going to say.

Catherine smiled. They had gently tiptoed around the preliminaries of the as yet unspoken subject, but Blake had reached the point from which he could no longer continue any further without asking the question that had been hovering in the air above their heads. It felt like a giant balloon filled with water just waiting for the exigencies of thin rubber or nature to suddenly take control and immerse them in a deluge of cold reality.

'So how did you find it?' asked Blake with more than a hint of precautionary restraint?

Catherine pointed to the garden swing hammock and they both walked back and sat down.

'It was interesting... but as you said, it stops at chapter three. I can definitely confirm that much.'

'What do you make of the story and the similarities to us?' he asked, still sounding a little constrained, as if he didn't want to hear the answer or at best wanted her to assiduously and fervently deride his suspicions as nothing more than vague conjecture and wild speculation, the product of an overactive publishers imagination. But, she didn't quite go that far.

'There were some, yes,' replied Catherine, but probably no different from many other people of our age.' She didn't sound completely convinced, but then she didn't seem overly concerned by the similarities either.

'Some of it could be down to generalities,' said Catherine, 'many people who grew up during that period probably had very similar experiences.' But even as she said the words, she knew it sounded improbable, there were too many specific references, which were obviously quite unique to Blake, to her and to their children and it would have been bordering on the disingenuous not to acknowledge that those details were germane and impellingly pertinent to Blake's uneasiness.

'Anyway,' said Catherine, 'with only three chapters it's not going anywhere is it? So unless the rest of the book miraculously appears, I think you should just forget about it and put it down to a "strange experience". She air quoted the words and smiled and that seemed to placate Blake's concerns. He nodded in agreement, and kissed Catherine.

Max and Claudia came over to the hammock and pulled at Blake's hands to get him to walk into the garden where they were playing in a paddling pool. He obediently went with them and sat down next to the paddling pool as they both jumped in and started splashing water about. He watched them both enjoying themselves, utterly oblivious to the ominous ruminations running around in his mind and realised that he could not let his thoughts and concerns detract from his enjoyment of these blissfully innocent times. He should take these fleeting moments spent with his children and treasure each one of them as they came and capture them in his heart, and hold them there forever. For they would soon be gone never to return and only the memories would remain as he grew older. He thought no more of Prospect Road that day, but not before checking over his shoulder one more time.

TO COMFORT HIM

Chapter 5

August 1982

Blake put the manuscript back into his study and did not look at it again for a couple of weeks, in fact he almost completely forgot about it. For some reason he didn't take it back to the office, which he had originally intended to do, but left it on his desk among a number of other newer scripts that he had brought home. Life continued to move on much as before. *TOWARDS THE END OF*

One Sunday morning late in August, Catherine had gone to her mother's for the day with Max and Claudia. Blake was left alone ready to enjoy a leisurely day in the sunshine. Prospect Road had somehow risen to the top of the pile of scripts on his desk ~~again~~ and once again, he found himself inexorably drawn toward it. Somewhat warily, he picked it up, with not unreasonable trepidation. Just for a few seconds his mind flashed back to the last conversation he had with Catherine about the book. *DECIDED TO GO TO AND TAKE M & C WITH HER*

He poured himself a large Jack Daniels from the bottle he kept in his study desk, took some ice cubes from the freezer in the kitchen, plopped them into his glass and clutching the manuscript, walked back through to the lounge. The French windows were open and a gentle summer breeze blew into the lounge and rustled the curtains for a few seconds. It was as if it were heralding the entrance of a character in some amateur dramatic stage production, but no one entered and the curtains became still again.

He sat down on the sofa and turned over the cover page and once again began to read this simple, yet elegantly strange story. Not for one moment did he consider flipping to the end, there didn't seem to be any point, so he just sat back and read the words, each one appearing evermore poignant, personal and pertinent than the last time he read it.

Once again, he became engrossed in the tale and as he did so, his left hand slowly edged its way towards the small table next to his chair to pick up the glass of bourbon he had placed there earlier. He took a sip and gently swilled the ice cubes around in the glass. Momentarily distracted, he glanced at the smeary threads of water and liquor interweaving like the golden strands of a Mobius circle, no beginning – no end, just an existence. Not dissimilar in some ways, he thought, to the story he was reading. Not the clearly documented, but nevertheless humdrum pedestrian story about his life from the age of five, that was just a superfluous outer shell; the protective covering, the wrapping paper that would eventually be discarded; ripped off in order to revel something far deeper, something that would slowly emerge into clear view… the reason for the story. It was leading somewhere, he was certain of that much, he just didn't know where or to what.

Once again, he was transfixed by the unsettling way in which the story so clearly documented his life. It appeared to have been even further enhanced from when he had last read it. It was as if it was now being re-edited by someone who knew his past life, as well, if not better than he did or had at least remembered it better than he had. But instead of removing the weaker parts of the story - the superfluous sections which only took up space and added nothing - the inconsequential elements that ruined the rhythm of the writing - the irrelevant phrases that didn't fit, it had added the finer detail. This brought, further into focus, the stark realism, clarity, and definition of the story, a story that already seemed alive. In the trivia - the minutiae - lay the credibility and the integrity, but more than that, there was something else, something on which so much in life depended… the truth.

The story began to recall little anecdotes and accounts of things that had happened long ago, things that he had completely forgotten about. Memories, that had laid dormant for so many years were suddenly being brought back into his consciousness. Once, when Thomas was about seven or eight years old, he had been invited to a friend's birthday party. But he did not have enough money to buy a present and his mother didn't have any money as it was near the end of the week, so he had wrapped up a book that someone had given him a few months earlier as a present. When he gave the neatly wrapped present to his friend at the party, he unwrapped it and immediately exclaimed much to Thomas's embarrassment and to the amusement of everybody else at the party, that this was the very same book that he had given Thomas only two months earlier. This identical experience had haunted Blake since the day it had happened and he had never forgotten it. *COMPLETELY* FORGOTTEN *H* *UNTIL NOW*

These were unimportant, inconsequential things, things that he would rather not remember, but the carefully chosen words added a poignancy, relevance, and sentient authority to the tale.

He arrived at the end of the story or so he thought, but on turning over the last page, the one he had signed only a few weeks earlier, he saw there was more. The blank pages of chapter four had now been populated with more words. The empty space that had so utterly confused and confounded him on previous readings had now been neatly filled with sentences - between the head title and the page number at the bottom, the story was moving forward, towards its inevitable end. *MAKE SURE / CERTAIN .*

He gingerly placed the manuscript on the sofa, stood up, walked over to the French window and looked out into *ALSO CERTAIN* the garden. He needed to ensure he was awake, not just dreaming. He really was not sure what was happening, but how could he check. He suddenly realised there was no way of confirming *ACTUALLY* beyond any reasonable doubt. Does anybody really ever know he wondered? Reginald Clanford had always jokingly advised him that, "Life, my boy was all an illusion made up of millions of stories, some true, some not and there is no way of knowing which is which. The only true reality is death..." In a more prosaic and less dramatic tone, he would normally finish this insightful moral precept with something along the lines of … "Now all we have to do is print a few of the really good stories and we would all make a jolly good living. And if by chance we can find just one story, the one that hasn't yet happened, but could - then all the better for us, for the most intriguing, captivating and enthralling of all stories would be the one as yet untold and that would make us rich beyond our wildest dreams."

It all sounded very whimsical and capricious at the time, just take a small selection of the stories that one way or another made up the flotsam and jetsam of somebody's life - stories that had been carefully distilled into a few hundred pages, publish them with an enticing cover and we would all be comfortable for life. The words just told the reader something that had already happened, the same story could be told a thousand different ways and probably would be over time, in fact, somebody once said that there were only really seven completely different stories and every written word was fundamentally based on one of them.

Now those words took on an entirely different perspective. Up until now, there had never been a basic story line, which rested almost entirely on the narrative predicting a future that had already been lived, but by its very nature one that could be changed.

If you didn't read the future would it still happen?

Blake sat back down in his chair and tentatively began to read... to wonder if...

Prospect Road 4

Chapter Four
written by
Anthony Theodore Clackle

1981

I had now been promoted to senior editor at the publishers now in charge of making decisions on the commissioning of potentially high volume sellers. Mine was the final decision on which books the company would select for a publication. With this elevation came a considerable amount of responsibility. The company were now depending entirely on my judgement as to whether we should adopt the risky strategy of spending large amounts of money promoting an unknown writer, one who they thought might repay this investment many times over with world-wide sales or alternatively, default to the tried and tested if somewhat predictable formulaic output of an established contracted author.

It was an onerous responsibility, but I felt confident that I could handle the pressure. The ultimate goal as with any publisher was to find the writer with the story that would change the world. The pot of gold at the end of a rainbow, the panacea for all ills, this was my quest.

To this end we conscientiously read everything that came into the office if one of my assistant's thought there was just a glimmer of hope, I would read it as well.

But still I couldn't find anything that inspired me, something that was worthy of the level of potential interest required to warrant the investment of vast sums of the company's money. This went on for years and many books were shortlisted and quite a few were even published, but there was never any realistic expectation of stratospheric sales. Some books are like that. They sell maybe a few hundred thousand copies, which was not unreasonable, in fact it was a considerable achievement for the writer, but for a publisher it would possibly only return him two pounds on a hardback and much less on a paperback. With all the marketing, albeit on a considerably smaller budget, and all the other overheads this did little more than keep the company ticking over.

What we desperately needed, to ensure our continued survival was a major blockbuster of a novel. One that would sell in the millions and be reprinted in every country of the world and possibly be turned into a film. A book that would continue to sell for many years finding new generations of readers who could reimagine it with consistent regularity.

This was what I was looking for and this is what I eventually found one day when I was passed a hand written manuscript. An unrequited love story between a gardener/handyman and a novice nun set in in Aix en Provence in the 1960's. The story was beautifully written and brought me to tears such was the passion embedded within the pages. Love stories were always good sellers, but with the subtle twist that this book contained it could not fail. I had found my Holy Grail. I read it over and over again to be sure of how I felt about it. To convince myself that I hadn't just settled on this out of shear frustration and desperation at not being able to find anything better, but it was good, it was very good, in fact it was the best story I had read in years, possibly the best ever. Each time I read it, I just became more convinced of the potential success it could achieve. I showed the book to the senior partners in the company and after reading it, they too agreed with me. They would publish The Chapter Room a love story, a story that hopefully would embrace the world and change Thomas's life forever.

MENTION GIDEOU DREN
WRITTEN BY

Chapter 6

ONCE AGAIN

Blake was becoming engrossed by the story and flipped over another page, but there were no more words, just as before the story ended abruptly. ~~He Blake~~ placed the manuscript carefully back down on the table. For some reason he now treated it with some reverence as if it were a treasured antiquity, but it wasn't, it was a diary of his life so far and now of things yet to happen, written by someone he had never met. Could this book - The Chapter Room - as foreseen in the book actually exist he asked himself. He had no recollection of seeing the book title in the office and could therefore only assume that this part of the story had not yet happened. *ANACHRONISM*

While he pondered over this enigma his mind drifted to *OFF TB* thoughts of how sadly, the vast majority of earths inhabitants wandered through life in quiet desperation never really knowing why they were here, but for him suddenly he knew there was a reason and it was being slowly unravelled before his eyes. No longer existential confusion, just mindful curiosity. He heard Catherine's car pull up in the drive and stepped outside to welcome them all back home. He felt relieved he was no longer alone with.....

'Hello daddy,' exclaimed Claudia joyfully, we've been to see Grandma and I made a cake.'

'Did you,' he replied, quietly, 'You're a very clever girl.'

'I helped as well,' said Max, not wishing to be left out of the free flowing adoration.

'No you didn't,' interrupted Claudia haughtily, while glaring demonstrably at Max. 'All you did was eat it before it was even cooked.' Blake looked at Max and Max just smiled back with an expression of insouciant innocence.

'I was testing it for quality,' said Max in a faux managerial tone, while wrinkling up his eyebrows. 'I have to keep an eye on her.' He suddenly sounded protective and mature for his age. Blake realised they were both already little people with views and opinions and attitudes, little people just waiting to be big people.

'Good day?' asked Blake, kissing Catherine and hugging her gently while squeezing her bottom.

'It was lovely, how was yours?' replied Catherine smiling and looking a little surprised at his uncharacteristic assault on her bum, 'obviously not too shabby... in flagrante extra domum, I am surprised.' It was a liberal interpretation, Catherine's Latin was a little rusty, but Blake understood what she meant.

'I tell you in a minute, nothing alarming just a little unusual,' replied Blake.

Catherine smiled with a slight hint of curiosity. Her eyes scrunched up a little into a quizzical expression as she unloaded a couple of bags from the car. She was obviously intrigued by his comment. She knew Blake better than he knew himself.

Blake grabbed the bags and they walked back to the house. Max and Claudia went straight out to play in the garden and Blake went in to the kitchen to put the kettle on to make a pot of tea.

'Do you two want a cold drink,' he shouted out of the back door.'

'Yes please daddy,' came the chorused reply. He poured out two orange drinks and took them out to the garden for Max and Claudia.

'So what have you to tell me,' said Catherine settling herself down at the kitchen table.

'Well, you remember that book I was reviewing, the one about... '

'Prospect Road,' interrupted Catherine, she knew instinctively what he was going to talk about, 'yes you gave it to me to read a few weeks ago, well the first few chapters anyway, that was the one that detailed the protagonist's life story some of which coincidently just happened to be a little similar to your dark and distant past.' She was being a little flippant.

'It was more than a little similar,' he corrected, 'it was precise and exact in almost every detail except for the names.' Blake had assumed a stern managerial almost pompous expression, one that possibly he thought commanded immediate respect and attention, one that he possibly would have used in the office when wishing to assert his authority, but it didn't work at home and trying it on with Catherine always made her laugh out loud.

'Was it?' asked Catherine whimsically, pursing up her lips into a tiny rosebud - definitely not taking the matter to seriously.

'Yes it was, you know it was,' said Blake indignantly.

Catherine acknowledged her slight disengenuosity. 'And...' she asked.

'Well I started to read it again today and...' he paused for a moment not for added dramatic effect, but to give him self sufficient time to allow his brain to quickly revisit the content of the four chapters, in particular the last one.. 'There's now a fourth chapter.' There, he had said it.

'A what,' asked Catherine?

'I just told you, there is a forth chapter.'

'Where,' asked Catherine sounding oddly suspicious.

'After the third,' replied Blake, who was still having a little problem believing it himself.

'After the third,' echoed Catherine, '... after the third chapter where? there wasn't anything the last time I read it?' It was beginning to sound like a sketch from a seriously under achieving television sitcom.

'Correct,' replied Blake.

'And when did it app.... materialise?' she asked, sounding more than a little curious.

'I came across the manuscript when I was tidying up and decided to give it another read while you were at your mothers and there it was...'

'And there it was,' she repeated with just a tiny hint of scepticism, but she refused to immediately surrender to the obvious. She looked Blake squarely in the eyes and realised that he was not messing around with her, he was troubled and uneasy in a way she hadn't seen before.

'Have you had a drink today?'

'Not a drop,' replied Blake firmly. *BUT HE HAD AND WONDERED WHO HE HAD LIED*

'Can I read it?' she quietly asked.

'Of course,' replied Blake 'I want you to read it. I think you need to, if only to bring a little sanity to this madness. If you can't, I don't know who can.'

'Right,' said Catherine summoning all her faculties together into a plan of action, which she was already formulating in her head. 'First thing - I'll make that tea...'

'Ah,' said Blake, 'sorry, I did boil the kettle.'

'...then we can sit down and read it together.' She made the tea and some more cold drinks for Max and Claudia, and then they both walked back into the lounge and sat on the sofa. She passed a cup of tea to Blake and glanced across at the empty whiskey glass on the small table. She said nothing, but Blake noticed.

'Lemonade, it was just a lemonade honestly, I wouldn't lie to you.'

'I believe you,' said Catherine.

'Thank you,' he replied a little timidly, almost as if he had been scalded for being a naughty boy. Catherine was not cross, but obviously the manuscript and Blake's preoccupation with its contents was now beginning to try her patience a little.

'I'm ready now,' said Catherine now sitting at the other end of the sofa so she could face Blake. He took a sip of tea. She smiled at him.

Catherine picked up the manuscript and briefly flicked through to the beginning of chapter four, and there it was where there was nothing before, there were now words. She looked up at Blake and in a less flippant tone than before and carefully choosing her words, she cautiously asked...

'I'm not for one moment saying you have...' she paused realising she was now treading on very dangerous ground, in fact, if theirs wasn't a marriage based on absolute

THIS WAS NOT HIM AT ALL. HE HAD ALSO

WHICH HE NEVER DID

unimpeachable trust, she would probably not have even ventured to float the question, furthermore she realised that just saying the words could do irreparable damage to their relationship. She knew their marriage was strong, but there was a breaking point for each and every bond, a point from which there was never any going back, when the invisible golden thread was stretched to its limit and then beyond, and at that point it was irretrievably broken. After that, you could only move forward, as if starting again. There could be no reliance on what had passed before, that would be gone forever all the trust built up over years would have been destroyed, that was the risk you take, sometimes the risk you had to take. Nevertheless despite all her misgivings she had to take the gamble and ask the question…

'You could you have written this today, while we were away…' the words seemed to hang in the air suspended on a slender thread of faith, fidelity and love. Catherine felt the air leave her body just as an inverted body is exsanguinated when the throat has been cut. She took another deep breath in preparation for what might come next, but Blake said nothing at first and Catherine knew instantly she may have made a terrible mistake, possibly the worst mistake of her *THEIR LIVES* life. It was a betrayal of trust, something that could never be reinstated.

His poker face said nothing, it was totally unreadable. His brain was working overtime, probably more intensely than it had worked in a long time, tumbling through the various possible computations that could be construed from those few words, but it was not conveying one speck of emotion or response to the far extremities of his body. It was as if he had been suspended in a moment of freeze frame animation, but a moment that was being unbearably extended.

'Yes,' replied Blake after a few more painful seconds, possibly some of the longest seminal seconds she could remember, seconds, in which their lives could have inextricably changed beyond all recognition… even possibly moved beyond a point of no return. It was the time it took a smiling President Kennedy, waiving from the back of limousine, a man who carried the hopes of the world in his hands, to change his expression to one of utter astonishment and disbelief. His life was instantly blown away and those few seconds changed the world forever, these few seconds could change Catherine's and Blake's lives forever.

'Yes you are right,' continued Blake turning to smile at her with quizzical admiration. This was, above all else, what had first attracted him over ten years ago when they first met, this feisty, no holds barred, rebellious streak. It was only afterwards, lying in bed, that he realised how stunningly attractive she was with her large dark brown Mediterranean eyes, eyes of molten lava that could burn right through him if he did her wrong.

'I could have written it,' continued Blake, 'In fact I was certain I had at one point, such was my disbelief when I read it; I am going mad, I thought, but then.... no, something else is happening.' Catherine slowly let the air out of her body, and began to breathe normally again. No damage appeared to have been done and she quietly said a little prayer to herself.

'I don't know what is happening, but I didn't write it, and as unbelievable as it sounds, and believe me I know how ridiculous this must sound, I didn't write it because the book...' Blake paused for a moment; he had to make sure he wasn't losing his grip on reality. But he was certain he was still sane... he slowly glanced around the kitchen and then looked at Catherine having absorbed all the things he recognized, all the everyday things he had always taken for granted, all the things now so precariously balanced on the tip of a knife and then he said the words...

'The book is writing itself.' There he'd said it, either he was completely round the twist, having suddenly developed some inexplicable schizophrenic condition or he was dealing with something way beyond his normal comprehension of literary phantasy.

Catherine stared at him, but said nothing.

'The book is writing itself...I swear,' he repeated, more slowly this time with heightened intonation. I thought somebody else was somehow writing the words and somehow slipping them into the manuscript, but that isn't what's happening.'

Catherine didn't know what to say. She had been temporarily struck dumb by his explanation of some supernatural phenomenon. This wasn't quite what she was expecting on her return home having been away for only two days.

She glanced downwards for a moment trying to get her head around what Blake had just said. She lifted her eyes back up and looked at the man who was now sitting at the end of the sofa. This man whom she loved and adored and who had just figuratively opened his veins and let the blood pour out onto floor, such was his incredulity at the circumstances that now seemed to be overwhelming him and taking control of his life and to a lesser degree hers.

'I believe you,' she muttered quietly. Blake looked at her for some kind of indication of what particular part she believed.

'That I'm some sort of sociopathic nutter who's managed to develop a multiple personality disorder in the course of a few hours or that I've magically stumbled across an incredible self-writing book?'

'I don't believe you are mad or that you are writing the book, there has to be another simple explanation. We just have to try and work out what that is.'

'How?' said Blake, having spent the last few minutes moving with terpsichorean agility from reality to abject desperation and back to reality.

'Let's read it again, all of it,' said Catherine, 'to see if there is something we've missed and then I suggest we lock it away in a safe, where neither of us can get to it, and we will come back to it in a month or two, and see if anymore has been written.' Brief, concise, practical, and logical. All the elements he seemed to be totally incapable of mustering together at this particular moment, but fortunately for him, all the qualities he so admired in her and which she had managed to martial together at the opportune moment in one crucial decision.

Catherine had remained undaunted - un-phased by the peculiar conundrum now facing them and had remained calm and unruffled by events. She had come up with a solution... no not a solution more a navigable route out of this maze of confusion and misdirection.

'That sounds good, brilliant... yes!' said Blake. He stumbled around for more suitable adjectives, but none where forthcoming; his brain seemed to have partially shut down. He moved down the sofa next to Catherine and slowly with some trepidation they opened the manuscript to page one.

'I'll make another cup of tea,' said Catherine, before we begin to read. 'I think we need it.'

'Good idea!' replied Blake, who was endeavouring to regain his composure and some of his sanity.

'We could have brandy,' suggested Blake, but Catherine's expression put paid to that. She made the two cups of tea and put them on the table in front of the sofa, before walking out into the garden to check on Max and Claudia. They had both fallen asleep on the hammock. Catherine came back into the kitchen.

'They're both asleep, so we should be uninterrupted for at least an hour.' They began to read from page one and continued to the end of chapter four without saying a single word to each other.

'So you started young,' mused Catherine, 'and you have another wife you haven't told me about.' She smiled. 'That wasn't there last time I read this, I would have remember that detail. So I agree, somehow that has been added, which means you would have to have had to retype the whole manuscript to squeeze in the extra details mentioned.' There was just a hint intrigue in her expression as she knew he was appallingly slow at typing, he "hated it with a passion" a phrase he often used in reference to the skill, and one, which he had carefully explained to her on one of their first dates when he was trying to impress her. The expression, so he had told her, originated from South America where the indigenous Indians threw Passion fruit at foreign explorers, not without some justification. But,

Catherine secretly harboured serious doubts about the credibility of the explanation finding it patiently ridiculous. She had not however ever mentioned her reservations to Blake.

Blake didn't answer.

'The bit about the book sounds interesting.'

'The book?' queried Blake.

'The Chapter Room,' replied Catherine.

'What about it,' asked Blake?

'It has a nice ring to it. Could be just what you need, a blockbuster, isn't that what you said a few weeks ago? If the book is writing your life, then maybe that's about to happen.' Catherine said this more as a diversion from what they were really trying to do. It was an interesting and welcoming interlude after the uneasy period they had just endured and one that gave Blake something on which to dwell. Adopting Catherine's suggestion could prove once and for all that he was neither an accomplice in some dark Machiavellian plot nor the instigator of this bizarre situation.

'Martin has a safe,' said Catherine, interrupting Blake's thoughts. Martin was a retired banker who lived next door and had been a good friend of theirs for many years. He and his wife Ruth had been regular Friday night dinner guests since before Max and Claudia were born, but not so much lately since Ruth had died.

'Perfect,' replied Blake. 'You take it round, just tell him,' he stopped for a second to think, '... you tell him whatever you think is best, but the one condition is he only gives it back to us if we are both together or to you, but not me.'

'That sounds good,' agreed Catherine. She smiled at Blake, the tide of anxiety and dread that had been threatening to engulf them over the last hour was now slowly, very slowly receding, their problem now partially resolved. She took the manuscript around to Martin and after explaining some, but not all of the details about the book, Martin agreed to place the book in his safe.

Chapter 7

RE Jig.

It must have been a few weeks after the Prospect Road manuscript had been safety imprisoned in Martins safe. Now it was being treated as a literary Edmund Dantes, a victim of suppression for simply trying to convey truth and honesty, but now all but forgotten about. There was a knock on Blake's office door and Jamie popped his head round the corner.

'Sorry to interrupt, but I have this one which you might like to have a look at.' He held up a manuscript.

Blake stopped what he was doing, looked up at Jamie, and made an expression of indulgent enthusiasm. He had been engrossed in something else he was already reading, and whatever it was it seemed to have partially retained his attention, but he beckoned Jamie to come in and take a chair opposite.

'We've all read it,' continued Jamie excitedly, 'it's that good so I thought it was about time I brought it to you to read.'

'What's it's about?' asked Blake casually, but still with the air of anticipation and expectancy that came with every new book passed to him after it had been through the normal office vetting system. He now trusted their judgement explicitly he had no option. By the time a book was passed to him for review he knew, with reasonable certainty, that it would at least be well written, articulate and hopefully interesting.

There was no longer any physical possibility that he could personally read every manuscript submitted to their office anymore, such were the number of manuscripts now being submitted. Surprisingly this is precisely what he had done when he first came to work a Clanford and Fox back in 1968, but the number of scripts sent through in those days were considerably less than now. The development of the word processor in the 1980's had meant a deluge of new works by less than gifted writers and a filtering system became essential to weed out the less than flawless efforts.

His decision as to what happened after he read a book depended almost entirely on whether he thought it had commercial viability or not and if it would sell it adequate quantities to make publication profitable. He had reviewed many books that ticked all the boxes, but for one reason or another had decided they probably wouldn't sell sufficient copies to make them viable. So much was now being written that the quality of the writing was not always the most important factor, sometimes something as simple as notoriety was enough to sell a book irrespective of the quality of the writing and that would be after it had been seriously edited. Many great pieces of literature were probably languishing, long forgotten in dusty old drawers somewhere after having been rejected by a number of publishers. Probably they would never see the light of day, but that didn't diminish one iota from the possible remarkable quality of the work. Such was the injustice of the business. ART ?

He often wondered what would happen if that feeling - that inexplicable frisson of electrical excitement that coursed through his whole being whenever he read something that was really good, suddenly deserted him. He would have to find something else to do, something entirely different, maybe become a gardener or a bricklayer something perfectly defined in what it produced, something TACTILE tangible, something you could touch and see. Something that no longer required imagination, for that element was essential to enable him to continue doing what he did. True success was the imagination of the writers intelligence having riotous fun with words and the publishers unqualified, unerring belief in the finished product, but without the benefit of any logical explanation or quantifiable rational. It was a religion above all other religions, the communicator above all other forms of communication.

He knew the only way to define the true worth of any story was to measure how much it effected a reader. Did the story make you want to change your life and be a different person - be a better person? Did it make you want to reassess how your presence effected other people - did your very existence bring joy and pleasure to others, even if only one person; or did it just bring sorrow and sadness? Could you identify yourself with one of the characters and was that good or bad. All these things come as part of the experience of reading a good story, and as Reggie Clanford had told him many years ago, "A good story starts at the beginning and finishes at the end, but a brilliant story starts long after it had begun and finishes well before the end. That way the reader, now completely enveloped in the narrative, is given the opportunity, with their imagination to write their own beginning and end and that turns the same story into a millions different story's, one for every reader. This was golden elixir of literary success.

'It's a love story - tragic finish,' replied Jamie, 'but it's slightly different from the normal dross. Nicely written, well-drawn characters. I actually found it hard to put down, which as you can imagine is normally easy for me, so definitely not that bad for a first attempt.' He almost sounded patronisingly Blasé about it, but held back just enough to remain on the upside of cautious.' But then publishers get like that. In one respect they were not dissimilar to literary critics, it was in their nature to be delicately cynical and respectfully critical, but never quite going the distance and actually committing themselves, just in case...

They seldom found anything perfect at first glance. These were the sort of people who would have described the bible as painfully loquacious - thin on plot - vague, unrealistic characterisation - obtuse, oddly derivative dialogue with incessantly rambling dialectic narrative coupled with an unfamiliar development format. Sort of thing Tolkien, Nietzsche or Gandhi might have cobbled up after a seriously heavy session on the old vino plonk.

'I think it could be great for the Christmas market,' continued Jamie. More books were sold during the Christmas period than at any other time of the year except the summer holidays.

'Yes, good, can you leave it on the desk,' replied Blake, still not quite hearing every word. He was actually in the middle of digesting the contents of the company's latest half-yearly sales report and going by the look on his face, it did not make for particularly pleasant reading. 'I'll have a look at it when I get back from my meeting.' He glanced up at Janine again and half smiled.

He was going out for a "media - marketing conference", (a publishers euphemism for a long drawn out boozy lunch affair) with Barrington Kane, one of Clanford and Fox's regular writers. He had just completed his ninth "Inspector Chang" Chinese detective stories and they needed to discuss how they would market this latest addition to the series. Invariably there would be a large number of bookshops to visit for short readings and book signings as well as television interviews and various other connected events. All this, even more significant now as there had been talk of a possible television drama series, this would inevitably boost book sales.

The Chang stories were always good sellers, although a little banal even for Blake's catholic taste and he often experienced tortured anguish at Barrington's misappropriation of the definite article in split infinitives. Nevertheless the prose worked and "as that was all he had", as his hero Raymond Chandler once said, "that was all that really mattered".

Never the less he was professionally and contractually obliged to read them and commit to memory every intimate, gory detail and in this respect, he had religiously and judiciously fulfilled his obligation.

There was something unquestionably compelling and strangely charismatic about this incompetent yet inscrutable detective with the glottal stop issue that intrigued readers. He was forever leaving out the two "t's" in butter or pronouncing "that" as "dat" as in 'Dat is very interesting, but dat doesn't make any sense.' Which was one of Chang's favourite catch lines before delivering a startling revelation.

He fumbled and bumbled around each investigation making calamitous errors, totally disregarding the perceived and obvious clues, most of which he invariably eventually disproved of or discarded out of hand. He was ably assisted by a very attractive Chinese girl detective who did all the running around and research required to solve part of each case and of course, she conveniently brought the element of sexual tension that was necessary to complete each story.

In the final chapter, with one staggering stroke of genius and panache, Chang would invariably deliver a highly relevant (but normally horrendously abstruse) ancient Chinese maxim that would, after Chang's painfully drawn out explication invariably lead him and the readers, to the guilty party. Samples of Chang's Chinese aphorisms for consideration were:

Cat with nine lives should never eat snow in June.

Man who falls into fast flowing river must quickly learn to sing.

Barrington did however have a large following of steadfastly loyal "Changies" and they were the sort of bread and butter readers that kept the company ticking over and Barrington in plentiful supply of beer tokens.

The real secret of becoming a financially independent writer (and Barrington had comprehensively exploited this truism to the nth degree) was to catch and retain dedicated readers who would religiously buy every book you wrote no matter what. This guaranteed continuous and ever increasing sales and therefore a steady income for writer and publisher. All the writer had to do was keep turning them out on a regular basis. Readers invariably stayed with particular writers they liked and it took some concerted and determined application by the writer to alienate faithful acolytes.

Barrington was the company's most popular writer apart from Desmond (Dezzi) Chandler, a lecherously rapacious middle aged chef with his own television program and a prodigious following of male and female fans, a large number of whom he had apparently bedded over the many years the program had been running. Dezzi would spend the vast majority of their lunchtime meetings regaling Blake, in great detail, with his latest conquests, which Blake, understandably, found embarrassingly insufferable

Regardless of natural predilection

Regardless of Predilection   COSMOPOLITAN ATTITUDE

Not APPARENTLY HAVING A Preference ONE WAY OR

and often in extremely bad taste, (no pun intended.) Unfortunately, this was an essential element of being a publisher. It was necessary, in fact absolutely essential that Blake endured this monosyllabic innuendo riddled diatribe at least twice a year, if he was to retain Dezzi as a client.

It was much the same routine with Barrington Kane, but without the ghastly details of his personal indiscretions shamelessly laid bare and then ladled over the linguine. He seldom ate much when out for lunch with Dezzi.

After lunch, Blake slowly made his way back to the office alone, musing contemplatively over the many topics they had lightly brushed over during lunch. He had left Barrington talking to a woman.

Barrington was actually a pen name, (his real name was Walter Measal.) The publicity department, in their infinite wisdom, had decided very early on that his name didn't sound quite rugged enough for a writer of detective story's so they had come up with the newer, punchier macho sounding one. He found Walter nee Barrington mind numbingly boring, but out of common curtesy had put up with him bleating on about his latest Inspector Chang escapade for nearly two hours when just as he was beginning to lose the will to live, their lunch, was somewhat fortuitously interrupted by a fan recognising him. She gushingly introduced herself at their table and Barrington invited her to join them. This was the opportunity Blake needed to leave and he quickly grasped the chance, made his excuses and left. As far as Blake was concerned, the interloper deserved all she would receive from Barrington for her bad manners.

As he meandered along the pavement, he quietly thought about the enormous sacrifice of valuable time he had to make in the line of fire, either suffering the ramblings of a sexually rapacious reprobate or the inane mumblings of an inveterate bore, but such was his life, the one he had chosen. Oh how he craved the conversation of an intelligent articulate writer.

A little worse for wear, and slightly shell shocked, he made his way up the staircase to his office arriving just after five to pick up some reports he wanted to take home and read that night, when he noticed the manuscript that Jamie had left on his desk. He picked it up - put it into his case and wandered back out of the office, saying goodbye to the remaining staff as he went. He arrived home just over two hours later. *Delays Due To Maintenance*

'Hi darling, how was your day?' asked Catherine as she walked up to kiss him hello. Wrapping her arms around him and pulling him in close for a cuddle.

'Same as always.' He replied squeezing her bum. A number of black coffee's on the train had sobered him up from his lunchtime meeting and returned him to some resemblance of normality.

'There were delays with the trains due to the unusual heat. That is what the station announcer said anyway. The trains had obviously been designed to run on lines with a different kind of heat.' He giggled to himself at his attempt at a witticism, fortunately, writing one-liners was not his livelihood, otherwise he would have been very poor and hungry. *or his forte*

'... I waded through the sales reports today; they were a bit depressing for the first six months. Things have slowed down quite a bit. All we've really have in the pipeline is another one of Barrington Kane's 'Inspector Chang Mystery's,' for the Autumn, which hopefully will boost things along a bit.'

'Oh I like those,' said Catherine, they're really funny…and quite naughty in places,' she added after a slight pause. It was a slightly stilted qualification. Blake made a mental note about her comment, it was after all singly objective, and he hadn't canvassed her for an opinion.

'How many is it now? Must be five or six,' she asked.

'Number bloody nine, would you believe,' He couldn't believe anybody liked the books, but they did. No accounting for taste he thought, but that was moving to dangerous ground. They were mostly badly written, the plots were weak, ill-conceived, half- baked and unrealistic. There were no tangible police procedures (which were precisely and accurately documented in all the other detective novels doing the rounds, and which most readers knew backwards these days) but despite all these flaws, they sold, in their millions.   AFTER SERIOUS EDITING

He privately, (he daren't let anybody in the office know his views in case it got back to Kane) compared the longevity of the Inspector Chang series to the Hayflick phenomenon whereby human cells will only divide a certain number of times until they cease to divide any further because the DNA structure had been so comprehensively degraded.   Blake thought the original ACTUALLY cracking storyline of the first book, which he had enjoyed, had now been over exploited and replicated so many times that it was now in danger of completely running out of all and any originality, in fact he was sure it had all but run out by about number five.   However the readers begged to differ and kept coming back to buy - in ever increasing numbers - poorly rehashed variations of the first book. Apparently Mr Change was on the road to perpetuity and Barrington Kane was well on his way to becoming a multi-millionaire.

Reggie Clanford had once told him that nobody ever went broke underestimating the bad taste of the general public. Here was the classic example in question to prove his point.

'Daddy!' exclaimed Max, who had been sitting quietly on the sofa reading, promptly castigating his father for swearing.

'I'm sorry.' said Blake contritely, while hunting around in his trouser pocket for a one pound coin which he immediately dropped into the pink pig money box that Max had suddenly produced from nowhere and was brandishing fervently under Blake's nose.   That was the financial arrangement they had come too which worked both ways, but more so in Max's favour, so Max was extremely careful with his language. He was making serious plans for the large quantity of pound coins now accumulating in the pig and had no intention of giving any of it back under the reciprocal agreement.

'I thought you liked them?' asked Catherine curiously

'I liked the first one, that was entertaining, but then it went downhill for me afterwards, but uphill for sales, so I stuck with it.' ᵀʷᴬᵀ

'It pays the bills,' said Catherine philosophically.

'It does indeed, and it's very ungracious of me to be so disparaging and pious about them, that is a tadge hypocritical I admit, but they are bloody boring.' The pig re-appeared on cue.

'Aaaaahh,' said Blake. ruffling about in his pocket for another coin. 'But's there's hope yet,'

'Oh,' replied Catherine.

'I have this.' He produced the manuscript from his case that he had picked up as he left the office.

'The new Inspector Chang,' asked Catherine with a wry smile followed promptly by an expression of benign anticipation?

'No, no it isn't actually,   it's... ' but he stopped, noticing that virtually all of the front cover was missing apart from a small area around the two punched holes. It looked as if the front page had been ripped off, possibly when he had put the manuscript into his case, but when he checked in his case, it wasn't there either. The rest of the manuscript appeared to be intact, but he checked the last page just to make sure it wasn't missing too, it wasn't.

'.. it's a new writer, Jamie thinks it's the best thing he's read in ages and apparently everybody in the office has read it and feels the same way. So that has to say something.'

'So maybe there is some   salvation,' said Catherine wryly. We may be able to afford a sausage and two feathers for Christmas dinner after all?'

'Yes maybe, we'll see,' replied Blake.

'Does it have a name,' asked Catherine?

'Yes, yes it does, but I don't know what it is or the writers name come to that, I've lost the front page, but it's a love story, I know that much, and it's   set in a convent in France. It's about a conman who is hiding from the police and working as a part timer gardener at the convent actually. He convinces the nuns in residence to sell the

SHOULD I REMOVE THIS

convent to a health spa company and retire on the proceeds to a luxury villa in the South of France and enjoy what is left of their lives. But he falls in love with one of the novice nuns and then everything goes wrong.'

'Oh,' said Catherine, 'well that's a little different. It does sound a bit far-fetched though.'

'Yes I thought so too, until I was told it was based on a true story.'

BIT OF

'Oh,' said Catherine, 'well that does make a difference.'

Blake sat down in the lounge and started reading the manuscript. It was intriguing from the first page and he found himself swept up in the story almost to the exclusion of everything else around him.

HAPPENING

Chapter 8

THE SISTERS OF MERCY
by Gideon Drew

Charlie sat in his cell reminiscing about all the good things that had happened in his life and how uncomplicated everything had once been - that was before it had all started to go terribly wrong. His memory of those days had been triggered by the exquisite fragrance of summer surreptitiously wafting up through the prison bars into his nasal passage to eventually settle somewhere in his brain, in whatever part of the somatosensory cortex processed these perceptions. His thoughts drifted back to a period just over a year ago, to when it had all began…

It was a day like any other day in Misericord, a tiny French village in the middle of nowhere.   The air was warm, still and heavy, and the spicy fragrance of the Dianthus and lavender that always seemed to overpower the other flowers, hung languidly in the air, as it did in most of southern France in late spring. The erotic pungent tang of Jasmine, the nocturnal accomplice and third member of the aromatic triumvirate that scented the country tended to be stronger in the evening, a time of passionate endeavour. The heady scented co-conspirators had now taken control of the countryside as they did every summer, a remorseless invasion of the senses by stealth and cunning intervention.

But it was the Dianthus that Charlie would always associate with long lazy lunches and intense discussions about politics, life and religion.   Such deliberations and debate always with his dear friend and confidante, Henri Pascal, owner of Café de Paris. The lavender reminded him of the febrile afternoons of inconsequential love and passion he had shared with so many women who had passed his way, women who were now nothing more than distant memories. Or maybe it was the other way around he wasn't sure, maybe he was becoming confused or maybe he just didn't want to remember anything or anyone anymore, all that is except for one woman.

The one who stole his heart, when he didn't think he really had one, his money, which he had never had until he met her, and his life, when he thought he was in complete control of it, but he wasn't, she just made him think he was. So much had changed and yet nothing had changed.

~~~

Charlie wandered casually down the dry dusty road to the village from the Convent of Le Sang de la Vie where he had been working that day. Dangling in his right hand was a half smoked Gitane cigarette, with the wisps of white smoke, like a recalcitrant fallen halo, curling up behind him.

His other hand was in his trouser pocket mindfully turning over some loose change. His beret was pulled down low and outwards in order to shade his eyes from the remorseless midday sun. He looked at the ground as he walked, but his thoughts were miles away, they were always somewhere else, never on where he actually was.

Charlie had been carrying out some general maintenance works and gardening during the morning, as he did most mornings, and now he was making his way to the Café for lunch.. A journey he made most days between the hours of 12.00 midday and 3.00 pm, when not otherwise engaged.

Today, the village was perfectly still. Still as if frozen in time and it appeared to be virtually deserted. All except that is for the sound of two obviously English women sitting at a table outside the café, under the shade of an Heineken umbrella, drinking wine and chatting animatedly. There was another man sitting alone at a another table reading a newspaper while sipping an expresso coffee. He didn't look up. Charlie began to…

'Dinner,' whispered Catherine, not wishing to disturb Blake any more than was necessary while he was reading. This was an understanding they had whenever he had started to read a manuscript during what were his normal working hours.

It was possibly a little regimented, even mildly dictatorial, but nevertheless absolutely essential to have such rules in place if he was to work productively at home. Normally he would be reading in his study, but occasionally, as today, he was sitting in the lounge.

'Oh great,' replied Blake, sounding a little surprised. He laid the manuscript down on the sofa. 'I'm starving.' As he got up he glanced at the old grandmother clock, it was ten past nine.

'Ten past nine that can't be right,' exclaimed Blake disbelievingly, maybe he had forgotten to wind it he thought. He looked at his watch to double check.

'Oh it is darling,' replied Catherine, you've been reading non-stop since you came home. You even missed the children going to bed... Blake looked a little stunned for a moment, his eyebrows dropping in bewilderment. Seldom, if ever, had he become so engaged with a story that it had prevented him from sitting down with his family to eat dinner or more importantly from saying goodnight to Max and Claudia.

'I am sorry, I just started on this and..' he apologised again most profusely picking up the manuscript and showing it to Catherine, 'I seemed to have just become totally absorbed by it, completely sucked in. It's a really wonderful story, I know our marketing people use the same old clichéd phrases of "can't put down", and "must read in one session, on half of the books we put out, but in this case it is actually true, it really is.' Blake was obviously completely intrigued by the story.

'So there's a chance I might be able to replace my old jalopy soon,' asked Catherine, with a pleading mournful expression. 'The old girl's just about on her last legs.' She wasn't being overly serious about her car, but the old Volvo estate was beginning to show its age and was breaking down on a more regular basis these days. She was having to depend more and more on Blake's car, which fortunately he left at home two or three days a week when he travelled to London by train. However if hers did fail it would invariably be on the day that Blake had driven in. Another niggling concern, was she would soon be taking Max to school every day and that was a round trip of eight miles down quiet country lanes where breaking down could be a real issue in the early morning with Claudia in the car as well.

'If there is any justice, this will fly and you can have a.. ' he hesitated for a moment '…brand new Volvo estate and I can have the Bentley convertible I have always wanted and we can have a decent holiday.'

'That's would be wonderful,' replied Catherine a little surprised at his bubbling jubilation. She did however ponder momentarily over the inequality of the choice of vehicles he had made.

'I haven't seen you this elated since… since Chelsea beat West Ham, and that was years ago.

'I am,' he replied, 'I really am. This could be it. The Holy Grail! This could be the one to put us firmly back on the publishing map once and for all.'

Things hadn't been brilliant almost since Reggie Clanford died. His timing was immaculate. He left just as their bestselling novelist died, not leaving anything unpublished behind. That was a golden opportunity that HAD just slipped through their hands through lack of planning.

They had Barrington Kane and TV personality Desmond Chandler and a number of other authors under contract who were all consistent bottom league sellers, but no major writer in the top twenty, which is where they had to be to make the serious money. So the company had been looking for someone to fill that top seller void ever since.

Blake sat down at the dining room table and they ate dinner together, albeit a little passed its best having been in the oven for a couple of hours longer than was strictly necessary. Blake poured a second glass of Niersteiner for Catherine and himself - they preferred the German Rieslings to the Austrian. He made a toast to the unnamed book and unnamed author. It was a bit odd toasting a book and an author without knowing either of their names.

'To the unknown writer… and his masterpiece,' They clinked their glasses together and drank the wine. Catherine smiled, she was glad to see some of the sparkle coming back in to Blake's eyes, just lately she had become a little concerned about his preoccupation with work and of course the matter of Prospect Road, which she knew was still troubling him, although he hadn't mentioned it recently.

'You can't be certain it's that good, you haven't finished it yet,' said Catherine.

'Oh I am.' he firmly replied. 'It's that good.' He smiled the smile of somebody who knew precisely what he had and what it could do for him, for his family, for the business and for his life. 'This book will change our lives, I am certain of that much.' Little did he realise just how much.

The next day, was a Friday and he caught the train into London and crossed as usual on the underground to Tottenham Court Road to get to Denmark Street and his office. On entering the office, he was immediately confronted by Jamie and two other assistant copy readers Julie and Rachel. They said nothing, but just looked at him.

'What!' He exclaimed. 'What's happened,' He naturally assumed the worst, and initially thought that maybe Barrington Kane had been murdered in some ritual killing, not dissimilar to one of his own storylines, but this one with the added credence of reality to give it some authenticity. Maybe it was a lover of literature that had chopped him up in to little pieces and fed him to his pet pig. Possibly as recompense for the untold damage he had not only inflicted on the literacy levels of his pulp fiction buying public, but more specifically on the degenerative effect he had had on the general standard of grammatical literacy, that he had so wantonly and blatantly encouraged. An assassin after his own heart. He drifted off, daydreaming for a few seconds, hypothesising on the various other gruesome ends that could have befallen Barrington. He had plenty of choice. Nine books (including the latest magnum opus,) that undoubtedly would now sell in incredible numbers with the additional unexpected marketing tactic of getting yourself murdered. That would certainly boost sales. With at least three grisly murder scenarios in each book covering the full spectrum of surprise demise he was spoiled for choice. Without doubt, a truly generous, noble and selfless act of bonhomie even, he pondered to himself.

'Is he dead?' Blake eventually blurted out, having now returned from a state of temporary wistful distraction and managing to string a few simple words together, with somewhat mixed emotions. He immediately realised that he was saying the words that he was thinking, and those words shouldn't have left his mouth. He had let his imagination run away with itself and that was unforgiveable in the circumstances.

'Who?' said Rachel, looking at him oddly and sounding a little confused.

'Barrington! Is he dead, was he murdered?' asked Blake quietly with a strained sense of empathetic compassion and concern whilst continuing unabated with his presumption of an untimely death and not yet able to let reality ease its way back into the conversation.'

'No!' said Jamie, 'Has someone told you something we don't know?'

'No, no,' replied Blake, ' It's just that... you - all standing here - to greet me, I thought....' Blake realised that he had completely misread the situation and that apparently Barrington was in fact perfectly fit and able, untouched by man eating pigs and probably half way through his next book.

'Did you read the book,' asked Jamie?

Blake took a deep breath. 'Book?'

'The Sisters of Mercy - the Gideon Drew manuscript,'

'Oh yes, yes I have, didn't know the names, somehow I had mislaid the first page.'

'I found that on your desk,' said Julie.

'Ah, that's where it was,' muttered Blake. He suddenly had a Deja vu moment. He could remember this same thing happened a few months ago with Prospect Road the book that he had temporarily forgotten about and which was now quietly resting in Martin's safe. The thought tempered his enthusiasm slightly.

'What did you think?' asked Jamie.

'What did I think,' answered Blake slowly with measured indifference. It was important he didn't appear too enthused or carried away, otherwise they might start talking about a bonus, which would obviously be a little bit premature at this stage. So best to be a little non-plus about it and deflate them a little, that would remove any immediate thoughts on that possibility. Of course, if the book did take off big time, it was customary to hand out bonuses, but all in good time he thought, it was early days yet, very early days.

'Yes it was quite good, I think we should have a chat with Mr....'. the author's name had, which either by deliberate intention or absent mindedness, temporarily escaped Blake. They staff were more than a little surprised and slightly deflated by his less than enthusiastic reaction, half expecting him to be as deliriously exhilarated as they had been by the book. Usually, he would be overly animated and bubbling with excitement after he had read something that he really liked, something, which had serious potential. But strangely, today he was not displaying any outwardly encouraging reactions.

Although he didn't immediately mention it to them, he had in fact stayed up all night and finished the book, such was the shear magnetism of the writing. Many books are touted as "one sitting book's that you can't put down,' this one truly was. He was totally exhausted by the end, such was the intensity of the writing. The dialogue filled his brain with an ineffable passion. The pure transience of the experience had seriously disturbed him almost to the point of inducing a state of paranoia, a fear of never again being able to achieve this level of visceral reaction and interaction with a written work.

He had been enthralled by a narrative that seemingly drew out all of his physical energy and dissipated it like a sponge soaking up his life, exsanguinating it into the space between the lines on the pages of the script. It was as if he were being slowly bled of his life force and the story was temporarily taking over his soul in exchange for the ecstasy of a sublime experience, one transient moment of totally unbridled exultation. It was a revelation, a sensation that he immediately realised could be replicated over and over again by every person who read the book.

The depth of characterisation was so good, he could swear he knew some of these people, intimately, he knew everything about them, every fault, every lie they had ever told, every indiscretion, every secret… every love they had ever known; they had become personal friends by 5am in the morning, which is when he managed to struggle to bed. By this time he had been reading nonstop for nearly eleven hours except for the short break for dinner and was beginning to hallucinate with the opiate of indescribable passion so cleverly embedded within the story. Such was his state of mind that he was finding it almost impossible to clearly distinguish between the people he had met in the book and real people who he conversed with every day, who in most cases he had known for years.

'It's Gideon Drew,' said Jamie, interrupting Blake's cerebral meanderings, 'I think he maybe American.'

'Oh,' said Blake, with a noticeable downturn in the tone of his voice. Almost as if, he were slightly disappointed for some reason. 'Gideon Drew, hmm, has a nice ring to it. Yes give him a ring and set something up. No! wait. He stopped for a few moments to gather his thoughts. 'Don't ring him, send a standard letter and ask him to arrange to come and see me. We don't want to seem too keen.'

Jamie looked at Blake a little oddly, he was not used to employing subtle psychological tactics when dealing with a potential new client especially one with a great book already under his belt and potentially many more to come. And of course there was every possibility the Gideon had already sent copies of the book to a number of other publishers and maybe they wouldn't be so tardy in responding if they felt the same way as he did.

He could see a small change in Blake's personality, it may have been infinitesimal, but it was there all the same, something he had definitely not seen before. A hint of ruthless manipulation and subtle misdirection. It was an uncharacteristic trait and it surprised him. He thought he knew every dimension of Blake's character having worked with him for over five years, but he had not encountered this aspect before. He took no further notice of his observation, and put it down to the elation of the moment. Maybe his brain had kicked out a few passive brain cells that had died and replaced them with a few aggressive ones. Who knows, he thought to himself.

'No problem,' replied Jamie, as he wondered off to organise the letter to be sent to Mr Drew.

Gideon Drew rang the office a few days later and a meeting was arranged for the third Thursday in September. During that period Blake had long discussions with the marketing, publicity and the sales departments on how best they could put together a major promotional campaign with maximum impact for an unknown writer. He hardly bothered with the editorial department as he firmly believed there was absolutely nothing they could add or remove that would enhance the book. In fact, their interference at any level could be considered to be degenerative, bordering on the derivative and could possibly reduce the flawless integrity of the piece. It would be a bit like asking a mongoose to edit Macbeth. That was probably a little disparaging he thought, comparing the mental agility and literary experience of his editorial team with a carnivore, but it sort of made the point in his head.

It was and this was something quite unique in all his literary experience a perfect manuscript without anything superfluous or irrelevant. There was no padding and the rhythm of story was as perfect as Ravels Bolero, building to a stunning crescendo that took your breath away and then brought tears to your eyes. It was just like having sex for the first time with a beautiful prostitute. Not that he ever had, but he had read about the experience in many books. He knew deep down that just like illicit sex, the book must have a flaw, a tiny imperfection, no matter how small, how indiscernible it had to be there somewhere, but he couldn't see it yet and that was what made it so perfect.

Blake was quietly excited, ecstatic in fact, but he kept his feelings in check. Some weeks later, the office received a telephone call from the Gideon responding to Blake's letter and an appointment was made for him to visit the office.

Chapter 9

Gideon Drew was a quiet, unassuming man in his mid-twenties. When Jamie showed him into Blake's office, he was polite and courteous to Jamie and didn't sit down until Blake asked him to. Blake looked at him and wondered why it was that so much talent, such an amazing gift should be gifted to one so young, Blake had tried himself to write a novel once but had failed miserably lacking the fire and talent to create anything truly original. He could see it in others fortunately and that was his saving grace, but deep down he felt bitter and frustrated that he had not been so blessed.

'Mr Drew, or can I call you Gideon?' asked Blake.

'Gideon is fine, thank you sir,' replied Gideon

'I'm not a sir Gideon,' replied Blake, 'please call me Blake, we're a big family here, it's all very informal.' He had an odd feeling he had heard that name before, but couldn't remember where. MENTION OF NAME ON PAGE 76

'Oh, I see,' said Gideon, 'right.' He actually seemed a little uneasy about the informality, which Blake quickly noted.

'Would you like some tea or coffee Gideon?'

'Yes please, tea thank you.' replied Gideon. Blake tapped on the intercom and asked Julie to organise some tea and biscuits.

'Right,' said Blake, 'let's make a start.' he smiled benignly at Gideon. 'Firstly I have to say I think it's a very good book. Everybody in the office has read it.' Not actually everybody had read it, only the editorial staff responsible for evaluation had, but it sounded impressive and inspiring, if a little obsequious.

A singular commitment by the company as a whole to one person's work. Blake nodded his head slowly as he spoke, a sort of brotherly gesture of comradeship. "They were all in this together, to make this book a great success." That was the message he wanted to convey.

'The story line is original, the dialogue is believable, which I can tell you is a real problem with many new writers, and quite a few established writers (he was thinking of one in particular) they tend to write as how they think people talk and not how people actually talk. It's surprising how many words people don't actually speak - they convey the message in other ways, and that is precisely what you have done, "little is more," and you have certainly grasped that concept.'

The Sisters of Mercy wasn't actually that long either, at just under seventy five thousand words it was, technically speaking, a novella rather than a novel, but that wasn't an issue worth worrying about. The Catcher in the Rye by Salinger, Breakfast at Tiffany by Capote, The Old Man and The Sea by Hemmingway, The Great Gatsby by Fitzgerald they were all considerably shorter and each one had managed to attain considerable cult status and all had made it to film (except the Catcher in the Rye).

'As for the characterisation, well I thought I knew those two people, well I knew all those people, but Charlie and Anna they just leapt out of the page and tore my heart out. They inspired me, they actually made me want to be a better person, and believe me, for a hard-bitten publisher like me that is some trick… no I take that back, this is no trick, this is pure genius.' Gideon thought back to some almost identical praise he had received many years ago.

Blake let that thought hang in the air for a few moments. He wondered whether he was overdoing it a bit, but what the hell - in for a penny… and to be perfectly honest that was exactly how he had felt the first time he read it anyway. The impact was in its immediacy and at times, unnerving ability to access areas of visceral awareness in the mind. The storyline activated emotions in a part of his brain that he was not even aware he had. Existential sensations that for most authors would be as alien as something from another planet.

'I think with the right marketing campaign this too could also be a major success, even, dare I say it, a possible classic!'

There, he'd said it. The magical words guaranteed to make the most hardened, cynical writer cry with happiness, (not that Gideon appeared to be either) the thought of immortality lingered listlessly in the air.

Even in measured quantities, sycophancy was a ploy he seldom defaulted to, but on this occasion, for reasons he could not fully comprehend, he thought it appropriate.

'We, that's the team and I, think it would appeal to a particular group, who are historically regular buyers and generally loyal customers to particular writers. This is where we see the continuity coming from, because obviously once we have a successful book, we need to follow it up with another one of the same quality - its keeps the reader focused and builds up a relationship between you and them. They come to trust you as a writer, and they get to know the characters, and therefore they buy your books on trust, once you have established your credentials with them. There is a bond between a writer's character and the reader. An invisible, intangible connection, a slender thread of commonality that links them together forever. It is like a love affair, a burning fire of desire, it just hangs on waiting to be satiated, a thirst that must be quenched.' Blake had lifted large sections of that diatribe from various books he had read recently.

'I understand,' said Gideon although he felt a little exhilarated by the overly dramatic approbation that was being heaped at his door, he was beginning to think it might envelop and suffocate him such was the intensity. He understood the importance of colourful, impassioned narrative in a story, it guided the reader in a particular direction as intended, but he was less prepared to accept delivery of such oratory fair.

'And to keep this love affair alive, we must feed the flame, this raging fire,' Blake was laying it on a bit thick, but he did this from time to time when he got into the mood. Deep down he was that frustrated novelist, but one who couldn't quite finish the story, whereas Gideon Drew had most definitely finished his.

'There is as always much more to publishing a book then just the printing element.' Blake paused for a moment to allow Gideon to absorb that thought. 'There is a lot psychology involved, are you with me so far?'

'Oh yes,' replied Gideon, I understand that. So how can I help?'

'Well actually you've done all you need to do at this particular time as far as the manuscript is concerned. Our people will brush it up as necessary, after contracts have been signed, and then send it to you for final approval before we publish. Right now all we have to discuss is the publishing contract and the financial arrangements, and we can do that today if you wish or leave it for a weak or two, it is entirely up to you. I can tell you what the basic terms will be now if you want?' Blake was purposely not being too pushy as he knew that generally, new writers grab whatever is going when an offer is made, having probably been rejected tens if not hundreds of times before by many other publishing companies.

It was a very much a dog eat dog business these days, and very few publishers took on new writers without some sort of established commercial or media celebrity value. Politicians, pop stars, film stars, footballers, soap stars, all these sort of people were guaranteed to make some sales irrespective of the quality of the writing. Even, if heavily ghosted and edited, the content was invariably lacking in depth and lustre, and no matter what you do or how much you spend - as he had always been told by Reggie Clanford - "You can't polish shit son." Reggie was a man of few words, but they were all wise words. Succinct and to the point. He was originally from Yorkshire.

This book did not need any polishing it sparkled like an enormous perfect diamond in the sky. Blake could see it, he could almost touch it and he could feel it in his bones.

Blake spent the next hour going over the specific details of the contract and what it would entail. It clearly set out the royalty rates for the first and following six books (they normally worked on a seven-book contract) and all the precursors and conditions, most of which seemed perfectly acceptable to Gideon. He did not try to renegotiate the royalty rates, appearing perfect happy with the terms of the offer. It fact he seemed to be more concerned about ensuring that Blake was happy with everything in the contract before he signed it.

Blake tapped the intercom and asked Jamie to pop in to witness the contract signing. Jamie arrived a few moments later. As he entered the room Gideon stood up and held out his hand, Jamie grabbed it firmly and shook it firmly.

'Great book, really enjoyed it. Those two people, Charlie and Anna, they feel so alive. Are they based on people you know? It was a genuine enquiry; Jamie really seemed interested to know how the intimate depth of sentient perception had been so cleverly achieved. Blake hadn't thought to ask that question.

'Yes they are, or were.... they are both dead now,' replied Gideon quietly, while drawing a small breath. His head dropped slightly, his eyes now looking at the floor, it was as if he were saying a prayer, maybe he was. He was obviously saddened by their passing.

That revelation sort of took the edge off things for a few seconds, and left an odd gloomy feeling lingering in the air. For a moment or two Jamie and Blake were both a little unsure as to how they should proceed, without causing any further distress, as Gideon, had obviously drawn heavily from this loss, of what must have been two very dear friends, for the characters in the book

'Oh!' replied Jamie, breaking cautiously into the stillness. 'That's so very sad, they were such inspirational people, makes you realise just how lucky we are.'

The compassion and empathy in Jamie's voice was clearly evident and seemed to reach out to Gideon. Gideon smiled.

'Thank you so much,' said Gideon, nobody else has ever said that, except for Blake,' he turned and looked at Blake and smiled. Blake smiled back.

'No, thank you,' said Jamie, shaking Gideon's hand once more before leaving the office, 'you have written a wonderful book.' He closed the door behind him and Gideon sat back down again.

'Do you have any more completed books?' asked Blake casually, not expecting a positive reply. He was a little saddened that there was unlikely to be a sequel to the book as the two protagonists had unfortunately died so tragically at the end. *Both*

'Oh yes,' he replied. 'I have two other books I am finishing. They all still need a bit of work, but I could have them completed with a month or two.'

'That's good, ' replied Blake, 'but there's no rush it will take three months before we can get this into the shops. So plenty of time.' He smiled at Gideon again and laid back in his chair. He could relax a bit now his work was done. The contracts were signed. *Sat. Leaned*

'It could be a hectic year for you promoting the book, so it's good that you have some writing already completed.' Gideon smiled again, but said nothing more.

Blake looked at Gideon, only now after nearly two hours of conversation did he really begin to see the person who sat before him. He had ceased to focus on the imagery, the creator of captivating prose, the writer and was now able to look at the man. He had dark features, short dark hair, a little goatee beard and large blue-grey eyes set back with bushy eyebrows. He was tall about six foot two, maybe three inches and there was a definite hint of the Mediterranean about him, possibly Greece maybe Italy, but definitely not American as Jamie had first thought. He obviously kept himself fit, he was a good looking man, there was no doubt about that, this would help when appearing in television interviews. He wore a gold wedding ring, but as he had not spoken about a wife, Blake thought it best not to say anything. If he had a wife, he would no doubt mention in due course. *it*

'You must come over to my house and meet the family sometime, we live in the country, so maybe you could make a weekend of it possibly over Christmas.'

'That's very kind of you,' said Gideon, 'I would love that very much, to meet your family.' Just for a second Blake felt a cold shiver run down his back, tingling the hairs. He looked around to see if there was a window open, but there wasn't. He thought no more about it.

They both got up and shook hands.

'Oh there is one small thing I need to ask,' said Gideon.

'Anything,' replied Blake, who was already thinking about going home and not really paying complete attention.

'The book title…'

'Yes,' said Blake,

'Well that was only a working title, but now I believe it to be a little ineffectual, so I have changed the name to something more appropriate, more relevant and more in keeping with the story, it relates to where they used to meet.' Blake was a little confused for a moment, he had read the book twice, but didn't remember anything about a particular meeting place just a room in the convent where the two main characters had met once to make love.

'Oh,' said Blake nonchalantly, he was perfectly happy with the working title, but he didn't want to upset the applecart now. 'I can't see that being a problem, what is the new name?'

Gideon didn't answer immediately, but slowly started to turn around as if he were pivoting on the spot, gazing at all the books on the shelves and the oak panelling, almost as if searching for inspiration. But he didn't need any incentive or stimulation for he already knew exactly what he was going to say, before eventually arriving back in the position from where he had started from to face Blake again, but now with no discernible expression at all on his face.

'I'm going to call it… The Chapter Room!'

Blake collapsed awkwardly into his chair, the words resonated in his head. His legs had turned to jelly and his whole body began to gently shake. The name, he knew that name…instantly he recalled Prospect Road, the manuscript now being held safely in Martin's safe and the book that had been mentioned in it. Oh yes he knew that name, that recurring nightmare that had been quietly haunting him for the last six months. The memory of that self-writing manuscript that he thought had quietly slunk back into the echelons of his distant memory, an area where it had no relevance and was no longer of any importance, but it was back yet again and with a vengeance. Blake looked up at Gideon, and noticed his face had begun to change. Gideon

AND THAT WAS WHERE HE HAD HEARD GIDEONS NAME

gazed back at Blake with a disdainful almost contemptuous glare that pierced right through him as if searching for his soul, his eyes were now burning with a fire an intensity that he could only compare with the flames of hell… for a split second Blake actually feared for his life.

'Are you OK?' asked Gideon innocently, apparently extremely concerned at seeing Blake suddenly fall unexpectedly back into his chair, 'Is that a problem?'

'I, I,…' Blake couldn't speak, but just muttered something almost inaudible.

Gideon rushed out into the main office looking for Jamie, who he could see seated at a desk.

'Jamie, come quickly something has happened to Mr Thornton.' Jamie ran across the room and into Blake's office. Blake, had by now recovered and was almost as he was before he collapsed.

'What happened,' asked Jamie, sounding very concerned?

'Mr Thornton fell back in his chair,' replied Gideon, appearing very apprehensive, I thought it was a heart attack or something. WRONG JAMIE AWAY

'Oh, it's nothing,' interrupted Blake, 'I just had a really odd dizzy moment, lack of food I think, working the brain too hard without nourishment, must be getting old.' He laughed self-deprecatorily.

'Do you want me to get you something?' asked Jamie.

'No, no it's OK,' replied Blake, still sounding a little confused, 'I'll pick something up in a minute, I was just showing Gideon out anyway.'

'I am sorry Gideon,' said Blake apologising profusely. He cautiously looked up at Gideon half expecting to see this bizarre manifestation again that he had just encountered, but Gideon appeared just as before the incident. He must have imagined the whole episode that was the only explanation he could think of, that and the lack of food. This really was a bit odd. 'Must be my sugar levels are down or something,' he mumbled as he got up. The words "The Chapter Room" kept turning over in his head, echoing in the distance, but he tried to block it out of his mind.

'Anyway Gideon, I won't detain you any longer, but I will walk down with you. I need to pop in next door for sandwich.' He smiled at Gideon again, a sort of reassuring glance. He hoped the episode hadn't frightened Gideon too much.

Blake politely ushered Gideon out of the office door and they wandered down the stairs to the ground floor chatting amiably about the weather as relative strangers do, despite neither of them being remotely concerned one way or the other. They stepped out of the lobby on the ground floor into the sunshine.

'This is what I miss,' pronounced Blake, 'being stuck in an office all day.' He lifted his arms up to the sky, 'Sunshine, wonderful.' He took hold of Gideon's hand again and shook it firmly.

'Are you sure you don't want to go for lunch?' asked Blake, 'it's a company expense now.' He smiled briefly, a sort of professional gesture, but Gideon didn't appear to understand the quip. Maybe he shouldn't of bothered, he wondered. He didn't want the Gideon to think they were about to immediately push the corporate entertainment ship of plenty out into the harbour having signed a brilliant new writer who was going to make them a lot of money. Maybe he had overthought that one a bit, it was after all just an offer of lunch. He was still a little on edge and that made him appear nervous, possibly even a little irrational.

'No, not for me, but thank you anyway.' replied Gideon calmly.

'It was really good to meet you,' said Blake, 'we are going to have a wonderful relationship I can feel it in my bones.' They smiled at each other again, it was a bit stilted, but that would fade with time as they got to know each other better.

'Yes we are,' replied Gideon.

'I'll let you know about that weekend thing,' said Blake.

'Yes, I'll look forward to that,' replied Gideon. 'Thank you.' 'Oh and the name change, that is OK? isn't it, you didn't say, what with the funny turn...' he smiled at Blake.

`No, no that's fine no problem,' replied Blake, 'and you are right it is a more befitting title.'

Blake wandered off to the sandwich shop and Gideon turned in the other direction, slowly walking away in the knowledge that his journey toward his avowed intent had now begun.

For some reason Blake suddenly remembered some words he had read recently and they made him shiver, he couldn't remember where they came from just the message they conveyed.

"He walks there quietly at your side and you don't care to even give him a second glance... and then he suddenly clears his throat and you are startled by his presence..."

Chapter 10

Blake picked up a chicken sandwich and ordered a large decaffeinated Americano, no milk. He paid the girl who had served him, picked up his tray and sat down in the corner, where he could see the rest of the room and opened the sandwich pack. So what was happening, he wondered to himself, was there something very unusual going on, or was this just his over active mind suffering from the constant intake of so many unfeasible stories. Maybe they were all beginning to morph into one outrageous story, no that was ridiculous. He promptly discarded that preposterously silly idea and took a sip of coffee, a bite out of the sandwich and then sat back and carefully pondered over the moments leading up to the incident. Maybe it was all one huge coincidence. He had probably encountered far stranger things than this before, but just couldn't remember exactly when. Probably, because they were of no relevance and had faded harmlessly into obscurity.

But he did have the script from Theodore Clackle in Martin's safe and he or more accurately, Catherine had locked that away back in August. That had clearly predicted a small part of what had taken place today and as much as he tried to rationalise the details that he had swirling around in his head, it just didn't really seem to come out any other way. Yes, he could put it down to coincidence, chance even, but on the basis of statistical probability the odds were heavily stacked against that possibility. It was almost as if it were all some elaborate carefully prepared illusion, a trick of the light, prestidigitation of the most elaborate form. The fact of the matter was, Prospect Road had clearly and unambiguously recalled much of what had already happened in his life that was beyond dispute, but could be explained away. But what was now apparently beginning to happen was the book was predicting what was going to happen in the future and to some extent controlling it, but was that really

EASILY

116

possible, this was what he now had to contend with, and that could not be so easily explained away.

The question now was, was this a good thing or bad thing. He took another bite out of the chicken sandwich and noticed the waitresses were all dressed up as stereotypical French waitresses. Black tights, stripy clinging tops, black berets, little red throat scarves, black high heels, and rouge lipstick. He looked around the room and noticed they had obviously made a special effort to give the coffee shop a French feel, probably because although it was late summer, it was still warm, or maybe they were celebrating a very belated Bastille day, but then nothing seemed to make any sense anymore.

They Café had slid back the glass panelled doors to the front and there were a half dozen tables outside with little umbrellas, all of which he had completely missed when he came in, so preoccupied was he with the events of the past hour. One of the waitresses' today was Susan, who he had got to know quite well over the years, but today he had not recognised her at all. From out of the dismal everyday utilitarian uniform she normally wore, she had blossomed into something quite beautiful and alluring. He watched as she slowly made her way around the café picking up trays and cups, provocatively bending over from time to time, (he felt sure for his benefit,) to pick up odd items that had fallen on the floor. Eventually she arrived at Blake's table.

'Good afternoon Monsieur,' she whispered quietly in a sultry French tone. 'I have been waiting for you,' spoken in that deliberately affected manner immortalised in the seventies television comedy series "Hello-Hello", but it was fun.

'Et comment allez-vous aujourd'hui,' asked Susan

'Tant mieux pour vous voir que j'aime vous regarder travailler,' replied Blake. She smiled, and he saw something in her eyes, something he had not seen before, but then maybe he hadn't been looking before. He was beginning to see everything in a different light.

'Peut-être que nous devrions nous amuser un peu plus,' said Susan

Maintenant vous jouez avec mon le Coeur,' replied Blake shyly moving is head slightly to one side.

Susan smiled and picked up his tray and Blake watched her as she sashayed slowly back to the counter, swaying her body slightly from side to side as she did. She knew he was watching. He finished his sandwich and the coffee, and bid farewell to Susan.

'Au revoir petit derrière,' Blake whispered as he left. She smiled seductively and blew him a kiss. Once outside he suddenly realised how out of character it was for him to even look at another woman let alone flirt with one. Why had he done so today, when he had been frequenting the coffee shop for the last six, nearly seven years and the thought had never crossed his mind. He was probably no more than a few words, a drink, and a furtive assignation away from committing adultery with Susan, and yet he had not realised it was happening. What was happening to him he wondered. Was the vague possibility of impending financial success distorting his moral compass? He was aware that some people would change their morality to suit a particular situation; a good Catholic who was perfectly happy to have sex without protection (as was the papal rule), would throw his arms up in abject consternation at the thought of the same girl aborting the child accidently conceived in a fleeting moment of illicit passion.

He looked into the tall thin mirror, part of the shop front of the café and stared at what he saw. He could see flashes of the man he was and who he used to be, but more disconcertingly, he also saw glimpses of the man he was becoming, and he didn't like what he saw. With all these troubling thoughts running around in his head he made his way slowly back up the stairs to his office to get things started on The Chapter Room. His previous concerns over the change of name now safely consigned to the rubbish bin.

That night he arrived home a little later than normal due to the initial discussions that had taken place in the office that afternoon regarding the new assignment; The sales campaign for Gideon Drew's book. He kissed Catherine and asked if the children were still awake.

'Claudia is asleep, but I think Max is waiting for you,'

'I'll go and say goodnight before we eat if that's OK,' Catherine nodded.

Max and Claudia were both still awake and jumped up and down when Blake went into their bedroom. He kissed and cuddled them both, before reading a short story, then kissed them both again having tucked them both into their beds. He was back downstairs at just after seven thirty.

'Look before we sit down for dinner could you pop next door and ask Martin if we could have the manuscript. I just want to reread the last chapter again, it's been nearly a month and I've forgotten precisely what it said. I'd go, but we did say that he wasn't to give me the book if I was on my own.' He smiled, self-deprecatingly at the absurdity of the peculiar arrangement that they had made. It now seemed so juvenile and immature to conceive of a situation where he couldn't trust himself. Catherine looked at him a little oddly at first, she had temporarily forgotten the arrangement. With hindsight it really didn't seem to make any sense. Reading the book last time had been quite disturbing, but more so for Blake than her. He seemed to have taken it quite badly at the time and she had even been concerned over his sanity at one point, although she didn't mention this to him at the time. The thought of revisiting and rehashing all that emotional tension again with all related trauma was not something she particularly relished, but he seemed to be in a confident, positive frame of mind, so possibly he had now come to terms with it, and wanted to move forward.

'You definitely want me to fetch the manuscript?' asked Catherine.

'Yes, if you don't mind.' He seemed quite insistent, but not in a belligerent way. He smiled reassuring at her.

'Why now,' asked Catherine sounding a little intrigued, and pressing the point a little further.

'I'll explain over dinner, it's nothing important just something odd that happened today.'

Catherine seemed mollified by his reply, any concerns she may have had now been assuaged by his calm reassurance.

Catherine dutifully popped into Martins, and came back ten minutes later, tightly grasping the manuscript to her breast as if it were something precious.

'Martin's going away on holiday on Friday for two weeks, so if we want to put it back into his safe we have to do it tomorrow at the latest, is that OK?'

Blake nodded. 'No problem, we only need to have a quick read. We'll have dinner and then a strong G and T, then see if there have been any changes or additions. You can take it back to Martin first thing in the morning, agreed?'

'Agreed,' replied Catherine, 'You make the drinks, I'll serve dinner.

'Excellent,' said Blake.

Over dinner Blake told Catherine about the events of the day, but not about the falling down in his chair mishap, it didn't seem relevant, it was, but he had convinced himself that his sugar levels were too low and that had been the reason for his collapse. He mentioned the book he had read a few weeks ago, and about how good he thought it was and that the author, had come to the office that day.

'Was that the one you stayed up all night to read,' she asked idly, while taking a sip from her gin and tonic.

'Yes, yes it was actually, shows you how good it must be to keep me riveted all night.'

'So you've met him?' she asked casually

'Yes, yes I have. He came to the office today, to sign a contract.

'Oh, it's serious then?'

'Very much so, as I said a few weeks ago I think we have a major blockbuster on our hands, as long as we promote it correctly it could make us a lot of money,'

'So what's the author's name, as I remember you lost the front page of the manuscript.'

'It's Gideon, Gideon Drew. He's a very nice guy, very unaffected by it all, he really doesn't know how good it is. It's actually quite refreshing to meet a writer, one who is better than he thinks he is, it's normally the other way round. I've asked him to come down to stay sometime, for a weekend, possibly in the November or maybe nearer Christmas, whenever it's convenient, when things start to move a bit, just so you can meet him, and I can get to know him better. I've signed him up for a seven book deal so it could be a few years that we're together in a manner of speaking.'

[handwritten margin note: MHCG Better THAN HE Realises]

'No problem,' replied Catherine. 'Just give me time to get the room ready, it's full of junk at the minute, we are starting to run out of room. The house seemed so big when we first moved here, but now....'

'When this takes off, we can buy a much bigger house with lots of bedrooms,' said Blake smiling. He sounded so confident and that reassured her. Finances had been a little strained recently.

'So what was the name of the book?' she asked.

'Ah, that's the interesting bit. It was called "The Sisters of Mercy", but Gideon thought that was a bit depressing and a maybe a little pious, so he came up with a better title.... it relates to the place where the two central characters have their encounter.'

'Where they have the "how's your father" you mean,' replied Catherine with her prosaic head on, but with a passing nod to the working class accent.

'Well yes, but Drew puts it a little more delicately thankfully.'

'Sex, Love and Violence and a bit of mystery, that's what sells. That's what you told me. Has it got all four?'

'Absolutely,'

'Then I'm ordering a new Merc estate next week.' replied Catherine, giggling.

'Ahhh got me there,' Blake smiled and they clinked glasses.

'So what's it called,' asked Catherine again, 'you still haven't told me.' Blake put his glass down. He didn't want a repeat of anything similar to the incident earlier in the day.

'It's called…' he took a deep breath, The Chapter Room.'

'The Chapter Room,' repeated Catherine a little surprised. 'That's a strange coincidence?' she paused for a moment to consider the change. She had immediately recognised the title from the one mentioned in Prospect Road, and she knew instinctively that that was why Blake had asked her to fetch the manuscript from Martin.

'That's the book mentioned in Prospect Road isn't it?'

The general light-hearted nature of the conversation up to that point seemed to change almost immediately and take on a slightly darker more sombre tone.

'Maybe, I not certain. That's why I wanted to read the manuscript again,' replied Blake with some hesitation.

'I see,' …I'm certain that's the book title mentioned,' repeated Catherine, now, not quite as self-assured as she was a few moments earlier. She thought for a few moments more before continuing. 'Now I don't want you to read anything untoward into this, but,' she paused for a moment realising she had made an excruciatingly bad, ill-timed pun purely by accident, but fortunately Blake hadn't noticed. She was aware that what she was about to ask was going to tread heavily and a little clumsily on his sensibilities, but she had to know the answer, the question had to be asked…

'So who's idea was it to change the name?'

'Gideon's.' replied Blake firmly, without even stopping for breath. He just carried on eating as if it were a detail of no relevance, completely inconsequential. 'Oh,' he suddenly added, putting his knife and fork down on the table, 'I see, you thought maybe I had suggested it.' He took another sip of the wine and put the glass down. He gave Catherine a reassuring smile, which in itself said so much more. 'No, Gideon came up with that. In fact, I was perfectly happy with the original title. I rather liked the seminarian - quasi-religious inflection, I think that's the right word.' He gazed upwards slightly to the left, invoking the medial temporal lobe to think about the word. 'Actually I'm not sure that is the right word, but anyway you know what I mean, novice nun about to be married to Christ when her religious and moral convictions are unexpectedly subjected to the ultimate challenge, possibly a challenge from old nick himself. So for me the "The Sisters of Mercy" worked really well. But he's the writer so….'

'Oh,' replied Catherine, 'I am sorry for doubting you, but with all that went on the last time we spoke about this, well I didn't want to see you in that state again.'

'I understand,' said Blake. But, now we know for certain I couldn't have written anymore, so if there is something, it's nothing to do with me.' Catherine nodded in agreement even though she was still unsure what was really happening.

They finished dinner and puts the plates and cutlery into the dishwasher, cleaned up the kitchen, then settled down in the lounge with the G and T's to read chapter four again.

'You read it first,' said Blake. Catherine looked at him, a little surprised at his sudden loss of curiosity.

'No,' she replied, 'We can read it together. We only have to cuddle up close.'

Blake smiled. 'You're not going to take advantage of me are you?' There was a naughty glint in his eye, something she hadn't seen for a while. This was more like the old Blake she knew, self-assured, confident even maybe a little bit arrogant at times, but weren't all men, she added as an afterthought.

'I might do later,' replied Catherine. Blake sniggered.

There was a lightness in his manner, as if he had temporarily disengaged from the more serious matter in hand.

This was more the way he used to be, back before the black cloud of Prospect Road had begun to overshadow everything. It seemed to be loitering ever present somewhere in the background just reminding them of its existence from time to time, like a tiny cancerous cough.

She could clearly remember that their married life had always been enjoyable, exciting and amusing, it was a also a struggle as well at times, but they endured it together. It had been like that for nearly ten years right up to early 1982 just before the Prospect Road manuscript had arrived. The stress that would be caused by the Chapter Room was normal, it came with every major new publication, but that normally quickly abated once Blake's job was done and the book was out, and he would return to his normal easy going manner. But the situation with Prospect Road had never actually been resolved by publication, it had just lingered in the air like a nasty odour that never really went away and slowly this toxic mist began seeping into their lives, into every tiny corner, it seemed to be waiting for something, waiting to do something, but she had no idea what.

Catherine longed for the good days to return, the happy days; days of carefree abandonment, when their love for each other was all that mattered to the total exclusion of everything else and even that euphoria was then further enriched by the births of Max and Claudia. Catherine could not believe how happy she felt, if was as if she were a princess who had found her prince charming and they would be living together in blissful harmony for the rest of their lives. The dream of most couples she thought, but how few actually achieve it she now wondered.

And then one day through no fault of their own everything began to change, Catherine had desperately tried to hang on to her dream, but she knew for reasons she couldn't explain that it now seemed to be very slowly slipping through her fingers like the sands of time, it was running out. Something was taking over her life, something to do with Prospect Road was taking control.

Before they began to read, Catherine said one small prayer quietly under her breath. A plea to whichever gods determine the outcome of such moments. The same god who decides who wins a lottery and who dies tomorrow when, for no particular reason, a piece of stone that has sat on the top of a building for a hundred years decides to fall and plummets to earth killing an innocent passer-by. Someone, whose life up until that very moment had been relatively uneventful, but now and for eternity   an honourable member of a very exclusive club.

In quiet desperation she was clinging onto the smallest possibility   that   nothing would have changed in the manuscript and that every word was just the same as when they had last read it. They could then   happily agree to arrange for it to be sent back to its author with the customary rejection note that is where a stamped addressed envelope had been included. However, many thousands of manuscripts that Blake's company received each year didn't and were therefore   considered to be of no worth to the authors and these would be consigned to be recycled into something worthwhile, something useful   like…. toilet paper. Yes that would be right and proper she thought, that is where this one belonged, that is all it was good for.

They skipped the first three chapters and began reading chapter four and came to the end….

Prospect Road - Chapter 4

*….This was what Thomas had been looking for and this is what he found when one day he was passed a hand written   manuscript   for   a   love   story   between   a gardener/handyman and a novice nun set in in Aix en Provence in the 1960's. The story was beautifully written and brought him to tears such was the passion embedded within the pages. Love stories were always good sellers, but with a subtle twist such as this one had it couldn't fail. Thomas   had found his Holy Grail. He read it over and over again to be sure of how he felt about it,   and to convince himself that he hadn't just settled on this story out of shear frustration at not finding something better, but it was the best book he had read in years. Each time he read it he just became more convinced of the potential success it could achieve. He showed the book to the senior partners in the company and after reading it, they too agreed with him. They would publish the book. **The Chapter Room**. A love story by Gideon Drew, a story that would embrace the world and change Thomas and Catherine's life forever.*

It was signed Blake & Catherine Thornton 13th August 1982 after the last line.

This was the point they had reached the last time they read the manuscript. Blake and Catherine's signatures were clear to see after the final word. But now there were more words after the signature, words that had definitely not been than the last time they had read it back in August. Catherine's heart sank, her prayer had not been answered, or maybe it had been, but not it the way she'd expected. Blake looked at Catherine as if to ask whether they should read on, but of course there was never really any option. They couldn't stop now even if they wanted to, so they continued to read the next chapter... Chapter Five.

Prospect Road 5

Chapter Five
written by
Anthony Theodore Clackle

KATE

HeR

Over the next few months Thomas totally immersed himself into the marketing and sales promotions for the forthcoming publication as well as the editorial elements that needed some fine tuning. The pressure at work meant he spent less time at home and she began to sense the first indications that he was drifting away from Kate. He would leave home at 6 o'clock in the morning, and not get back home till nine, maybe even ten o'clock in the evening, absolutely shattered and with little interest in eating his evening meal.

Fortunately he was eating out most days having working lunches with the various associates and business people connected to the publication, these tended to be lengthy affairs sometimes stretching out for two or maybe three hours. When he did eventually arrive home, he seldom wanted to engage in any normal conversation, it tended towards utilitarian matters such as household repairs or bills that required paying or something to do with children. Under normal circumstances, Kate would not normally bother mentioning these matters to Thomas. She would usually just deal with them herself, but in an effort to open some kind of meaningful dialogue she would now mention everything that involved him in the hope that it might move the conversation in the direction of something more personal. But it never did and it was now beginning to feel as if her attempts at re-establishing communications were doing more harm than good.

It was all to no avail. Their relationship had lost direction and momentum and was now almost totally devoid of any emotional dimension, it was as if they were acting out the final scenes from a domestic television tragedy where the inevitable end was now clearly in sight.

During the course of an evening, a few curt words might be exchanged and then they would go to bed. She would lie awake gazing out of the window looking up at the moon wondering why and how their once blissful existence had so suddenly and without any warning suddenly slipped away and left her in this desolate, lonely place. Only their children and a few friends and neighbours helped to ward of the feelings of absolute hopelessness and futility that was now fast overtaking her. But friends and neighbours with all their good intentions were still a poor substitute for the sense of fulfilment she once derived from the close relationship she had with Thomas. The thought of his laughter and their conversations during the evenings and weekends and their interaction with their children, all those things that were once sufficient to sustain her during the lonely days and nights when he wasn't there were gone, now nothing more than a distant memory.

She could remember a time when they would be lying in bed together and sometimes he could be a million miles away and she would just reach out and touch him gently and he would be there in an instant, back with her and he would ask her; SHE WOULD SAY "COME BACK TO ME"

EXPAND

'How did you know where I was.'

And she would just smile and say 'I just know.'

But now she would lie beside him in the dark just before they fell asleep and wonder what he was thinking about. She knew he was somewhere else again, a million miles away, but she didn't have the courage to reach out and take that chance anymore, the fear of possible rejection was now too much to bare. There were no words that could heal his pain. She still craved the warmth and tenderness of his love and affection and she held onto a faith that one day he would come back to her. She still believed in miracles and even if there were no words spoken, deep down she knew there had to be a tiny thread of hope, something for her to GRAB OF HOLD ~~hang on~~ *to and pull him back, but she just didn't know how to find it anymore, so she patiently waited day after day.*

She could recall things he had said the night before or even the weekend before, things they should do, plans they were making for the future or arranging to go out with friends, all this would keep her mind occupied and comfort her soul. The joke he would have made a few days ago would come back to mind and make her laugh again, possibly many times, but now there were no humorous asides to recall and her days were spent without amusing reflections or memories. She would look over to Thomas, but he would have fallen asleep almost immediately. Kate was now completely alone with her thoughts....

'Hi, sorry I'm late darling, it's just so hectic at the moment getting this book ready. We have had so much interest from other countries from the proof copies we sent out that we just never seem able to get on top of it all. I'll be glad when it's published, at least we won't be under so much pressure in the office, It will be the printers with the problems then.'

But the conversation was lame, pedestrian, soulless and laboured, it was just words, hollow words with no meaning, just noise to fill an empty space where once there had been more, so much more. This was the path the dialogue and mannerisms would quickly take night after night, futile gestures and meaninglessness acknowledgements, and it seemed to deteriorate even further into this trough of despair as the months slowly passed, as if that were possible.

When they spoke now it conveyed nothing of Thomas's real feelings for Kate...nothing about how they used to be, nothing about anything really.... It was just a monochromic snapshot of their existence in a particular point in time. But without the benefit of any clear cut definition between black and white – it was all shading and tonal variation - a mishmash of inconsequential greys fading to darkness.

For some reason he was no longer able to convey the way he once felt, it was as if that element, that invisible conduit of communication that had always flowed between them had now been irretrievably severed....

...There were forces now in play that neither of them could understand, and there seemed to be nothing left of what had once existed between them when they were so much in love. This was the course and the nature of their

existence night after night and after nearly four months it had already inflicted irreparable collateral damage to their relationship.

Kate was once a serene and understanding wife, being fully aware of the pressures her husband was constantly under, but she was losing patience and it was beginning to show. She desperately required some tiny indication of his love or at the very least an acknowledgment of her existence as a person not just the keeper of the house. But even this she was being denied. So many nights she sat alone waiting for Thomas to return and when he did there was nothing. They continued in this state of abject limbo, where their life had all but put on hold, as if into a state of suspended animation. The flame of their love for each other almost burnt out like the flickering candle burning the last remnants of wick before it dies.

So intense and real did this illusion become that at times she began to imagine she could actually step back and see what was happening to her and Thomas as if she were another person looking in on them, she had become a Edward Hopper voyeur peering into their own life, their very existence through a distant window.

This peculiar disorder continued for another three months, and she began to consider the possibility that maybe she was truly losing control of her mind, such was her detachment from the life that she had been accustomed to. She even considered suicide at one point, but thoughts of the children held her back, but still she slipped further into this spiral of depression. She even considered darker thoughts, but pushed them from her mind. But how long she wondered, before they returned with vengeful retribution for being denied that which they desired...

Catherine and Blake both stopped reading at the same moment and turned to face each other with an expression that clearly conveyed the same question they were both about to ask. Maybe it was another coincidence, but why now, why at this particular juncture, just when   Blake and Catherine - Kate as he occasionally called her in moments of anger - were also navigating their lives through a period of turmoil, chaos and confusion. Would they too, now fall into the well of emptiness and despair, this atrophied existence - just as Thomas and Kate had done. This troubled Catherine deeply, but she said nothing.

Blake looked at Catherine, 'This will not happen to us,' he swiftly reassured her, knowing instinctively what she was thinking, they had, as do so many relationships, began to understand what the other was thinking moments before they said it. This was a part of what being together - soul mates - kindred spirits was all about, this indescribable, unfathomable sixth sense of communication. Completely intangible and scientifically not possible, that was as far as the scientists were concerned. But they only ever dealt with quantifiable evidence to disprove a theory, not that indefinable something, that untouchable, unseen, intangible force that deep relationships thrive and depended upon.

We won't let it happen!' continued Blake His eyes opened wider, she could see tiny the crinkles in his forehead, his eyelashes moved upwards coming to attention as if responding to a command, his cute little ears twitched. He was firm and assertive, instantaneously responsive for he had a good idea what was going through Catherine's mind, and he chose to confront the issue head on, not side track it or try to deflect it down some dark alleyway where it would fester and grow into something more damaging like apathy or indifference. This was Blake, her husband speaking. Blake the man she loved, had always loved.

'What?' said Catherine, her heart leapt at his magnanimous announcement. She was a little surprised at his directness and candour. He was saying there might be problem, a small problem, but we will not let it take over our lives, we are stronger than that, much stronger. Catherine was so relieved. Blake had said the words she so desperately wanted to hear, he had reached out and touched her and answered the questions she wanted to ask, but dare not, for fear of what the answers might be, now, she didn't need to.

He was making a statement, a reassuring affirmation of their relationship, and something that was a far cry from the debilitating, demoralizingly and soul destroying nature of Kate's thoughts in the chapter of Prospect Road they had just read together.

'What this is saying,' He threw the manuscript on the floor and it came apart, 'We won't let this happen.' But somehow conversely, in that very statement, he was acknowledging that Prospect Road somehow seemed to have taken some control of their lives.

'We will take the shrivelled little gonads of this nasty little monster and fry them in boiling goose fat that will make them nice and crispy.'

'It was an absolutely ridiculous declaration to make, one that didn't make any sense, but it made Catherine laugh out loud and it comforted her soul.

'None for me thank you,' said Catherine politely, with an expression of extreme disagreeableness. Her eyes squinting at the thought, the corners of her mouth downturned in jovial revulsion. They both laughed out aloud again, together.

This was the Rabelaisian ingenuity she was more accustomed to, and which she much preferred to any wimpish concession to the apparent mystical premonitory power of the words in the manuscript that now lay on the floor is disarray.

'This is all bollocks,' said Blake, 'pun intended.'

'I agree,' said Catherine. 'But let's not give up now. Let's just read it to the end and then we can decide what to do with it,'

'Right.' said Blake, firmly agreeing with her proposal. He knelt down and started gathering up the scattered pages of the manuscript that had become detached and put them back in the correct order.

'We need a drink,' said Blake firmly.

Catherine went to get to up, but Blake touched her arm. 'Not tea, I think maybe something a little stronger?' Catherine nodded and Blake got up and went over to where they kept the spirits and poured another G and T for Catherine and for himself a large bourbon, then he sat back down. They clinked glasses, smiled and both took a large swig before putting the glasses down and   continuing to read to the end of Chapter Five and then they continued onto Chapter Six.

Prospect Road 6

Chapter Six
written by
Anthony Theodore Clackle

[handwritten annotations: Released to change HER HABIT; 1) IF WORD MAINTAINS STILL THE HABIT?]

And then one day quite unexpectedly Thomas came home early, just after five o'clock. As usual, it was a routine now, an automatic, spontaneous response to hearing the noise of his car pull up on the gravel drive and despite the way things had so deteriorated over the last nine months, she, as always greeted him at the front door. Today, their two children, Michael and Carol were also waiting at the door, ready to greet him as they had not yet gone to bed.

'Hello Daddy...' they chorused, as soon as he entered the hallway, 'we love you very much, and we miss you lots when you are away working.'

This had not been rehearsed and Kate was as taken aback as Thomas was by this completely spontaneous and unexpected display of affection. She glanced at Thomas with a mixed expression of wonder, concern and astonishment, fully believing that he might possibly have been maddened by this unforeseen outpouring of emotion. But he was not. He seemed to acknowledge, without question, that it had not been orchestrated by her. He was in fact, completely disorientated and a little humbled by this ingenuous greeting. Try as he may, he could not hold back the tiny tears of joy that suddenly welled up in his eyes. He suddenly realised he had completely lost touch with his life, his wife and his children, the only things that really mattered. Could he, maybe recapture those halcyon days he wondered..

'Please can we play together daddy?' plaintively chorused Michael and Carol, again in perfect unison and once again sounding as if they had been coached, but they had not.

Thomas dropped his case by the door, and gazed at Kate with a hollowed expression of lachrymose contrition suffused with and consumed by the fearful shame he was now experiencing, suddenly realising the damage he had been inflicting and what had been happening to their relationship. He knelt down in the doorway and threw open his arms to embrace his children, holding them closely, desperately hugging them tightly to his body as he stood up. The tears were now rolling down his face. He looked at Kate and saw the woman he loved, the only woman he had ever loved and she was lost and confused, and he knew this was his doing. Something had taken hold of his life and had nearly consumed his soul. It had threatened to drag him down into a sea of oblivion and he had not seen it, he could not see it for he was blinded by misdirection. He gazed at Kate, searching for forgiveness, some kind of redemption for the pain he had inflicted on her and she gave it to him, in an instant he was absolved and he beckoned her over to join them. She cautiously stepped forward into his outstretched arms, the children still clinging to his neck and he kissed her passionately in way he had not kissed her for many, many months...they all embraced, the children not really understanding what had happened, although they now felt much happier than before. The embrace never seemed to end, the tears rolled down Kate and Thomas's faces and they kissed again and again. His crisis of faith, his carapace of dark confusion had been broken, it was over, they were happy once again... for now. BREECHED

Thomas's company published the "The Chapter Room" two weeks later and within a few weeks it rose to the top position for weekly sales. It stayed there for nine months eventually selling over seven million copies, before it was released worldwide where it went on to sell another twenty eight million copies in the first year. It was the biggest selling book the company and ever published and had become one of the largest selling books of the last five years. Thomas was asked to become an equal partner in the company, his life would never be quite the same again.

Just six months later Thomas and his family moved to a much larger country house on the outskirts of Oxford. Some major changes were now being made in the office and a number of new people joined the company in anticipation of a continuing flow of more successful authors joining the company. Kate and Thomas were now much happier than they had been for a long time and they settled down to enjoy their new house and increased income. All was well for nearly a year until one day while he was at the office he received a telephone call from Kate, she seldom rang him during the day, so he knew it must be important. With some trepidation, he picked up the call, which had been redirected to his office phone, and listened intently as Kate explained what had happened. He slowly replaced the receiver in its cradle, picked up his case and walked out of the office without saying a word. One of his colleagues tried to speak to him, to ascertain whether there was a problem and whether there was anything they could do to help, but he appeared not to hear them, so engrossed was he in his thoughts. He paused for a moment at the office door and turned to look back into room, he started to say something, but stopped and then with a look of incomprehension and disbelief he left...

Chapter 11

And there once again the story came to an abrupt end. Blake looked at Catherine a little confused, for although the manuscript had once again documented what was possibly going to happen, there was nothing particularly epiphanous or revelational in the predictive nature of this chapter. Had it been more incisive in its content there was a possible advantage to be had from the information as detailed, but there was little more than generalisation and supposition. They were however still faced with the profound conundrum of how the book was self-writing itself to consider. This obviously concerned them both and it was something that had to be explained, there had to be a rational answer, but what was it! yet

'What should we do?' asked Catherine after a few moments.

'What can we do,' replied Blake. 'What have we actually got?... nothing but words. We will just have to wait and see how accurate it is. The only problem is we don't know how long we will have to wait.

'It has to be the same book,' said Catherine, 'it's the same name that's too much of a coincidence and surely that will be coming out very soon anyway,' asked Catherine.

'Hopefully,' replied Blake, 'We do have some last minute issues to sort out first, which could mean a few late nights for me at the office though but..'

'Oh,' said Catherine, a tiny cold shiver shot down her back.

'Like Thomas?' She asked gingerly..

'Well yes, I suppose you could say that, but it's not going to be four or five months, it'll be a few nights at most if that.'

'Good!' said Catherine. 'We don't need to play into its hands...' She stopped suddenly, 'Oh my God!' she whispered under her breath. She seemed to be glaring into space.

'What?' exclaimed Blake, looking anxiously around expecting to see something, but there was nothing.

'I just acknowledged the existence of...

'What?' said Blake

'Someone or something.'

'There is nothing,' said Blake reassuringly. 'You're just getting a little spooked by a few clever words, that's all.' Catherine smiled. Blake was right, the manuscript has just put her into an nervous frame of mind, for no rational reason. Her concerns were based almost entirely on nothing more tangible then some cleverly contrived passages in the book.

'That's what good writers do,' said Blake, after a few moments, 'they make you challenge your beliefs, everything you hold sacred, they..... they make you re-evaluate what is really important in life. Every good story has to be a morality play, a metaphor for life. It must have a reason to exist and that is to show us something, something that invariably we may have lost or forgotten along the way, humanity - compassion - kindness, the characteristics that make us human, it could be anything. If it does not, then it just becomes a large collection of meaningless words. Maybe that's what Prospect Road is all about I don't know.' He smiled at Catherine and kissed her on the forehead.

'...And of course there is the fact that this chapter seems to end reasonably well?'

'Yes,' replied Catherine cautiously, 'I suppose that's some small consolation,' although she didn't appear overly convinced by that observation.

'We can take it back to Martin's now for safe keeping,' suggested Blake.

'Good idea,' said Catherine. Catherine put the manuscript back into its envelope.

'Wait,' said Blake, 'can you take it back out?' Catherine wondered what Blake was going to do. Nevertheless she did as he requested. Blake produced his fountain pen.

'We still need to sign it... for what is worth...' Catherine nodded and took the pen.

Having both signed and dated it on the page with text, ON IT LAST they replaced it into its envelope.

'Come on you two,' shouted Blake to Max and Claudia who were playing in the garden. 'We are just popping over to Uncle Martins for a few minutes. Max and Claudia came in from the garden and they proceeded to walk over to Martins house. ONCE

When they arrived Max and Claudia went straight out to play in Martin's garden, and out of earshot of Max and Claudia, Catherine and Blake confirmed that the ongoing provision that it should only be released to Catherine still prevailed and that it should not be handed over to Blake under any circumstances if he was alone. Blake nodded his agreement.

Martin gazed at the two of them with a slightly confused expression, but said nothing. He did wonder what might happen if Blake did ask for it and he had to refuse, but he put the thought to the back of mind for the moment.

He continued to be quietly bemused and a little perplexed by the specific nature of the condition, but did not query the instruction. He was after all an ex-naval officer and had been conditioned to taking orders and instructions during the war, without question, many of which he never fully understood. His was not to reason why blah di blah, he mumbled quietly to himself as he placed the manuscript back into the safe and spun the dial.

Catherine still had serious unresolved concerns over how the manuscript was continuing to self-write further chapters, and Blake was still at a loss to explain the peculiarity, so the rules of release were still very relevant to both of them.

'Drink, you two nutters, asked Martin, turning and smiling to himself while pursing his lips together in a quizzical manner?

'Yes why not said,' said Catherine, now relieved that "Prospect Road" was safely back in his safe.

Martin poured out a gin and tonic for Catherine and a bourbon for Blake, which he knew were their normal tipples and handed them the glasses, before pouring himself a whiskey and soda, which he immediately took a sip from.

'Cheers,' said Martin.

'Happy days,' replied Blake. Catherine smiled.

'I must apologise for our strange behaviour,' said Blake, 'I think maybe you deserve some sort of explanation.'

'Don't' worry about me old boy,' replied Martin, 'I've never been the overly curious type, it's being in the navy you know. Teaches you not to ask too many questions. I remember what happened to the pussycat.'

Catherine and Blake were a little confused for a moment.

'Pussycat,' enquired Blake cautiously?

'Tiddles,' replied Martin with a sombre expression.

'I didn't know you had a cat,' said Blake sounding a little confused.

'I don't, not anymore, it's all very sad.'

'Oh,' said Blake empathetically, 'What happened to it?'

'It died! Fell down the bloody well didn't it?' Martin was deadly serious and firmly held the look for a few moments, while sipping his whiskey.

Catherine and Blake didn't know what to make of it, not sure as to whether they should make some token gesture of sympathy for a feline pet that they had never known about, but apparently one that had been very close to Martins heart, before the penny dropped and they all laughed.

'You haven't got a bloody well,' said Blake.

'He hasn't got a bloody cat either,' said Catherine still laughing.

Max popped his head round the door, 'That's two quid you owe me dad.'

The next day Blake went to work as usual. The advertising and marketing schedule for the official launch of The Chapter Room had now been set. Various interviews had been arranged with television and radio chat programs to interview Gideon and discuss the book alongside a countrywide billboard and bus campaign.

& rebinour

Blake was certain that with Gideon's strangely enigmatic personality, his appearance on the media platforms could only enthral and entice potential buyers, women in particular, to purchase vast quantities of the book. The vagaries of success or failure in the publishing world so often turned on such nebulous elements.

This was it... everything the company had and considerably more was being staked on the biggest gamble of Blake's life. The turn of one card could dictate how the rest of his life would play out.

If the book subsequently failed to make the sales as he had predicted, the company would be in debt for years, probably forever and Catherine would never get her new Merc. A failure was inconceivable, if this crashed Catherine might even leave him, unable to face the ignominy of near poverty for the foreseeable future. Maybe that was a little melodramatic, but such were the disparate thoughts running through his mind. He suddenly realised just what a risk he was actually taking, not just with his personal life, but his business and his career. For it was certain that if it turned into a monumental disaster he would never work in publishing again, the business would collapse, nobody would employ him, he would become the iconic Jonah figure, the one to avoid at all costs. The one who sank the ship by dropping the golden anchor straight through the bottom of the hull.

He began to have some niggling doubts about his decision. Had he possibly lost control of his normally acutely astute business acumen he wondered? He started to wonder if maybe for some ludicrously egotistical motive he had lost track of all reason and objectivity and had just blundered ahead committing the company to a massive marketing budget way beyond what they would normally spend on what was after all, a debut novel, by an unknown writer. But of course, he couldn't mention these concerns to anybody now, it was far too late for that. And anyway, everybody he had spoken to was of the same opinion as he. Indecision and prevarication at this stage of the game would be counter-productive, it would be fatal, the kiss of death. "Stand by your guns and prepare for action" as Nelson had said at Trafalgar or was that Davy Crockett at the Alamo, he wasn't sure.

Nevertheless, despite his reservations, outwardly he displayed no visible concerns whatsoever about any remote possibility of The Chapter Room not performing as well as he had predicted, or even receiving a pedestrian or mediocre reception.

Blake's unwavering confidence in the absolute runaway success of the book was at times a little awe inspiring and overpowering and at the same time a little intimidating. It was as if to even think of anything other than complete success was a sin worse than blasphemy, a desecration of his belief, a sacrilegious profanity. Blake had lifted the mind set of everyone in the office to a level where they now truly believed this was one of the greatest novels written in the last ten years and they were the privileged few who were bringing it to the attention of the world. A masterful piece of subliminal psychological promotion.

As the day drew closer the atmosphere in the office became tense and electrified with anticipation. You could feel magic in the air, and it began to percolate out to the media, a rumbling giant was about to be unleashed on an unsuspecting public, a story that would move people to tears for years (as the advertising went) and then one Tuesday morning in early November it started.

Chapter 12

(handwritten: SOME SHOPS SOLD OUT BY 9.15)

The book had been released on the Monday night and a number of reviewers had stayed up all night to read it and were appearing on the television breakfast shows at 7-30 am on the Tuesday morning. Their appraisals, plaudits, praise and reviews were way beyond even Blake's wildest expectation, it was as if a new Bible had been written and released that day, such was the tsunami of emotion and hysteria with which it was greeted. Blake had predicted possible sales of a half million books in the first year… *(handwritten: SOLD)* there were twenty thousand orders by 9.10am (ten minutes after most book shops opened) advance orders had already been taken for nearly a hundred thousand copies which Blake's office had not been aware of. The floodgates had opened and the cascade of frenzied customers had begun to feed. *(handwritten: Four)*

A guardian angel had been watching over him and the angel made sure that everything was right, and it was. The angel would return one day for settlement, but not just yet. *(handwritten: MILLION)*

Sales in the first month crashed through the three hundred thousand mark *(struck through, handwritten: million)* bolstered up by some further remarkable reviews, which at times even surprised Blake. These were critics that gave established writers a hard time for decent books, but without exception, they all applauded the creation of the book as one of the seminal moments in literature of the twentieth century and Gideon Drew as the new messiah of heart rending prose. A popular if somewhat clichéd sobriquet.

The printers were initially unable to maintain supplies such was the demand. There were fights breaking out in bookstores when copies became available.

Blake couldn't believe the opprobrium that was being heaped at the writer's door and by association the foresight, sagacity and courage of the publishers for taking such a chance with a totally unknown writer. Sales continued to rise as they approached Christmas, customarily the busiest period of the year, the bandwagon was galloping ahead at full speed and he had to run very fast to keep up with it.

Catherine had had a few sleepless nights, when Blake had arrived home very late in the weeks just prior to publication, but any concerns she may have had quickly faded into obscurity the moment the book was published. It was all Blake and his staff could do to fend off the torrent of approaches from other established writers who had been awestruck by the support that the company had given to Gideon Drew and by the marketing strategy of their company. It was an enormous gamble, but it had paid off.

Catherine had a surprise for Christmas that year, a brand new top of the range Mercedes estate car appeared on the drive on Christmas morning complete with a very large pink bow wrapped around it. They had a fabulous Christmas day especially as the receipts from sales were already starting to trickle into the company's bank account; the bank manager even rang Blake on Christmas day to update Blake on receipts. He was old school and liked to keep clients advised of major changes in their accounts personally, in this particular instance it was to advise him that the balance had passed the half million mark in what was only eight weeks since the release date. He had never experienced anything like this before and he was as excited as Blake was at what was happening.

Gideon Drew had arranged to come over to stay for a few days from boxing day and Catherine and Blake were looking forward to spending some time with the creator of the phenomenon that promised to change their lives beyond all recognition. He was secretly hoping that Gideon would turn up with the manuscript to his next book, but he couldn't be too pushy, they were unable to cope with what was happening at the moment with The Chapter Room. Publication of another book would have to be delayed by at least a year if not longer in order to maximise on the current sales campaign.

Gideon arrived at midday as arranged. Blake, had half expected him to bring his wife or girlfriend, possibly even a boyfriend; these were enlightened times and Blake was prepared for all eventualities, but Gideon arrived alone. He wore a long black leather coat that brushed the floor, black leather boots with shiny brass buckles, a pale green silk scarf wrapped around his neck and a large fedora hat with a small fawn coloured feather sticking rakishly out of the rim on the right hand side. He now carried himself with the air of some ungodly character from an obscure eighteenth century Transylvanian horror story hell bent on vengeance for an unspoken act of debauchery against the will of an innocent virgin. Blake was drawing that from something he had read recently, something he did from time to time when the opportunity arose, which was very often at the moment.

He could not help but stare awkwardly at Gideon for a few moments - somewhat bedazzled and yet pleasantly surprised by the sartorial manifestation that stood before him. His expression of mild puzzlement changed to a smile of admiration at the transformation and he found himself immediately starting to apologise..

'I do apologise but..'

'Please don't,' interrupted Gideon, 'I realise it's a little over the top, but you did mention something about having some minor reservations about my unexciting and introverted appearance at interviews. So I thought I had better make an effort to liven things up and go for something different... the outrageous rock and roll superstar look,' he smiled at Blake, looking for approval.

'Is it OK?'

'It's wonderful. You will sell thousands with that,'

Blake felt relieved at what was potentially an embarrassing moment. He ushered Gideon into the house and grabbed hold of his suitcase and placed it in the hallway. Gideon took off his coat and hat and gave them to Blake who dropped them on the hall table.

He was a remarkably handsome man. Blake remembered that he was good looking, but he was different now, his whole appearance had changed quite dramatically, so much so that he hardly recognised him. His shoulder length tousled dark hair (it had been much shorter when he had last met him) and tanned skin gave him the appearance of gypsy pirate, something that would undoubtedly engender him to women at book signings. His eyes were a piercing blue, which was a little odd because Blake thought they were greyer the last time he saw him, but he was probably mistaken or had forgotten.

Blake's mind seldom drifted to far from the mechanics of the business. Inwardly he was slightly bemused and a little perplexed by Gideon, but nevertheless gladdened by the reformation.

He had previously harboured some minor reservations about the possible marketing issues of the shy and retiring nature of the reclusive author when making public appearances, as he knew that interesting, unusual, gregarious writers sold far more copies at signings and on promotional tours than boring ordinary looking people did. This was an unfortunate fact of life, but had to be born in mind with all marketing decisions. Sales were already very high, but natural declension could soon set in unless a high public profile could be maintained. But any concerns he may have had were quickly dispelled for he knew beyond any doubt that he would electrify an audience with this reimagined characterisation of a romantic tragedian author.

The perception of mystical charm Gideon now conveyed, intermingled with the readers instinctive curiosity would undoubtedly intrigue them and entice them to buy. Any concerns Blake may have had about Gideon's saleability were now firmly consigned to the waste bin and he felt a tiny paroxysm of recalcitrance take hold of his spirit and gently lift it up and hold it at a level he had not experienced for a long while.

Gideon's carriage and persona had changed beyond all recognition from their last meeting. He had somehow acquired the aura of someone far less apprehensive than previously, someone daring, risqué with an element of overt yet measured precociousness and charm.

It was as if, he had miraculously acquired, in just a few short months, a mantle of cultural eloquence. Something that would normally take a lifetime to attain conventionally, but one that apparently perfectly suited him and befitted his elevated position in the literary world, however transient and illusionary that might be. Everybody he would meet would be swept up and carried away on this chariot of mistaken sensory perception. It was perfect.

As they made their way through to the lounge Blake noticed the strong aroma of Bay Rum and lilies about him. A strange sweet pungency, with a delicate pall of age and death. This was a man who probably functioned best when alone - he didn't really need anybody else, such was the aura of self-possession and confidence that he carried so adroitly before him. He was a man in control of his own destiny and his own mortality.

As before, on the previous occasion when they had met at Blake's office, Gideon was polite, quiet and unassumingly enigmatic. On meeting Catherine, he gently took her hand and kissed it softly - his lips never quite touching her skin - while bowing his head slightly, but never loosing eye contact with Catherine. His piercing cornflower blue eyes seemed to be searching for something, possibly something he had now found.

It was an old-fashioned propriety, something Catherine had seldom encountered, except in Bronte' sisters novels. His smile was totally disarming, and yet strangely engaging, almost as if they, alone, shared a dark intimate secret. His eyes, which now seemed to be burning a pathway straight into her soul, reassuringly conveyed a message, "even under threat of death he would not reveal their secret to a living soul". Of course there was no secret, but that didn't matter for she had already begun to falter and yield to the gravitational pull of his erudite charm.

Although the manner of Gideon's greeting surprised Blake a little - he took it to be no more than an academic eccentricity, having assumed, incorrectly that Gideon had attended one of the red brick universities where he had probably witnessed such foppish traits and mannerisms at first hand. He neither approved or disapproved, but simply found the gesture amusing. He had however completely failed to notice the subtle effect that Gideon was having on Catherine.

She, felt confused, unsteady and suddenly embarrassed by the unexpected attention she had received from Gideon - feelings to which she was not now accustomed. Blake generally tended towards the more prosaic elements of love and amity, he was caring, considerate and attentive and when they made love, she felt a warmth and satisfaction that only comes from years of intimately knowing all the secrets of someone else's body and them knowing all of yours.

She no longer swirled with Terpsichorean ecstasy when they fucked, no longer lost in that euphoric chemical high of the neuropeptide hormonal opiate induced by the release of endorphins, neither of them did, but that didn't matter...

That was the opening gambit of the courting stage and that would soon pass, the first months of any relationship were always a whirlwind of confusion when the mind was being obsessively controlled and driven by the body's basic demands, desires, cravings and requirements.. But despite the absence of gregarious visual affection, she still passionately loved him. Sex was now just fun and amusing and entertaining, for the corrosive elements had not yet taken hold.

Nothing as ephemeral as a few days in the company of Gideon Drew would deflect her from this persuasion and she strenuously maintained her composure giving nothing away. But then she found herself slowly beginning to weaken as she became enthralled and beguiled by notions of becoming embroiled in a passionate love affair, such was the state of the light-headedness he had somehow managed to induce. This was a schoolgirl flight of fancy, an adolescent evanescent crush, nothing more, but why now, why today after nearly ten years of happy marriage was she suddenly being sapped of the strength she desperately needed to resist to defend herself from this intruder who had somehow, so easily charmed his way into her humanity. She took a deep breath and opened her eyes a little wider for a moment, struggling hopefully to eradicate these unwarranted fantasies and visions that had with reckless abandonment, licentiously inveigled their way into her brain with each fresh inhalation of oxygen.

But the "Tusitala", for that is what he was, a word she had picked up a holiday in Samoa and often used to describe the better story tellers, had cast his spell. She wondered whether her close proximity to fiction in general and to meeting the author of The Chapter Room in particular, a novel which she had read several times and found to be truly enchanting and captivating was having some sort of profound metaphysical effect on her. Each time she read the story she found different aspects of the narrative that seemed to relate directly to her and nobody else, but this was part of the riddle of the book - its inherent ability to connect directly with every woman and man that read it. *but each in a slightly die way*

Maybe she had been unknowingly intoxicated by the pure romanticism so deeply imbedded within every page of the book and she was confusing idealistic prose with the reality of life. This, after all was the definitive intention of every author, to engage the reader so deeply, so intently that they became temporarily suspended from reality, transported away from the mundane certainties of their *pedestrian* ordinary lives for just a few hours.

This sort of thing had not happened before, but then she had not read a book like that for some time, if ever and she had never met anybody quite like Gideon Drew. He was definitely having an inveigling effect on her and for reasons she could not yet clearly fathom.

Having recovered from her moment of tangled disorientation, she introduced Gideon to Max and Claudia who both smiled a little warily at first, being also clearly mesmerized by his presence. Never before had they met someone with such an overt mystical charm. To them he was more than just simply a story teller. Blake had previously told them that a friend of his who wrote stories was coming to stay for a few days and he had embellished his portrayal of Gideon in order to make him sound mysteriously interesting, this however had proved to be totally unnecessary, as he was already beginning to realise.

Max and Claudia had previously discussed the imminent arrival of the visitor and had concluded from Blake's description that he was from another age and was somebody who could regale them with dark tales of dragons, demons and monsters… and white knights.

After they had all been introduced, Catherine took Gideon upstairs to show him his bedroom, closely followed by two seriously entranced children.

Blake remained in the lounge gathering his thoughts and was just about to sit down when something odd occurred to him. Gideon had mentioned that Blake had said something about "minor reservations about my unexciting and introverted appearance at interviews", and that being the reason for him making this extraordinary effort to reinvent himself and change his image, but in fact Blake had not said anything at all to Gideon about his image. He wouldn't have been so crass as to even mention something directly that might cause personal offence. He had however definitely discussed the issue in some depth with Jamie and some of the staff in the marketing department and they had considered various options to reimagine his persona, but nothing had been settled.

He wondered how Gideon appeared to be aware of the specific details of a conversation he was not a party to, in fact Gideon wasn't even in London at the time of the discussion, as far as he was aware…

Over the next three days, the whole family got to know Gideon very well. They found him to be an affable personage with many interesting and invocative tales to tell. The spellbinding manner in which he told them tended to enthral Max, Claudia and Catherine more so than Blake. It was as if the cynicism of age, the day to day pragmatism of life, the harsh realities of business and the worldly wise perspective he had acquired over the last few years had somehow censored and cauterised his ability to enjoy whimsical diversions. Gideon could create intricate tales from miniscule incidents and the tiniest fragments of life, which he would slowly extrapolate into sweepingly cloudless legends. These would engross Catherine, Max and Claudia sometimes for hours. This in itself made the stories almost believable, it was sometimes very hard to distinguish precisely where fact ended and fiction began, such was his story telling ability.

He could entice you into his world of purposeless splendour and make you believe you never wanted to leave.

He made you realise that what really mattered was not how many times you breath in a lifetime, but how many times your breath is taken away. Gideon was a true Tusitala, a teller of tales and weaver of dreams, and Max and Claudia in particular were very reluctant to depart the realm of quixotic utopia he so easily created. He spoke little of his next book, only to say, somewhat strangely, that he found it to be even more captivating then the Chapter Room. It was another love story was all he would say. But this one was set in England in and around Oxford.

It was odd to hear him talking so objectively about something he had created - as if one half of him wrote the books and the other half critically reviewed them. A unique and enviable characteristic if it could be accomplished, which in the case of his first novel he had succeeded in doing so with admirable impartiality. BUT THEN IN A WAY

THAT IS WHAT ALL WRITERS DID

The First night.

Gideon came down For dinner at 7-30 pm as requested by Catherine. He had already mentioned to them that he liked to write between 3.00 pm and 7.00 pm as he found this to be the best time for him and he did not want to break his normal work pattern, so the timing for dinner was perfect as far as he was concerned.

'Take a seat Gideon, I am just about to serve,' said Catherine speaking from the kitchen which abutted the dining room. Gideon didn't sit down immediately, preferring to wait until everybody else had arrived.

Blake, Max and Claudia were just coming across the hallway from the lounge.

'Evening Gideon,' said Blake.

'Good evening Blake,' replied Gideon, with the hint of a restrained smile, one, which held something more than just a casual pleasantry, but Blake didn't notice, '...and good evening to you two,' continued Gideon, addressing Max and Claudia who both quickly seated themselves at the table.' They both smiled at him a little coyly.

'It's a lovely room, beautiful view to the woods. In fact it's a very lovely house, you are very lucky Blake...'

ABSURD?

Blake was going to say "well we hope to move someone bigger soon, but thought better of it".

'The woods have some sort of historical importance, something to do with a battle during the English Civil war I believe,' he muttered instead.

'Interesting period,' murmured Gideon.

'We're having lamb I hope you like it,' said Catherine, interrupting.

'That sounds lovely, thank you,' said Gideon. 'Do you have any mint sauce?' … he added as an afterthought

'Yes we do,' replied Catherine smiling. 'I like mint sauce too, Blake doesn't though, he hates the vinegar.' Gideon nodded and they sat down and began eating. This was the way the evenings would play out over Friday and Saturday night. Casual unobtrusive non-invasive ordinary conversation. Questions - answers views and opinions, but nothing that really revealed anything of any consequence. But on the Sunday night something changed…

'If you would like to sit down,` asked Catherine, smiling at Gideon as he came into the dining room precisely at 7.30 as he had the two previous nights. `I will bring dinner through.'

'Wine,' said Blake, who was already sitting at the table, offering to fill Gideon's glass.

'Thank you,' said Gideon, Blake filled his glass and Catherine and Gideon sat down and began to eat dinner. After they had finished dessert Blake offered to take Max and Claudia up to bed, which was a little unusual, but Catherine just smiled, happy to stay seated and relax after dinner and drink her glass of wine.

'Will you tell us another story before we go to bed?' asked Max.

'I think you have had enough stories for today,' interrupted Catherine. Gideon had been regaling them with stories from just after lunch time till he went to his room at 3pm.

'Maybe Gideon will tell us some more tomorrow,' she glanced at Gideon to make sure she hadn't inadvertently committed him to an arrangement to which he might not be willing to partake, but he appeared perfectly amenable to the proposal, 'but you must go to bed now.' She then realised, somewhat embarrassingly, that she had rescued him from one obligation only to bind him to another.

Max and Claudia kissed Catherine goodnight and both politely shook Gideon's hand, which seemed to amuse him. They then both smiled, and flounced up the stairs to bed.

'I will read them a story, to keep them happy,' said Blake wandering up behind them. 'You keep Gideon amused.' it was a throwaway line with no agenda, but Catherine suddenly felt warm. AND EXCITED

Gideon and Catherine watched them all as they walked up the long staircase to the landing before disappearing from sight. Catherine turned back to Gideon.

'I will have to be leaving about three tomorrow to get back home if that is OK.' said Gideon sipping his wine.

'Of course it is. I know the children would love you to stay, but you must have work to do.' she paused for a moment, she knew it was a leading question, and had surprised herself by phrasing it that way, but she had.

'What about you?' asked Gideon.

'Me?' replied Catherine surprised by the question.

'Would you like me to stay?'

'I am sure Blake wouldn't mind,' said Catherine evasively. She smiled at Gideon. 'So tell me Gideon, pouring more wine into his glass, and deftly changing the subject, 'where did you get your idea for the book, how do you write something like that, it seems so personal?'

'From people, people I knew… people I know and some from people I don't know.'

'But how?' said Catherine, sounding intrigued.

'I watch them, people in love and see the things that they can't see.' VENTURING

'What sort of things,' asked Catherine prodding a little deeper into unchartered territory.

'Sometimes things they want me to see; things they want everybody to see, signs of affection... the touching of your hair as you pass or just a transient stroke of your body. I suppose if you really deeply analysed it... it's probably something to do with possession... you know, this is mine - I can touch, but not you - that sort of thing. It's all body signs. Catherine smiled, but said nothing.

'Sometimes I see tiny infinitesimal things they don't want me to see. The cold glance of remonstration, disapproval, hesitation... minute hand movements and mannerisms, the turning away and reluctance to answer a question... and sometimes I see things they cannot see, things that could mean all is not as it seems, little idiosyncrasies that could indicate they may not even realise what is already happening. And sometimes I see the same identical things, but they mean something entirely different, - a desire - a yearning, I see all these things even though they may try to keep it a secret, and they do manage to hide it from most people, but it's always there if you look close enough and you know what you are looking for.'

It was a harsh appraisal of his remarkable abilities to delve deep into the psyche of a relationship and in some ways she found it very disturbing to listen to somebody who could glean so much relevant information about a relationship just by careful observation. She felt exposed, vulnerable, almost naked before his gaze.

'Oh,' said Catherine, sounding a little surprised. He had not alluded to Blake and Catherine in particular, but the inference was there nevertheless.

Gideon smiled... 'It's all to do with the things that go into making a relationship work, that delicate fusion, that... balance of emotion, feelings, passion, ... and need between two people.'

Catherine hesitated before continuing the conversation, aware that she could figuratively speaking, be boxing herself into a corner from which there was no escape only submission. But curiosity and his charismatic manner drove her forward like a chariot of fire hurtling towards the cliff edge. On the surface she wanted to save the occupants, to scream out and tell them to jump to safety, but deep down in the darkest part of her soul she had already surrendered to something else, something she cared not to think of. The cinematic imagery and verity of the raging flames and the tormented cries of anguish from the trapped passengers was all to enthralling – to enchantingly beguiling to resist, so she stood by quietly and said nothing and watched and enjoyed the moment.

'I can understand emotion and feelings even the passion and desire,' she murmured, looking downwards for a split second as she spoke the last words, ...but need... isn't that a bit like dependency, a weakness?'

'Why did you look away when you mentioned need,' asked Gideon?

'Did I?' asked Catherine, sounding surprised, 'I wasn't aw...' she stopped, realising what she had just done. Gideon smiled.

'I don't know why,' said Catherine. 'But isn't need just a weakness,' she asked again?

'No, it's something entirely different. Need exists in the absence of weakness. I see pure need as something that is added to the relationship equation, not taken away. It's like oxygen. We all need it, and yes, we are all dependent on it, but without it, we would simply be dead. But that doesn't mean we are lesser mortals because we have that need, it's just essential to continue living. We can't function without it, does that make sense?'

'Yes, I can sort of see that.' replied Catherine. She went quiet for a few moments just looking at Gideon while she prepared what she was going to say next. 'So are you really like a voyeur?' she continued, mischievously grinning, 'secretly peeking through keyholes?'

Gideon smiled, 'No, not a voyeur, I'm.... I suppose you could call me an observer... of life, a witness... and when I see something interesting, I makes notes... in my head.

'To use in your next novel?'

'Possibly,' replied Gideon.

'Were they very much in love...?'

Gideon looked at Catherine intently and then dropped his gaze to the table, thinking about what she had said, the sudden change in direction had caught him a little unaware.

'Yes they were…'

The question seemed to trouble him slightly and Catherine could sense this. She decided to move the conversation in another safer direction.

'Do you watch everybody?' asked Catherine smiling. Gideon lifted his eyes to engage Catherine's, the blueness radiating a luminescent almost ethereal light.

'It depends.'

'On what,' asked Catherine?

'On whether they interest me.'

'Do we interest you?' asked Catherine tentatively, she had stopped smiling now. She was asking a perilous question, she knew that and she was fully aware that those few words could lead her to somewhere unanticipated or expected when they had first sat down for dinner that evening. Up until now conversation had been generalised and non-specific just typical dinner talk coupled with the inevitable curiosity on how a writer does what he does, but now it had moved onto a more personal level. Catherine was venturing into new terrain. Gideon moved his hand a few inches across the table and gently stroked the area just in front of her hand with little circles He purposely did not touch her … Catherine felt a very peculiar feeling on the back of her neck, a sensation she couldn't ever recall experiencing before. She instinctively looked towards the staircase to see if Blake was coming back down…

'Yes, you both interest me very much, but you interest me more.' He looked directly at Catherine as he spoke.

'I am falling in love with you…I want to be with you, when can we be together?' In a few brief words he had summarised precisely how he felt and what he wanted to do, leaving only one decision to make. It was like the clever car salesperson who always asked; when would you like to pick up your new car? - not if you actually wanted to buy it, he had already made that decision for you.

Catherine had to think about his words for a few moments. She wasn't sure whether he had actually said what she thought he had or whether she had just imagined it. She'd had a few drinks that night, and she did have a tendency to wander off at times lost in her own dreams. Maybe she had misheard him, but no, it was so blunt and honest and without a hint of ambiguity that the only conclusion she could come to, was that he had actually said it, she just hadn't been prepared for it.

'I don't think I've ever read a story with so much intensity,' she answered in confusion, her head now spinning with his words. Changing the subject was the only available tactic open to her, she needed something to give her time to think.

'Being in love is intense and should remain so. When that has gone all you have left is two people who know each other, they may even love each other, but they are not in love.'

He'd done it again, succinctly summarised her state of mind into a few carefully chosen words. How does he know how I feel she asked herself? Was he talking about the book or them? She wasn't sure, she wasn't sure of anything at the moment.

'Are you in love,' asked Gideon?

'Yes, yes I am,' replied Catherine quickly, grasping for simple words.

'Are you, really?' asked Gideon again.

'You can't ask me that,' replied Catherine.

'But I have, you see. I'm looking for the passion the desire, but I can't see it, not between you and Blake... so how can you be in love?'

'How are you two getting on?' asked Blake coming back down the staircase into the dining room.

'Fine just fine,' replied Catherine, breathing a small sigh of relief at the momentary respite from Gideon's tender inquisition.

'Gideon was just making a few suggestions...' she hesitated for a few moments looking playfully at Gideon, '...about running away to sea, to get away from everything.'

'Damn good idea if you ask me,' replied Blake, 'we could get away from all this chaos and the mayhem in the office, it's all your fault you know.' he smiled at Gideon.

Gideon and Catherine smiled at the idea. But what they were thinking was not what Blake was thinking.

'Are the children asleep,' asked Catherine?

'Yes, they are just, at last, I had to explain all of your stories to them again,' said Blake looking at Gideon again. 'You've so completely enthralled their minds that you are going to have to come over again to retell your stories, sometime in the very near future, if you can manage it. If you don't, I'll never be forgiven.'

'No problem,' replied Gideon, it will be a pleasure,' he smiled at Catherine. They continued to talk and drink long into the night, before eventually getting to bed around midnight.

The next morning, Gideon came down for breakfast and after they had finished, Blake, Max and Claudia said their goodbyes before walking off to the village, leaving Catherine to clean the breakfast things and see Gideon off. As he stood at the front door, he referred to the previous night's conversation, which had not been finished at the time.

'Remember what I said last night, I meant it.'

Catherine smiled, slightly embarrassed by his comment. She had sobered up now and was clear in her mind that the previous night's flirtatious conversation was nothing more than the wine talking, the tranquil surroundings and the poetic licence of a romantic novelist working overtime and was therefore of no consequence. But the sincerity in his words left very little uncertainty as to his intentions.

After Gideon left, Blake, Catherine and the children spent the last few days of the holiday visiting estate agents and collecting details of houses for sale within ten miles of where they currently lived. Catherine put all thoughts of Gideon out of her mind. He had now gone back to his boat on the Thames and it was very unlikely they would meet again in the near future.

Chapter 13

Catherine liked the area very much and didn't want to move too far and with the change in fortune for Blake's company. Anything, within reason, was now a possibility. It was Catherine who found the house, a beautiful seven bedroom Victorian manor house in three acres of land with a swimming pool, tennis court and within walking distance of the village. They arranged to view the house a few days later and before they had even entered the house, they knew it was the one. The interior was everything that Catherine had dreamed of, apart from the normal requirement for a new kitchen and a couple of new bathrooms.

There would obviously be many other cosmetic things to change, but the layout was exactly how Catherine had always imagined it, it was what she had always wanted. Rather curiously, it was almost identical to a house that Gideon had visualised in one of his many stories.

They moved in just over three months later in late April when the air was just beginning to warm up after a hard winter. The work began immediately to make all the changes that Catherine had planned.

Meanwhile Blake was now back in the office in London orchestrating the European, Japanese, Chinese and American publication of, The Chapter Room. UK sales for the hardback had reached an astonishing two million copies and now the paperback edition had pushed sales through the three million mark. As publishers, they received nearly two pounds on every hardback copy that meant Blake's company would receive over four million pounds just from hardback sales alone. This was virtually unheard off in the industry.

It was while he was at the office one day in late April 1983 that he received a telephone call from Martin, his old neighbour. Martin informed him there had been a serious fire at his house and nearly everything had been destroyed, but fortunately, by some curious twist of fate, the safe in which the manuscript for Prospect Road was held had withstood the fire and the document was unaffected. Martin wanted to know if Blake would like to pick it up sometime and of course, Blake immediately agreed. They arranged to meet that weekend at The Lodge hotel and restaurant near to where they used to live, and where Martin was now living until the builders had completed the rebuild of his house.

After Blake replaced the receiver he thought back to the last time he and Catherine had read the manuscript and the details mentioned within the final pages. It had accurately predicted the critical acclaim of The Chapter Room, the high volume of sales, even their move to a village just outside of Oxford. It had also mentioned a very tense period between Thomas and Kate, but Blake and Catherine had not experienced anything quite as traumatic as was mentioned in the book so it appeared to be less than accurate on some details. Neither had the book mentioned a fire. Maybe it was all just coincidence, he thought. He tried to put it out of his mind, but it wouldn't go away. There was still the nagging question of the riddle of how the manuscript was being written, and that was something he had yet to solve. He tried not to think about it anymore that day and pushed the matter to the back of his mind. Maybe it would all make more sense if they read the manuscript once more. Each time they had read it before, *previous* parts of it became clearer.

On the Saturday, they drove over to the hotel where Martin was staying. As they pulled up they could see Martin sitting on a bench outside having a drink in the courtyard area in the front of the hotel, taking in the spring sunshine. His appearance was that of someone who seemed perfectly at ease, almost without a care in the world, but then that had always been Martin's general predisposition to life. He never really took anything too seriously anymore, not that they could remember anyway and that was despite the loss of his wife some years earlier, which they had thought would change his freewheeling attitude, but fortunately it had not. He didn't socialise quite as much as he used to when Ruth was alive, but he still kept in touch with close friends.

As they got out of the car, Martin stood up and started walking toward them.

'Catherine, Blake, wonderful to see you, and you two,' looking at Max and Claudia. He kissed Catherine on the both cheeks and shook Blake's hand. From nowhere he produced two lollipops and gave them to the children, but not before glancing cursorily at Catherine to make sure that was OK. She smiled her approval.

'Hello uncle Martin,' said Max and Claudia in chorus, he wasn't actually their uncle, but Catherine and Blake had encouraged them to call him that as he had been in their lives since they were born. He now lived alone and what little family he had, lived many miles away and seldom visited him. He was now in his early seventies, but still extremely agile and animated, which amused Max and Claudia. They all sat down.

'Let me get you a drink,' said Blake.

'No, I'll get these,' chipped in Martin, 'there's a sexy little barmaid here and I could be in with a chance, she thinks I'm loaded.' He laughed at the self-deprecatory delusion, making a sad clown like expression, which amused Max and Claudia, who obviously didn't understand the hidden agenda (or so he thought). 'I don't want to disappoint her, well not just yet anyway.' He laughed again and Blake and Catherine smiled back. 'It's not my money,' added Martin, 'I have a subsistence allowance from the insurance company, so it's on them, mind you I don't know how long that will last, the food's very expensive here, but very nice, so I'm getting my three meals a day at the moment, with wine,' he laughed. 'Normally only eat at dinner time. He pulled a funny expression as if he were a naughty boy who had stolen some sweets from the tuck shop. 'Stopped eating breakfast and lunch after the old lady died.' He was talking affectionately about his wife, who Max and Claudia had liked very much. Martin went into the hotel and came back a few minutes later with a tray full of drinks.

'Right, there you go lemonade for you two,' he passed the drinks to Max and Claudia then passed a beer to Blake and a gin and tonic to Catherine. 'Happy days,' said Martin picking up his beer. He seemed in remarkably good humour considering the disaster that had befallen his house.

'So how did the fire start, have they told you yet,' asked Blake, wiping away a bit of froth from his mouth?

'Well that's the strangest thing,' replied Martin, 'well the second strangest thing actually. I was out for the day… do you remember Derek the postman?'

'Very vaguely,' said Blake shaking his head.

~~Yes, replied Catherine~~, 'you wouldn't remember him darling, you're were gone long before he ever arrived,' *SAID CATH REP?*

'Ah,' said Blake acknowledging the point.

'Well anyway he was cycling up the drive just after eleven o'clock and suddenly there was an enormous explosion which destroyed about half the house according to his statement. Apparently a gas leak according to the fire brigade on their first inspection.

'Nasty,' said Blake.

'Then what was left of the house burst into flames.'

'You've upset the *village* mafia haven't you,' suggested Blake wryly, taking another sip. *WOMENS INSTITUTE ANACHISTS I HEARD A FEW HAD JOINED*

'It's no laughing matter,' said Catherine gently scolding Blake, 'Martin's lost everything he owns, all his memories, photos.' Blake lost the slightly jovial expression and apologised to Martin. But Martin did not seem overly concerned, but then he never was.

'No it's not as bad as all that.' I kept most of that sort of stuff in one of those four drawer metal office filing cabinets in the garage and as you probably remember that's quite a few yards from the house, or where the house used to be anyway.' He laughed at his quip. 'I did lose a few photos, but there is plenty left. We took thousands of each other over the years, but no one ever looks at them, I don't think anybody actually looks at photographs to be honest. I think most of us remember people in our heads, I know I do.' It was an odd statement to make, but inherently true.

He lifted his pint and took a sip. 'Now one of the really odd things was the safe!' *PLACE NEEDED REDECORATING ANYWAY*

'The safe?' echoed Blake.

'Yes, the safe where I kept my real valuable's and of course… your document.'

'The manuscript,' replied Catherine and Blake in unison.

'Correct,' replied Martin.

'Can we play in the garden?' interrupted Max, he pointed to a small area just to the right of where they were sitting, where there were some swings, a climbing frame and various other amusements for children.

'Yes of course you can,' said Catherine. They both finished their drinks and ran off to the play area. Martin leaned over to a brief case by his side, took out the manuscript, passed it to Blake at first, and then slid it to Catherine. BEFORE REMOVING HIS HAND

'It that right?' he queried. A little unsure if he had inadvertently embarrassed Blake.

'Yes, yes it is,' replied Blake. 'Look I think you deserve an explanation for our..

'All in good time,' interrupted Martin, I haven't told you everything yet, not quite.'

'Oh,' said Catherine, wondering what else there could be to tell.

'Well… after the fire brigade had put the fire out, and the structural people had checked out what was left they found something very odd.' He stopped for a moment with a hint of theatricality in order to allow the tension to build. This was typical of Martin, never one to miss an opportunity to over dramatize an experience. In fact, he had appeared in a few local amateur dramatic productions, when Ruth was still alive, usually as the imperious ex-major or an overbearing Judge, so he tended to rely on a few hackneyed theatrical affectations from time to time to emphasise something or make it appear a little more interesting. It was a habit that he had picked up from various play directors.

He knew full well Blake was a crime fiction publisher among other genres so he was endeavouring to make it sound a little mysterious like a thriller novel would be, just to make it a little more interesting.   Blake didn't

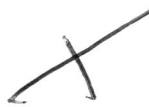

immediately realise that Martin was making light of his story, he had obviously dined out or at least had a couple of pints on the back of his recollection of events. He continued… 'When they got to my study, where the safe was they found the room was virtually untouched. The rooms on the other three sides had been completely demolished or burnt out, but the study was… as it was, even the ceiling was still there. And what's more, there was a burst water pipe sending a fountain of water directly over the safe, as if to protect it from any harm by the fire. It was all very odd.'

Blake looked at Catherine, but said nothing.

'If was as if by some sort of divine intervention your documents were being saved by a higher force.' He added emphasis to the last two words by delivering them slightly slower and a couple of semitones lower, in order to produce an element of cod theatrical gravity. He looked upwards and then furtively left and right looking not dissimilar to an espionage agent out of a Graham Green novel.

Blake and Catherine were no longer as cheery as they had been when they first arrived. In fact for a few moments they were completely lost in their own introspection, contemplating the unusual circumstances surrounding the survival of the manuscript.

'So,' said Martin, 'what were you going to tell me?'

In the light of what Martin had just told them, Blake thought it wiser not mention the unusual attribute that the manuscript appeared to have. Martin had suffered enough trauma for the moment. He didn't need to have something else to worry about. Martin finished his drink.

'It was nothing of importance,' replied Blake, 'Would you like another drink Martin?' Martin looked at his glass.

'No, I'm OK at the moment thanks,' replied Martin. 'Oh, there was one other peculiar thing about the explosion though.'

'Yes!' Said Blake cautiously.

'No gas!' Replied Martin abruptly.

'No gas,' replied Blake, momentarily mystified, then he suddenly remembered, 'of course, we didn't have any gas either did we,' he looked at Catherine who just nodded in agreement.

'The gas company has never put the service into our area, so nobody has gas.' said Martin.

Blake thought about that for a second or two, 'so how did the..'

'... Explosion happen,' finished Martin. 'That was the other thing I was alluding to earlier. The fire brigade investigators couldn't find the reason for the explosion, they were certain it was gas to start with, but eventually they had to rule that out, when they found there wasn't any. All very odd.

'Odd indeed,' said Blake, deep in thought again.

'So what caused it?' asked Blake quietly.

'They don't know, think it might have been a build-up of methane gas or something from the farm, but that's some way away so even that's a little improbable, as I said a bit of a mystery.' Blake and Catherine both smiled, but with an air of quizzical confusion.

'Anyway we must be off,' said Blake, 'but you must come over to see us sometime, any weekend is good, just give us ring.'

'I will,' replied Martin, 'that's very kind of you.'

'When you are all sorted out, we may ask you to take safe keeping of our manuscript again,' suggested Blake. You protected it very well so far.' Catherine gave Blake a reproachful glance, but said nothing.

'Glad to be of service.' replied Martin.

'Have the builders said how long it will take?' asked Blake.

'Yes,' replied Martin a little despondently, ' about six months so November time. Definitely back for Christmas I hope,' he paused for a moment then smiled, 'still, gives me plenty of time to work on the barmaid.' He laughed, and Blake and Catherine smiled.

'Max! Claudia!' Shouted Blake, 'we're going now, come and say goodbye to Uncle Martin. They both sauntered over and said their goodbyes. Blake picked up the manuscript.

'Thanks again,' said Blake.

'Yes, thank you very much for everything,' said Catherine, she kissed him on the cheek and gave him a reassuring hug, possibly a little more intently than was necessary, but she was feeling very uncomfortable about the grief and destruction that she now firmly believed they may have unintentionally brought to his door. They all made their way back to the car, waving as they went.

'Anytime,' said Martin, 'anytime.' smiling amiably, as they turned to walk away.

Max and Claudia waved back as they skipped their way to the car and Blake placed the manuscript in the back of the estate. The ride home was a little subdued for Catherine and Blake as they both contemplated what Martin had told them, but by mutual unspoken agreement they chose not to discuss in the car, as they didn't want to mention anything in front of Max and Claudia.

After they arrived back home, Max and Claudia went to play in the back garden and Catherine went into the kitchen to make a cup of tea.

'So,' said Catherine, 'this manuscript not only documents your past and predicts the future it..

'Predicts the future,' interrupted Blake, a little surprised by Catherine's statement. 'I think that's overegging it a bit.'

'Well I don't think so,' said Catherine, firmly, 'It did foretell all of this,' she waved her arms around indicating the house they were standing in, 'and the success of The Chapter Room.' Blake pretended he had forgotten, but he too had been thinking about it since the telephone call from Martin. So much had happened since then, he wasn't sure how much had been actually documented in the manuscript and how much was real, albeit that everything was real one way or another - more or less.

'Are you sure,' replied Blake.

'Yes I am, just read it, you will see how close it is.' There was a sense of concerned urgency in her voice that Blake had not noticed before. The mysterious explosion had obviously unnerved Catherine. 'But of more concern now is that it appears to have a guardian angel protecting it.'

'Well not quite,' replied Blake quickly discounting that suggestion, 'why would a "guardian angel", ' he flicked his fingers in the air to indicate it was in inverted commas, ' try to blow it up and then set fire to it.'

'Maybe that was a message,' said Catherine after a few moments thought, pursing her lips together in an odd expression of intrigue and mystery. She rolled her eyes around a bit to enhance the suggestion. She was desperately trying to make light of the incident, but deep down there was a tiny niggling doubt, a suggestion of uncertainty that she couldn't ignore.

'What kind of message?' replied Blake, still in a whimsical state of mind, but now taking careful note of Catherine's odd facial contortions.

'"Don't ignore me, or this is what I will do!"' replied Catherine, using more inverted commas, and adopting a strange effected nasal tone to her voice.

'Don't ignore me,' said Blake, thoughtfully. Any previous air of flippancy in his tone no longer evident. He was carefully considering what Catherine had said even if it was a little, melodramatic, but maybe she had a point.

'What do you actually mean,' asked Blake.

'Well maybe, it wants to be read, and you haven't read it for a while, so it got annoyed and the only way it could attract our.. ' she thought about that for a few seconds then changed the pronoun to "your" attention, was to…boom! She threw her arms up in the air emulating an explosion. So maybe it's time you did have another look.' Catherine seemed to have now accepted that something unusual was happening, she also realised how ridiculous that last statement sounded, but rather than try to explain it what she was trying to say was… "run with it, let it be your guide."

This was the real difference between men and women and why they had to have come from different planets, thought Blake. Men function in a practical world encapsulated within an imperious vacuum, like a large soapy bubble floating a few inches off the ground, impervious to anything that defied convention, accepting all the illogical rules as presented. But a woman can function without reason or accountability and will challenge almost anything if it has no tangible purpose. They will also quickly re-adjust their subjective opinion if there is a possibility this action could solve a problem. They were neither stubborn or intransigent and were usually unconcerned about losing face. Sometimes, Blake wished he could be more like Catherine, more like a woman in the way he dealt with some things. Her way, sometimes indisputably worked despite the illogical methodology

[margin notes:] REMOTEST COURSE OF ACTION

'But I thought you thought I was writing it, sort of sleep writing or something,' asked Blake still trying to get his bearings on exactly where they were with it.

'It did cross my mind just once, but not since and definitely not while it was in Martins safe.'

'Right,' said Blake 'OK.' Case in question he thought to himself.

'So what do we do?'

'Read it,' replied Catherine with disarming pragmatism. Blake realised he was being a bit obtuse.

'And weep?' he offered, mis-paraphrasing a cliché. Catherine ignored him.

'So, just so that I'm perfectly clear on this, what you are suggesting is the manuscript indirectly arranged to blow up Martin's house because we have...

'Not we,' corrected Catherine hastily, 'definitely not we, you, it was sent to you not me.' For whatever reason, Catherine was now consciously endeavouring to place some sort of metaphysical distance between herself and whatever it was that was causing the incidents, it was as if she had suddenly become a little unsure of something that she originally had no issue with.

[margin note:] SPACE

'OK, sent to "me", and all this is happening because I haven't read it for a few months?'

'Nearly six I believe,' said Catherine.

'Six then.' agreed Blake reluctantly.

'So we'll read it again tonight after the children have gone to bed,' said Catherine. Blake nodded his agreement.

'In fact you don't need me to read it, you read it, if anything relevant happens tell me, and then I'll read it.'

Blake looked at Catherine for a moment unsure whether he was comfortable with that suggestion, but Catherine gave him an expression of reassurance, so he smiled back and began to read… *complete*

Prospect Road 7

Chapter Seven
written by
Anthony Theodore Clackle
Mary Drayton's Story

When Thomas arrived home, Kate met him at the door and kissed him.

'I'm sorry darling,' said Kate 'It was last night, all very unexpected according to her neighbour, apparently she had been to Bingo and seemed perfectly OK, but when her neighbour popped in this morning she was gone.'

'I haven't seen her for month's... with all this going on,' replied Thomas, 'I should have gone to see her, shouldn't have left it so long.'

'We all leave it too long for somebody,' replied Kate philosophically; quietly attempting to ease the remorse and regret that Thomas was obviously feeling. She had been badgering him constantly to ask Mary to come over to the new house and stay for a while, but he had just never got around to it and now she never would.

'I haven't told the children yet, ' said Kate.

'I'll do that,' said Thomas.

'We can do it together,' said Kate, Thomas smiled. Kate had never really got on that well with his mother, but she had never let that become an issue....

'We will have to go down tomorrow to sort things out for the funeral,' said Thomas, 'I will ring the office in the morning and tell them I will be away for a few days. I'm sure they can cope without me for a little while. Could you ring your mother to see if she can have the children for a couple of days?' Kate nodded.

The following day, Kate and Thomas arrived at his mother's house at just after seven o'clock in the evening and were met by an tall elderly woman, the lady that had spoken to Kate on the phone the previous day and who had arranged to meet them. She was carefully dressed in a

NEATLY

tweed skirt and jacket with dark brown stockings and sensible shoes, not exactly obsessive, but precise nevertheless in a practical sort of way, which suited her demeanour and candour. She appeared a little austere, but that was to be expected under the circumstances. Definitely not English thought Thomas, who couldn't quite place her, but thought he recognised her. She introduced herself as Adrianna and she opened the front door for Thomas and turned the light. ON . THE CURTAIN HAD ALL

HAS TO

'I am sorry for your loss,' she declared rather abruptly. 'I was your mother's friend, but I wasn't here when... she died alone unfortunately.'

Adrianna delivered the line more as a statement of fact rather than as affirmation of amity, but that was probably just her way. Maybe, thought Kate, as we grow older we become more crotchety, more impatient, less inclined to waste what precious time we have left on the trivia and mundanely banal eccentricities of polite conversation and etiquette. Maybe civility is unintentionally sacrificed at the altar of honest intent, bluntness ~~at the cost of civility~~ maybe that was the order of the day. And maybe she was just making benevolent excuses for an old lady and was just trying to be helpful, but had forgotten, possibly mislaid, temporarily, the essential niceties that were necessary to carry it off successfully. Kate suddenly thought how sad it was that somebody should die alone, with no one to talk to in the last few moments of lucidity - the last few minutes of light just before she slowly slipped away into the obscurity of the darkness behind them. And the last opportunity to plead for forgiveness, expiation and atonement for sins unspoken.

PROCRAFTIN

Bluntness not enough to the ople of the day

Thomas thought about some words he had read somewhere recently...he couldn't remember where, but for some reason they had stuck in his mind and kept coming back. "He walks there quietly at your side or behind you in the shadows and you don't care to even give him a second glance... and then one day he suddenly clears his throat and you are startled by his presence..." Was she startled by his presence? probably not. Did she have things she *should have told him before she died? probably, but now he would never know and probably it was best that way.*

'We used to spend our days together talking. I will miss our conversations... I will miss Mary.' *Kate and Thomas turned around to where Adrianna was standing, she appeared oddly reluctant to enter into the house before they did.*

Adriana paused for a moment. 'I live just next door, if there is anything you need please knock.' *Thomas didn't seem to hear her speaking. Adrianna turned as if to leave.*

'Thank you,' said Kate, realising that Thomas appeared to be preoccupied and had unintentionally ignored Adrianna. He was gazing at the front door and Kate presumed that maybe he was preparing himself for the moment when he would step back into the house, the house where he had spent his childhood years from the age of nine. This time however, his mother would not be there to greet him. For the first time in nearly twenty five years he would enter the house and be met by a deafening silence. Mary had always loved classical music and the radio would be turned on first thing in the morning and the music would resonate around the house all day long, only to be turned off at around seven in the evening when they would sit down to watch some television. His love of Debussy, Grieg and Brahms had been nurtured by this subliminal indoctrination, but he was glad of this because his appreciation of the great composers had continued long after he moved away and had continued to this day. Something else he had to thank her for.

'I remember you,' said Thomas suddenly returning from his momentary introspection, 'I must apologise, I was just thinking back to when I lived here. You moved here just before I left didn't you?'

Adrianna turned back to face Thomas. 'Yes that's right,' she replied.

'I must have met you a few times over the past years?'

'You didn't come here very often,' replied Adrianna with a hint of gentle remonstration, 'Mary always looked forward to the times you did visit.' *Thomas felt a little*

Guilty

embarrassed, Adrianna was right, his visits were rare, occasionally he would make a flying visit at Christmas and maybe twice in the last ten years he had managed to pop down for a few hours in the middle of summer. But Mary had not seen her grandchildren as much as she would have liked, and now she never would. Thomas pondered over the lack of consideration he had afforded his mother. He had denied her the true joy and pleasure of seeing her grandchildren, probably one of the few pleasures she had left in her declining years, when all it would have cost him was a little time. He began to realise that not everything was conditional on a return on investment. Mary had never shown anything, but love and care for him and he had repaid her with abjuration. On this, a very rare occurrence for him, he felt himself begin to well up and he began to experience the bitter pang of loss, a loss that could never be replaced.

'Oh I forget to give you these.' Adrianna passed Thomas the house keys she had been holding and a business card.

'That's the chapel of rest where Mary is, I told them you would probably pop in tomorrow, I hope that's OK. Oh and I left some milk, bread and eggs and a few things in the fridge, there's wasn't much left and what there was I had to ditch...it was beginning to...'

'Yes thank you,' said Kate, thank you for sorting everything out.' Adrianna smiled then made her way back to her own house.

Thomas stepped into the small hallway and continued through to the lounge and Kate followed him. For a few moments he stood in the middle of the room looking around at all the reminders of his youth, is was if he was half expecting his mother to suddenly appear.

'Let's get the bags,' said Kate, then we can...' but she didn't finish, not sure what to say.

'Yes, yes of course,' replied Thomas suddenly returning from wherever he was. He went back to the car, collected the two small suitcases they had brought with them, shut the front door behind him and took the two bags upstairs to

his old bedroom. The room was just had he had left it all those years ago when he last stayed, but it was smaller now, much smaller than he remembered. Mary had put in a new double bed some time ago in anticipation of Thomas and Kate staying over for a few days, but it had never happened, the bed had never been used.

Chapter 14

Blake stopped reading and looked up at Catherine; 'Thomas's mother has just died… and they hadn't spoken for a long time, it was very unexpected… apparently he had stopped visiting her for some reason.'

Catherine was only to aware of the similarities with Blake and his mother. They too had not spoken for some time and she too had become quite frail the last time he had seen her.

'Maybe you should call her,' whispered Catherine, reading the unspoken thoughts hanging in the air. Blake had an obstinate look in his eyes.

'The last time we spoke, we had a row… about you,' he spluttered.

'I know, but I can't help it if we don't get on, she doesn't like me.'

'It's not you, it's her, why does she always have to say unpleasant things, it annoys me, it winds me up and then we have a row.'

'It's what mother's do; they only want the best, especially for their only son. That's what they do, it happens to lots of mothers as they grow old, they can only see the son they had, the son they looked after from birth and now they see somebody else getting all the benefit after they have done all the work, she only wants what's best for you.'

'You are,' replied Blake.

'I know that, you know that,' said Catherine a little tongue in cheek, 'She just doesn't know it yet.'

'But when?' said Blake, still a little furious with his mother's belligerency.

'As long as it takes. She doesn't worry me, don't let it worry you. Just get her over, for a few days, maybe this weekend, we can break her down slowly over time, we will just have to be patient with her.' she smiled, and Blake leaned across and kissed her.

'I'll ring her tomorrow, I promise,' said Blake, Catherine smiled. He continued reading...

'I'm going to have a bath,' said Catherine. 'You carry on and tell me what happens when I come back down.' She got up and kissed Blake and wandered up the stairs.

Blake continued reading...

INC   INTO   CH 13

Prospect Road 8

Chapter Eight
written by
Anthony Theodore Clackle
Mary and Julian's Story

Thomas's old bedroom was quaint rather than functional as are most rooms in thatched cottages. There is always the illusion of size from the outside, bolstered up by the depth of the thatch, but inside the rooms were invariably very small with lots of awkwardly positioned beams, which although appearing to exude oldie world charm were very restrictive and could be a real problem for people of normal height. His mother stood at 5'2" and had no such issues, but Thomas had to duck under the head of the doorway. Cottages like this were built for country folk who were a lot shorter two hundred years ago, but the builders obviously hadn't considered the possibility that people might grower taller in years to come.

SCRAP.

'Do you want something to eat,? I'm starving,' said Kate, calling up the stairs to Thomas... 'Adrianna said she left us a few things in the kitchen.'

'Whatever you can find, I'm not all that hungry at the moment.' He came back down into the lounge and sat at his mother's desk and casually pushed up the roll top cover while Kate prepared some food in the kitchen.

There were ten compartments each one neatly labelled. Household bills, Insurance, Circulars, Letters, Legal, Motor car, Will & Private Papers, Repairs etc. She had become very methodical after Jonathan, Thomas's father had died, wanting to know precisely where every important document was so she could get to it quickly in an emergency, a habit that served her well and obviously would serve him well in the next few days. He took out the envelope marked "Last will and Testament of Mary Florence Drayton" and looked at the words. He wondered what testament actually meant. It had biblical connotations, which somehow did not seem that relevant *anymore. He pulled out the paper knife from the compartment marked "Letters" slit open the envelope and took out the document*

'Scrambled eggs on toast OK,' shouted Kate from the kitchen, unaware that Thomas had come back downstairs.

'Yes, that's fine thank you.' replied Thomas quietly.

'Oh,' said Kate a little surprised, turning round to see Thomas seated at his mother's desk. 'I didn't realise you were back down.' WHAT HAVE YOU FOUND

Thomas smiled and continued to unfold the document.

'It's Mary's Will, I thought I should open it.'

'Yes, yes you should.' replied Kate.

He began to read what was in affect her final "To Do" list the only one that she would not be able to complete herself, due to the prevailing circumstances, so one that REWRITE *she would entrust to her son to fulfil. It was all as he had expected, with the majority of the estate coming to him apart from a few bequests to the two grandchildren, Adrianna, the local cats home and a donkey sanctuary. Mary had always loved donkeys. He flicked through the other compartments and everything seemed to be more or* Been *less as he would had expected from* Had *his mother, always a meticulously tidy person, even more so since her husband's demise. He carefully refolded the will, replaced it in to its envelope, and placed it back into its compartment.* It was *then* that *he noticed the small bundle of letters in the Private compartment, all carefully tied together with a faded red ribbon, not unlike the ribbon used by solicitors for tying up defence barrister's briefs. Someone had told him that was where the phrase "tied up in red tape" came from. White ribbon was used for a prosecution brief. A detail he remembered from a short spell working as a clerk in chambers when he was much younger. He idly wondered whether the colour of the ribbon tied round the letters had any similar connation or significance.*

They were probably letters between Mary and his father Jonathan going by the way the ribbon had been neatly tied and by the careful attention to detail on the way his mother's name and address on the first envelope had been

written.   He pulled the bundle of letters out,   quickly flicking through them, not actually intending to read them when he noticed that alternate letters,   presumably the corresponding replies that she had written to his father were not in fact addressed to him at all. They were in fact addressed to a Mr J. Clackle at an address that he didn't recognise and yet it was definitely her handwriting. Curiosity got the better of him and somewhat reluctantly and with some trepidation he opened the first letter addressed to his mother that was dated 12th July 1950, one year before he was born. This oddly, on closer inspection, was in a handwriting, which he did not recognise. He briefly flicked to the last page of the letter which was signed "Your ever loving Julian", not a name he could recall. The letter was well thumbed and had obviously been read many times. Thomas   wondered who this Julian Clackle might be as he began to read the letter.

But To

Relay

Kate came through from the kitchen with two plates of scrambled eggs on toast and placed them on the table.

'Dinner darling, I'm sorry it's a little unadventurous, I'll pick a few more things up tomorrow.' She went back to the kitchen and brought back two cups of tea. Thomas placed the letter he had started to read back down on the desk. The room was eerily quiet so Thomas got up from his chair and walked over to the Roberts radio perched on the sideboard, occupying the same space it had inhabited for as many years as he could remember and turned it on very low, a piece by Debussy was being in introduced. They sat down at the dining table to eat dinner.

After a few moments the sound of Clair de Lune slowly filled the room,   perfectly matching his contemplative mood. Thomas pondered on how fortuitous it was that this particular piece of Debussy was being played at that particular moment. The melody perfectly matched the way he was feeling, the slow heartbeat rhythmic tempo of the piece gently caressing his tormented soul.   She had dedicated so much of her life to ensuring that he had peace and tranquillity in his childhood protecting him from the harsh realities of the world until he was ready to face them. Now he was beginning to realise just how much he had neglected his mother in her closing years and hardly repaid her at all for all she had done.

He was becoming engulfed by a wave of guilt and remorse, and that was something he was going to have to live with. Nothing could now alleviate the thoughts running around in his head, only time would ease the sadness and feelings of regret he now felt. They finished dinner, cleared away the dishes and Kate washed them in the sink. Thomas sat back down at the desk in the lounge and resumed reading his mother's letters.

'I'm going to sort the bedroom out then have a bath,' said Kate making her way up the staircase. Thomas looked up from the desk and half smiled.

'I'll come up and scrub your back,' he replied quietly. There was solicitous tone in his voice with just the tiniest hint of innuendo, but he hadn't really applied himself to the suggestion - his mind was elsewhere.

When Kate came back down she took out a book she had brought with her and began reading. Thomas was still at the desk, but was now retying the faded red ribbon around the bundle of letters, just as he had found them. He carefully placed them back into the compartment in the desk. He wondered why Mary had not destroyed the letters.

Some people grow old and become fixated with making preparations for their death and feel obliged to tidy up their affairs as best they can while they are still able. Some people meticulously prepare their own funeral preparations down to the last detail in order to be certain that the final farewell is conducted precisely in the manner in which they had intended. They prepare detailed instructions about which hymns they would like played and which people should be contacted, and who should be advised of their death. If was as if they were afraid that their passing would go unnoticed, unseen, unmarked if the final ceremony they would be attending was not planned properly. Mary would have wished her entrance to eternity be trumpeted with blaring horns and raging chariots. His thoughts turned to Dylan Thomas's verse, something he and his mother had read a thousand times together, but until now, never really appreciating the defining relevance.

"Do not go gentle into that good night, Old age should burn and rave at close of day; Rage, rage, rage against the dying of the light." (Mary always added an additional "rage" when she recited the poem) truly believing that Thomas had made a unforgivable miscalculation in the lilting cadence of his greatest verse. She was not adverse to making comments about any of the great poems, books and classical music if she felt it warranted criticism, guiding advice or partial rewriting as was the case in question.

Some people become obsessed about leaving behind anything that might show them in a less than perfect light if they were to be found after death. Best to remove indiscrete photographs taken at a time when, the potential embarrassment sixty years hence, had not been a consideration at the moment of inception. The carefully prepared closing imagery held intact. The paradox being that the removal of the evidence also removed the portal through which personality, character and temperament could be clandestinely observed.

Oddly, if discovered a hundred years later such objects would be feted to be nothing more than quaint, highly collectable items of harmless or possibly slightly risqué ephemera from a bygone age and of little or no consequence to the memory of the original protagonists. Even something possibly to enhance a faded reminiscence, a moment of startling revelation and honesty never previously envisaged.

Thomas turned to Kate and quietly, without any intonation apart from an underlying sense of confusion, said the words that had been running around his head since he had placed the letters back into their compartment in the desk.

'I'm not sure I know who I am anymore.' Thomas's eyes appeared to focus on something far, far away in the distance, a long way from the Mary Drayton's lounge.

'Sorry darling,' replied Kate putting her book down, 'I don't quite understand.'

'My father may not have been my father after all, my father could be somebody else altogether.'

'Things happen,' replied Kate, she was still a little unsure precisely where this might be going so she decided to reply in a lighter, slightly whimsical, more prosaic vein.

'Things Happen!' exclaimed Thomas a little surprised by Kate's remark.

'Well, you did say you hardly ever saw him, wasn't he away all the time anyway - and didn't you say you thought he was a little bit gay or something?... , even in the best of families things happen. I can't see any point in getting upset over it now.' She wondered if maybe that had made her sound a little bit vacuous, which she definitely didn't think she was.

Thomas was a little taken aback by Kate's casual almost blasé acceptance of what to him was a relatively momentous and significance development. His whole life had suddenly been turned upside down and all Kate could say was "things happen". He did not think he was being particularly melodramatic about the revelation in fact he thought he was being surprisingly objective and considered about it. 'You can't be a little bit gay no more than you can be nearly a virgin! replied Thomas a little indignantly, picking out the obvious contradiction in terms. ' Either you are or you're not. It's like saying someone is slightly dead ....it's a definitive.' He paused to immediately apologise . 'I'm sorry, I didn't mean to snap, it's just that I had always assumed that despite his predilection I was his son, but now I find it would appear, I am not and it just drops another layer of confusion over my entire life.'

Kate shrugged at his apology as if to say his interpretation of what he had read was probably wrong and continued reading. But after a few moments she realised she may have been a little harsh and insensitive in her assessment and maybe he had come to the right conclusion, he had after all carefully read the letters, which she had not, and he was not someone who would normally jump to conclusions or make rash judgements. She put the book back down again and looked up at Thomas... 'So if your father wasn't your father who was? I presume it's something in those letters you've been reading, that is causing you some concern.'

'Well yes, sort of..., possibly,' replied Thomas hesitantly. 'I don't know.' His eyes sunk to the floor as if in despair.

Kate look even more confused. 'Nothing good ever came from reading other people's private letters.' Kate spoke in that homily style accent she often adopted at moments like this and which Thomas hated with a passion that bordered on the psychotic. Her vague disparate nature, innate philosophical cliché's and natural resistance to over react to almost anything drove him to a state of near apoplexy at times, but of course he knew she was absolutely right which only made things worse.

Thomas looked up at Kate, but with his head still in his hands and still slightly bowed and talking through the tops of his eyes he continued..

'What I don't understand is this... If she didn't want me to read the letters, she could have burnt them, that would have been an end to it, but she didn't, which meant she did and that means she must have had a reason.' He had to run that over in is head a couple of times immediately after he had said it just to make sure it actually made sense. He could be just as obtuse and obfuscated as Kate could be with her bumper sticker philosophy, when it was called for.

'But does it really matter?' asked Kate, effectively ablating Thomas's carefully considered rational with a few simple words.

'Of course it does, where we come from defines what we are and what we will eventually become.' It was a sweepingly profound statement delivered with intensity and simplistic clarity. 'We are what are parents were, but more so. It is the very nature of life that, each generation becomes stronger and cleverer. Survival of the fittest - natural selection and all that. Those with a propensity to survive have a propensity to survive and flourish. If it were not so we would all be condemned to oblivion.'

'*I didn't realise you thought so strongly about it,*' replied Kate a little surprised by this unexpected heart felt philosophical outpouring.

Thomas half smiled. '*It would have been nice if she had told me while she was still alive, I could have asked her some questions about him then.*'

'*Like what?*' said Kate, curiously.

'*Well, who he was, what he did, what became of him.*'

'*Wasn't that in the letters, she must of mentioned his name?*'

'*Well yes, there's lot of information in the letters about him and about his life,*' replied Thomas, '*but that doesn't really tell me anything about him.*'

'*But you had a father, a real father doesn't that count?*'

'*Yes of course it does, but...*'

'*Well what was his name,*' asked Kate?.

'*Clackle, Julian Clackle and he was married to a lady called Rosemary.*'

'*Clackle,*' said Kate running it over on her tongue, '*Strange name,*' and he was married?'

'*Yes, so it appears,*' replied Thomas.

How odd thought Blake. I wonder why Anthony Clackle should introduce somebody else with his surname into the book. He made a mental note to mention that to Catherine when she came back down and carried on reading...

'*Katie Clackle.*' pronounced Kate authoritatively rolling the words around in her mouth and testing the sound they made. '*Kay-Te-Clack-Cool,*' pronouncing each syllable as if deciding which was the best way to deliver the words. `*Christ! what a mouthful that would have been, I would have sounded like a demented harridan.*'

Thomas laughed.

I've decided, I'm perfectly happy with Drayton, that's just fine,' said Kate.

Thomas smiled. Maybe he was going a bit over the top about the whole thing, while Kate as usual was being sensible and taking it all in her stride.

'It's still odd she never mentioned it though,' said Thomas.

'She must have had her reasons.' said Kate, 'Maybe she just didn't want to tell you while your father was still alive and after he died... well maybe she thought what would be the point.'

Thomas pondered over Kate's words, which in way seemed to make some sort of sense.

'I wonder where he came from,' said Thomas thoughtfully 'I wonder what happened to him?' ......

'What else did the letters say?' asked Kate.

'Well Julian Clackle or daddy as maybe I should now call him,' he looked up at Kate and grinned, '...well he mentions various things, personal stuff mainly, between him and Mary, but amongst all that he starts to write about something else, something that happened quite a long time ago.'

'When exactly?' asked Kate, slightly flippantly, but obviously intrigued by Thomas's attempt to introduce a mysterious element to the proceedings, 'are we talking a few years?'

'No, not exactly,' replied Thomas a little condescendingly, 'no it was around the turn of the century actually.'

'Right, well that's a long time.' said Kate.

Thomas nodded.

Kate, decided that it might be better if she were to listen with a little more solemnity. She pursed her lips together for a couple of moments in a semi-contrived act of languid contrition, smiled disarmingly with the most inventive expression of engrossed interest she could muster and with a playful magisterial flick of her hand engendered Thomas to continue...

Thomas responded accordingly. 'Oh and by the way, I have a brother, well half-brother.'

'A brother?' exclaimed Kate with a quizzical expression.

'Yes, well half, Mr Anthony Theodore Clackle no less.'

'This gets better and better,' said Kate.

~~~

Blake stopped reading just as Catherine came down the staircase, with her dressing gown on and her head covered in a towel in that unique way that only women can wrap a towel around wet hair.

'This is all very peculiar,' said Blake laying down the manuscript for a moment, 'The letters that Thomas found and read now mention Thomas's real father, was a Julian Clackle. Apparently Mary had an affair with him, became pregnant and Thomas was the result, but Mary never told her husband about the affair or who Thomas's real father was, just pretended that her husband was the father.

'And never told him?' asked Catherine.

'No, never from what I can make out. Then Julian Clackle has another son with his wife proper, a half-brother to Thomas and they call him, and this is where it becomes very confusing… Anthony Theodore Clackle, the writer of the story!' Blake looked blankly at Catherine.

'So the book is a sort of autobiography?' said Catherine a little bemused, 'but what then is the connection to you and why is it foretelling events that are happening in our lives?'

'I don't know. It's all very confusing,' replied Blake. He picked the manuscript up again and started reading further.

'Then the letters mention a writer called Gideon Drew, and something that happened back around 1912. Apparently this Gideon wrote a book which his publishers stole from him and published through their company, but under their own names.'

'Can they do that?' asked Catherine.

'No! they most definitely can't, but apparently they did.' Blake read on…

~~~

Thomas and Kate

'Oh,' said Kate, musing over what, if any ramifications that might denote. 'Well that's something you didn't know, what else do they say about him? Do they mention where he is?'

'No they don't, well not so far, but this is the part of the letter I want to tell you about.' He took a sip of the whiskey he had been slowly pouring into his glass ... 'Julian goes on to talk about a young author back in the early 1900's who sends his first novel to some book publishers called, Clanford and Fox...

Blake and Catherine

Blake stopped reading for a moment and stared at the words… Clanford and Fox … his company, why was this book now talking about his company.

'Now it's mentioned the business,' exclaimed Blake, looking totally mystified.

'What?' replied Catherine

'It now mentions a publishing company called Clanford and Fox, my company.' Catherine said nothing. Blake continued reading becoming increasing intrigued by the coincidence.

Blake read on…

Thomas and Kate

.. there were two partners in this company - it was newly formed and apparently they didn't have much money

– *anyway they read the novel and agreed that the book was that good it could become a really big seller. But then they suddenly became gravely concerned and began to have some doubts as to whether the writer would stay with them once he had realised how small a company Clanford and Fox was and how new to the publishing business they were. They had no record of accomplishment at all and Gideon would quickly find this out if he came to visit them, which he would have to do at some stage.*

'And,' said Kate a little precipitously, now becoming more absorbed by what Thomas was telling her.

'They thought they might lose their very first client before he had even signed a contract and they would then continue to struggle for years to become established, but they also knew that publishing this book would virtually guarantee them immediate success. So they decided to do something about it and Joshua Clanford proposed a plan. It was illegal, unprofessional, unscrupulous, unprincipled and highly unethical, but they were new to the publishing world, and they were very hungry for success, so they pushed any concerns they had to the back of their minds.

'What did they do?' said Kate, Thomas now had her full attention.

'They decided to steal the book and claim they had written it themselves, or to be more accurate Joshua would claim to be the writer and they would then publish it through their own company.'

'But surely that's illegal, its theft – plagiarism, they couldn't possibly get away with it,' said Kate sounding seriously disturbed at the thought, especially as that was Thomas's profession. The fear of something like this happening, always loitered in the darkest corners of the minds of all aspiring writers. Many believing, somewhat erroneously on most occasions, that the novel they had sweated over for maybe two or three years and believed to be a unique masterpiece, was in fact little more than an extremely large collection of disjointed sentences. In most cases they would be tenuously and rather precariously strung together into a spurious and highly implausible narrative that would be finally embellished and polished off

with completely unrealistic dialogue. But of course that wasn't always the case as was the situation with this book..

'Yes it is,' replied Thomas, 'all those and more, but you see in those days, most writers only ever wrote one copy by hand and there were seldom duplicates, so it made things much easier for a book thief with no moral integrity to operate and even flourish with relative impunity. Even Shakespeare occasionally "borrowed" from other writers and he was already a famous writer.'

'Then what happened?' asked Kate.

'Well the book "A Sacrifice of Souls", was published in 1912 by Clanford and Fox purportedly written by... Joshua Clanford. They never really expected it to be anything more than a moderately successful novel. They thought it would make them financially independent, but not enough money for them to worry about the original author making a big fuss.'

'But it made a lot of money,' speculated Kate tentatively.

'Oh yes, an enormous amount of money for those days as it began to sell in prodigious numbers all over the world.'

'Then what happened?' asked Kate sensing there was something ominous looming up on the horizon.

'Well the author, Gideon, did turn up at their offices about a year later and was justifiably outraged at what he claimed they had done. There was a furious argument about authorship, but of course, he had no evidence to back up his claim. Eventually they had to have him forcibly ejected from their office after he became violent, they never saw him again.

The last thing that Gideon did as he was being thrown out, was swear to take revenge on them for what they had done.'

'And did he?' asked Kate.

'Well apparently not. The next thing anybody heard was about a year later. Gideon's wife had left him after their daughter died of something or other, the letters don't

say what exactly, probably tuberculosis, anyway he couldn't afford any treatment for her, as he had no money and there was no NHS in those days and without money you died from nearly everything.

By now he had stopped writing and was working as a casual labourer and had started drinking heavily and then one day he just disappeared. One of Julian's letters mentions that his estranged wife heard a few months later that Gideon had joined the army and that he had gone to fight in Turkey where he was promoted to sergeant, this was around 1915.

Nothing more was heard of him after a battle at Mesopotamia, his friends thought maybe he was dead or that he had just simply disappeared again, but nobody was sure. That was until news filtered back to his wife that he had been promoted to lieutenant and had been transferred to France around 1916 where apparently he was killed not long after at the age of twenty four years and seven months. It had been an unbelievable act of heroism - he had single-handedly saved the life of his commanding officer, carrying him back on his shoulders for nearly four hundred yards across the battlefield whilst under relentless gunfire from the enemy, and had then been shot by German sniper, just as he arrived back at his lines. But it was all very vague and for some reason not clearly documented, so the story could have been just fictional for all anybody knew, a muddy mix of mysterious conjecture, speculation, assumption and harmless fabrication. A year later his estranged wife died in poverty, all very wretched for all concerned.

'And was that the end?' asked Kate.

'Well no not quite, in fact this is where the story becomes even more intriguing. You see Julian "my father" (Thomas made an air quote sign), starts to explain that around 1920, the writer, Gideon, turns up again., his full name was Gideon Drew by the way did I mention that?

'No,' replied Kate, but it meant nothing to her.

'Anyway....

Chapter 15

'Christ!' exclaimed Blake with a confused look in his eyes and his mouth half open as if he was about to say something. His head turned to look at Catherine now standing by the open fire in her dressing gown while gently rubbing her hair which she had wrapped up in a towel.

'What?' replied Catherine with casual indifference.

'…now this mentions Drew.' Blake scratched his head.

'What?' repeated Catherine, unsure what Blake had just said.

'Gideon Drew, the book now mentions Drew,' replied Blake sounding understandably surprised.

'But I thought the story was about Thomas Drayton and his family and some letters he had found.' Catherine felt a cold shiver run down her back at the mention of Gideon, her heart missed a beat. All of a sudden she found herself paying far more attention to what Blake was saying then she had previously.

'It was,' replied Blake, 'but…'

Catherine interrupted, 'and I thought Prospect Road was written by an Anthony Clackle.'

'It is,' replied Blake, trying to explain, 'that's what I was about to say, Anthony must be Julian's Clackle's son. 'It's some sort of denouement for things that happened in the past. I think he has written Prospect Road not only to explain the events that brought about his very existence, but possibly to atone for what his grandfather did.'

Catherine was beginning to understand what Blake was trying to say, but there still seemed to be no rhyme or reason to any of it. Nothing really made sense and of course in the back of her mind, in fact never really even at the back, more the forefront, there was still the recurring mystery of how the book apparently continued to self-write itself with what now appeared to be a gathering and prescient momentum. That mystery remained unsolved.

Although she had had some reservations about its authorship previously, at least she was now reasonably certain that Blake had nothing to do with writing it. She walked over to the half open window and gazed out into the garden. Her head full of questions, but which could she ask and which should she leave unspoken. The sky had begun to cloud over and there was a slight drizzle starting to fall. She could hear a gusty summer wind blowing up and then just as quickly die away as if endeavouring to blow an approaching armada away from its intended invasion of Crete or Iraklion.

Catherine had recently read a book about the Trojan wars and the invasion of Troy and how the Gods controlled the winds and how they had made such a difference to the outcome of the invasion. Whenever she heard the winds swirling she thought of the Gods that were ultimately in control of all elements. It always sounded and felt a little unusual for this time of year. It was still warm and the heavy air had the indefinable sense of peace and tranquillity about it that you only ever experience in summer, but in the distance just the faintest sounds of rumbling thunder could be heard, the sounds that heralded a change.

'But the book was sort of predicting our future and what has happened in your past…and now you say it's talking about Gideon so how does that connect to you and when did all that happen? didn't you say it was…..'

'It was over seventy years ago?' interrupted Blake again, 'it's something to do with Clanford and Fox, they are the publishers mentioned in the letters, they are the people that stole the original book that's the connection. My company is the link...'

'But why does it suddenly mention Gideon Drew now,' enquired Catherine a little hesitantly, 'That just doesn't make any sense.'

'I don't know I haven't a….' he lifted up the manuscript and started reading again. 'Maybe it's …' but he did not finish apparently caught up again in the context of the letters.

After a few minutes Catherine interrupted Blake again... 'Does it say anything else about him?'

'Who?'

'Gideon, Gideon Drew.'

Blake looked up, intrigued by her question, 'no not so far why?'

'It's just very odd that it should mention him isn't it?' She paused for a moment, as if looking for some sort of affirmation, 'don't you think so?' Catherine was clearly unnerved by this completely unexpected development, it was obviously playing on her mind. A film of prescient guilt seemed to hang in the air, but Blake didn't notice. She had also sub-consciously - unintentionally, referred to the manuscript as an animate object. No longer just an abstract collection of words and recollections that had been slowly forming a syllogistic assumption in her mind. But what the assumption was, she wasn't too sure, and now, she was even less so. Putting two assumptions together did not always produce what you expected.

'I have to admit that it's a slightly spooky coincidence that the manuscript mentions a Gideon,' replied Blake deep in thought, 'and that I have a highly successful client with the same name. But the book they are talking about was written around 1912 so Gideon would have to be well over ninety years old if he were the same Gideon and that's laughable. So obviously it's a different Gideon or he as aged extremely well.' A grin crossed Blake's face at that suggestion. 'I just pop up to the attic for a moment and check,' he added light heartedly, but the Wildean reference was completely lost on Catherine who was otherwise engaged.

'Yes, yes he would have wouldn't he,' Catherine murmured quietly, having completely missed the last part of his glib remark.

'.. and that's ridiculous because Gideon can only be in his early twenties, twenty five at most, I'm sure of that.' Her mind flashed back to Christmas and the proposal that Gideon had made.

Blake glanced at her for a second, a little surprised at her precise and remarkably explicit assessment on his age. He had never mentioned it before and if anything Gideon looked younger than his age.

Blake read on…

Prospect Road 9

Chapter Nine
Written by
Anthony Theodore Clackle
The Letters

Thomas and Kate

'Look, do you want me to read the letters out aloud darling,' asked Thomas, 'it might be easier for you to understand what is going on rather than me giving you a brief summary on the contents, I'm probably missing some important elements.'

'But should you being doing that,' asked Kate? 'They are private after all, if your mother has left them for you then I think it's reasonable to assume that she only meant for you to read them. I can't see how very much can be gleaned from pouring over some old love letters anyway. I wouldn't like it if somebody looked at ours not with the...' she didn't go any further. Thomas thought over what Kate was saying.

'I understand what you are saying, but I still think my mother must have left them for reason. I think either you should read them or I should at least read some of the important parts so that you know exactly what I know.'

Kate mumbled something incomprehensible, and Thomas started to read the letters out.

~~~~

'I'll only read the letters out that make sense,' said Blake reiterating what Thomas had just suggested to Kate in the manuscript, while desperately trying not to sound as if he was being patronising. 'I think that may make it easier for you to understand.'

Catherine nodded and took another sip of her wine.

FIRST LETTER 12th July 1950

from Julian Clackle to Mary Drayton.

My Dearest Mary,

I felt I must write to explain my behaviour last week and beg your forgiveness. I realise you may not wish to see me again, but I hope that somehow you can find it in your heart to forgive me.

You were so kind in allowing me to unburden a problem that has been troubling me for so long, something I have not been able to discuss with another living soul.

Now at long last, just as I feel there is a chance I can put all that has happened behind me and move on with my life, I have yet again fallen back into a trough of despair. Secrecy and half-truths, hiding behind a cloak of anonymity that has engulfed me for so long and continues to threaten to consume my very existence.

I know I can trust your discretion and I feel and hoped that you felt the same way about me as I about you. I truly believe we have grown closer together each time we have met over the last few months.

I know when I told you last week that I was already married and had been since 1946, that you were understandably more than a little surprised that I hadn't told you before, but there was a reason for that. I did not intend to deceive you or hide the truth these past months, but the problem was, the closer we became the more certain I became that if I tried to tell you the truth you would consider this to be a first betrayal and you would finish our relationship and not wish to see me again. The first lie does so little harm, a tiny slip of the tongue that remains uncorrected for the sake of expediency. But it grows exponentially with each further lie to support the first, each one not only creating its own trail of deceit and deception, but profoundly enhancing the previous lie and expanding the deceit to levels never anticipated at inception. I feel this maybe a failing of many men never realising at the beginning how something good might end so bad. If only I had the strength and courage to have been candid and honest at the beginning, but I was not. Possibly this is due to cowardice or foreboding apprehension or the fear of losing you, I don't know - I will never know. But if it can be of some small recompense to you I would like to try to explain the intricate details of my past and hopefully then this will help you to understand what happened and why I have acted the way I have.

If you do not wish to continue with our friendship and I will understand if that is how you feel, then so be it, but if you believe we can overcome this together, then to my dying day, I will be forever in your debt.

Please write and let me know how you feel and whether you can forgive me for my weakness in not being more honest from the start.

Your ever loving Julian

SECOND LETTER
Mary to Julian.
22nd July 1950

Dearest Julian

Your letter arrived today and for many hours I deliberated on whether I should open it at all. After considerable heart-searching I eventually did pluck up enough courage and did so. I have read and reread the contents initially with some bewilderment and concern, but my feelings have now segued into thoughts of hope and deliverance and optimism for the future.

When you first told me you were married and had been so for nearly four years and that you also had a son, my immediate thoughts were that our relationship should end before it became even more complicated than it already was.

You have Anthony to consider and your wife Rosemary, who, as far as I understand and despite what you have now said, you still feel some affection for and this is the aspect that confuses me and throws into doubt any possibility that our relationship can continue. I feel that we are maybe just passing through a phase in the journey of life and that soon this part will be over and we will both have moved on and gone our separate ways or possibly just continued on the paths we were on originally.

But then I think back to the first time we met in the park. We seemed to talk for hours about something as innocuous and as innocent as the amazing colours of the flowers and the beauty of trees and how year after year they return just as beautiful, if not more so, than the year before and how wonderful life would be if it were the same cycle of life for people.

It seems so ridiculous now, but in those first few hours of meeting you I realised that not only could I so easily fall in love again, but more importantly, that I wanted to fall in love again. I told you within those first few hours of meeting you that although I was married, I was imprisoned within a loveless relationship. I thought I did love him when we married, but I was only eighteen and I did not really know what love was and still didn't until I met you.

As I told you when we first met, after nearly six years of being together our relationship had changed to one of total indifference toward each other. I felt I wanted to leave, but I had nowhere to go so I stayed. Jonathan works hard, and we have all the things that everybody wants, but we never enjoyed our own company and for some reason we were unable to have children which may also have made a difference. I felt oddly trapped in a place where there was nothing to stop me walking away, but the fear of freedom and loneliness. Some days I feel I am just enduring a very short joyless life and in reality, it is nothing more than an intermission before the eternal infinity of death resumes. But now I feel there is a reason to live and a reason to enjoy every moment of our short existence on earth, that is what you have done to me, how you make me feel.

When we spent that first afternoon together in that hotel, something glorious happened to me, something that I find hard to put into words - suddenly I felt alive again. I felt a passion and a longing inside my heart that I have never felt before, and yet somehow deep down, I know it is something I have always wanted. They were feelings that I was certain could last a lifetime and when I looked into your eyes I saw the happiness that you were feeling and knew that you wanted what I wanted.

Catherine felt an odd feeling in her stomach as Blake read the words. It was almost like a forewarning a premonition of something, but she didn't know what.

Please write and tell me if there is anything you want to tell me that might help me to understand. I want to see you again, but I think it would be best if we know everything there is to know about each other before we can meet again. I hope you will understand my reluctance to allow this to develop further before I can surrender my heart and soul to you unreservedly, but experience has taught me that everything comes at a price and I just need to know what price has to be paid, for the happiness we both desire.

I will always love you no matter what.

Mary

xxx

Third Letter from Julian to Mary
7th August 1950

My Dearest Mary

Thank you for your kind reply and the thoughtful words, which mean so much to me.

You deserve an explanation and the best way to do this is for me to start at the very beginning and try to explain what has happened to bring us to this wretched juncture in our lives.

Firstly I should tell you that I was adopted by Hilda and Harold Clackle, when I was one year old. My real father, (or I should say the person I thought was my real father was called Joshua Clanford).

In 1911 Joshua Clanford and his partner Obadiah Fox formed a publishing business. The company struggled for a while before suddenly finding success in 1912 after publishing an extremely popular book called "The Sacrifice of Souls", which you may of heard of. The book was written by Joshua Clanford or so everybody believed at the time

In early 1916 Joshua Clanford . (I prefer not to refer to him as my father and I will explain why later) began courting my mother Madeleine Allbright. My mother had inherited a small fortune from her father after he died in 1915 and in reality it was this that had first attracted Joshua.

It was no coincidence that this relationship was only formed just as the royalties and income from book sales of Joshua's book, The Chapter Room, had begun to diminish. The small fortune that had been generated by the book since 1912 had by now been almost completely squandered by Joshua and Obadiah Fox with their debauched and extravagant lifestyle. Joshua and Madeleine were married in September 1916

For a while Madeleine had found Joshua to be attentive charming and captivating and she was very happy, in fact happier than she had ever been in her life. She never envisaged for one moment that he could ever change, but he did, soon after they married. He quickly resumed his previous lifestyle of heavy drinking, gambling and womanising having now replenished his wasted fortune. But she truly loved him, never being one for seeing the failings in others only in herself and for this reason she was always prepared to forgive him for his failings and erring ways. She believed that for some reason he was a soul in torment, hell bent on personal destruction, but she could never find out why and so she continued to support him in any way she could despite his actions. There were times when he was still very kind to her, but they were becoming less frequent.

I should mention, and I say this not as a plea for mitigation or justification for my mother's actions; that according to my adopted mother Hilda, Madeleine was completely faithful to her husband for over four years despite the fact that he continued to engage in his debauched life style frivolously and irresponsibly spending her money entertaining other women.

Then one day in 1920 by chance Madeleine met somebody, somebody who by all accounts really cared for her and she suddenly found herself falling madly in love with him, but she refused to leave Joshua. Then she became pregnant and I was born one of twins the other being my sister. Because she wouldn't leave her husband, Madeleine's lover broke off the affair and she never saw him again.

At first with the new arrivals, Joshua changed back to the way he used to be, temporarily engrossed with the joy of having two children. He became caring and more attentive toward her again, but then somehow he found out about Madeleine's affair and realised that he was not our father, he demanded that Madeleine put us both up for adoption.

Joshua wanted nothing whatsoever to do with the legal procedure and left it all to Madeleine. He just wanted us out of his life as soon as possible and it was left to my mother to arrange what must have been the most heart wrenching and traumatic event in her life.

Hilda and Harry Clackle adopted me when I was just nine months old in 1921 another couple adopted my sister. Joshua and Madeleine were never intimate again and began to live separate lives in the same house seldom speaking and never socialising together, but then they had never socialised before so there was little change there. Madeleine's day to day existence became very subdued now virtually subjugated by Joshua. Her only release from the interminable incarceration being the clandestine journey she took once every week, without fail, on a Thursday afternoon to the other side of the town.

You may wonder how I know all this and the reason is because Madeleine used to visit my adopted parents Hilda and Harry Clackle on a Thursday. Joshua always went out to his club on Thursdays and never returned until the early hours of the next morning. Madeleine would play with me and talk for hours to Hilda about the things that Joshua had done. I never realised that Madeleine was my birth mother as she always pretended to me that she was just one of my adopted parent's friends. This was the arrangement she had agreed with the Clackle's in order not to confuse me over my parentage..

Somehow Joshua found out that she had been secretly seeing me for nearly three years and he immediately forbade her from making any further contact. I never saw my real mother again, neither did I find out who she really was or that I had a sister until many years later. Madeleine obviously couldn't tell me while she was visiting me at the Clackle's. A little time after this my mother, in what I can only presume was a severe state of depression threw herself under a lorry and was killed instantly. At the age of thirty two Joshua had driven Madeleine to the point of no return.

A lonely woman who had done nothing to warrant this sad end to her life, except to fall in love with the wrong men. One, a man who's only agenda was to wreak pain and anguish on the families of Joshua Clanford and Obadiah Fox.. publishers, the other a thief, rapacious philanderer and disreputable opportunist lacking one iota of common decency who was slowly sinking in to a turgid sea of moral turpitude.

Joshua Clanford paid little heed to my mother's death it was of absolutely no consequence to him according to the Clackle's. His life carried on much as before.

Hilda and Harry attended the funeral along with a small number of other mourners one of whom was a gentleman who spoke to Hilda and introduced himself as Gideon Drew. He mentioned that he had known Madeleine some years before and a little oddly he had asked after my wellbeing, which is why Hilda remembered him. Hilda and Harry remembering that Madeleine had told them she was devastated when Gideon deserted her after he found out she was pregnant, thought it was best they didn't mention that they were in fact his son's adopted parents. Joshua did not attend the funeral.

Joshua now had all her money, and that was all he had ever wanted. A few months later in 1927 he married Olivia. Just over one year later Olivia gave birth to a son called Reginald in 1928.

For the next twelve years life continued without incident with my adopted parents until just before I left home to join the RAF in 1940. My mother fearing the worst, but saying nothing about her own concerns to me, told me some of the details from my past that she thought I should know. That was when I found out who my real mother was called Madeleine Clanford and she was married to Joshua Clanford, but my real father was Gideon Drew after she had had an affair with him. Hilda also mentioned that Joshua had forced her to give me up for adoption after he found out about the affair.

Hilda knew very little else about my real father only his name. So on my nineteenth birthday probably only months away from my own probable death I now knew the truth about myself and the mother I had never spoken to, but by now she had been dead for sixteen years and I never would... tan pis.

On the 20th May 1941 both my parents were killed in one of the last air raids on London. I had been flying with the RAF for over a year by then(which I can tell you was some achievement in itself) and I was based near Chichester. It was there that I met and fell in love with Rosemary the girl I would eventually marry.

The one thing my adopted mother didn't tell me, the one thing she probably didn't know and I didn't find out until much later was that I had a sister and that sister was Rosemary the same woman I was to marry in 1946

Rosemary obviously didn't know she had a brother either, her adopted parents had never told her, they probably never knew she even had a brother.

I only found out the final bits and pieces of information that filled in the blanks due to a chance meeting in 1949 when I met a stranger on a train travelling to London. We got chatting and I happened to mention I was in publishing, one thing led to another and it eventually transpired that this stranger had actually known my mother Madeleine back in the 1920's and he had also met her husband Joshua Clanford, my erstwhile father before the revelations had been revealed that had changed everything.

He also told me that as he remembered Madeleine and Joshua Clanford had had twins and they were both adopted one was called Julian, but he couldn't remember for certain the "girls" name, but thought it might have been.. Rosemary. This as you can imagine came as a shock to me. He also mentioned that as far as he could remember, Joshua had also had another son by his second marriage to Olivia, this was after Madeleine had died, they called him Reginald.

It was an odd encounter as the man only appeared to be in his mid- twenties, but obviously he must have had a good war or an easy life because he would have to have been at least forty five years old to have known my mother. It was only afterwards that I began to consider the remote possibility that he may in fact have been my father Gideon Drew, if it had not been for the fact that he was far too young, no older than I was in fact.

That was when I put two and two together and working out all the names, dates and places in my head realised that I had in fact married my sister Rosemary Brierly - previously Clanford. But by then it was too late to do anything about it. Our son Anthony had been born in 1947 and was now nearly two years old. Anthony had been born with some minor retardation, hearing problems and severe physical problems, which gave him an unusual limp. We were told that his disabilities would become much worse as he grew older, but obviously we didn't know what had caused them.

This secret and the reason for his disabilities have tormented me ever since, realising that his problems and his tortured life were all of my making..

I immediately ceased all intimacy with Rosemary and after a few days we had a long conversation and I explained everything as I believed it had happened. As you can imagine Rosemary was absolutely devastated, not least by the fact that she still felt she was still deeply in love with me, but in time she came to realise that everything would have to change quite dramatically from that day forward. My whole life has changed beyond all recognition since I met that stranger on the train and I was beginning to think the nightmare would never end, and then I met you.

I still felt incredibly close to Rosemary and I still do. She had done nothing wrong neither had I, but know I only feel affection in a brotherly way and all we have left is the tangle of absolution to unravel and our son Anthony to look after, but we couldn't stay married it wouldn't be right, and so we divorced nearly a year ago.

I hope you can understand what has happened and maybe after reading this you will be able to see me again and we can talk.

I look forward to your reply

Your ever loving Julian

xxx

Blake put the manuscript down and looked over at Catherine.

'So what do you think is happening?' Blake sounded very confused. 'The whole thing is just becoming curiouser and..' he abruptly stopped himself from playing out the Dickensian cliché, which would have undoubtedly doused the ember of credibility, and relevance that he was endeavouring to attach to the document. Catherine didn't answer, she was miles away deep in thought.

'Catherine!' Said Blake

Catherine suddenly came back from where ever she had gone and looked directly at Blake with a slightly glazed expression of surprise.

She gestured for him to continue reading...

'Are you sure you want me to read this to you aloud, wouldn't you prefer to read it yourself?'

'No, no I'm fine I can think more clearly when I am listening to you, please go on.' So he did..

'That was the last of the letters it just goes back to the story now,' said Blake.

Prospect Road 10

Chapter Ten
Written by
Anthony Theodore Clackle
1920 Joshua's Story

After Gideon disappeared in 1915 nothing more was heard from him. Everybody assumed he was dead possibly killed in the war, but he was not. He turned up again in 1920 and by now had acquired considerable wealth apparently from his interest in a gold mine in Africa.

The first thing he does on his return is to purchase a large elegant town house in London's Mayfair from where he begins to quickly develop a circle of influential friends; friends who facilitate his aspirations to immerse himself with pernicious intent into the society crowd and the places that the Clanford's and the Fox's frequent. But he now uses a different name and his appearance and manner have changed considerably from when he first met Joshua Clanford in 1912.

Due to the traumatic experiences he has experienced during the war, he is no longer the shy, timid and withdrawn person he once was and Joshua does not recognise him when he meets him again at a gambling club.

Joshua Clanford and Obadiah Fox have by now made a considerable fortune out of the book they stole from Gideon Drew in 1912, but they have also spent a large part of the ill begotten gains on their hedonistic lifestyle.

It is often found that those who illicitly come by vast amounts of money which is not rightfully theirs, are invariably less than prudent with the proceeds than they would be if they had acquired it legitimately.

They have a tendency, possibly out of a sense of guilt, to try to inveigle others into becoming tacit accomplices to their crime albeit unknowingly, by allowing them to enjoy some of their illegitimate rewards. It salves their conscious. They have a tendency to be far more generous than those who have had to work long and hard and industrially for their wealth.

However, by 1916 and having no luck at finding another major writer to boost their ailing finances and as the sale receipts from the book's sales were rapidly diminishing after three years success, Joshua and Obadiah decide on another plan of action in order to support their life style and their ailing publishing business. To this end they draw straws as to who should propose marriage to a Miss Madeleine Allbright an extremely rich, but remarkably unattractive, eligible heiress, of whom they have both wasted no time in making the acquaintance.   They are aware that she is not only available, but also eager to marry.   Joshua drew the short straw, proposed and they were married some months later in October 1916.   The fortunes of Clanford and Fox temporarily restored.

Gideon Drew, by all accounts was an extremely good looking man, refined, rich and well read. And with his easy manner and soft tones, it was no problem for him to strike up an innocuous relationship with Madeleine, who by 1920 had suffered four years of being virtually ignored by her husband.   He embarked on a passionate affair with Madeleine   a   woman   not   adverse   to   responding appreciatively to anyone paying her attention and also someone whose affections could be easily manipulated, bearing in mind that Joshua was by now not paying her very much attention and spending his or more accurately her money on other women.   Gideon and Madeleine's ardent, but for obvious reasons, clandestine affair lasted some months and   resulted in Madeleine becoming pregnant at which point Gideon immediately terminated the affair and made a hasty withdraw from the scene. His work was done. The first part of his plan accomplished.

Madeleine had twins, a son and a daughter by Gideon, which Joshua and Madeleine decide to call Julian and Rosemary. The birth came as a pleasant surprise to Joshua as he has no recollection of having had any intimate contact with his wife for a number of years, preferring to satisfy his carnal desires with various other more attractive women he was having affairs with or even the occasional whore when he became really bored. However as he quite often arrived home very drunk he assumes that he must have had intercourse possibly while he was unconscious. He thinks no more about the matter for nearly six months happy in the knowledge that at least his wife has managed to produce a son and heir and a spare. However one afternoon while snoozing in his club with a copy of the times draped over his head, he is awoken by a raucous and rumbustious conversation accompanied by much hilarity between two other members discussing the rumours that he, Joshua, has been cuckooed and is unknowingly bringing up the offspring of the liaison as his own.

'Did you hear about old Clanford?' exclaimed Major Erskine-Blythe.

'No, what about the chap?' replied Judge Matthews picking up his sherry and taking a sip.

'Rumour is mamsab was tubbed by her lover, in her husband's bed while old Clanford was out playing around of golf would you believe.'

'How did he do?' asked Judge Matthews.

'Hole in one I imagine,' replied Erskine-Blythe.

The judge spat out his sherry in surprise, 'Wasn't she the plug ugly one?'

'And some,' replied Erskine-Blythe, 'probably why old Clanford kept her at home under lock and key.'

'Thought she might frighten the dogs,' replied the judge grinning. They both laughed out aloud.

'I heard she had a few bob, and Clanford's publishing business wasn't doing too well... he does like the gee gee's and the tables and he's not adverse to a bit of hokey- pokey either, and that's not cheap.'

'Ah I see,' replied Judge Matthews, 'still he should have done the honourable thing and kept her pleasured at least, could have popped a brown paper bag over her head if she was that doggy.' They both laughed out loud, much to the chagrin of the other sleeping members.

'Quite right, fair do's I say, fair do's if he wasn't doing the decent thing then....'

'Do you er ... keep the old girl.. you know,' muttered the judge a little indelicately?

'Me? God no,' replied Erskine-Blythe, 'dear little thing hasn't got a brass farthing to her name, so don't need to bother, anyway can't be doing with all that lark not at my age, upsets the indigestion.'

'Right.. right.' said the judge, 'understandable... well I think it's very decent of the chap to take them on. All that responsibility for the next twenty years without any reward or compensation.'

'Or nookie for that matter,' added Erskine-Blythe.

'Well not from the wife anyway, she obviously gets all she wants elsewhere.' They both fell about laughing again, despite further disdainful looks from the other members who were trying to sleep.

Joshua stood up and stormed out of the club much to the embarrassment of the two members, who were obviously unaware he was in the club and were left looking rather sheepishly at each other before they burst out laughing once again.

He immediately returned home to confront his wife with the slanderous rumour he had heard. They had a raging argument and she eventually conceded that Joshua was not the father of their children, but blamed this on his inability to perform. Madeleine argued vehemently to keep the children, but Joshua refused to agree and eventually she reluctantly agrees to give both children up for adoption, Julian to a family called the Clackle's and Rosemary to another family.

So Julian Clanford(Gideon's son) became Julian Clackle. Despite Madeleine's affair Joshua refuses to divorce her only to aware that she still has indirect control over the remains of her inheritance, the part he hasn't yet managed to spend, this strained existence continued, Madeleine with the money and Joshua needing it until Madeleine eventually committed suicide.

'Oh I see,' said Kate, 'so a tale of infidelity and treachery, deceit and money, all very interesting but, hardly earth shattering and definitely not very original. All

very much the same as today really. She appeared a little deflated by the story, somehow expecting something more. Her harsh and oddly cynical appraisal and generalisation on the morality of mankind caught Thomas a little by surprise. He had always thought of her as someone with a balanced non-judgemental perspective on life, but this uncharacteristic outburst displayed a dimension he had not seen before.

'That's not the end,' added Thomas a little guardedly , at which point, Kate's interest perked up again.

Thomas read on... 'then in 1928 in furtherance of his plan, Gideon Drew embarked on another affair, this time with Emily Fox, the wife of Obadiah Fox, Joshua's partner in the Publishing Company.

One year later Emily had a son and Gideon was the father, but this time the husband, Obadiah Fox didn't find out immediately, but tragically six months later Obadiah and Emily Fox were both killed in an horrific hunting accident and eaten by lions while on safari in Africa. Twenty five percent of the shares in the company automatically reverted to the Joshua Clanford and the other twenty five percent of the shares were passed down to their son Freddy who Joshua Clanford offered to raise. Freddie committed suicide in 1966 while high on LSD and his shareholding in the company passed directly to Reginald Clanford.

Chapter 16

'This Gideon Drew sounds like a right bastard,' exclaimed Catherine.

Blake looked up at Catherine, a little surprised by her outburst of indignation about a character in a novel.

'He's not getting to you is he?'

'No not at all, it's just that he seems to be ruining everybody's life and...'

'It's only a story,' said Blake calmly reassuring Catherine about its provenance, but nevertheless still a little surprised at her unexpected reaction to the way the story was developing, 'it's not like you to become so involved and animated about a fictitious character, sounds like he's getting to you. Praise indeed for Anthony Clackle.'

'You forget,' interrupted Catherine, this story also details our lives as well; and this Gideon character sounds very un-fictitious to me.'

'In parts its similar to our lives, yes I agree,' replied Blake, 'but that is just coincidence – serendipity – chance even. Different writers often write similar story's simultaneously without ever seeing the others work. Anyway he hasn't ruined our lives at all, in fact, just the opposite.'

Catherine didn't answer, Blake was right on that particular detail, but she knew that more in the book had happened to them then Blake knew about and possibly more might happen in the future.

'I can only imagine that the Gideon they speak of in the book is possibly the grandfather of the Gideon we know,' said Blake, 'that's the only explanation.'

'Well it's one explanation,' replied Catherine, gazing unconvincingly at Blake and by implication proposing another far more bizarre option.

'No! that's ridiculous,' replied Blake, 'immediately becoming aware of what Catherine was eluding to. He picked the manuscript up and carried on reading. The manuscript appeared to be self-writing much faster than before and he could see there were a large number of new written pages for him to wade through. 'Maybe there's an explanation in the pages I haven't read yet.'

'Maybe,' said Catherine, but she was no longer so concerned with what had been written so much as what had yet to be. 'Maybe we should give the book to Gideon to read, maybe he will give us an explanation?' Blake didn't answer, but just looked at Catherine thinking about her proposal. He finished reading the newly written pages of the manuscript then passed it to Catherine for her to read... but kept her "off the cuff" suggestion in the back of his mind for further consideration.

Prospect Road 11

Chapter Eleven
written by
Anthony Theodore Clackle
Hilda's and Harry's Story

On a warm summers day in 1940 a few days before he was about to leave them to start his training for the RAF, Hilda and Harry Clackle sat Julian down in their kitchen and Hilda started to tell him a story.

'Before you leave... there is something which we think we should tell you, something that may be of great importance to you.' Harry nodded, but looked uncharacteristically solemn which unnerved Julian a little, it was not expression he had seen very often. Once when he was fourteen he had seen that same look just before his father had sat him down to tell him that his pony "Perfidia" had died during the night. It didn't bode well. Julian loved his mother and father dearly, they were gentle folk, simple farmers and they loved him dearly, he knew that. The saddest thing he had ever had to do was to tell them that he had signed up to join the RAF three months previously and that soon he would be leaving them. That had broken their hearts, but they realised that if that is what he wanted to do they should not stand in his way. Being a farmer, he was technically exempt from conscription, but he was not the sort of man who would allow a small technicality like that stop him from serving his country.

'We are not your real parents,' said Hilda a little reluctantly, obviously uncertain as to how he would react, 'we adopted you when you were very young.'

'Adopted! he exclaimed, but I don't understand, how? I have always lived here for as far back as I can recall. I don't remember anything else or anybody else come to that.'

'You were just one year old when we...' Hilda hastily added.

'Oh I see.' replied Julian. He went quite for a few moments while he endeavoured to pull his confused and rambling thoughts together. This revelation had caught him totally unawares, but was it really that important now he wondered.

'So does it really matter,' he asked? 'You are my parents, you are all I know, whoever my other parents were, they obviously didn't want me and you obviously did, so is there any more to say?' It was all very matter of fact, more than Hilda and Harry could have possibly hoped for.

Julian cared passionately for many things, but he was also a pragmatist not someone to dwell on what had gone before, he was far more interested in what was going to happen now and in the future. Hilda and Harry were heartened by the knowledge that he didn't think they had kept the secret from him for any other reason than that it would have served no purpose in him knowing at that time.

'Do you want to know the details? asked Hilda 'it's only right that you should know if you want to, but it's up to you.'

Julian got up from the table and walked over to the window and looked out on the farmyard courtyard. A few chickens were fluttering about and he could see the cows in the low field just the other side of the lane happily chewing the cud. It all seemed so peaceful and idyllic. And yet behind it all there was a world war going on where thousands of people had already been killed and more were probably being killed at that very moment somewhere, and yet here right now it was a warm quiet summer's day, and now there was this revelation, the last thing he could have expected. The whole world seemed to be in chaos.

Julian turned round 'Yes maybe I should know, it will probably make no difference, but.....' he didn't finish the sentence choosing the let the words remain unspoken.

Hilda took a deep breath, 'Your mother... Madeleine was her name and she was a very lovely lady... she was married to a man called Joshua... Joshua Clanford he was a book publisher.' Hilda stopped momentarily just in case Julian wanted to ask a question, but he didn't and so she continued... 'Madeleine, we got to know her very well over

*the time that we knew her,' Julian should have noticed the
subtle reservation in the context, the hidden missive
between the lines when he wondered about the odd
phrasing, but he didn't, not straight away; 'she had an
affair and that's where you came from.'*

*'She betrayed my father?' exclaimed Julian sounding a
little obdurate and not unjustifiably judgemental. His first
thoughts were that his mother had acted adulterously and
he had suffered the consequence of her deceit, but this
didn't seem to reconcile with how Hilda had initially
described her as being "A lovely lady", so he held his
thoughts in check.*

*'No.. no it wasn't like that, not at all, it's not that
simple.'*

'So what did happen,' asked Julian.

*'She had the affair, and you were born and for a while
your father Joshua...' Harry looked down at the floor a
little saddened by the phrase Hilda had used, 'was happy,
they were both very happy. And then one day Joshua found
out about the affair which had by now ended, but assuming
that you weren't his although he had no proof, he ordered
Madeleine to put you and your sister up for adoption.'*

'I have a sister, where is she?' asked Julian.

*'We don't know, we never knew, Madeleine gave her to
another family, we could only afford to take one child so we
chose you. The other family moved away soon after and
Madeleine never saw her daughter again, but she started
visiting you.'*

'She visited me?'

*'Yes, she came here almost every week for three years,
and it brought her so much joy. We could see how sad it
was for her only being able to see you for a few hours each
week, when she could get away, and even then she had to
stand back and not get too attached, because she knew it
could never become anything more than just a friendship.'*

'But why didn't I know who she was?'

'Madeleine insisted that we didn't tell you, you thought she was just a friend of ours that came to visit us, but really she was coming to watch you grow up.'

'But weren't you afraid the maybe one day she would come along and say she wanted me back?'

'Yes we had thought of that, but as I said she was a lovely lady and honourable and we were your legally adopted parents so, we thought it would do no harm. We had what we had never had, a son, and she had what she needed which was the opportunity to see you, which would have been denied her under any other circumstances. It seemed to work and there was never a problem'

'Are they still alive?' asked Julian.

Hilda went quite for a moment then looked at Harry and then back at Julian..

'Joshua is still alive, but he is not your father... Suddenly for no apparent reason, Madeleine stopped visiting you. Then she sent us a note to say that Joshua had found out about the meetings and had forbidden her to make any further visits. So now she had no contact with either of her children. A year later she committed suicide. She sent us a letter that arrived on the day she died... all it said was as she couldn't go on not seeing you anymore her life was over.

Julian went very quiet for a few moments.

'And my real father, did she never say who he was?'

'Yes she did. His name is Drew... Gideon Drew, but we don't know anything else about him or what happened to him.

'And what about my sister, do you know anything about her' asked Julian?

'I'm sorry,' said Hilda, 'but we don't know anything about her not even her name.'

Prospect Road 12

Chapter Twelve
written by
Anthony Theodore Clackle
Julian's story

'What else is there?' asked Kate trying to put everything in its right place.'

'Well as you can imagine when Julian met Gideon in 1979 they were both getting on a bit Julian was fifty eight and Gideon was...

Kate interrupted Thomas just to show she was keeping up 'Well your father must have been nearly sixty and Gideon... she stopped for a moment, looking a little bit confused, 'well no, he must have been nearly... nearly ninety years old.' She looked a bit stunned for a moment running over the numbers and dates in her head just to make sure she hadn't got it wrong, 'surely that can't be right?'

Thomas looked at Kate and with no discernible expression he slowly uttered a few words that would change everything '...well actually about twenty four.'

'Twenty four, what do you mean twenty four, that's not possible, he wrote the book that caused all the problems in... 1900 and he was about twenty years old then, if not older,'

'That was what Julian told Anthony, he also said something more,' replied Thomas

'What more was there?' said Kate now sounding very confused.

'He said....' Thomas paused 'This may sound a little ridiculous and extremely far-fetched, but..' he paused again carefully collating all his thoughts and assembling them in some sort of logical order. 'When Julian married Rosemary in 1946 a stranger turned up at the wedding and introduced himself as Gideon Drew, saying he was an old friend of Julian's real mother Madeleine. Julian knew he

was adopted, the Clackle's had told him that much when he was twenty one. They had told him that Joshua and Madeleine Clanford were his real parents, but the Clanford's had not told the Clackle's all the truth and never explained why they wanted to have their son adopted. The stranger at the wedding, Gideon Drew was the same age as Julian. So Julian assumed that maybe Gideon wasn't actually a friend of his mother, but was in fact another son that the Clanford's for some reason had also given up for adoption. Julian didn't realise that Gideon was his real father. Not least because Gideon and he were both in their mid-twenties.

'Well that doesn't make any sense,' said Kate

'No, I couldn't understand it either,' said Thomas.

'So your real dad was Julian Clackle not Jonathan, after your mother had an affair with him, and you now have a half -brother Anthony, and your grandfather was really this mysterious Gideon Drew who never seems to get any older.

'More or less,' agreed Thomas

'So is this Gideon Drew still alive?' asked Kate.

'Well he could be, but as you said, he would have to be nearly ninety years old,'

'He sounds like a very unusual character, your granddad,' said Kate, 'don't the letters mention when he died?'

'No,' replied Thomas, 'No they don't.'

'So he could still be alive then?'

'Yes I suppose he could, but....

Chapter 17

June 1983

And there the story ended. Catherine placed the manuscript on the sofa and looked at Blake. They didn't know what to make of it anymore

Next day at the office it was as busy as ever with the planned release of Chapter Room in the United States. The assurances of the night before now forgotten.

The day seemed to roar away from him especially after two o'clock when the American publisher's office opened. Then just after three he had telephone call put through to him from Catherine, which was a little unusual. He half expected her to say his mother had rung and she was coming over for a few days, but she hadn't. She had died suddenly, earlier that morning. At first it didn't seem to have any effect, all of the commotion in the office was completely misdirecting his sensory awareness, he was reacting, but not evaluating. His mind was running at full capacity nearly on overload and he was unable to absorb anything more at that particular moment... and then from an unexpected quarter came one tiny scrap of information. Just three little words found their way into the specific part of his brain that dealt with incoming grief and suddenly it all made some kind of sense.

'Your mother's dead,' said Catherine as compassionately as she could, only to aware of how that might affect him after only reading about Thomas's mother's death in Chapter 7 of Prospect Road last night.

'What!' he cried. The first reaction - nearly everybody's first reaction at receiving a message like that was complete disbelief and incredulity. Amongst all the cacophony in the office and confusion in his brain, he had received a message that didn't register it just didn't make any sense at all. It was all gobbledygook.

'What did you say?'

'I'm sorry,' said Catherine, 'The police have only just rung me, I thought you would want to know straight away. Blake didn't answer immediately, letting the words sink in.

'I..... I'll leave now, should be with you in about an hour or so.' The past began to whirl around in his head. Suddenly he was thrust back to coronation day. He was dressed up as a little Indian prince, wandering up and down Prospect road. He could see his mother polishing the cardinal red front door step and then she was beating him with a cane for some unfathomable reason. He could see the salvation army band moving down the road in slow motion, their feet not quite touching the ground they seemed to be hovering just above it. The music was all very peculiar fading in and out, loud then soft, distant then very close, he couldn't make any sense of it at all... 'Blake..... Blake.... are you OK?' He couldn't see where the words were coming from, was it from somebody in the band he wondered... He turned around and he could see Jamie standing in front of him. Years ago back in the 1960's he had once experimented with the hallucinogenic drug LSD, which dramatically changed his perception of reality, this was what was happening now... a distortion of everything that normally kept him firmly on the ground.

He knew this was coming, he knew this was going to happen one day, but he couldn't process the information, for some reason he couldn't do anything about it... How did he know... he scrambled around in his brain looking for an explanation and then he remembered last night, reading the manuscript... that's how he knew, Theodore Clackle had told him in the story, but he wasn't really listening, not really taking any notice, but he was now.

Nine days later Blake buried his mother in the little village cemetery next to St Mary's Church Bindle-Dean near to where his father had been buried four years previously. It was a warm summer's day and there was a gentle southerly wind blowing through the trees. An idyllic setting for a burial if there can be such a thing. There must have been at least two dozen of Florence's friends there, in the main, people he didn't know, or didn't think he knew, some of them must have been from when they lived at

Prospect Road and Wadham Road. They all spoke of her as a second mother and they all seemed to remember him.

'Haven't you grown up then.' said one of the ladies.

Yes I've noticed that he thought.

'I don't suppose you remember me, but I used to bounce you on my knee.' Em...

'You were a lovely little boy then..,' another one of the ladies chipped in. Was that a backhanded way of saying, you look like a miserable bugger now, thought Blake.

Blake wondered just what their relationship had been with his mother, had it been more than just a friendship, but it didn't really matter much now. They were happy to have known her, so she must have brought some joy into their lives and not many of us can say that.

Standing by the graveside, he thought about the manuscript and how it was now effectively up to date for want of a better phrase. Yes it had predicted a few things might happen and they had come to pass, but was there much further it could go, if indeed it was going anywhere at all. Could today be a final valediction before the manuscript finally left his life forever or at best, ceased to have any effect on it. He hoped so.

Nearly all those attending the service came back to Florence's house afterwards and enjoyed the normal fare of cucumber and salmon sandwiches, tea and sherry, which had been prepared by one of Florence's neighbours who was also a good friend. Coincidently, the ladies name was Adrianna, the same name as Mary Drayton's neighbour in the manuscript, but neither Blake or Catherine felt inclined to mention the letters or the strange premonition to her.

Intermittently, during the course of the afternoon, one by one the ladies, who Blake scarcely new, came up to him again to warmly shake his hand, thank him for something unspecified and pay him compliments about his mother. This was a little unnerving at times as he was becoming increasingly uncertain as to what precisely they were alluding to or thanking him for, so initially he just acknowledged their comments and remarks, but then he began to feel a little guilty and awkward about receiving their praise such was the honesty and sincerity imbued within their words. These were people speaking about his mother in a way that he had never seen her, but they had. Was there more to her than he knew, he wondered. He wasn't aware of it, but the evidence he was being repeatedly confronted with today indicated otherwise. He should have made more of an effort to try to heal the differences between them, but he hadn't. Maybe she had written the book to attract his attention. She knew all the facts, yes that must be it. That was definitely a possible explanation. She could have been masquerading as Anthony Theodore Clackle sending him chapters and possibly coming round adding chapters when he was out. She didn't have a key to his house, but that was of little consequence to a woman such as Florence, someone who was always very enterprising in her endeavours, showing remarkable initiative and never one to be thwarted in her quest by such mundane trivialities as keys or access to a safe.

That would so neatly answer so many of the questions he had, it all seemed so obvious to him now. It all fitted nicely into place, that was why he hadn't seen it before. All these so called ladies were probably in on it as well, all part of a massive conspiracy, they were probably going to continue sending him chapters, probably chapters Florence had written before her untimely demise. The only question was why, and that had been answered comprehensively by them all being here today, all except his mother in a manner of speaking, she obviously was there, but only in spirit. It was all a rort to get them back together. How devious, how clever he thought conspiratorial cunning worthy of the Borgias, she was so much more than just a mother, so very much more. But why the praise from her friends he wondered that didn't quite fit any pattern.

'We must be going now,' said one of the ladies all dressed in black, most of the ladies were not dressed so formally, but five of them were, and she was one of them.

'We've had a lovely day saying goodbye to Flo, she was such a lovely lady.' The four other ladies, all dressed in black, nodded uniformly in agreement looking not dissimilar to a row of nodding dogs in the back of an old

Ford Cortina, such was their synchronicity. They all smiled at the same moment. An odd vision of Macbeth's weird sisters, the goddesses' of destiny, with two additions suddenly sprang to mind for no particular reason. He furtively looked around for a boiling cauldron, but there wasn't one. There was also something else odd about them. They were all aged around fortyish, whereas his mother was nearly sixty, so they were little more than teenagers when she knew them… it was an unusual relationship.

'Thank you for coming, and for being so kind,' said Blake.

One of them, I think her name was Nancy, stepped forward, obviously this was pre-arranged as the others stayed back, preferring to observe what Nancy was going to say without becoming directly involved, but still emanating the impression of cognizance of what was going to be said.

'Florence loved you very much, you know that? Blake didn't answer, but nodded his head nonchalantly.

'She was hoping to mend things before she….'

'She was a hard woman to understand,' interrupted Blake, defensively.

'We all know she could be stubborn, and she didn't mince her words, but she has helped nearly every woman in this room one way or another, so we tended to see past the bluff exterior, and see her for who she really was. All that other stuff was just a façade, something to protect her. It's sad you didn't see what we could see.

'I tried to, I was going to…' started Blake, but it was pointless to continue, "I was going to", and "if only's" and "what if's" are all so very sad because they all mean the same thing…. it's too late to change something that has already happened, and there's no going back. He followed them to the front door and bid them farewell as they left Flo's house and his life forever. As evening wore on the rest of the mourners slowly left and by seven o'clock it was just Blake and Catherine left to clear things up.

'It's very odd the way they spoke of her,' said Blake washing the cups as Catherine dried.

'They loved her, she was a good friend,' replied Catherine.

'Was she more though,' queried Blake?.

'More, what do you mean,' asked Catherine?

'I don't know, it's just that, well I don't remember her mentioning any of those people.'

'Well you wouldn't, you hardly ever went to see her.'

'Em,' said Blake, meditatively. 'Do you think she wrote Prospect Road?'

'I don't know, it would seem remarkably farsighted of her, especially the premonitory bits. I mean how could she have predicted her own death, when it was due to natural causes,' that still some trick?

'Em,' replied Blake again, weighing up the odds. 'Some people have done it before.'

'Have they?' replied Catherine unconvinced.

"Right, we'll better be going, the baby sitter will be wondering where we are.'

They locked the house up and left.

Chapter 18

Sept 1983

With some reluctance Blake had put the manuscript for Prospect Road into the house safe after collecting it from Martin and there it had laid undisturbed since the funeral.

A few months had passed and it was now the beginning of September. The summer had been very warm, but was now cooler and not so humid. Catherine was at last getting the new house into some sort of order. Blake had been very busy in London with The Chapter Room American publication and was getting home very late most nights. Martin had rung and left a message to say the rebuild of his house was coming along really well and hopefully it would be finished by October and would they like to come over for dinner and to celebrate the completion of works sometime in November. Max and Claudia had spent the summer exploring the house and gardens finding lots of old sheds and out-houses scattered around the grounds that had not been mentioned when they purchased the property.

Nothing out of the ordinary had happened since the funeral and Catherine and Blake were both beginning to think that maybe it was more than a coincidence that since Florence's death everything had gone a very quiet. Neither of them however had mentioned this stillness for fear of upsetting the karma, or more accurately this peculiar state of tranquillity that now appeared to exist. But of course they also hadn't bothered to read the manuscript for some time... there had been no reason to. Then one day out of the blue sometime near the end of September, in fact is was the 24$^{th...}$ Catherine's birthday, she received a telephone call. She picked up the receiver expecting it to be Blake apologising once again for being held up at the office and not expecting to be home till late, but it wasn't.

'Hello Catherine, how are you?' asked a quiet gentle voice on the other end of the phone.

It was one of those extremely rare moments in her life. Some weeks earlier, she had been browsing around in an old backstreet antique shop in Guildford, when she had come across one of those heavily distressed, hand painted signs painted with a philosophical quote burnt into it. The sign read, "What really matters in this life is not how many times you breath, but how many times your breath is taken away." Today the breath in her body had been completely taken away, sucked out as if she were a suddenly deflated balloon. She immediately thought back to that shop and the sign, which for some reason, although she loved the sentiment, she had not purchased. For one fleeting moment air didn't seem to exist anymore, she felt she was drowning in her own existence, but she wasn't and then she inhaled and everything went back to normal or as normal as she could expect in the situation.

She immediately recognised his deep, soft, mellifluous, intoxicating tone, but she didn't answer straight way, she was physically unable to. Her throat had suddenly been rendered bone dry, totally devoid of moisture. Her brain was also a little befuddled and racing with confusion. This was precisely not what she was expecting and she was correspondingly unprepared...

'I'm fine' she eventually answered in a faltering tone bordering on the circumspectly cautious, but with a hint of surprised anticipatory optimism. She instinctively knew that even remembering his name could prove to be a psychological disadvantage, but nevertheless she surrendered to his expectant tenor it would have been churlish to respond any other way, 'it's Gideon, Gideon Drew isn't it?' She affirmed in her best attempt at insouciance and vague detachment, but it didn't really work.

'Yes, yes it is. I'm surprised you remember me after all this time.' replied Gideon quietly. Touché thought Catherine that'll teach me to try to be clever.

He wasn't surprised, but he knew better than to appear overconfident, that would smack of arrogance, or worst still manipulative contrivance.

She had thought about him almost every day since their last meeting, maybe for only a minute or two each day, but he was never that far out of mind.

'It hasn't been that long, it was only Boxing day when you came to stay,' replied Catherine a little too swiftly, just before muttering something incoherent under her breath and nearly biting her lip. That was the second mistake she had made. She castigated herself. She couldn't afford to make a third mistake, that would make her sound like some brain dead schoolgirl totally out of her depth with the preliminary verbiage of a relationship. Christ, what has he done to me she thought. She should have dithered half way at least for a few moments just to add a tiny element of inconsequential indifference, a hint of haziness, but now she had more or left confirmed that she had been counting the days, hours and possibly the minutes and seconds.

'Yes that's right,' replied Gideon slowly and quietly, perfectly happy to allow the conversation to progress in this strangely casual manner, 'but that was last year, over nine months ago.'

'Yes it is isn't it,' she pretended to sound surprised, 'how time flies, so tell me how have you been,' inquired Catherine in a courteously innocent tone. 'Blake tells me the book is going really well in America… and Australia I think… you must be very happy.' That was better she thought, just a touch of uncertainty.

'I could be happier,' replied Gideon. In everyday conversations there are always cleverly constructed questions with an opaque agenda. Some, are quite deadly, often with no obvious means of escape, but more lethal are the cleverly fashioned answers. Answers that can ensnare the unsuspecting victim in a trap, especially when uttered from behind the cloak of invisibility that a telephone conversation affords the enquirer; no chance to gauge the true agenda from a fleeting expression or casual involuntary gesture.

'Oh,' said Catherine, 'are you unhappy?' Christ she thought to herself, closing her eyes momentarily in disbelief at her own crass naivety. I've done it again, said too much. Now I've invited him to pore his heart out and we've only been speaking for less than a minute. Gideon didn't answer her question. Catherine was relieved, somehow, for some indefinable reason he had chosen not to pursue the inevitable path that the conversation could have taken.

'Would you like to go for a drink sometime?' he asked. Having just been excused one potentially embarrassing moment she was less inclined to refuse his invitation. It was a clever tactic by Gideon. Why had he not continued, she wondered, he could have struck while the iron was hot, but he chose not to, maybe there was no agenda after all, maybe she was just being paranoid even cynical. She cursed herself for the negativity in her mind.

'Blake rarely gets home before ten most nights, so that could be a bit..' Gideon interrupted.

'I meant just you.' Gideon was oddly blunt, as if to infer his invitation was obviously just to her anyway and surely, she must have realised that.

'Oh, I see. I wasn't expecting that. I am a married woman you know,' replied Catherine playfully, but that was exactly what she was expecting. She twirled her fingers in her hair girlishly, while carefully taking stock of the situation.

'What were you expecting?' enquired Gideon who was now beginning to realise this was a kind of mind game.

'Oh I don't know, as I said I wasn't expecting anything and I definitely wasn't expecting to hear from you so…' replied Catherine. Maybe I've just about recovered from the opening catastrophe she thought, gently clenching her fist and mouthing a silent "Yes".

'It's only a cup of coffee, so will you come?' asked Gideon again.

'When?' said Catherine nonchalantly.

'Whenever suits you?'

'I usually do some shopping on Thursday and the child minder stays all day in case I get held up so she picks Max and Claudia up from school, so that would be good.'

'I could meet you in the Lodge Hotel restaurant in Lansbury say one o'clock do you know it?' asked Gideon.

'Yes,' replied Catherine a friend of ours is living there at the moment, his house is being rebuilt after a very strange accident.'

'Oh,' said Gideon, 'You must tell me all about it next Thursday.'

'I will,' she replied, the conversation went quite for a moment.

'Till next Thursday then,' said Catherine filling the void.

'I look forward to it,' replied Gideon, 'oh, and a happy birthday for today.'

'Thank you, replied Catherine a little surprised, 'but how did you know?'

'You mentioned it at Christmas.'

'Did I?,' said Catherine, who had no recollection of mentioning it.

'During one of our conversations over dinner. I have one of those memories for dates and places and things.'

'Oh,' said Catherine still a little stunned.

'Bye-bye,' said Gideon, once again a little abrupt, but that was his way, not his intention.

'Bye,' said Catherine, She hung up the phone and sat back on the sofa in silence trying to remember when precisely she had mentioned her birthday, but nothing came to mind. Then she thought about the lunch date with Gideon... should she tell Blake she wondered, of course she should, why wouldn't she and yet for some reason she felt the urge to maybe not tell him, but why she thought, it was all a little confusing.

Prospect Road 13

Chapter Thirteen
written by
Anthony Theodore Clackle
Julian's Story cont…

Julian went off to war and didn't return home until after the war had ended in 1945, except that is for the odd weekend and on one other particular occasion. He fought a long, hard and ferocious Battle of Britain during 1940, four months of nonstop attrition, which took the lives of nearly all his friends and a good many younger pilots as well. He felt old and weary at twenty two, when boys aged eighteen had joined up, learned to fly, gone to the local pub for their first pint and to have a singsong around the old piano and then were killed within six months.

He often laid in bed and wondered why it was that he had managed to survive five bitter years of conflict when so many others had perished. Had he been granted this reprieve for a reason? he didn't know, he just thanked God every day for his deliverance. By the end of the war he had, despite the odds, managed to survive and had been promoted to squadron leader, but tragically Hilda and Harry would never see him proudly showing of his new uniform. They were both killed in the very last German raid over London in 1941 and so the last connection he had, through which he could exercise his inalienable right to find his real father had been severed, all bar one.

After the war ended, Julian tried to find his father, from the scant information he had, but there was no trace. He wrote to Joshua Clanford on a number of occasions, but not unsurprisingly it was all to no avail and he never received a reply. Then one day, out of the blue in late 1947 Joshua, sent him a letter asking to see him. They arranged a meeting at Joshua's house in London.

When Julian was ushered into Joshua's drawing room he was confronted by the sight of an old man now imprisoned in a wheelchair and looking very much as if he were not long for this world. He was by Julian's calculations still only about fifty five years, but he looked nearer a hundred such were his infirmities, but it was hard to tell for sure because the curtains had been drawn and the only light in the room was from an open fire and the candlelight from a number of candelabra placed around the room.

There was a heavy, overpowering stench of putrid urine in the air, which somebody was obviously attempting to neutralise by having bowls of freshly crushed lavender juice scattered about the room. This, if anything had made the problem worse, not better.

The resultant stomach wrenching aroma brought back memories of an horrific episode from his past, the images just unexpectedly popped up in his head. Hidden away for years in one solitary cell deep in his brain and then suddenly they were back, re-activated by a smell. That's what some smells do, take you back to another life. How he wished he could permanently erase those images, but he could not.

The incident happened when he had been based at RAF station Tangmere is Sussex, just outside of Chichester in 1943. He had to experience one of his friends dying, trapped in his overturned burning Spitfire, which had crashed in a field of rotting cabbages just to one side of the runway.

Try as he may, he couldn't get close to the aircraft and was unable to save his comrade from the flames. He had no option but to stand back and listen to his screams as he was slowly burnt to death. All the while he was inhaling the smell of the decomposing vegetation intermingled with the acrid stench of burning flesh and oil. It was an incident that he would never forget and up to today, the most repulsive odour he had ever encountered.

Initially Joshua's face appeared to be moving, but only when Julian drew closer did he realise why. His bloated face was heavily pockmarked and inflamed, covered in erupting pustules, many of which were slowly oozing a yellowy greenish puss. His nurse, who never left his side carefully wiped away some of the discharge with a small towel and dabbed cream onto his face, probably some form of antiseptic was Julian's guess. His hands were also bloated and riddled with arthritis, his fingers the shape of small bananas.

'I like to sit in the candlelight and do you know why...' he paused for a moment, he understood the value of timing, and Julian didn't answer or respond.

'...it enhances my charisma,' continued Joshua.

Julian still said nothing, he thought if he stayed quiet Joshua would simply continue to speak... he did.

Joshua laughed, it sound a little croaky, the nurse smiled, happy to see her patient laugh.

'I commend you for your good manners sir, your patience, your fortitude and your intellect...'

He paused for a few moments to see if Julian would react, but he did not. 'I am jesting with you dear fellow, nothing could enhance my appearance. I am as ugly as a gargoyle sucking lemons.'

Julian now smiled at Joshua's self-effacing remark. It was not what he was expecting.

Joshua beckoned to a chair and Julian sat down.

'So why are you here boy?' asked Joshua.

'Because you invited me, because I want to know about my parents, and you appear to be the only person who knows anything about them.'

'I will tell you what I know, but I doubt if it will be of any comfort, if that is what you seek.

Julian said nothing.

Joshua began to explain what had happened over thirty years ago and how Madeleine had betrayed him with Gideon, but Julian had his own version of this account, one which he had lived with for many years and one which he preferred to think was probably nearer the truth. Julian couldn't believe the lies he was being told, he thought maybe the dementia that had now taken hold of him had distorted the facts in his brain, just as the syphilis had distorted his face, maybe this was just some more bile that he wanted to leave behind to fester and grow after he had gone.

After he had finished retelling the story Joshua took a drink of the water by his side and looked directly at Julian.

'Leave us,' said Joshua to his nurse. She obediently left the room.

'You are a fine looking man Julian Clackle,' remarked Joshua, 'Looking at you now I realise I may have been a bit hasty and impetuous in allowing you to be adopted, I should have been more forthright and kept you and thrown your mother out, but she insisted.' He was lying, but that was the privilege of the old and dying, if they chose to exercise the option at that point in their life.

'But you weren't my father, I thought that was the problem all along?' said Julian.

'Maybe you were maybe you weren't, we'll never know now will we?'

'My mother killed herself because of what you did.'

'I didn't do anything, she killed herself because she couldn't be with him, she didn't care about you or me.'

'That's not the way that I was told it happened,' replied Julian defensively.

'Everybody tells the same story about the same event from a slightly different perspective, and each version will contradict the others, isn't that the way of life?' Put ten men in a circle and a ugly naked woman standing still in the middle, and ask them to describe what they can see of her and also the parts of her they cannot see and I guarantee you that each man will describe her slightly differently depending on where they are standing.' Joshua tried to look up at Julian, waiting for his reply.

'I only want to find my father, my real father, the man who loved my mother... your wife.'

'But maybe I am your father,' said Joshua, he was enjoying this moment... tormenting Julian. Probably the only activity he had left to indulge in now he was housebound and confined in a wheelchair. His days of decadence and debauchery a misty memory now. All he

had left to play with was what he knew and what Julian didn't.

'No you are not my father, I would know if you were. All that you have told me is a lie, my father is Gideon Drew.'

'Ah the mysterious Gideon Drew,' sighed Joshua taking a deep breath and wheezing a little, 'the man you have been searching for, but for one reason or another have been unable to find. Maybe he doesn't really exist anymore, had you thought about that?'

'What do you mean,' asked Julian?

'Well you have said you can't find any trace of him so what does that mean, you tell me? I never knowingly met him and when I did he was masquerading as somebody else. I only wish your mother had never met him, and if she were alive today I wager she would rue the day she did, that was the worst day of her life.'

'I would have thought that was the day she committed suicide,' replied Julian bitterly .

'That was caused by Drew,' retorted Joshua.

'The way I heard it you forced Madeleine to give up my sister and I for adoption because you weren't our father and then when you found out she was visiting me at my adoptive parents you stopped that as well... that sounds like a convincing argument to blame you for her death.'

'That's all lies.'

'Did you know I married Rosemary?' asked Julian.

'What!' exclaimed Joshua.

'I married my own sister, Rosemary, because I didn't know who she was when I met her and we had a son.'

Joshua was too stunned to say anything.

'That was your fault as well,' said Julian, 'placing us with two different families and then somehow making sure they never met, I don't know how you did that, but that was the result.'

'That was nothing to do with me; Madeleine dealt with the adoptions, not me.'

'You were in control, you were always in control.'

'Ahhh,' said Joshua screeching in pain, 'get my nurse I need some ointment on my face,' Joshua appeared to be in some sort of distress.

'In pain are you?' asked Julian, not moving.

'Yes, excruciating pain all the time.'

'He's retarded you know, crippled, in constant pain and deformed and all because I didn't know who I had fallen in love with.'

'Who's crippled?' asked Joshua. disconsolately and sounding confused.

'Our son Anthony Theodore Clackle, that's who.'

'That's not my fault either,' said Joshua. 'Get my nurse.'

'I think it is, I think everything is your fault. Somehow you have brought this all down on your own head and now there is some retribution for what you have done and somewhat fortuitously, I am here to see you suffer it.'

'Believe what you like.' shouted Joshua, wincing in agony.

'What did you do, to cause so much pain to so many people, that's what I want to know.'

'Get me that fucking nurse,' shouted Joshua again, his face appeared to have erupted with puss oozing from every boil.

'You are dying of something that smells revolting and looks disgusting, my mother, your wife committed suicide, my son is crippled, your partner and his wife both died horribly in Africa eaten by lions I heard, their son Freddie, committed suicide, your second wife drowned at sea shall I go on....?'

'I told you, none of that is my fault,' replied Joshua.

'I don't believe you,' said Julian.

'Believe what you like, I don't care anymore.'

'I don't think you ever cared for anybody except yourself.'

'Can you go now,' pleaded Joshua, 'and leave a dying man in peace?'

Julian smiled at Joshua's discomfort, taking pleasure in the moment, he knew it would not come again. He stood up and walked towards the door, opened it and beckoned the nurse to come back in. He turned back to Joshua, 'I will find him one day and when I do I will know the truth and if you are responsible I will wish you to hell.'

'To late I'm there already,' replied Joshua.

'Not yet you're not,' said Julian.

'Will you find him?' replied Joshua, I doubt it, and let me give you one last piece of advice...' he slowly lifted his head once more with every ounce of strength he could muster to look at Julian. The soft glow of the candlelight throwing a soft cream glow over Joshua's face highlighted the grotesque gargoylian features that Julian could now see had taken over his whole body. He coughed and a little more blood dropped into his handkerchief, ... ' be careful what you wish for boy, be very, very careful, for you may find things you wished you hadn't found.

'His head slumped forward as he fell into a deep sleep. The nurse smiled at Julian as if to say 'you'll get no more from him today, so Julian left Joshua's house never to return.

Joshua died a few days later in excruciating agony apparently possessed by a demon right up to the end and constantly screaming out the same phrase "You may never take my soul," until his very last breath.

Julian continued his search for Gideon, but he wouldn't find him, not until many years later.

Chapter 19

Isabella arrived as normal on Thursday at just after ten and after some updates on village life and a cup of tea she started on the cleaning.   Catherine went upstairs and carefully picked out what she would wear for her coffee date with Gideon.   She tried various outfits trying to balance elegance with the practicality of shopping and eventually settled on something that she thought was attractive, but not too obvious.   She then addressed the matter of underwear, considering the various options and the obvious possibilities available.   But having let her imagination briefly meander whimsically into the realm of fantasy she eventually, after considerable deliberation, settled on something sexy, but practical.   There was definitely no requirement for an alluring, but not particularly comfortable G string today.

She left at just after eleven to do the shopping and arrive at the Lodge Hotel and Restaurant a few minutes after one o'clock.   As she walked from the car park towards the seating area in the front garden, she could see Gideon waving from a table.   She made her way towards him with some unexpected trepidation.   She had mentioned the meeting to Blake so there was no reason for feeling anxious, but never the less she still was.   In fact, Blake had been only too pleased that she had found the time to entertain Gideon as although he would normally take clients (especially his bestselling authors) out to lunch on a regular basis, he had been rather busy recently and had neglected this particular publisher-writer responsibility.

Gideon looking as majestic as ever, gently embraced Catherine and kissed her softly on both cheeks.   She could smell the heavily scented cologne on his body, but beyond that there was something else, something warm, sultry and aromatic.   It deceived her senses momentarily, distorting reality, transporting her to somewhere exotic, conjuring up, as if by magic, the distant sounds of an Arabian market place.   Tingling bells, and wisp's of marijuana smoke entwining with the exquisite flashing colours of the night and whirling dervishes dancing faster and faster as if they were about to sacrifice their souls into a swirl of infinity in order to defend their very existence. And all this from just one inhalation of the air that surrounded his body, but then maybe that was the intention.

'I am so glad you came,' he stuttered, a little uncharacteristically. There was an unexpected air of vulnerability and nervousness about him that she found enchantingly endearing. She immediately forgot about any concerns she had, her mind now slightly more at ease. Maybe her recollection of their last meeting, like so many remembrances of things past, was not how she had thought it had been after all; maybe she had simply got it wrong.

It may have been a rash assessment, slightly romanticised; distorted by wine and seasonal emotion, as if looking at a familiar object through a smoky glass prism. She had obviously completely misread the signs.

Today she could plainly see the difference in their ages – Gideon must have been in his early thirties according to the occasional comments that Blake had made in passing, but he looked no more than twenty five. (There had to be a portrait tucked away somewhere in an attic, she thought a little disingenuously, immediately berating herself for being so petty and for thinking like a petulant child and anyway Blake had already made that very same comment a few months ago, so it wasn't even original.) How little did she know how close to the truth she really was.

She was nearly thirty nine, happily married, a mother of two children, but dangerously close to ringing the half time bell and in the cold light of day, the innocent naivety of her quasi adolescent infatuation was clearly apparent. Christ! She thought, with a not unreasonable stretch of the imagination, I could look like his mother for God's sake. She quickly looked around at the other diners to see if anyone was watching them, but none were.

Notwithstanding the fact that she had taken the lords name in vain twice, in the space of one sentence, which, being a good catholic, she quickly castigated herself for, she realised the situation was untenable. The prospect of her and Gideon never being anything more than acquaintances riled her sensibilities, it was an affront to mortal equality. Nothing more than the tangential osculation of two diaphanous circles colliding in space.

Why should she be denied the intimate affection of a man she signally desired just because she had suffered the misfortune of having been born at the wrong moment in time. With some reluctance and a footnote to the dissimilitude of the singularity of cultures, she reluctantly let the moment pass

'Would you like a coffee,' asked Gideon.

Catherine smiled, 'yes please, I'll have a skinny latte… thank you.' Gideon went into the restaurant to order the coffee.

Catherine tried to relax and began to think about things to say when he returned.

'One skinny latte,' pronounced Gideon on his return, as if there were some agenda to her request.

'I have to watch my figure after two children. I could go to seed very quickly if I'm not careful,' she half smiled. She wasn't deliberately pitching for compliments, but immediately realised how crass that sounded.

Gideon smiled, but did not answer with the hackneyed reply she was half expecting. They both took a sip of coffee in silence.

'Is that expresso?' asked Catherine looking at Gideon's black coffee, hastily attempting to fill the void, 'I've always thought expresso was too strong. Blake drinks it that way. I prefer it much weaker. I'm sure it keeps him up at night.' Gideon smiled at the accidental innuendo she had thrown in at the end, but said nothing. Catherine realised she was talking in short, monosyllabic spurts, lacking fluidity and bordering on the edge of inane superficiality.

This was harder than she thought it would be, it was not how she normally was, she would have to make a conscious effort to breath deeper and talk slower.

'He likes to read to three or four o'clock in the morning sometimes,' continued Catherine, still a little too hurriedly, almost by way of explication, 'if he has a good story that is. Sometimes I'll wake up in the morning and he's still reading - not even bothered to go to sleep. 'Do you...'

Gideon put his forefinger to his lips and made a gentle shushing sound. Catherine felt a little embarrassed for a moment, she realised that she had been rambling on a bit, probably sounding like a ditzy schoolgirl with a crush on a teacher. She even thought she was going to blush for an instant, and then found her brain talking to her heart and telling it she was thirty nine and she didn't do that kind of blushing anymore.

'Have you ever seen Rosencrantz and Guildenstern are Dead.... it's a play by Tom Stoppard,' asked Gideon? Catherine was a little surprised by the sudden change in direction of the conversation, she wasn't expecting that.

'Yes, once or twice.' replied Catherine a little unsure where this sudden puzzling diversion was leading.' She took another sip of coffee, '.. I first saw it just after I left uni. .. and again a few years ago I think.'

'What do you make of it,' asked Gideon, it was a rhetorical question - he probably knew the answer, or let's just say he knew the answer he was expecting. There was a certain beneficence, a generosity of spirit in the voluminous question, it was as if he were trying to bridge the invisible divide between them that only she could see, but he could sense.

'What did I make of it?' she repeated, 'I don't really know to be honest...nobody has ever asked me before so I....' Catherine stopped and thought about this strange question and her mind began to backtrack to the last performance she had seen nearly three years ago.

'As I remember it was about two off stage characters from Hamlet, minor characters as I recall, anyway they are discussing and re-enacting various scenes from the play to demonstrate the confusion and loss of morality in life in general and their lives in particular, while waiting for their scenes to arrive. It was like an alternative view to the Hamlet story to the one the audience sees. The exact opposite in fact, the view from the other side of the play if that makes any sense, from two people who could see the play and the audience at the same time and watch how each reacted to the other. A sort of a play within a play about a play if that doesn't sound too abstruse or pretentious.'

Gideon smiled as a sense of calm serenity seemed to wash over him. He appeared enthralled by Catherine's explication, it was as if he had been searching all his life for a kindred spirit, someone who understood things the way he did and now, at last he had found that someone, somebody who could fulfil that role, that vacancy that had remained unfilled for so long since...

'That makes perfect sense,' he replied, 'that's precisely what I thought for so many years until one day I read it again and then I've found something else, something even more important.' Catherine felt exhilarated. She so enjoyed this feeling of worth and enablement, this sense of intellectual empowerment that he so easily instilled in her. She felt she was becoming part of something more, something strong, something powerful, it engendered a sense of invincibility – immortality that she had never felt before, she was being tantalized by his words, but she was unable to resist the tsunami of verity and actuality that was sweeping over her soul.

She had never felt undervalued by Blake, and her life fulfilled everything she had ever dreamed of, but this was something entirely different, this involved exploring regions of her mind, areas into which she seldom ventured and probably thought she never would.

'I believe it's about the inevitability of coincidence - chance - fate. Serendipity if you like,' continued Gideon, slowly ensnaring Catherine in to his labyrinthine plan. 'How small decisions can affect the whole of our lives and sometimes beyond. Can you see how that could make a difference?' he asked.

Catherine said nothing, not sure as to what he was now alluding to, but nevertheless completely entranced by his words of simple honesty and truth...

'…They could have taken control of events and the outcome would have been entirely different, instead of which nearly everybody dies.' Gideon looked at Catherine and smiled just for a moment and then in an instant the smile was gone, replaced by something else, and for the first time she felt a cold shudder of uncertainty trickle down her spine, she saw something she had not seen before and then it was gone.

'But then if they didn't die… it wouldn't be Hamlet anymore, it would be something entirely different,' said Catherine.

'Yes it would, you're absolutely right and that's my point...' Gideon was demonstrative and assertive, he wanted Catherine to understand his feelings '…but Shakespeare wanted it that way, so that's the way it is.'

'Em,' replied Catherine lamely, still unsure where this was going, but certain of one thing and that was that she was now falling inextricably under his spell, intoxicated by the passion of his words.

'I am so sorry, I do blabble on sometimes,' remarked Gideon apologetically in what was obviously an attempt to lighten the intensity that had settled on the conversation.

'Blabble?' said Catherine smiling and scrunching up her nose, never having heard the word before.

'Yes blabble, it's a nonsensical fusion of gabble and blabber, it's a word I made up, but that's what I do… when I'm anxious, when I feel vulnerable.' It was a clever subterfuge and it worked.

Catherine laughed at his creation. She muttered the word a couple of times to hear the sound of it ripple over her lips and laughed again.

'So you're anxious?' said Catherine sounding surprised, 'I thought I was the anxious one.' They both smiled and took another sip of coffee.

'He only wrote comedies and mediocre drama until his son died you know, after that he started writing tragedy's, the first was Hamlet.'

'I didn't know he had a son,' queried Cathrine.

'Hamnet... that was his name oddly, died of the plague when he was about eleven years old.' Gideon pronounced the words slowly in an oddly stark – matter of fact manner that lacked any depth, feeling or compassion, which just for a second or two surprised Catherine. She somehow, for some reason, had half expected some kind of empathetic intonation, on such a detail, but there was nothing, just cold, lifeless, soulless pragmatism.

Gideon continued, 'You see in a way we may only have all the best tragedies ever written because by chance or fate, whatever, his son died and then his mind-set changed. It was a sort of a creative trade off... To feel, to understand pain and grief he needed to experience it first-hand that was the deal he accepted.'

Catherine thought that was an odd thing to say.

'Had his son lived... then we would probably only have ever known him for comedies and nothing else and what a tragedy that would have been?'

They both laughed at the lame witticism.

'Do you think that everything in life is a trade-off?' said Catherine.

'Possibly, maybe a compromise.'

'Between what,' asked Catherine?

'What you want, desire, need and what you eventually settle for.'

'Have you settled for something?' asked Catherine.

'Oh yes, I definitely settled for something, something I want, something I need.' Gideon leaned half way across the table and kissed Catherine gently on the lips. She could feel the warmth of his body seep into her soul through the conduit of two tongues gently exploring new unexplored territory. She didn't resist, she didn't know how to.

He leaned back slightly and smiled, then continued talking.. Catherine couldn't take her eyes off his. She needed to understand what was happening.

'...In fact we probably wouldn't know him at all apart from being an irrelevant footnote in the annals of literature. It would be as if he didn't exist, not like us...'

'We can't do this,' said Catherine suddenly pulling back, sitting bolt upright in her chair.'

'Do what?' said Gideon, with an expression of childlike innocence.

'This,' Catherine replied waving her hands in small Pope like gestures. 'Making small talk… talk that always leads to somewhere… somewhere I don't wish to go.'

'But we just have,' replied Gideon. 'We can't just go back and pretend it didn't happen, it did, the moment has passed, it is now enshrined in our memories forever, it can't be expunged, time has moved on and so have we.'

'But it's wrong on so many levels,' pleaded Catherine, she sounded desperate to redact the moment , but it was no more than a token gesture and nowhere near adequate to have any tangible effect.

'I must be ten possibly fifteen years older than you, I'm married, I have two children, a lovely house and my husband is your publisher and..'

'You haven't mentioned love?'

'Love? I don't love you,' replied Catherine firmly and looking a little surprised.

'Not me,' replied Gideon quietly, 'Blake… you didn't mention love.'

'Oh I see…' replied Catherine suddenly realising she had made an explicit omission, for a fraction of a second half her brain processed the comment while the other half tried to rationalise the implication. 'of course I love Blake, that's a given.'

'Is it?' replied Gideon. 'I would never consider love as a given, it has to really be there, not just assumed or taken for granted. You have to see it every day, in a smile or a word or a kiss or a touch, but it has to be there, or you have absolutely nothing.'

'You don't understand marriage, it's not all just wine and roses, there's lots of things that make it work, many other boring everyday pedestrian things as well as nice things, it's a melting pot of different emotions and..'

Gideon leaned across the table again, gently took hold of both her upper arms and slowly, firmly, drew Catherine back toward him and kissed her passionately, not like she'd been kissed for a long, long time. She could sense the desire in his mouth, she could feel the strength in his arms, latent and under control, but waiting. She knew how to resist, but her brain was malfunctioning and was not passing the message to her body.

At that precise moment, the world she knew began to slowly crumble. The next thing she clearly remembered was lying naked in the hotel bedroom having made love to Gideon for what seemed like days, but was in fact just a few hours. All the rest that had passed before that moment now seemed to be very hazy.

She vaguely remembered him kissing every inch of her body and tasting every opening, but perfect clarity seemed to have become lost in the delirium of ecstasy she had experienced, no not experienced she thought, experiencing for that's what she was doing, this wasn't over. This feeling was constant, insatiable, relentless and unforgiving. By six o'clock they had been making love for over four hour's non-stop, something she had never done before, not even when she was teenager. Gideon made love to her in ways that made her feel as if she had never actually made love before, only been a willing participant in an act of proprietary sex. This was many things, but never just sex. His strength and stamina had quite astounded her. She never realised the levels of ecstasy she could achieve, the frenzied heights of passion to which she could be taken when wilfully encouraged.

At just after seven they dressed and made their way back downstairs to the lobby where they kissed and parted with very few words. Everything they had to say that day had already been said.

Catherine made her way to her car still a little hazy with the miasma of somnolence that had begun to overwhelm her, still unsure exactly what had happened that afternoon. She lowered the front windows before driving off, to allow the rushing air to revitalise her senses as she drove home eventually arriving just after eight. Walking back towards the house she could feel the gentle pain in her lower back, thighs and hips where her legs had either been apart or manoeuvred into so many different positions during the afternoon, but most of the time wrapped around Gideon's waste.

She thought back to Gideon's words about inevitability and chance and wondered whether this day had been preordained, whether it would have happened no matter what she did, maybe she had no choice maybe this was the way her life was now going to be irrespective of anything that had gone on before. She didn't have the good fortune of Rosencrantz and Guildenstern, unable to evaluate cause and effect and probable outcome if circumstances changed, but she knew she would have to continue down this path she had taken no matter what. Nobody could know what could possibly happen and nobody would know what had happened. She was determined that nothing would change, her life would continue just as before, but now with one glorious additional dimension.

She arrived back home just after eight. Isabella was still there, Blake was obviously running late.

'The children are in bed, I read them story, and I have made you some lasagne for dinner.' She was very precise in all she did and said. Although Romanian by birth, she had spent a number of years in Germany and had absorbed some of their Wagnerian almost Germanic traits in her mannerisms.

'Do you need me for anything else Mrs Thornton?' asked Isabella, 'You look like you have had a very hectic day,' she added the comment in all innocence. 'I can make you cup of tea if you wish.'

'No, no thank you' replied Catherine, possibly a little sterner than was necessary, I'm sorry – I just need to sit down. Thank you very much for today, I will be fine.' Isabella smiled and Catherine smiled back, a smile that turned to a grin when she thought about what Isabella had said when she first arrived. Yes it had been a hectic day, one she would remember for a very long time and no doubt there would be moments in the following days and weeks when the odd twinge in her thighs would also make her smile discreetly to herself again.

Chapter 20

March 1984

Two weeks later Blake went to the office as usual, but today he took the train. He had removed the Prospect Road manuscript from the safe, while Catherine was still asleep and slipped it into his case. Blake had not mentioned this to Catherine as he wanted to read the last few chapters again unhindered by the constraints of their previous arrangement. He was perfectly aware that this innocuous mutual agreement was simply to dispel any possible concerns over whether he was secretly writing the new chapters in the book. But, he knew he wasn't writing the book so it didn't seem make any difference now. Chapter Ten had summarised much of the background detail and filled in a few more of the spaces, but one of the central unanswered questions revolved around Gideon Drew, the character mentioned in the Prospect Road story and his relationship with the novelist of the same name that he now represented, that was what interested him most.

There was also the question of why this mysterious un-contactable Anthony Clackle had sent him a manuscript and had then made himself completely unavailable.

Blake mulled over everything that had happened to date and what had been foretold in the manuscript and then, while idly gazing out of the train window at all the trees frantically rushing by, suddenly realised something. If he concentrated hard enough, he could see the dense woods just beyond the trees and all that was happening thereabouts. If was almost as if the train wasn't moving at all, the trees that were much closer to the train became a blur and the harder he concentrated on the woods, the less he could see of the trees that were close to the track, they almost seemed to disappear. That was it he thought, it was a seminal moment… there was a bigger picture, but this had been totally obscured because he was looking to closely at the details that were obvious, to notice what was really happening.

He made some quick notes in the margin of the script about what had just occurred to him. It seemed to make a lot of sense, admittedly in a very abstract quixotic manner, but it still made sense to him. He made a mental note to discuss his thoughts with Catherine when he got back in the evening.

It was just after lunchtime when the telephone rang, the house was very quiet, Max and Claudia were at school and Isabella had finished for the day. Catherine was sitting in the conservatory drinking a glass of wine, contentedly daydreaming, her thoughts somewhere else entirely and totally unaware of how much her life – all their lives in fact, would change for ever after she had taken this call.

She casually reached across to lift the receiver and put it to her ear, but before she could say anything a voice came on the line, a resonantly evocative tone that she immediately recognised.

'Catherine… it's Gideon.'

Catherine said nothing at first. It had been nearly two weeks since that afternoon. Since then she had heard nothing from him, at one point even entertaining the nebulous possibility that their brief liaison was nothing more than an overly contrived one night, no, one afternoon stand, although, somewhat whimsically, she noted they had not remained standing for very long. A tiny smile crossed her face.

For a few moments, her mind flashed back to those few delicious hours of passionate enrapture - more specifically to the memory of his naked, sexually aroused body prowling round the bedroom, never taking his eyes off her. Stalking her like a lion before it pounces on its mesmerized prey – she, the victim unable to defend herself against the onslaught that would follow. She could remember his long dark mane of hair flailing restlessly as they gyrated in a rhythm of ecstasy, he seemed possessed of an energy that she found increasingly impossible to match, he was beginning to engulf her body and inveigle her soul and she was losing all control over what was happening. His constant incantation, a charm like spell of words she did not recognise exsanguinated every other thought from her mind, her body felt as if it had been flensed to the bones with enchantment, as a sense of declension of her very being began to overtake her. It had all become very confusing as she became lost in the euphoria of the illicit assignation.

She could remember drifting in and out of semi-consciousness, a state of mind that had not been artificially induced by drink or drugs, but by the remorseless demand on her body's reserves of energy being demonstrably sequestrated by the eroticism of their love making. She had never experienced anything as intense before, never in her whole life, not even when giving birth to her children.

After what they had experienced that afternoon, she found it impossible to believe that he wouldn't want to see her again. She knew she shouldn't see him, but the gravitational magnetism was pulling her into the centre of something she couldn't comprehend, something malevolent, dark, evil, a centrifical force swirling faster and faster and far too strong for her to resist. As the moth is inescapably drawn to the naked flame and eventually burnt to death so too did she feel the inexorable inevitability of the vortex she was being drawn into.

Her mind raced in circles thinking about what had been said the last time they met. Christ she thought, I'm already thinking about sex and he's only spoken three words. All these thoughts passed in a split second…

'Gideon.. it's nice to hear from you, how are you?' There was a stilted formality in her tone, she was not sure of the protocol under these circumstances and thought it best to appear semi-formal until she could evaluate the reason for his call. He could, for all she knew be ringing to speak to Blake. But then again he would also know that Blake would probably be in the office at that time of day, so maybe not.

'I was wondering if we could…'

'What!' interjected Catherine in a half-hearted attempt to chastise him, 'You tell me you love me, you take me to a hotel, fuck me all afternoon and leave me so exhausted I can hardly walk and then you ignore me for weeks and have the nerve to...' she realised she didn't know what he was going to say next..

'I am sorry I didn't call, but I love you Catherine, and I need to see you again, I need to explain.'

Some words can take your breath away and these did. They took the wind out of her sails and the anger from her heart.

'Explain what? asked Catherine, now settling down a little after her initial outburst.

'I want to hold you in my arms and feel your naked body beneath me, I want to make love to you all day and all night...'

The words hung in the air… Catherine knew what they would mean and above all else, to the exclusion of all others, she desired the same, to be with him again. 'You haven't rung me for nearly two weeks and I thought… I thought, I was just one of your dilettante dalliances and that was it.' She had vented her anger at being ignored, but it was a submissive retort and lacked the essential venom to validate its integrity.

'I understand how you feel completely and it wasn't a casual fling, I..' he paused to compose himself, before continuing to speak, but now a little slower than before. It would give Catherine time to process the depth and veracity of his words.

'I took advantage of our relationship and Blake's kindness and generosity and I thrust myself onto you and your family…' it sounded almost as if it were an act of contrition for the sin of desire, but inexcusably the mention of the word thrust for some reason instantly excited Catherine. She tried to inwardly rebuke herself for her obtuse thought, but failed miserably.

Not since her schooldays had such a simple innocuous word had such an affect. 'It was juvenile and embarrassingly pathetic and she had taken the word completely out of the intended context. It was the sort of mis-interpretation of a perfectly innocent remark that would have produced a lamentably absurd giggle from prepubescent   teenager with a low intellect,   which was possibly to be expected, but not from a mature woman with two children, but that is what he did, and could do to her.

She felt mildly embarrassed, but she could also feel this strange alien sensation, a tingling in her pelvic region, not something she had experienced very often, but she could feel it now and she liked it.

Gideon continued, 'I felt guilty for betraying Blake and for taking advantageous of you and I wanted to leave you both alone for a while to let you come to a decision on whether we should stop this now or continue.'

'I want to see you and I want to be with you,' replied Catherine without taking a breath. There was no hint of hesitation or a moment's indecision, this was what she wanted and she wanted it now.

And so the affair began...

After a few months, they had settled into a regular routine. They would meet at "Clanford" Gideon's new house,   well it wasn't exactly a house more a palatial mansion set in nearly thirty acres of land and ornamental gardens and only just over twenty minutes away from Blake and Catherine's house. Somewhat coincidently the mansion had once been owned by Joshua Clanford the original partner in her husband's company Clanford and Fox back when the company was formed in 1911. Joshua had died many years before and the house had stood empty for a long time. Gideon had bought the house just over a nine months ago and had completely restored it to its original Edwardian glory. Gideon had moved one step closer to his ultimate intention, ironically it was also one step closer to nothingness.   They would meet   every Tuesday and Thursday afternoon at one o'clock and spend the rest of the day either eating, drinking champagne, dancing or making love, but mainly making love.

Isabella stayed late both days to collect the children from school. Blake normally never arrived home much before eight in the evenings, but occasionally he would come home even later if they had had a marketing, media and development meeting, which happened twice a month normally on a Thursday. These normally ran on for a few hours after the office had closed.

Life was exiting again for Catherine and she seemed to have completely forgotten how much in love with Blake she once was. It was as if Gideon had cast a spell over her. The delirium of the affair continued for nearly six months until one day just moments before reaching an orgasm while riding on top of Gideon, she shouted out at the top of her voice "we're having a baby". She was so overjoyed at making the announcement and simultaneously climaxing that she didn't notice the subtle change of expression on Gideon's face. The pleasure he was now experiencing was beyond Catherine's comprehension.

She gently uncoupled herself from Gideon and they embraced passionately for a few minutes before falling back down on the bed to rest.

'That is wonderful news,' said Gideon, 'just what we were waiting for. That completes everything.'

'Yes it does,' replied Catherine, unware of exactly what Gideon was referring too.

'What shall we call the baby?' asked Catherine, lighting a cigarette. She never used to smoke, but had started too whenever in his company.

Gideon thought for a few moments, staring languidly at the ceiling, seeing visions that only he could see. 'Mephisto, I would like to call him Mephisto, I have always liked that name. It commands respect.' He thought about his first meeting and the contract they had made, now nearing completion, but he should still be able to extend it for another fifty years or so if he played his cards carefully. A smile touched his lips, but Catherine didn't see it because she too was staring at the ornately plastered ceiling, but she was watching the painted cherubs playing innocently in a heavenly setting.

'Mephisto?' replied Catherine, sounding surprised. 'I've never heard that name before.'

'It has a Greek origin; it's a favourite family name.'

'I've never met any of your family,' replied Catherine 'in fact I don't remember you ever mentioning any of them before.'

'That's because they are all dead!' Gideon was oddly blunt almost abrasive with his reply as if he were completely unconcerned by their existence.

'Oh,' said Catherine apologetically, 'I am sorry I didn't realise.'

'Nothing to apologise for,' said Gideon still gazing upwards with an odd expression on his face somewhere between immense satisfaction and bitter regret.

'And if it's a girl,' asked Catherine a little reluctantly, now a little wary as to what name Gideon might propose?

'Not very likely, but if it is I will leave it to you. I have always loved the name Alicia…' he paused for a few moments, 'that's another family name that's very close to my heart.' A tear formed in the corner of his eye, but Catherine never saw it.

'That's a lovely name.'

'But it will be a boy, I am sure of that,' replied Gideon. He appeared incontrovertibly convinced that it would be a boy.

'Oh,' said Catherine, a little surprised, 'right. I should break the news to Blake and start making arrangements.' It was a clear declaration of intent, but she paused for a moment to think about whether she should next say what she was thinking, but before she knew what had happened the words had passed over her slips. 'Should we move in together?' It came out sounding a little sheepish and she wished she had thought about it a little longer and made it less passive. It had the ring of a submissive plea, that was not her normal manner.

'Oh, I hadn't thought about that…' replied Gideon sounding slightly alarmed at being caught off guard by Catherine's proposal .

Catherine was a little surprised at his reply, believing for one reason or another that moving in together was inevitable, a natural progression, whereas in reality it now appeared never to have been on the agenda. For a brief moment, she wondered whether she had misunderstood the situation and her mind began to race with unanticipated uncertainty and confusion. Had she completely misread the situation altogether she wondered? This possibility had not been factored into the plan that had been forming in her head.

'…You could move in here I suppose,' continued Gideon with a smile, after what seemed to be an interminable pause. His qualified suggestion alleviated her immediate concerns, and yet she had still detected an almost infinitesimal hint of reservation in his tone. Catherine's ear was acutely tuned to notice these incongruences. The same words said with different inflections produced entirely different meanings.

'Yes,' replied Catherine, 'that would be wonderful, this is an amazing house, the children….' Then she stopped, suddenly realising that she had two other children, two children who had completely slipped her mind and this was all becoming a little unreal… there were many more things to consider in this complicated proposal that she had not foreseen. There was also Blake and how would he react to all of this.

'How far have you gone with this?' asked Gideon.

'How far!' she replied unsure what he was referring too. It seemed an odd question.

'The baby, how far gone is he?'

'You're absolutely sure it's a boy then,' replied Catherine smiling with just the tiniest hint of disbelief.

'Absolutely, I have knowledge of these things,' he replied enigmatically.

'Do you?' she replied smiling curiously, 'nearly three months,' 'Three months! exclaimed Gideon, 'why didn't you mention it earlier?'

'I needed to be sure,'

'And is it…?' he stopped.

'Yes, it's yours,' answered Catherine, ' "we", Blake and I that is, haven't had sex since your bloody book went ballistic last year. Blake is too tired to do anything by the time he gets back home except sleep.'

'I will have to send him another manuscript to keep him busy,' said Gideon smirking.

'Yes you do that,' replied Catherine rolling over to perch herself back on top of Gideon once again. 'And in the meantime…' Catherine started to slowly move up and down on Gideon's manhood, smiling with all the enraptured passion of a woman totally entranced by the joy, happiness and fulfilment she was experiencing at that particular moment, completely oblivious to the dark capricious clouds forming on the horizons.

Chapter 21

Catherine arrived back home at just after seven thirty. Isabella had already put the children to bed and had prepared a simple spaghetti Bolognese for their dinner. She would normally prepare something, if she knew Catherine would be coming in late. The table in the kitchen had been laid, as they tended not to eat in the dining room unless they had guests staying over.

'Hi Issy,' said Catherine 'is everything OK?'

'No problem Mrs Thornton, everything fine.'

'Good, good,' replied Catherine, smiling to herself for no obvious reason.

'Are the shopping bags in the car?' asked Issy curiously, noticing that Catherine had not brought any in with her.

'Oh no,' replied Catherine, suddenly realising her oversite. 'I… I met an old friend I hadn't see for ages and we had some lunch, got chatting, you know, and I never got round to it. I'll get something tomorrow, it doesn't matter.' Such fleetness of mind was occasionally necessary to maintain the illusion, but it was getting harder. She usually picked up some shopping on the way home to support her Thursday alibi, but with the thoughts of everything spoken about that day, including the game changing decision she and Gideon had made regarding their domestic living arrangements still running around in her head she had completely forgotten.

'I understand Mrs Thornton.'

'Catherine,' replied Catherine, 'Please call me Catherine, Mrs Thornton sounds so formal it's as if as if we weren't friends, but we are friends aren't we?' asked Catherine plaintively. Catherine had asked her many times before to call her by her given name, but all to no avail. Isabella preferred the detachment of formality.

'Yes, off course we are,' replied Isabella smiling, but sounding a little apprehensive. Catherine had never specifically mentioned friendship before, it had just been taken for granted. Catherine smiled back.

'So you will remember,' asked Catherine? She spoke with a casual laissez-faire conviction, a temperament undoubtedly brought about by the earlier consumption of the best part of a bottle of Madam Clicqout's magical elixir of life. Champagne quite mysteriously deceived her brain into believing circumstances were invariably far more convivial than they actually were. Conventional social barriers would simply dissolve or cease to exist, until sobriety eventually returned. Such was the case today. But she wasn't so much as drunk on alcohol she was as elated with her vision of the future, however much of an illusion that may have been.

It was an odd question thought Isabella, of course, they were friends, but there had to be clear demarcation lines when one person employs another, no matter how close the relationship may be. It was necessary, in fact essential for the borderlines of delineation to clearly exist in order that clarity could prevail; it demonstrated the perimeters of each of their responsibilities. No ambiguity, no inconsistencies and therefore no misunderstandings. But today, for whatever reason, Catherine desired something different, the introduction of a little haziness on the borders, a touch of greyness on the edges. Calling Catherine - Mrs Thornton seemed inappropriate, but nevertheless if that is what she desired.

'I will try to remember,' said Isabella.

'Good,' replied Catherine, 'good.'

Isabella started to put her coat on as Catherine disappeared into the walk-in-larder in search of a cold bottle of Pinot Grigio.

'Drink before you go?' asked Catherine suddenly reappearing and brandishing a bottle she had liberated from the wine cooler? She had been steadily drinking champagne (Gideon refused to drink anything else) during the course of the afternoon, which had no doubt considerably enhanced the pleasure she had derived from their afternoon of lovemaking and now she just wanted to extend, for just a little while longer the sense of euphoria she was currently experiencing.

'Yes that would be nice,' replied Isabella, a little surprised at the gesture as Catherine normally let her go the moment she arrived back home. She took her coat back off, placed it on the chair and sat down at the table. Catherine poured her a large glass of wine and a small one for herself.

'To… life.' toasted Catherine, 'To the love of life.'

Isabella picked up her glass, still feeling as if she should be a little restrained and clinked it against Catherine's… 'To the love of life.'

'You seem very cheerful today?' asked Isabella.

'I am, all my plans are slowly coming together. There will be a few changes soon but…' she thought for a moment and took another sip if wine, 'it will all be for the better.' She smiled again at Isabella.

'I am glad, replied Isabella,' I am happy that everything is going so well for you.' Catherine had never really listened to the eastern European inflection in Isabella's voice before, the intonation, emphasis and nuance was all wrong, but her dedication, reliability and honesty was beyond question. She had been their children's nanny as well as their cleaner and occasional cook since they had moved to the new house back in early 1983. Max and Claudia had taken to her almost immediately as had Blake and Catherine.

'If I tell you something, can we keep it between ourselves?' asked Catherine.

Isabella didn't answer immediately, but took another sip of the Pinot. 'A secret?' she asked inquisitively?

'Yes,' replied Catherine.

'From whom?' enquired Isabella whispering over the rim of her wine glass. There was a clearly evident hint of caution in her tone. The confidant had now become the erudite inquisitor.

'Everybody,' replied Catherine, 'for now,' she added as a qualification.

'Is it important?' asked Isabella with a subtle hint of caution.

'Very much so,' said Catherine.

Isabella took another sip of wine finishing the glass and put the glass back on the table.

'Would it jeopardise my position?' she asked with measured restraint, the sagacious Germanic influence now coming into play. She was as curious as any woman would be a similar position, someone who could be about to be entrusted with a confidentiality that would strengthen the bond between employer and employee, but with any secret comes responsibility, accountability, obligation and risk. Once you were partnered to a conspiracy there was an implied mutual declaration of intention to deceive and absolutely no going back to the ways things were before. The dynamics of a relationship change from that point forward and whatever dye had been cast could not be uncast. All this weighed on her mind. She wondered if maybe she had overinflated this simple request way beyond its own importance. Possibly, possibly not, but she had been asked once before to keep a secret and it had not ended well.

'No, not at all.' said Catherine, refilling Isabella's glass to the top while waiting nervously for her reply. She too began to wonder whether she may have disturbed the delicate equilibrium that currently existed and had now compromised their relationship by engendering Isabella to answer a question that she may not wish to answer, in fact a question she may not even have wished had been asked, but that moment had passed. The question was in reality already answered for if Isabella declined to answer she would forever be in possession of knowledge of unspecified information and therefore by default considered to be an accomplice to something despite being unaware of what precisely she was an accomplice to.

'You can tell me if you wish,' replied Isabella reluctantly. She reasoned that on the balance of probability if was more likely than not to be something innocuous and of no consequence.

Catherine didn't answer straight away; in her mind she was attempting to carefully choreograph what she was about to say, so that the salient facts were unveiled in the correct order of significance. How she revealed and conveyed what she was going to say was almost as important as what she was about to say. She took another sip of wine then slowly placed the glass down on the table. 'I'm having another baby.' she waited for Isabella's reaction.

'Oh!' exclaimed Isabella loudly,' she was stunned for a moment her lips drifting slightly apart in astonishment, before her face lit up in relief and joy as any hint of the apprehension that had previously dominated her thoughts quickly faded away. All thoughts of something unpleasant gone in a flash, all instantly replaced by the simple joy of Catherine's impending birth. 'That is absolutely marvellous,' said Isabella, 'I am so happy for you, for you and for Mr Thornton and for Max and Claudia, you are all so very lucky. This will be a lovely time for you all, I am so..

'So how far pregnant are you.'

'Three months,' replied Catherine smiling as she tried to work out in her mind which particular day it had been and where they were.

'Oh,' said Isabella, 'should you be…?' she gestured to the wine glass Catherine was holding.

'No,' replied Catherine, 'no I shouldn't.'

'So it will be here for...'

'There's a little more…' interrupted Catherine, now looking a little pensive.

'More?' said Isabella, still looking overjoyed at the news, 'don't tell me… it's twins, yes? If you are worried about me I can help you with them, babies are not a problem. I will be here to help you all the time you need me no matter what.'

'This could be a problem,' muttered Catherine.

Isabella's expression changed almost immediately. 'A problem, oh I am sorry…' her hands shot across the table to take hold of Catherine's, holding them both tightly. 'We can deal with this together if you want, now I understand why a secret.'

'No, I don't think you do,' said Catherine.

'So what is the problem?' asked Isabella.

Catherine didn't speak straight away, but looked at Isabella and carefully studied the genuine concern and honesty in how she spoke and how she looked, and wondered if all that would change immeasurably possibly even irretrievably once she had told her what she was about to say next.

'Blake is not the father.'

'I'm sorry,' said Isabella, not certain if she had just heard what she thought she had just heard.

'I said.. Blake is not the father, I've been having an affair with… and well… he's the father.'

'Oh, I see,' said Isabella, now a little subdued and confused by the confession. 'But how, why… or maybe I shouldn't ask,' but she continued, suddenly realising her revised position in the arrangement. 'Do you want to tell me more, or do you want to just leave it there?'

'Of course I have to tell you more, I want to tell you everything, I don't really know what is happening, that is why I wanted to talk to somebody, to you, the only person I can trust with this.'

'Don't you have close friends or family you can talk to?' asked Isabella.

'No, not really and it would put all our friends in a very awkward position, we have known all them for so long. That's why I needed to tell you.'

'I see said,' said Isabella. She took hold of Catherine's hands again and held them tightly, 'Do you love him?'

'Yes,' replied Catherine, 'I love him more than anything in the world, I have never known a love like this, I… I would give up my children for him if I had to.'

Isabella was slightly taken aback by the that stark declaration, she had in her past had many relationships, some with married men and had known many friends who had had relationships that had come and gone, but none as far as she was aware had ever come close to avowing such a sacrifice for another man.

'What do you mean?' asked Isabella.

'I have to be with him and our baby, I can't continue to live with Blake... hopefully he will allow me to take the children with me, but if not...'

'I am sure it would never come to that.' replied Isabella reassuringly.

'Probably not, Blake is not an unreasonable man. He will see what is best for them.'

'Are you going to tell him tonight?' asked Isabella.

'No, I'll tell him tomorrow, we'll then have the weekend to decide what is going to happen.'

'So you don't need me to come over?'

'No we'll be OK, I'll call you Sunday night if anything has changed, if I don't I call you, I'll see you on Monday as usual.' Catherine picked up the bottle, but it was empty. 'Ah,' she turned to Issy, 'should I open another?' before remembering she had just indicated that she wouldn't be drinking anymore for a while.

'I can open one just for you,' said Catherine.

'No, I had better go,' said Issy 'I don't want to be arrested for being drunk in charge of a bicycle and you will have to give up the wine as well... for a while.'

'Yes I know, I have been easing back slowly anyway, but now...' she made a "cut the throat" gesture with her hand and frowned. 'I will have to give it up completely.'

'I can drink yours for you and tell you how it feels if that would help,' suggested Issy. They both laughed and then Issy got up and put on her coat. She turned to Catherine who was now standing, but in floods of tears. Isabella took hold of her and they both held each other very tightly.

'I really don't know what is happening to me Issy, this is just not like me at all. I've never looked at another man not since the day I first saw Blake and then suddenly, a few months ago, we met and now my head is all over the place, it's almost as if he has cast a spell on me.'

'We'll talk some more next week, but if you want to call me over the weekend that's OK any time.' Issy picked up her bag and left and Catherine sat back down in her chair and stared out of the window, trying to figure out what had happened over the last seven months almost without her realising it. In fact it had really started before that, but she just hadn't realised it.

She went back into the larder and brought out another Pinot Grigio and slowly inserted the cork screw, thinking about what she had said and what she had done. Then realising that she shouldn't have anymore, she pushed the cork back into the bottle and put it into the fridge.

Chapter 22

April 1984
Saturday.

The next morning Blake was quietly sitting at the desk in his study idly reading the newspaper when Catherine came in with two cups of coffee, one of which she placed on the desk. She took a sip from her cup before sitting down opposite Blake.

'Thank you darling, are the kids up yet? said Blake looking up.

'No not yet, I wanted to have a word with you first, there is something we need to talk about.'

'Oh,' said Blake light-heartedly, laying the newspaper down on the deck, 'that's sound a bit ominous.' He pulled a curious "have I been a naughty boy" type expression,' to humour her, but noticed she didn't appear to be responding as he had expected, in fact she didn't appear to be responding at all.

'Is this important?' asked Blake, now a little concerned about her expression or to be more precise the lack of.

'I think it is,' replied Catherine quietly.

'Oh,' said Blake, the corners of his mouth quickly dropping, as he adroitly adopted a more sombre expression. 'Have you dinged the car?' he ventured in a cheerful, but restrained vein, 'because if you have, that's really not important.'

'No I haven't dented the car, it's nothing like that.'

'Oh,' said Blake now in mortal danger of an accusation of over use of the interjection. He could sense that this conversation was drifting into the realms of unchartered waters.

'I have a confession to make,' said Catherine, who for some peculiar reason was beginning to sense the initial anxiety and apprehension that had kept her awake all night, was fast fading away and being swiftly replaced by an unexpected inner strength, a strength she never knew she had. For a brief moment her mind flashed back to thoughts of Gideon and to them making love, and for some reason this too seemed to stimulate and energize her to continue unabated with what she had decided she must say and do today.

Blake didn't say anything sensing that this was not the opportune moment to speak. He opened the palms of his hands to her as if to say "the floor is yours."

'I'm leaving you… I've met somebody else, we're in love and I want to move in with him… and I'm having his child.' There she'd said it all. Succinctly, no rambling, no vacillation or prevarication.

'Oh,' said Blake, for the fourth time, but the threat of mortal danger had already flashed passed having now cut him down in its wake. 'You're leaving me?… You've met somebody? I don't understand.' His arms fell to the table. 'Is it something I've done? because I'm a little confused… I wasn't really aware we had a problem.'

He looked stunned and couldn't have moved out of his chair even if he wanted to. His body had turned to lead, so heavy he didn't have the strength to do anything… it felt much the same as that moment eighteen months ago when Gideon had told him in his office about the change of name of The Chapter Room. It was so totally unexpected and immediately brought to mind all manner of disconnected thoughts that had been quietly dwelling in the back of his brain, suddenly they were coming together and starting to make sense.

'And you say you are having a baby? but how? I don't mean how, I mean when, when did you even find the time, no that's the wrong question. What I want to say is are you really leaving me and is it an irretrievable situation?' In these situations all the right questions are asked, but they always come out sounding wrong.

At the very moment that he was being confronted by a full frontal attack on his life and virtually every aspect of it he was already looking for ways to resolve the problem and retrieve the situation. This was Blake the man she had fallen in love with and these were the personal traits that she had always so admired in him. It was his honesty, his integrity, his ability to make her laugh when everything was going wrong and his resolute refusal to except anything that was detrimental to their relationship that had so overwhelmed her when they first met, but there was little chance of a witticism rectifying this situation.

They, Catherine at first and then Max and Claudia had always come first, everything else always a distant second. That had been the priority for nearly ten years up until nearly two years ago when all of a sudden everything had begun to change, starting almost exactly at the same time as The Chapter Room had first appeared in Blake's office. But that was all in the past, and today all that would count for nothing, for she wanted something else now, something that apparently only Gideon could give her.

'Yes, I am leaving and it is an irretrievable situation. I am truly, truly sorry, but I met him and we have fallen in love and I'm not in love with you anymore… it's as simple as that. It's nothing to do with you, no I'm sorry that's not what I mean, what I meant to say was, you have done absolutely nothing to cause this, you are the innocent party, this is all me, all my fault. I drifted into something I didn't really understand and now I have completely lost control. I can't live without him, I am so sorry.'

'As simple as that?' You've met someone else,' replied Blake picking out the phrases that seemed so unreal. 'You make it sound so matter of fact, it's almost clinical the way you have conceived this... this plan, this devious plan and then executed it with utter brutal efficiency completely fulfilling your objective without a shred of compassion or consideration for the enormous devastating consequences it will have on us all. Do you know what? I am absolutely stunned beyond belief by this. For the first time in my life I am at a complete and utter loss for the right words to say to convey exactly how I feel.' It was as if his cognitive powers had been temporarily withdrawn due to overwhelming pressure and he had been left floundering around, flapping like a stranded fish on the mud when the tide had suddenly left it behind, he was having to default to pedestrian anecdotal aphorisms and clichés.

'How long have you planned it?' he exclaimed, his voice now raised slightly which was unusual for him. Blake could feel the vitriol building up inside, something he thought he would never experience, but here it was, the bitterness the venom the anger and the hostility, manifesting bile out of nothing and delivering itself in plentiful supply.

'I didn't plan anything, it just happened.'

'How long as it been going on for?' asked Blake, now totally bereft of any feeling and temporarily lost deep in thought juggling days and times in his head. Of course, it had been possible, he had been working late two or three nights a week on Gideon's book for well over a year, as it continued to sell at a prodigious rate all over the world. Sales had now passed the thirty million mark, and they were now deep into negotiations for the screen rights with three separate companies, but it all required intense personal involvement and direct management. That meant even more of his time, time that he had deprived his family of and now he was paying the price for that act of abject carelessness.

'Just over seven months as an affair, but it started really before that.' Catherine was being brutally honest which if anything made the pain even worse.

'What do you mean it started before that? when did it start?' shouted Blake.

Catherine pulled back slightly, a little surprised at his raised voice, it was undoubtedly fully justified, but she couldn't recall him ever shouting at her once in all the years they had been together. This was the final straw that had broken the donkeys back. Suddenly she became a little reluctant to be more specific, but she had no choice. The proverbial genie was now out of the bottle and all the nasty little grubby details would come out eventually, so she might just as well get it over with and make a clean breast of it now. Not an idiom that she would normally use, but that was the first thing that came into her head. She quickly wracked her brain to ensure she was correct with the dates... before continuing...

'Boxing day 1982,' she declared with perfect precision.

'Boxing fucking day? How the fuck did you meet somebody on…. oh fuck me… its fucking Gideon isn't it?' He was usually a little more inventive with expletives when the need arose, but today, at this particular moment nothing else would have served as well. Nothing else existed in the English language, he knew that much. The Anglo Saxons had much to be thanked for in that department.

'Catherine said nothing, but that was enough.'

'So that little bastard that I have been working my bollicks of to make rich repays me by shagging my wife.' There had to be some sort of metaphorical analogy in the irony, but for the life him he couldn't see what it was.

'It wasn't quite like that, it didn't start out like that it..'

'It never does, does it?' interrupted Blake 'but that doesn't matter now, it's how it finishes that matters.'

'Quite,' said Catherine, staring intently at Blake trying not to second guess what he would say next. Blake appeared to have settled down a little now.

'I can't believe what he has done to us, I can't believe what you have done to us.' Blake was quieter now, the moment of fiery condemnation had now subsided, he hadn't come to terms with it, but he realised the shouting and swearing wasn't going to get them anywhere. 'So what's the plan?'

'Well I don't know actually, this isn't a plan, we just agreed that I should tell you today and then work it out from there.'

'What about the children?' asked Blake realising that they were as much a part of this as he was.

'I was hoping you wouldn't object to them coming with me, off course you will be able to see them whenever you wanted, and we won't be living that far away. Gideon has a..

'I know where Gideon's fucking house is,' interrupted Blake bluntly, but with remarkable sanguinity under the circumstances.

'Yes, of course you do, I forgot, I'm sorry.'

'I'll not fight you over the children...' Blake looked remarkably calm now, almost disturbingly so and strangely in control of the raw emotions which were no doubt boiling up inside.

'But I thought that..' started Catherine sounding a little surprised.

'No, I would love them to stay here, but if we went to court I would lose, men always loose and probably be even worse off. And obviously Gideon now has far money that I do to spend on lawyers.'

'I promise you, that you will have all the contact you want with them,'

Blake smiled, one thing he knew about Catherine above everything else was she kept to her word, and if he had that than that's was all he needed. She had been totally upfront with him about the affair, and she had bitten hard on the bullet of anguish and broken the news to him face to face, when she could of so easily just have slipped away during the day, any day.

'OK, OK,' said Blake, 'I will leave it to you to let me know when...'

'Thank you,' said Catherine.

'What for?' said Blake.

'For being so civilised about it all.' Blake smiled.. 'I love you Catherine and this changes nothing, you may not be here anymore, but I'll still love you remember that, and there is always hope, where there is life there is always....'

It was an unusual thing to say thought Catherine, but Blake was an unusual man in so many ways.

Catherine began to feel a tear welling up and turned to quickly leave Blake's office before collapsing in tears in the lounge, but this time unlike all the other occasions when she had begun to cry, Blake didn't come out to comfort her, for he was already crying his heart out too, but alone.

Chapter 23

Sunday.

Blake sat alone is his study on the Sunday morning watching the sun come up and listening to the dawn chorus. He had tried to get some sleep in the spare bedroom, but that had not proved particularly successful. He had spent the majority of the night raking over what had happened and how it was that the manuscript of Prospect Road had so methodically detailed the events of his earlier life and then segued almost seamlessly into predicting the events that were happening right now.

The manuscript appeared to be the instrument through which those changes had been applied. He considered whether not reading the book could have any effect on the eventual outcome. Maybe the events only became real once he had read them. Maybe he should stop reading it, no he couldn't do that, maybe he should destroy it, no he couldn't do that either, there would be absolutely no going back then, at least at the moment there was a chance.

Blake began to formulate a pattern, a sort of paradigm for what was happening, but it still didn't make any sense. Somehow he knew that everything that had happened over the last few years appeared to be part of a much larger plan. Somehow the book was trying to communicate with him… send him a message, but what was the message, that's what he could fathom out. It all seemed to go back to when Reggie had died in December 1981 and Blake had taken over the company, that's when everything started to happen. The manuscript for Prospect Road arrived only a few months later and then in August 1982 Gideon Drew's manuscript arrived.

It wasn't just Catherine leaving him, that was just a tiny part of something much bigger, but what and why and more importantly how could he find out. If he could answer that question than maybe he could change everything. Maybe even put it back to the way it was. Every plan no matter how meticulously it is designed has a flaw, a minute flaw that if carefully exploited could ultimately bring about the destruction of the entire plan.

The Germans, the Romans, the Greeks, Napoleon and the French, Attila and the Hunnic horde, Genghis Khan and the Mongols, even the English, they all had plans to conquer world, but each plan had a tiny flaw and each plan eventually failed quite profoundly. It was a vague analogy out of all proportion to his situation, but it was the first to come to mind. There had to be a link, a thread of commonality between their demise and his situation.

There was also the element of chance, the unknown factor, that too could affect the final outcome.

It had all started with the manuscript for Prospect Road and it's writer Mr Anthony Theodore Clackle. Blake's office had never managed to contact Clackle despite many attempts and there had to be a reason for that, that was where he would begin.

He opened the wall safe in the study, took out the manuscript for Prospect Road and laid it down on the desk.

He would need to read the whole manuscript again to try to figure out what the hidden message was, but before he did anything he would make a fresh pot of coffee. It was all very quiet upstairs, so Blake made the black coffee making the least amount of noise possible and took it back into his study.

He turned over the first page and then out of habit, a ritual that he had only adopted when reading this particular book, he flipped the pages over to the end page. He couldn't see his signature so he flipped back a page and there it was at the bottom of the final page of Chapter fourteen. So in the space of only a few weeks one more page had been added to the story. It wasn't in fact a whole page just a heading and some notes...

<u>Notes for Prospect Road Chapter Fifteen.</u>

In this Chapter Kate decides to leave Thomas after starting an affair with the writer Gideon Drew.

She discusses affair with her housekeeper?

Expand..... ....

Thomas considers suicide.?

Kate discover she is pregnant with Gideon's baby?

Kate Moves in with Gideon.

Gideon has cast a spell ???

Who is the mysterious Gideon Drew?

Julian searches for Gideon. Does he find him?

Is anybody going to die?

What would happen if Gideon...?

The details were almost identical to what was happening now, some were a little enigmatic, but the warning was there, clear to see but he had not realised what Anthony had been trying to tell him. He wondered how long they had been written.

That was it short and sweet. Just a few words on what the next Chapter could bring. In fact life had moved on well past this point, for the first time the reality had overtaken the fiction. Then Blake thought about that for a few moments. Maybe as the full chapter had not yet been written, there was a possibility that the chapter content, i.e. the characters, narrative, plotline and final outcome could change radically, if so how exactly could he do that. There was possibly a time element involved, but how would he find that out.

Clackle had to be the answer, he knew he had to find him, he was the only person who could provide an answer to this puzzle. Maybe there was a chance he could save his marriage, his sanity and probably his life if he could work it out in time.

Chapter 24

Monday.

On the Monday morning he spoke briefly to Catherine before leaving for the office and she confirmed that she would not be moving out until the beginning of the following week to allow them to prepare the children for what was happening and to make all the other necessary arrangements. It all sounded remarkably affable and civilised, but Blake refused to be baited by the calmness with which Catherine appeared to be handling the transitional stage. As before on the Friday night it had all been conducted with a frighteningly detached and dispassionate air. It was as if they were just arranging to go away on holiday to Devon for a few days, not making what was for him the most dramatic change in his life ever.

When Blake arrived at the office at just after ten, he almost immediately pulled out the file they had on Theodore Clackle. It was still very thin.

Jamie popped his head round Blake's office door

'Morning Blake, good weekend? Blake just mumbled something incoherent.

'Good, good...' replied Jamie not taking too much notice, 'look I need to go over some figures with you sometime today. It's the calculations the lawyers have come up with for the screen rights for "The Room" so...'

The office staff invariably reduce a book's title to something slick and catchy given half a chance, the easiest option normally being the book titles initial letters or possibly the last word. It all sounded very clicky and buzzy and invoked a sort of "in the elite club" aura for the people dealing with a particular publication. It was completely artificial, all very pseudo and occasionally harmlessly derogatory, but it gave them a sense of self-importance, which probably helped compensate for the paltry wages they received for working on blockbuster books of dubious quality. In any publishers office you can always find a few members of staff who truly believe their own humble scribblings are nothing short of unpublished masterpieces..

'…we need to get everything finished off before we can present it to Gideon,'

Blake looked up, 'No problem, just give me a couple of hours to go through this.' He waved the "Road" file at Jamie.

'Prospect Road?' said Jamie, I thought we'd dumped that one on the back boiler, isn't half of it still missing or something, bit of a dead duck?'

'No I've…' Blake hesitated for a moment. There had been considerable confusion the last time they discussed the manuscript because of the missing chapters, and they had turned the office upside down looking for it, without success. It would now appear a little unusual for Blake to suddenly produce a large proportion of the missing section out of fresh air, without a reasonable explanation, and of course he didn't have one, not one he was prepared to throw into an open arena for discussion.

'I was just wondering if there had been any more communication from Mr Clackle, I thought we could follow it up if…' He was fumbling around and didn't sound particularly convincing. Jamie gave him a curious glance.

'I would have thought you had enough on your plate right now with The Room,' asked Jamie curiously.

'I do, I do, but that won't last forever I just thought...'

'We did receive a letter from him about a week ago, it's in there,' he pointed to the file. 'I didn't mention it because we were a bit busy with…'

'Oh, right I have a look then. Come back about twelve and we can go out for some lunch and go over the figures OK?'

'Right,' said Jamie, smiling while shutting the door as he left the office.

Blake opened the file again and took out the letter that he had never seen from Clackle and read it.

June 14th 1984
Clanford & Fox Publishers Agents
Denmark Street
London

Dear sirs (or madam),

Many apologies for troubling you, but I was wondering whether you had had a chance to read my manuscript for Prospect Road. I appreciate that certain elements of the story may appear a little far-fetched, even for "Fiction", but I can assure you that this story is based in part on first-hand information from a very reliable source. I felt driven to write the story as I believe my time left on this earth will not be for much longer and I must finish it and hopefully find a publisher before I am done.

I have no idea who the story is really about, but I know that it relates to somebody who must be aware of what is happening to them and there is also a family connection.

This is a simply a message to that soul or souls. There are forces in play that militate against me for writing this letter to you and I feel their powers growing stronger day by day as they try to impede every word I right, but nevertheless I feel I must do the best I can to have the work published even at the risk of death.

Please excuse the histrionic quality of this letter it was not intended that way, but that is genuinely how I feel about it. Hopefully you will be able to respond to let me know whether you would be interested in considering publication, but if not I would be grateful if you could return the manuscript as I do not have the strength to write another copy and I would like to send it to another publisher. I am still physically able to discuss this book with you, if necessary, but am not sure for how much longer.

Best regards
Theodore A. Clackle
Farthingales,
Guildford

The address was in a little village just outside of Petersfield, which wasn't actually too far away from where Blake lived, probably only about forty five minutes by car. It appeared to be some sort of hospitalisation facility. Blake made a note of the address and put the letter back into the file and dropped the file on his desk.

On the Tuesday he phoned the office and left a message to say he would be in late as he was visiting a client.

He stood outside of the towering main entrance to Farthingale's Dignity and comfort Care Centre and looked up at what had obviously once been somebody's ancestral home, at a time when money was no object to maintaining such a grandiose property, and every stately home had aspirations beyond its station. A once beautiful building set in glorious grounds now sadly reduced to being an "utilitarian establishment" for the care of the wealthy elderly and infirmed he presumed. He made his way in to the main reception area where he saw a very large smartly dressed woman in a business suit and sensible shoes remonstrating with someone who appeared to be a cleaner. On seeing Blake enter reception, she immediately curtailed her conversation, made a small gesture to the other person and proceeded to marched towards Blake in a distinctly military fashion with what could only be described as a "business smile", type expression.

'Can I be of any assistance,' she politely enquired, leaning her head slightly to one side as she said it, 'My name is Brenda, the senior day manager.'

'I must apologise for not making an appointment, but I wonder whether it would be possible to speak to one of your...' he paused for moment not sure of the correct nomenclature... 'Patients?' he tentatively tendered.

'We prefer to call them house guests,' replied Brenda, still smiling, but now with just a tiny hint of snobbery. It was obviously a very expensive establishment, if it had this sort of defence system in place, thought Blake.

'Yes,' replied Blake, 'A guest by the name of Clackle,'

'Clackle,' enquired Brenda, 'ah you mean Anthony Theodore, don't you?'

'Yes, that's right Anthony Theodore Clackle.'

'We prefer to use their full names here, it avoids possible confusion.'

'I understand,' replied Blake demurely.

'A very nice gentleman if I may say so. I had the pleasure of meeting him when he first contacted us that was before...' her expression suddenly changed and she hesitated about going any further before reaching for a register under the desk.

'Oh,' said Blake, unsure where to go with that observation.

There was silence for a few moments while Brenda flipped through some records. Blake glanced around the impressive reception area, which had obviously once been the grand entrance to the house. Probably once filled with classic antique furniture and family portraits before the removal of the classical arrangement and the installation of some smaller temporary offices, two other reception desks and various company marketing posters and paraphernalia. All of which, somewhat abrasively raped the original style of a room that had stood proud for hundreds of years until now. He wondered if any of the great events of history had begun life within the walls of this impressive building.

'Yes, he's in the Waterloo Wing, in....' said Brenda, interrupting Blake's historical meanderings. She flipped over another page, 'The Copenhagen Suite.' She glanced up at Blake with an air of superior intellect and pronounced, this with a smiling expression as if it were some sort of rarely known fact, which she had probably heard on a television quiz show. 'That was named after...'

Blake interrupted, `The horse, ridden by The Duke of Wellington at Waterloo 1815.'

'Ah' said Brenda, acknowledging that it was obviously more widely known than she had anticipated. 'Not to many people know that.' Her smile had now turned to a frown.

'He was stuffed,' said Blake blankly.

'Who, the Duke of.. replied the lady a little indignantly and sounding surprised before Blake interrupted again.

'The horse, the horse was stuffed.... after it died that is, not the Duke.'

Brenda half smiled, and murmured something quietly to herself.

'Are you a relative?'

'No, just a business acquaintance... and a friend,' he promptly added. He lied a little, believing it to be a necessary falsehood in the circumstance.

'Oh I see, well he's not particularly communicative you know.'

'Oh,' said Blake, 'What do you mean?'

'He's virtually paralyzed, head to toe.'

'That's strange, he wrote to me only a few weeks ago and he sounded perfectly OK then.'

'Things have changed somewhat dramatically since then I'm afraid,' replied Brenda.

'Can he speak?'

'Not really, not now, as far as I am aware.'

'Oh well, we will have to get through as best we can with sign language wont we,' replied Blake optimistically. He had come this far and he wasn't going to give up now.

'He can't move his hands,' said Brenda reinforcing her previous statement.

'We'll manage,' said Blake, smiling.

'Follow me, it's quite a long walk.' Blake obliged and fell in beside her, briskly marching down the main corridor.

'Interesting term Dignity and Comfort Care Centre, is it a hospital or a recuperation unit?' Blake asked innocently.

Brenda stopped and turned to face Blake with a vacant expression of curiosity.

'Neither. Do you not know what he is here for? she asked, once again appearing a little indignant, but that was her way.

'I know he's ill,' replied Blake bluntly, instantly realising that, that statement sounded a little crass.

'He's dying, and soon. That's what we do here, we help them in their last few days.'

'I apologise, I didn't realise he was that ill.'

'He wasn't,' she replied sharply. 'He came in to see us about a month ago and told us that although he looked perfectly fine and there was nothing wrong with him, he had had a premonition that he would suddenly deteriorate very fast and probably die before the end of this month, it was all very precise.'

'He paid for everything upfront including collection from the hospital, and then on the exact day he had predicted he collapsed, was diagnosed with a terminal brain tumour and was brought here.'

'But it's the twenty eighth today,' said Blake.

'Quite,' said Brenda, with a very scornful smile that said "You're quick aren't you" but she didn't actually say the words. 'So we are not expecting him to last beyond Friday, he's been right on everything else so far, so we see no reason to doubt that he will be correct with that as well.' She exuded a sense of matriarchal wilful arrogance.   A defender of the dying and her job was to ensure that guests died in comfort and dignity and hopefully on time, but while under her care they would be extended every possible curtesy, and the living well they were of secondary importance as far as she was concerned at this stage. She resumed walking and Blake followed her.

After a few minutes of twists and turns they arrived at "Waterloo" and made their way to The Copenhagen Suite. She showed Blake into the suite and proceeded to leave before giving Blake one final instruction.

'Try not to tire him out, he's only got three days, so he deserves to spend them peacefully.' She obviously really did care about her guests. Maybe he should book up for here for when his time came he wondered, but hopefully not just yet he added as an afterthought.

The nurse who was just finishing feeding Anthony smiled charmingly at Blake, before pushing the meal trolley towards the door. She closed it behind her and they were alone. He walked over to the bed to see a man who looked roughly the same age as he was and yet he was preparing to die. Blake suddenly realised how short life really was.

Anthony just stared forward, his eyes appeared glazed and fixed.

'My name is Blake Thornton, I work for Clanford and Fox book publishers, you sent me a manuscript.. Prospect Road.' There was no response.

'You've written the book about my life, but I don't understand how you know so much about me and why.' Still there was no response.

'I have met Gideon Drew and we are publishing his book The Chapter Room, the book you mention in Prospect Road...'

Almost at the moment Blake mentioned Gideon's name Anthony's head began to turn very slightly towards him and his eyes widened, suddenly becoming alert. He started to say something, but it was no more than a faint whisper. Blake drew closer to Anthony and he spoke again.

'You may never take my soul...'

'You may never take my soul,' repeated Blake.

'Clackle smiled as best he could with his eyes for his facial muscles no longer functioned.

'Who?' said Blake.

Clackle look disturbed, obviously frustrated that he couldn't just pronounce the words. Blake was beginning to understand.

'Is it Gideon?' asked Blake. Anthony relaxed and his eyes smiled again. So it was something to do with Gideon.

'The manuscript you sent me, it appears to be writing itself... is that really happening?'

Anthony's eyes smiled, they had a form of contact, if he smiled it meant yes or he agreed.

'Why is it doing...' he stopped, he couldn't ask a question he could only put the assumption, that made it harder and he would have to think about how to reword the questions as assumptions if he was to get anywhere.

'If… ' he paused for a second not sure if he wanted to know the answer to his next question, if it wasn't the answer he was hoping for than all was lost anyway so what had he too loose… 'If the manuscript that I have only writes a brief summary of what might happen in the next unwritten chapter does that mean… ' he paused again… 'Does that mean that.. the chapter could turn out differently from the initial brief summary.' It sounded like a complicated question, but there was no easier to put it. Anthony thought about the question for a moment, he almost seemed to be running the option through his mind, to make sure he understood before answering. His face was still turned to Blake as slowly a smile came into his eyes. Blake's heart almost skipped a beat, at last there was a chance he could change everything, he just need to know how to change it.

'How can I change it?' asked Blake before realising he couldn't ask that question.

'Is there a way I can change it?' Anthony's eyes smiled

'But how? I don't know what questions to ask.' Now Blake was feeling frustrated almost as frustrated as Anthony must have felt.

Anthony's lips began to open and Blake drew closer.

It was almost inaudible, a ghostly whisper of just one word "share" it seemed to linger on Anthony's lips like a final breath slowly fading away, but what could that mean. Must he share something with somebody, but what and with whom and how could that make a difference, he was more confused now than when he had first arrived. Anthony may have given him some of the answers to the puzzle, but he had now replaced those with more unanswered questions.

Anthony turned his head back to face forward and his eyes closed, he was not going to utter another word that day.

There were so many other questions he wanted to ask; Would the rest of the Prospect Road still carry on writing itself if Anthony died? Why had the complete book been sent to the publishers in the first place with an ending, but now only the first fourteen chapters could be seen; Why in fact had the book been sent at all? Who was Gideon Drew?

Blake got up and gently touched Anthony's face. 'Thank you, thank you for everything.' Anthony's eyes smiled but Blake couldn't see it as Anthony's were shut. Blake said goodbye to Brenda who was now back at her main desk by the front door and gave her a card and asked her to contact him when….

Blake Drove home knowing that he had to have a discussion with Gideon at some stage, but he would have to reread Prospect Road first. There had to be a clue in there somewhere, relating to Anthony's final word that day.

Chapter 25

Tuesday.

Blake arrived home just after three o'clock, which was relatively early for him, but the desire to return to the office especially after visiting Anthony had, for obvious reasons declined dramatically over the last few days. He had always been a highly motivated individual and an enthusiastic employer to work for. His driving passion had always enthused everyone to work as industriously as he did and this is what had made the company successful. No one complained about occasional late hours that had to be worked to get a project finished or even coming in at weekends if necessary, that was the commitment you signed up for, it was never going to be a nine to five job.

Book publishing was not a profession for the faint hearted, in fact it wasn't a profession at all - it was an art form almost a vocation as much as writing was. It required complete and absolute dedication, it was nearer to a religion than a business. The publisher has to believe in something, when there is absolutely no tangible evidence available one way or the other, that the work in question had any commercial worth. He has to rely on his own gut instinct and very little else. That is what all publishers depended upon, this and their judgement based experience.

Their business succeeds or fails, lives or dies on this alone. There is nobody alive who can truly read a book and say with absolute certainty that it will be popular and be a success, but everyday publishers make that call, because that is what they do, their very existence depends on it.

It was for this reason that Blake decided it would be better that he did not go in, not at least until he had come to terms with the proposed changes that were about to take place in his personal life. His frustration and bitter frame of mind would undoubtedly spill over in the office, and that would create a tension, which would affect the efficacy of what they had to do. He would return when certain matters had been resolved.

Max and Claudia greeted their loving father at the front door hugging him and chattering away about the things they had done that day. But Catherine, for the first time ever, held back in the hallway, not exactly cowering in the shadows, but carefully monitoring the situation and watching her family go through the routines they had gone through so many times before. Just for a split second Blake glanced upwards and caught her eye and gently smiled. Not the imposters triumphant grin over the minor victory of being greeted so warmly by his children when she had chosen to desert him, but the simple expression of joy and happiness and gratitude at being greeted at all. Something, which they had created together over the last ten years. It was magnanimous and generous and honest and courageous and it hurt. He wasn't sure how he would be greeted today.

She could feel bitter tears welling up behind her eyes and so quickly returned to the kitchen to carry on preparing dinner. Gideon had warned her that there would be distressing moments like this, during the few remaining days that she had agreed to stay at the house, so she was half prepared for it. But nothing could fully prepare her for the emotional trauma she had elected to receive. He had also told her that there would be moments when she would experience feelings of self-doubt and even thoughts of self-recrimination for what they were doing, but that too was a natural emotion in anybody as caring and considerate as she was, and she should take no notice. Standing back and quietly watching this act of theatrical drama play out in front her, Catherine wondered how it was that Gideon was so knowledgeable on such intimate feelings, had he possibly once experienced the same familiar situation that she was going through right now? If so when she wondered. Maybe she should ask him… or maybe not, maybe that could endanger the relationship that now existed between them. But then surely the essence of a long term relationship was the ability to be able to share all previous experiences without becoming emotionally involved in what was the past. Only by exposing them to daylight and open discussion could they be truly relegated to the position they truly deserved which was a part of ancient history, a part that had no place in the here and now. She would have to ask him one day when the time was right.

Eventually the greeting was over and Max and Claudia returned to the lounge. Blake popped his head into the kitchen.

'How are you, sorry about all that, I realise it was a bit...' asked Blake.

'I'm fine, fine thank you. You're early?' she seemed a little surprised, but no overly so.

'Yes I went to seem somebody and by the time I'd had some lunch it seemed pointless going to the office, so I thought I would call it a day.'

'Right,' said Catherine, she took a deep breath and plunged in, 'I've spoken to Gideon and he has said I don't need to take any of the furniture, so I will just be taking my clothes, some personal things, the children's clothes and some of their toys, but I will leave enough for the weekends, if that's OK?' she waited with some trepidation for his reply...

'Yes, yes that's fine,' replied Blake sounding surprisingly sanguine about her pronouncement almost as if he were not really concerned about the pedestrian trivialities of separation as he knew she would hardly pillage the house, that wasn't her way of doing things.

'Look..' said Blake continuing he was oddly hesitant, 'If you don't object, and I will understand if you do, but I would like to have a chat with Gideon, on neutral ground so to speak, just to discuss everything, you know what with me being his publisher and his agent and us having contracts and things...'

'That's not a problem Blake, I am sure we can work this whole thing out so that everything is just f...' she nearly said fine, but realised that that would be pushing his sensibilities just a little too far at this stage. 'We can talk, you can talk to him, I'm sure you won't come to blows, I will call him if you want me to and...'

'That would be good,' said Blake. 'Thank you.'

'Dinner won't be till five,' said Catherine, not really knowing how to continue the conversation, it was moments like this that were always going to be a bit awkward until she had left.   Tip toeing around on eggshells very accurately described the situation, something he was not accustomed to.

'That's fine,' said Blake I know I'm back a little early, I've got something to do anyway.   I wanted to start rereading a manuscript I have.'

'Oh,' said Catherine, trying to make conversation, 'which one, anything we've spoken about?'

'Prospect Road actually,' replied Blake.

'Prospect Road oh,' repeated Catherine, 'the odd unfinished one about…' she stopped, she didn't need to finish. He knew what she was going to say.

'Yes that's right, in parts it was, wasn't it?   All a little unusual, but then life has been a bit unusual lately.' He smiled then went to his study. He opened the manuscript for Prospect Road and began to read it until Catherine called him in for dinner at just after five. They all sat down and enjoyed the meal much as they always had done on weekends, when he wasn't working. It reminded him of just how much things were about to change, but he didn't let it show.

'I've spoken to Gideon and he has suggested that maybe you meet him at the Green Dragon in the village,' said Catherine as she was clearing the plates away.

'Can we come to see Uncle Gideon,' chipped in Max.

Blake looked at Catherine slightly surprised at Max's comment, 'Uncle?'

'That's what I've told them to call him for now, and they do know him…'

'But Uncle?' said Blake with just a touch of indignation.

'It's all I could think of,' apologised Catherine.

Blake shrugged his shoulders and let that go, 'when?'

'Can you do lunchtime tomorrow? I know you have the office but maybe..'

Blake interrupted, 'That's not a problem, in fact I've decided not to go in again until you move out next week, I won't be able to concentrate with what's going on, so it seemed pointless. Don't worry, I won't cause you any..' he paused for a moment searching for the right word, 'difficulty,' he landed on, but not very convincingly, 'you know what I mean.'

Catherine smiled, she knew Blake well enough to know he would keep his word. Blake smiled back at Catherine then returned to his study to continue reading Prospect Road.

~~~~

Wednesday

The next day Blake arrived at Green Dragon at the appointed time. Gideon was already sitting outside nursing a pint with another one on the table.

'I got you one in, bitter isn't it?'

'Yes that's fine, thank you,' replied Blake.

'He spontaneously put his hand out to shake Gideon's and immediately withdrew it realising that the gesture was not appropriate under the circumstances, historically the reason was to show you didn't have a weapon in your hand, he didn't have, but had considered it. Gideon made a mental note and smiled at Blake.

'I understand,' said Gideon, 'look… Blake,' said Gideon firmly, delicately managing to encapsulate the essence of condescension and patronage into one word, this wasn't what I had expected to happen, this whole thing came out of nowhere, it caught us both unaware, I hope you can understand that?'

Blake didn't answer immediately, but just sipped his beer. 'I am here because I don't want to upset my children by having arguments with Catherine in front of them. I know the way this works, I've read it enough times in the books I read every week to know all the likely scenarios and the ways these things play out so, that's why I am taking it like this.'

'Right I see,' said Gideon, taking a sip of his beer. sounding slightly relieved at Blake's admission.

'I do however have a couple of questions to ask, and I would be interested to know the answers if you are willing to help me,' said Blake with an oddly curious expression, 'it would help me to understand things much better if I could just clear up these anomalies.'

'Anything at all,' said Gideon, 'if it's about money or anything like that I can assure you, I will look after Catherine and the children, you need have no fears there.'

'No it's not about money, I know you have no problems in that department, I am your agent and your publisher after all, and as for my children, well I will have them at weekends and some of the holidays and obviously I will continue to support them anyway.'

Gideon half smiled his acknowledgement. 'So what is it?' asked Gideon.

'I went to see a man yesterday another writer as it is, his name was Clackle, Anthony Theodore Clackle, have you ever heard of him?'

'No can't say I have, why?' replied Gideon.

'That's odd because he seems to knows you, and it would appear in some detail.'

'Oh,' said Gideon, appearing perplexed.

'Nearly two years ago, he sent me a manuscript, about the life story of a man called Thomas Drayton and his wife, her name was Kate.'

'And?' said Gideon.

'Well it's odd you see this manuscript he sent me, it a very unusual manuscript for a number of reasons.'

'Oh,' replied Gideon, 'please explain?'

'Well firstly, and this is quite bizarre, the book recalls all of my past life right up to the present day, but under the pseudonym of this character called Thomas Drayton.'

'That is very unusual, but…' Blake interrupted

'That's not all you see it also writes itself.'

'I don't understand,' said Gideon, 'If this Clackle guy sent you a complete story then surely it's already written?'

'Well yes you'd think that wouldn't you,' said Blake, 'that sort of makes sense, but as I said this one is different.'

'How?' said Gideon sounding intrigued, but not overly so.

'Well when he sent the original manuscript to the office somebody else read it, Jamie if fact, you know Jamie my assistant don't you?'

'Yes of course, we speak most weeks.'

'Quite,' said Blake, 'well when he read it, it was complete, it was finished I fact. He liked it, so he gave it to me to read, and that's when it went a bit odd. You see when I read it, there was only two chapters and then nothing else just blank pages, but the next time I read it a few weeks later another chapter had appeared and the first two chapters had been filled out a bit more. You know how it works with writing and that's the way it went on up to chapter fourteen which was quite recent and that is where I am now.'

'Very mysterious,' said Gideon, 'that's really fascinating.'

'Ah no, that's still not the mysterious bit, that's yet to come. Getting back to Theodore Clackle, who as I said, I went to have a chat with, well he couldn't actually talk to me, he was completely paralyzed you see. Struck down very suddenly by a brain tumour, which oddly the doctors couldn't see only a few days previously, when he first complained about severe headaches, but hey presto a few days later it suddenly appeared and it's goodnight Vienna or Mr Clackle in this case.'

'Tragic,' remarked Gideon, continuing in his trite laconic vein, which was beginning to annoy Blake a little.

'Is he dead now?' asked Gideon.

'No not yet, but soon I think.' Blake thought that was an odd question, but didn't pursue it any further. The odd thing was Mr Clackle had already booked his place in the care facility a few weeks earlier, at a time when he was perfectly OK, he told them that he had had a premonition that something unpleasant was going to happen to him and he wanted to be fully prepared. You can imagine the care facility manager was very reluctant to process Mr Clackle's request on such a nebulous and unsubstantiated diagnosis of his imminent death, but never the less Mr Clackle insisted and offered to pay them in full in advance and so the booking was processed.

'Very proactive of Mr Clackle, it's a shame we don't all get similar premonitions, would make exit planning a lot easier,' said Gideon.

Blake thought that was also an unusual thing to say, not so much what he said, but more the way he had said it, it was almost as if he was aware of an option, but of course that wasn't possible. 'Anyway,' continued Blake, 'I happened to mention you and your book The Chapter Room in passing and do you know what, just those few words seemed to rally him round for a few moments. It was quite inspiring actually, his eyes lit up and he even managed to move his head slightly, which must have taken some considerable effort according to the nurse, and then he said something to me and do you know what he said?'

Gideon casually threw his arms up into the air in a mock expression of surprise and replied, 'I've absolutely no idea, but it must have been a seminal moment for you.' For the very first time Blake could see a small weakness in Gideon's lambent armour, it was just a tiny chink of darkness in a shining light, but something he hadn't seen before it was not alarm or even anxiety it was unease, he suddenly looked a little uneasy about something that he had said.

'It was very enigmatic almost cryptic, he said...' Blake paused to look directly into Gideon's eyes, he wanted to carefully gauge any reaction.

'Share,' quoted Blake in his best theatrical tenor.

'Just that and nothing else,' asked Gideon?

'No just that, but he appeared very anxious about it.'

'Probably delirious, it's the drugs they can do that.'

'Possibly, but to me it seemed to be the mention of your name that stirred him.'

'Well maybe he has read my book and was making a suggestion, that's the effect I am told it has on some people or maybe it's one of those philosophical things that people mutter in their last lucid moments on earth, lambent advice to those still living on how to live a better life?'

Blake thought that was oddly arrogant, but didn't comment.

'Yes, yes it does, that probably explains it's,' said Blake in a sort of conciliatory fashion, but his heart wasn't really in it, Gideon was still his biggest client, so he couldn't exactly tell him what he really thought.

'Anyway he goes on to mention a Julian Clackle who I believe was Anthony's father who could have been very helpful to me with the queries I have, but unfortunately he died about four years ago so I can't speak to him.

'So it's a sort of semi biographical novel?' asked Gideon.

'Yes, you're right, that's what I thought. Anyway, Julian and Rosemary, that's his wife had a son, who I am pretty sure was Anthony, but Julian also had an affair with a Mary Drayton the wife of Jonathan Drayton and they have a son called Thomas who marries Kate. They are the couple I mentioned earlier that appear to be similar to Catherine and myself. They also appear to be the main protagonists in the story.'

'It's getting complicated,' remarked Gideon.

'A bit, but if you can just bear with me I'm nearly there now, ' Gideon nodded, now here's the strangest thing, you see the character Gideon Drew, not you obviously because in the book this Gideon drew was born in eighteen ninety and he would be about ninety four now at least, and you...' Blake smiled wryly, 'obviously are not that old...... are you?' he added the last few words after a long pause.

'No I'm only twenty five,' said Gideon totally expressionless.

'Yes I realise that,' said Blake, 'Just twenty five, so lucky to be that young aren't you?'

Gideon didn't answer straight away, but just smiled while carefully mulling over what Blake had said. 'That is a fabulous story. And I'll tell you what, if by any chance your Mr Clackle doesn't finish it, and that's beginning to sound highly unlikely. And assuming it doesn't finish writing itself,' he made a strange fascial expression. 'I would love the opportunity to make a contribution and tidy it up for an acknowledgement of course before you publish it, if you want me to of course.'

'That's very generous of you Gideon, I will keep that in mind. Anyway I'm still not quite finished with the story, it turns out that Julian, that's Gideon's son had a sister, but for some reason they were split up at a very early age and adopted by different families. Julian meets Rosemary during the second world war somewhere down near Chichester in Sussex and not realising they are related they start a relationship which lasts throughout the war and eventually in nineteen forty six they are married and one year later have a son Anthony. Unfortunately, Anthony was born was with some retardation issues and physical problems which the doctors can't explain. Now not very long afterwards, it must have been about three years, by a stroke of incredible bad luck or unbelievable misfortune, whatever, Julian runs into a stranger on a train and they start talking and this stranger tells Julian something, something that he never thought possible.'

'What?' said Gideon a little prematurely.

'Well it was a long story, but to cut to the chase, he tells Julian that he and his wife Rosemary are in fact brother and sister and of course realising this, it immediately explains Anthony's problems. Not long after they get a divorce.

'Who was the stranger? asked Gideon.

'Can't remember, but it's in the manuscript, anyway that's it more or less it.'

'It's a wonderful story,' said Gideon.

'Well in a way yes I suppose it could be, but I still haven't mentioned some other minor details in the letters from Julian Clackle to Mary Drayton, you see in one of the last letters it mentions a Joshua Clanford...'

'Clanford.. my house is called Clanford, that's an odd coincidence,' remarked Gideon.

'Not really,' said Blake, 'You know him in a manner of speaking.'

'Do I?' replied Gideon, 'Who is he? asked Gideon innocently.

'Well he's the Clanford in Clanford and Fox Publishers, but of course he's dead now.'

'Now that is an odd coincidence,' remarked Gideon.

'Yes I thought so to start with, but there's a little more, this will probably help you quite a bit if you to decide to finish off Prospect Road. Apart from being a plagiarist, Joshua Clanford was a bit of a charlatan, drunk, gambler and a womaniser by all accounts and while he was out playing every night his wife Madeleine started an affair, and do you know who she had an affair with? and believe me this will surprise you...'

'I've no idea,' said Gideon, 'it all sounds absolutely fascinating.'

'Gideon Drew no less.' replied Blake, with an expression of abject surprise blended with the absolute certainty that it was no surprise at all to Gideon.

'Amazing,' said Gideon, 'My name sake no less, now that really is a good story. This Gideon sounds a right bastard.'

'Yes he does, doesn't he, but what I don't understand,' continued Blake, 'is why this Gideon should start an affair with Madeleine because by all accounts she was really very ugly, a bit of a gargoyle by all accounts. That is the mysterious bit that I don't understand, so if you could come up with a reason for Gideon taking up with Madeleine in the first place then we could be on our way to another winner.'

'Yes, we could,' said Gideon, 'I see what you mean.'

'Anyway, I will no doubt see you soon, so I will leave you with that conundrum and maybe you could think over the proposal re Prospect Road. If you want a copy let me know and I will have one sent over, and with regards to Catherine, well I do hope you treat her well, she doesn't deserve anything less despite what has happened.

'That's very magnanimous of you Blake and I really appreciate you taking such a civilised view on things.' Blake smiled even though deep down his heart was breaking, but there was no way he was going to let Gideon see that, he still had a few things to do before everything was completely settled. He finished off his pint and stood up to shake Gideon's hand and then walked away leaving Gideon for once in his life a little perplexed. Gideon stayed there for another half hour wondering why Blake was being so reasonable and accommodating, it wasn't something that he had factored into his plan.

Chapter 26

Wednesday.

Blake arrived back home just after four o'clock having driven around the countryside for a while running over the events of the past five days, but more particularly the last few hours. He thought back to last Friday when he had arrived home for the weekend with expectations of an enjoyable weekend, possibly visiting a country pub or maybe a country fair on Saturday and probably doing a bit of the essential shopping with his family. On Sunday in the summer, he and Catherine would probably do some gardening, but normally he would spend the time with Max and Claudia, catching up on what had happened in their lives during the week and taking careful notice of the tiny physical changes that had invariably taken place over the course of the week. Changes that he seldom detected during the week as more often than not he arrived home mid evening, by which time they would already be in bed.

  New important words may have been learnt during the week, now permanently committed to memory, ready to be rolled out at any opportune moment. New abilities learned, new goals achieved, old problems conquered or overcome, to crawl, then to sit up, and then for each of them,   the momentous day when they would take their first unassisted steps, and then before he knew it, they were wilfully running everywhere with gay abandon, oblivious to the vagaries, exigencies and cruelties of life.

He remembered the first day they both began to walk, a treasured memory hopefully only ever witnessed once in a child's lifetime… but in just a few days all that had changed possibly never to return.

Weekends spent in their company would be the only opportunity for him to experience the infinitesimally small changes in their characters, changes that may have taken place during that week, the refinement and development of tiny idiosyncrasies that would intractably and yet imperceptibly mark out their individuality for life.   Max was now seven and Claudia six, but already Max, who was by far the quieter of the two, much preferred to curl up in a chair with a book than watch television. He had begun to show a remarkable ability to not only read and absorb books, but to question their credibility, integrity and their validity in a world of words. He had already somewhat astutely come to the conclusion, that it was important to keep an open mind when reading anything, invariably the writer, whoever he was, would only ever postulate his personal view on the subject matter and that could be severely tainted by a lack of objectivity, undoubtedly there would always be other interpretations. Max hadn't quite put it that way, but that was the message that he had tried to convey.

Blake found this incisive observation profoundly exhilarating in one so young, especially as it was his own son. He harboured a secret desire that one day he too might come to work in the family business, in readiness for when the time came for him hand over the reins and stand back. Sometimes, he would propose outlandish or ridiculous scenarios in order to observe how Max would rationalise the argument and find the weaknesses. He found these moments to be immensely pleasurable, bringing him and Catherine great happiness, happiness far in excess of almost any other pleasure they had experience or expected in their lifetime apart that is from the joy of being with each other… but even that was now under threat.

These were the little things he would now miss, the growing up part. Yes he would still see them at weekends, but only alternately, for one weekend in two would now be spent alone, with endless hours to reflect on how things used to be. Would this change in circumstances change Max's and Claudia's view on life he wondered.

The house was eerily quiet. Catherine had mentioned before he left for his meeting, that she was going to do some shopping and would take Max and Claudia with her as Issy would have finished by then. He poured himself a large bourbon without ice and sat down in his study to mull over Prospect Road once again. After about twenty minutes he wondered back out in to the lounge and poured another large bourbon, he didn't normally drink so fast at this time of day, but the first glass didn't appear to have the dulling effect he so desperately craved. He sat back down at his desk and took a large sip from the glass and laid back in to his chair.

The room slowly began to turn and for a moment it felt like he was on a carousel ride at a travelling fair. He made a mental note to slow down his intake of whiskey, he had gulped down a glass and half in no time at all and that was never a good idea on an empty stomach. He closed his eyes for a few moments, to stop himself from feeling giddy, but that didn't seem to help. Then he noticed some of the books had started to float out of the book shelves and gently spiral around in the middle of the room, one by one different books he had published over the years came sharply into view and then withdrew to allow another to take its place. Most of the books eventually made their way back into the book shelves from whence they came leaving just three spiralling around in front of him… Prospect Road, which he knew he hadn't published yet, but he could clearly see the cover… then came The Chapter Room, he knew this one well, it had made him and Gideon very rich and then a third book hove into view… The Sacrifice of Souls…. he could just remember the title, he hadn't published the book himself, but that was the first book that Clanford and Fox had published back in the beginning of the twentieth century over seventy year ago.

It was the sale proceeds of this book that had cemented the continued existence of the company and had made Joshua Clanford and Obadiah Fox very rich. By a stroke of genius Joshua Clanford had written the book, in fact the only book he ever wrote, at just the right moment in time. The three books then seemed to morph into one single volume that then began to glow red hot before an image of Gideon appeared before him hovering in the air, with the one single volume swirling around his head. His eyes were on fire and seemed to be raging and then suddenly the book burst into flames and the image grew larger and came closer as if it were about to engulf him, but Blake fought back with all his might…

The next moment Blake was back at university wandering around outside looking confused and noticing that everybody else was staring at him. He ran up to the top of a stone steps leading in to the front entrance to the main building and then he slipped and began to slide all the way back down the stairs on his heels. When he reached the bottom he stood up still slightly bewildered and dazed. In the distance he could see a girl peddling furiously towards him. When she arrived he realised it was Catherine, but she was only eighteen years old, but he never knew her when she was eighteen and then...

'Blake.. Blake are you OK?'

Blake opened his eyes 'What?'

'Are you OK? You were asleep in your chair waving your arms about. I thought you were having a seizure or something?'

Still half dazed he looked around the room, 'I was fighting off monsters, killing the demons,' he exclaimed, his eyes look petrified.

'What?' replied Catherine, looking confused and a little concerned for his sanity.'

'I was..' then he realised what he was saying. Fighting off monsters, Christ that's for children, I'm not a child anymore, I put monsters away when I became a man, I'm no longer a child... but now he knew what he had to do, some of it had already been done, he just had to finish it off if he was to win Catherine back...

'...I was having a nap, no I must have fallen asleep and had a dream.'

'Looked like a nightmare to me,' said Catherine.

'Yes, yes it was, but I think it's nearly over now.'

'You are OK then?' said Catherine, completely missing the grammatical implication of his reply.

'Yes, yes I'm fine,' said Blake. He had to focus his mind for a few more moments, as he still wasn't a hundred percent certain where he was. Had the last few days all been a horrible nightmare, from which he had just returned or had he in fact just returned to the nightmare?

'Have you been drinking,' asked Catherine?

'Yes I did have one, possibly two,' replied Blake.

'I've told you before not to drink on an empty stomach, you know how it affects you.'

'I know, I know,' replied Blake apologetically, but he was certain he hadn't drunk that much.

'You will have to look after yourself when I'm...' she didn't finish the sentence.

Gone, thought Blake, finishing her sentence for her, that's the word, gone. Can't you bloody say it? He was feeling a little belligerent, and the bitter feelings of recriminations were beginning to well up inside, but he said nothing and just gently bit his lip.

He smiled, 'Yes of course I will and it's just like you said, I didn't eat, I was reading and I forgot.'

Catherine glanced at him, a token expression of reproach and concern flashed across her face, she may have embarked on a raging affair with Gideon, a man who she was now madly in love with, but that had not extinguished all the feelings she still had for Blake.

'I've arranged to see Gideon tonight, I hope that is alright?' It sounded almost like a request, but it was not, it was a clear declaration of intent. It was all so matter of fact for Catherine in this new relationship, it was almost as if she had been drugged or was in a trance and she was not really aware of what had happened or was going to happen or how it would affect other people. It was probably not the best of timing, mentioning this now, but sooner said the better, she thought. Now was not the time for hesitancy or indecision. The executioner who procrastinates, inflicts infinitely more pain and suffering than the one whose aim is swift and true and kills quickly with a single cut.

No confusion any longer, thought Blake, this was reality. He had returned to the nightmare, and he would have to ease back on drinking in the afternoon, that much he knew for certain. But what was that dream all about? He could recall almost every detail, every moment, it was so vivid, it can't all have been generated by alcohol he reasoned... The Sacrifice of Souls? Why had that featured in his dream, he had never given that any thought in the past, Maybe he would have to read it.

'Fine no problem,' replied Blake. For some reason Catherine's declaration of an intended adulterous liaison didn't register as being of any concern at the moment. In fact it didn't seem to register at all. There was a time when he could not have conceived hearing those words without being devastated and emotionally destroyed, but those feelings were now being held in a sort of cryogenic suspension. There were now far more pressing matters whirling around in his mind that had to be addressed.

Chapter 27

Thursday.

Catherine arrived back at the house at just after eight o'clock in the morning. It was all very quiet. It was Issy's day off. Fortunately it was half term and the children weren't up, as they didn't have to go to school. Blake had been up most of the night reading and drinking, despite the previous days reprimand, and had fallen into a deep sleep before waking up and eventually getting to bed at just after three o'clock. Catherine, had already showered at Gideon's, so she went straight to the kitchen and started to prepare breakfast.

'Breakfast in fifteen minutes,' shouted Catherine up the staircase after a few minutes, she could hear movement upstairs so she knew they were awake. Ten minutes later Max and Claudia wandered down the stairs still in their pyjamas.

'Aren't you dressed yet,' asked Catherine, it was rhetorical question which Max responded to with a confused expression, Claudia didn't answer. They smiled sweetly then dropped down into their chairs. Blake came bounding down the staircase a few minutes later, fully dressed and apparently unaffected by the previous night's drinking, but then even if he had been, he would have been ill advised to have mentioned it.

'Morning Catherine,' said Blake, smiling without a hint of reservation, it was almost as if he had forgotten everything that had happened, but he had not.

'What are you up to, asked Catherine casually, but not with any real intent? It was a suitably vague enquiry, as she was fully aware that she no longer held the franchise on asking in depth questions about his private life.

The sacrificial lamb of innocence and verity had been well and truly slaughtered on the altar of betrayal and that particular baton of privilege had now been passed firmly to Gideon.

'Nothing at all, I just feel......... I feel good.' He smiled at Max and Claudia and they returned the gesture a little warily. Catherine was still a little unsettled by Blake's tacit acceptance of the situation and it continued to quietly unnerve her that he had only once raised his voice with her over the whole dramatic rearrangement of their lives before totally embracing them with what appeared to be, to all intents and purposes, virtually no visible resistance. Blake's cheery disposition permeated through to Max and Claudia who both became almost sanguine about the whole matter. Catherine and Blake sat down at the table to a strangely enjoyable breakfast. Blake enjoyed these rare moments, he always had.

'Anymore coffee or orange anybody?' asked Catherine.

'No thanks you,' replied Max and Claudia in unison. 'Can we go over to see Uncle Gideon today.' continued Max. Blake pushed his cup and saucer over to Catherine, and as he did so he looked up into her face and she could see his expression had changed, not dramatically, but sufficiently to register some hurt deep down inside on hearing Max's plea. For a few brief moments Catherine didn't look away, but continued looking at Blake hoping that she might be able to gauge precisely what he was thinking, but for some reason she couldn't, not on this occasion. That tenuous bond, that fragile golden thread of commonality that ran between them had been surgically severed. For Catherine this was an new experience, one she had not encountered before. In the past she could usually peek inside his mind and speculate with reasonable accuracy what was going on, but not today. A miasmic haze of impregnable confusion precluded clear sight of her objective.

'I don't know, we will have to ask daddy.' They all looked at Blake.

'I have a meeting later on this morning that will take a couple of hours, so no problem for me. What time do you expect to get back?' It was a peculiar question to ask and the implications were not lost on Catherine.

'I'll just go for a few hours, so we could be back say by one o'clock if that's OK.'

'Are you staying there tonight,' asked Blake blankly?'

'No not tonight,' replied Catherine.

'OK, I see you this afternoon,' replied Blake smiling.

They cleared the breakfast things away and Max and Claudia went into the garden. Blake went into his study and opened the safe, where he still kept the manuscript for Prospect Road, he lifted it up, but didn't remove it and scrabbled around for a large old brown envelope underneath the manuscript and took it out. On the front of the envelope in a large handwritten scrawl were the words Company Documents. Underneath were a small list that had been typed onto a white label.

1) Articles of Association & memorandum.

2) Certificate of Incorporation.

3) Minutes of AGM's.

4) Share certificates.

Blake put the envelope into is leather satchel and dropped the two self-closing tags. He glanced around his study looking to see if there was anything else he needed, but having satisfied himself that he did not, he walked back out and across the hall into the kitchen, where Catherine was tidying up after breakfast.

'I be back about one all being well, the traffic shouldn't be too bad today.'

Catherine was about to ask where he was going, but for some reason changed her mind.

Chapter 28

Taylor Bedridge was one of the new breed of split discipline practices dealing with accountancy and law within the same office. Blake had found this to be of great benefit to him as it saved a considerable amount of time when dealing with the number of legal contracts and accountancy affairs for the growing number of clients, most of whom they also acted for as agents.

Many newly successful writers were unaccustomed to dealing with the financial vagaries of the publishing and writing world and directing them to John Taylor of Taylor Bedridge had solved a large number of niggling problems over the years.

John came into reception and shook Blake's hand.

'Good to see you Blake, please come on up. John led him through the labyrinth of offices up to the first floor where his office was situated.

'Take a seat,' said John pointing to a chair. John's secretary came through and asked if he would like some tea.

'Yes please,' replied Blake, 'White, two sugars, thank you.' The secretary smiled and left.

'So,' said John, 'You've intrigued me. You mentioned a disposal on the telephone, but with a rather unfamiliar prerequisite.

'In a nut shell I need to know whether it can be done without the recipient knowing,' asked Blake?

'Before I can tell you with any certainty I need to fully understand precisely what it is you want me to do, because what you are asking… well it's highly irregular to say the least, and I need to be certain I have not misunderstood your instruction. I am having to check whether it is even legal. But, on the basis of what you have told me so far, I don't think that is going to be an issue. Of more importance, as far as I am concerned are the financial implications, which to put it mildly are extremely serious and need to be very carefully considered. They will impact immeasurably on Catherine, the children, and everybody that works for you, you do realise that?'

Blake nodded, but said nothing. He was listening to every word, every syllable and absorbing the ramifications that were being painstakingly explained to him.

'The worst case scenario could see you bankrupt and losing everything you have, if whatever it is you are planning doesn't work. I have presumed that behind all of this there is a plan, a reason?' He looked emotionlessly and sternly at Blake to ensure the he fully understood what he was proposing. Now was not the time for indecision or uncertainty, there was absolutely no room for manoeuvre or recourse or retreat after the transaction had been completed.

'I fully understand everything you have said,' replied Blake, '...and if necessary I will sign a declaration exonerating you from any responsibility whatsoever for my actions.'

'Can you tell me why,' asked John?

'I can't, if I did, first you would think I had taken leave of my senses or gone mad and...

'I already think that,' said John interrupting. Blake smiled.

'...and secondly you wouldn't believe it. But I promise you this much after it is all over one way all the other I will explain... if I can... if I am able...' John was a little unnerved by the last few words, they smacked of Machiavellian melodrama, but this was no play-acting this was real, of that much he was certain.

'When do you want this matter concluded?' asked John.

'The sooner the better,' replied Blake. 'I can't break this enchantment until your part is done and I have finished my part.' It was an oddly enigmatic phrase to use, almost sounding like some sort of analogy, but of what, he had no idea.

As far as John was aware what he was being asked to do would change everything, there was nothing else.

'I will have a small document drawn up before you go it will only take a few minutes. You will need to sign it and have it witnessed by a third unconnected party and then returned to me, I will then arrange the transfer.'

'My bank is just across the road, if I have the manager witness it is that OK?' asked Blake.

'That would be fine,' said John.

Blake got up from his chair to leave, but before he had taken a second step John had jumped out of his chair and quickly walked around the desk to grab hold of Blake's hand and as he did so he put his other arm around Blake's shoulders and pulled him close to hold him in a tight embrace. Blake embraced him back, he needed an ally right now and John was there when he needed him, he would not forget.

'Be careful my friend,' said John, 'I have a very odd feeling about all this, will I see you again afterwards?'

'Of course you will, it may be a while, but you will.'

John smiled. 'If there is anything else just let me know, we have been friends for a long time and...'

'Thank you,' said Blake,. 'but you will have done enough.'

John said nothing, but clasped Blake's hand with both his hands and shook it one more time. Blake left the office to return home.

Chapter 29

Thursday afternoon.

Blake arrived back at the house at just after one, but Catherine had not yet returned. He went into his study and picked up the telephone and called the office.

'Hi Carol, could you put me through to Jamie,'

'No problem Blake,' replied Carol, there was a short delay while the extension rang.

'Blake,' said Jamie, 'How are you?'

'Not too bad, sorry I haven't been in this week, but something cropped up.'

'No problem, we just about managing the empire without you, but we will need you next week there's a few..'

Blake interrupted, 'Jamie I have something very important to ask you to do.'

'Yes,' replied Jamie, 'you're the boss.'

'I know this is going to ridiculous and it won't make any sense at all, but I need you to do something for me.'

'No problem,' said Jamie enthusiastically.

'Well you don't know what it is yet,' said Blake.

'You want me to murder somebody?' asked Jamie.

'No,' replied Jamie, it's not that bad.'

'Right,' said Jamie, 'Then it's not a problem.'

'The company published a book many years ago, it's still on our back catalogue for occasion reprints; it was a big seller back around the early 1900's.' It's called A Sacrifice of Souls.

'You want be to get a copy from the archive?' asked Jamie.

'No… it's a little more than that, I want you arrange for a small reprint run of say one copy.'

'One copy? The printers can't print one copy, I think the minimum is a hundred copies,' replied Jamie, 'but we probably have a few copies somewhere that haven't been pulped.'

'I will have to have a hundred then. There's going to be some small amendments, so we will need a new print run.'

'No problem,' said Jamie, 'Are there many changes or can you tell me over the phone.'

'I'll fax over the details. How long will it take?' asked Blake.

'If it is still on their reprint list a few days maybe a week.'

'Good,' said Blake. I'll send over the details as soon as I've finished this call and leave it with you to arrange, oh and I won't be in till Wednesday or Thursday next week, very busy here for a few days.'

'No problem,' said Jamie. 'Hopefully we will have the reprints here by then.'

'That would be good,' said Blake. 'Thank you.'

'No problem,' said Jamie, 'anything else?'

'No, no thank you, I leave it with you.'

'See you next week then,' said Jamie.

'Yes next week, bye, bye,' his mind seemed to be somewhere else.

Blake put the phone down and slipped a single sheet of paper he had previously typed into the fax machine and punched in the office fax number. The machine made some funny noises, then the sheet of paper slowly disappeared from sight. He sat back in his chair and wondered what next week would bring. Had he set something in motion, something that would have been better left alone, maybe it would all come to nothing and this was all a tremendous waste of time and effort, but then maybe not.

The whole thing was based on a whimsically capricious notion that had come to him in a dream and he began to wonder if maybe he had read too many stories over the years and he was now confusing reality and life with make-believe.

Whatever the possible outcome would be, he couldn't sit around and wait, he had to take a chance, life is about taking risks, the important thing was whether the gain was worth the risk. He didn't really have any option, and anyway it was all in the lap of the Gods now, everything was. There was never any going back.

There was however just one last thing he had to do.

Chapter 30

Friday.

Blake awoke early on the Friday, once again he didn't sleep much during the night. The imminent departure of his family and the plan he had now set in motion all playing on his mind. Over and over again he replayed the possible scenarios in his head. He was as certain as he could be that the likeliest outcome was the most probable outcome. But that still didn't alleviate the unmistakeable feeling of trepidation, foreboding and fear… but fear of what precisely, that is what he kept asking himself, the unknown, the conclusion that he had not considered, the reaction from Gideon that he had not factored into the equation, all these played on his mind. Each one taking its turn in the forefront of his mind before slowly slipping out of view to be replaced by the next.

During dinner the night before, Catherine had mentioned that she wanted to start packing up some of her clothing and personal things today and some of Max and Claudia's clothes. She had arranged for a number of large cardboard boxes to be delivered on the Friday so that she could make a start and hopefully finish it over the weekend. She had also arranged for a removal lorry to transfer the boxes over to Gideon's house on Monday morning.

'Is there anything you want me to do?' asked Blake. It was a situation he clearly didn't know how to respond to. He was floundering a little, endeavouring to ascertain what exactly the correct etiquette was, under the circumstances.

Should he assist his wife who was about to leave him and thereby effectively become an accomplice by default in the conspiracy to break up his marriage, or should he stand back and let her do everything, which seemed the more natural and yet belligerently unaccommodating option. He just didn't know.

'No, we can manage,' said Catherine. She felt as awkward as he did. 'Look I know this is very distressing for you, why don't go out for a few hours while I make a start on this, it might be a little less traumatic for all of us if...?'

Oh great, thought Blake, you want me to bugger of and sit in the pub and get drunk all day while you pillage and plunder the remnants of my life, our life. He knew she wouldn't do anything unreasonable or remove any item that meant something to both of them, but nevertheless he was well aware that once she had concluded what she was doing there would be little spaces and voids everywhere. Where once sat a familiar photograph or a curio, a memory of different times, happier times, there would now be a void, something would become conspicuous by its very absence.

Fundamentally, each room would still look the same. Only when subjected to closer examination would the subtle idiosyncrasies that make the dwelling space of each one of us unique be noticed. Only then would each room appear to have lost something, something that had once made it warm and welcoming. Each room now a few shades closer to the cold clinical detached colour of a hotel room. The aura and the atmosphere of a house occupied by a family of four would be demonstrably and immeasurably different to that of a house occupied by a lonely man. Nothing could hide that.

'I have a few things to do as it is,' said Blake, 'so we can have breakfast and then I'll leave you to it.'

'That would be good,' said Catherine, I'll put some coffee on.

They sat at the table and ate toast and drank coffee in silence, for there was little more to say. Just as they finished Max came downstairs.

'We are going on a long holiday to Uncle Gideon's,' said Max.

'And me,' said Claudia, suddenly appearing from nowhere.'

'"We" means all of us,' retorted Max, 'except daddy, he's not coming, he is staying here to look after our house.'

The innocent words almost immediately reduced Blake to tears. He hurriedly left the room, so as not to let his children see him crying.

'You will both be coming to see daddy is looking after our house every week,' said Catherine in a slightly louder voice to ensure it carried a little further in an attempt to lessen the pain that had been unintentionally inflicted.

Our house, thought Blake, was that a gentle hint that it was jointly owned, he wondered, possibly an overture before impending matrimonial proceedings. Divorce? He hadn't even considered that aspect yet, but they would have to discuss it before long, living in some sort of suspended animation was not an option. Even that possibility was subject to the consequential outcome of his arrangements and he had no idea at all as to how this all might end despite what he had done.

Blake went back into the kitchen.

'Right, I'm popping out for a few hours, be back around two, OK?'

'Yes said Catherine, I can only do so much each day I am feeling…' she didn't finish, but Blake knew what she was trying to say. He kissed Max and Claudia and left.

The weekend passed with little incident. Catherine carried on packing her boxes and as the sun shone most of the time, Blake sat in the garden and read and Max and Claudia played.

Chapter 31

Monday.

On the Monday morning the removal people rang very early to say there lorry had broken down and would it be convenient to make the collection on Wednesday. That was the day that Catherine had intended to move out anyway so she agreed to the rescheduled arrangement. She made a telephone call to Gideon to tell him about the rearrangement and said she would pop over that night.

During the afternoon there were a couple of telephone calls.

'Blake,' shouted Catherine from the house, 'It's Jamie at the office.' Blake made his way back to the house and picked up the receiver.

'Jamie?'

'Hi Blake, how are you?'

'Fine, taking in the sunshine at the moment.'

'Sounds good. It's horrible up here, the air cons broken and it's as stuffy as hell on a busy day.'

Hell on a busy day, thought Blake... good name for a book... he never really switched off. 'How can I help you?'

'That book "A Sacrifice of Souls" they've arrived, what do you want me to do with them?'

'Ah,' said Blake mulling over the options, 'I could come up tomorrow, yes that would be best, can't trust the post as I need them by Wednesday.'

'Are you sure?' said Jamie.

'Yes, yes I am I need to pop into to see John at Taylor Bedridge, so I can kill two birds with one stone.'

'Fair enough I'll see you tomorrow, enjoy the day.' Jamie hung up and Blake stood for a few moments with the receiver still in his hand pondering over how he would stage manage the next part of the plan.

'Did I hear you say you were going to London tomorrow?'

'Yes, so I'll be out for most of the day.'

'Would it be OK if I took Max and Claudia over to Clanford House for the day, as you won't be here?' asked Catherine cautiously. For some reason she didn't say "Gideon's," but simply referred to the house by name, somehow it seemed less offensive, less of another shard of humiliation tearing into his flesh to avoid using his name, '…if you don't want me to I….' she began.

'No problem,' interrupted Blake, 'I won't be here so.. what time do you think you might be back?' It was all very civilised and adult, but somehow still smacked of falsehood and treachery, those thoughts were never really far from his mind. Not Catherine or the children, they were innocent parties, nothing more than convenient bystanders to Gideon and his devious machinations, pawns in the game of life he was now playing. Gideon was the instigator, the controlling personality the man he had to confront, the man he would eventually have to face when the last cards was to be played.

Chapter 32

Tuesday.

Catherine woke early and went down to the kitchen to make Blake some strong coffee, which was her normal routine if he was going to London. Blake was already dressed and sitting at the table reading the newspaper.

'Can I speak to you for five minutes?' asked Blake, which seemed a little odd as they were drinking coffee together. But the inference was that he wanted to discuss something of significance.

'Off course,' said Catherine looking a little guarded.

'Look this is a bit embarrassing, but I would like to ask you to do something for me.'

'What?' said Catherine.

'When you next see Gideon could you discuss whether he would be prepared to set up some sort of arrangement to protect you and the children until such times as the divorce comes through and I presume you get married. Just in case something happens in the...

Catherine interrupted, 'He's already done so.'

'He has?' queried Blake.

'Yes. He has changed his will so that if anything happens to him we will be provided for, I know you would not see us starve or be without a roof over our heads, but I didn't want to take the house or half the business from you that wouldn't be fair and Gideon has agreed.

'So you have already discussed this,' said Blake.

'Yes, yes I have, I thought it was important to get that sorted out as quickly as possible to avoid aggravation later.

'Oh I see,' said Blake.

'In the event of his death...' she paused momentarily just too allow the word sink in, it was so emotive, 'he has left everything he has to me and the children, he has no other family so, you have nothing to worry about.'

'Good, good.' said Blake. I'm relieved by that, it has been playing on my mind a bit. Catherine smiled at his continued concern for her, then thought about what he had said and realised just how hard that must have been.

'Looks like a nice day to go to the office,' said Catherine gazing out the window and changing the subject. It was a comment simply to fill time, superfluous packing, irrelevant but that's how it is sometimes.

Blake smiled, finished his coffee, stood up and leaned forward instinctively to kiss her, before suddenly withdrawing and apologising profusely. Just for a fraction of a second his brain had temporarily disconnected itself from reality.

He quickly put his jacket on, grabbed his leather bag and left without saying another word. Catherine went back to bed for an hour mulling over the odd moment in the kitchen.

Blake arrived at the office at just after ten o'clock. He greeted everybody with his customary smile as he passed through reception and the front office to his own office at the back. He sat down at in the old brown leather chair, the chair he stubbornly refused to replace, the chair that Reggie Clanford, his predecessor had used and the one he had always considered to be his lucky chair, the one he sat in whenever he made major decisions. It had also served him well so far. He looked at the silver framed photograph of Catherine and the children, the present she had given him on his thirty fourth birthday, a time when everything had been perfect. He smiled for a moment at the memory and then the smile disappeared, replaced by one of a sullen and angry tormented soul. Jamie popped in.

'Hi Blake, good to see you, everything good?' asked Jamie

'Getting there,' replied Blake.

'The book, it's over there.' Jamie pointed to three boxes next to one of the bookshelves, 'I put one on your desk, for you to check the changes.'

'How come the..'

Blake interrupted, 'it's a long story, a very, very long story, I will explain it to you soon, just not today if that's OK.'

Jamie looked intrigued by Blake's entreaty and left it at that.

'I'll get you a coffee,' said Jamie.

'That would be great, I want to read this just once more.' He took out the tattered manuscript for Prospect Road from his bag and laid in on the desk alongside a copy of The Chapter Room by Gideon Drew, which had now sold over thirty million copies in hardback and paperback. Then he pulled across a brand new edition of A Sacrifice of Souls, a novel by Gideon Drew. Inside the book on the second page there was a small addendum and corrigendum, something never seen before in any of Clanford and Fox's published works.

Corrigendum

When this book was originally published, the author was stated as being Joshua Clanford. The publishers at that time had no reason to doubt the veracity or the integrity of that claim of authorship and no counterclaim or objection was ever received by the publishing company by any other party claiming authorship. The publishers therefore proceeded with the publication of the recognized work in the full and honest belief that it should be fully attributed to the pen of Joshua Clanford.

However, further investigations by Clanford and Fox Publishers during 1983-1984 revealed serious doubts on the author's original claim and these have now been fully substantiated. We are now certain beyond any doubt whatsoever that this book was unequivocally and indisputably written by Mr Gideon Drew in 1911 and we now acknowledge Gideon Drew as the true author of this work. We humbly apologise to any living members of the family of Mr Gideon Drew for any personal pain, suffering, anguish and contempt they may have suffered or which may have been caused by this error.

We are now pleased to acknowledge Mr Gideon Drew as the true author of this book. Prescribed copies for libraries and institutions will be replaced with the corrected edition in order to fully authenticate the copyright.

Blake Thornton

Clanford and Fox Publishers and Publishing Agents.

About three o'clock in the afternoon Blake had a call put through to him from Taylor Bedridge. John confirmed the transaction had been completed and the details lodged at Companies House.

Chapter 33

Tuesday.

Blake arrived back home at just after five o'clock, to be greeted by Max and Claudia at the front door. He kissed them both, took of his shoes, dropped his bag on the chair by the front door and walked hand in hand with them into the lounge.

'We have had a lovely day at Uncle's Gideon's, and we are going to stay there for a holiday from tomorrow,' said Max. Claudia smiled in agreement, however she seemed a little subdued, definitely not as jubilant as Max appeared to be.

'Will you be coming with us daddy?' asked Claudia.

'No, no I won't. I have a lot of work to do here and I'm very busy at work, but I am sure you will have a wonderful time.' Claudia seemed oddly reserved and a little disappointed.

'I love you daddy,' said Claudia out of the blue. It was simple and plaintive and honest and it hurt like hell. Blake felt a lump come up in his throat, and he knew immediately that despite her tender years Claudia had managed to detect something was amiss by the tone of his voice.

Like all women, she had an inbuilt highly developed sixth sense, a natural instinct that told her when something wasn't quite right, but she still didn't quite know what it was. Max had missed the hidden engender altogether, but then men often do.

'Gideon has a swimming pool,' said Max

'Has he,' replied Blake, 'well that will be great fun for the summer.' He was just going through the motions for their sake. He refused to put a dampener on Max and Claudia's expectations, they had done no wrong and they didn't understand what was going on. There was no way that he could ruin their expectations just because his life had been virtually destroyed, that would be selfish and callous to say the least and he would not stoop that low no matter what.

They all sat down to what was effectively their last meal together, a quite affair, with Catherine not saying much at all. After dinner Blake went to his study to carry on reading A Sacrifice of Souls, while Catherine, Max and Claudia watched television. Max and Claudia went to bed at around seven thirty and Catherine carried on watching the television, more as a distraction then for the content, before putting her head round the corner of Blake's room and saying goodnight before heading off to bed at nine thirty.

'Do you have a few minutes Catherine?' asked Blake.

Catherine looked a little surprised as they had had plenty of time to discuss anything he wanted to talk about over dinner, but he had not raised any topics instead he had remained relatively subdued.

'Yes, of course,' she replied. She entered his study and sat down.

'I'm not going to lecture you or anything, you know how I feel about what is happening, but there are some things I think you should know.' Catherine looked a little uncomfortable as she had half expected something like this at some stage, but due to the proximity of her departure she had anticipated that it probably wasn't going to happen.

Catherine acknowledged what he said.

'There is something very unusual about Gideon, something I can't explain, something you need to know.'

Once again, Catherine said nothing, but acknowledged what he was saying with a half-smile in anticipation of some kind of revelation.

'I don't know who Gideon is,' said Blake.

'I don't understand,' said Catherine, You're his agent, his publisher and a sort of friend until.. he's a writer, a good one as it turns out and a nice person, he gets on well with the kids, he has a nice house, what is there to know?' Catherine sounded a little confused by Blake's statement.

'Gideon wrote another book…'

'He hasn't mentioned that,' said Catherine.

'It was a very successful book sold millions of copies,' said Blake.

'Are you sure? asked Catherine now sounding a little intrigued.

'Why have you never mentioned it, I thought you said The Chapter Room was his first novel.'

'That's what I thought, until I did some research and also of course the book is mentioned in "Prospect Road".

Catherine became slightly subdued for a few moments as she recalled the self-writing manuscript they had both been reading a few months earlier, that manuscript that had predicted various events in the future as well as describing the parallel lives of two people who seemed to be very similar to her and Blake.

'I thought we had agreed that that was all coincidence an example of literary synchronicity,' replied Catherine defensively.

'Possibly it is, but "A Sacrifice of Souls" isn't.

'A Sacrifice of Souls,' repeated Catherine.

'That's the first book that Gideon wrote.'

'How come I've never heard of it?' replied Catherine now having a few doubts on the accuracy of what he was saying.

'He wrote it some time ago,' replied Blake, 'In fact quite a long time ago.. in or around 1910.'

'What do you mean 1910, that's nearly seventy five years ago. You must have got him muddled up with someone else, someone with the same name, maybe his father, well no it would have to be his…' she thought for a moment, working out the possibilities in her head , 'No that would have to have been his great grandfather, that's who must of written it.'

Blake said nothing at first, he let Catherine run her mind over what she had just said.

'We published the book.' said Blake.

'You... how,' replied Catherine?

'Not me precisely, but Clanford and Fox, it was the first book they ever published, but originally the author was stated as being Mr Joshua Clanford, the original owner of the publishing business. He stole the book from a Gideon Drew and published it under his own name.

'But why? said Catherine.

'Money,' replied Blake, just money, it's as simple as that.'

'How do you know all this?'

'It's in the final chapters of Prospect Road, but more importantly… if you ask Gideon, I doubt very much if he will deny it.'

'So what happens now?'

'Well nothing much, I have redressed the matter of the true identity of the writer and I have had a new amended edition printed with an apology for what happened, on behalf of the company.' Blake leaned down to the floor and with some trepidation he lifted up a copy of A Sacrifice of Souls, and placed it on the desk in front of Catherine.

'It's not a bad book I read it over the few days.'

Catherine picked up the book and handled it with some care looking at the front cover and flicking through the pages. 'I should give this to Gideon.'

'You should, it rights a lot of wrongs,' agreed Blake.

'Will he be pleased, do you think? asked Catherine.

'I think his tormented soul will at last be at peace,' replied Blake.

'Do you think so?' asked Catherine sounding a little unsure as to what he meant.

'I know so.' replied Blake.

'But what about the year's thing, that still doesn't make any sense to me.'

'I am sure Gideon will explain everything to you if you ask him, what reason would he have not to?' asked Blake. he said the words as if he didn't have an explanation either, but he did have one, but one he was not inclined to discuss today, or any day for that matter, so he didn't mention it.

'Thank you Blake, for what you have done, you didn't have to do this, I realise that, but it will make such a difference to Gideon, I know that.'

'I know that to,' said Blake, 'I know that to,' he repeated quietly. Catherine went to bed and Blake poured himself a large bourbon and sat back in his old green leather captain's chair and thought about what he had done and what might possibly now happen, but he didn't know for sure, in fact he had no idea at all, it was now all in the lap of the Gods.

Chapter 34

Wednesday.

The removal lorry arrived at eight o'clock on the dot and once the three men had had a cup of tea they commenced removing all the cardboard boxes that Catherine had so carefully packed. Blake sat in the garden while they did their work, drinking coffee and reading the newspaper. He appeared to be unconcerned about what was happening appearing almost sanguine about the whole matter. When they had finished the lorry drove off and Catherine came out into the garden with Max and Claudia to say goodbye.

'We'll going now,' said Catherine.

Blake jumped up, actually appearing a little surprised.

'Oh right, well you all take it easy, and don't work too hard today unpacking and things, there's plenty of time to do all that in the weeks ahead, I hope it all goes well.' He leaned forward to pick up Claudia and gave her a tight cuddle and kissed her, and then he picked up Max..

'Now you two have got to be strong little soldiers today and help mummy, as she is going to be very busy in your new house, do you promise me?'

'Yes dad,' replied an extremely confused Max. 'I don't understand what's happening dad?'

'Mummy will explain everything to you, there is nothing to worry about.' That seemed to reassure him and put his mind at rest. Blake smiled at Catherine.

'I love you both, don't forget that,' and looking up at Catherine he said, 'I love you too Catherine always remember that, no matter what happens in the future I will always love you.' It sounded a little ominous to Catherine and she gave him an odd look.

'You are going to be alright aren't you?'

'Yes, I will be fine, you are the one setting out on the adventure into the unknown, not me.' That seemed to satisfy Catherine's concerns. She kissed him on the cheek and then she left with Max and Claudia walking out of the Garden for the last time.

It must have been around eight o'clock in the evening when Blake drove up the driveway of Clanford House. It was a very imposing driveway with Copper Beech trees on both sides. Blake had always favoured the Copper Beech because of its unique Golden reddish brown leaves in summer, which reminded him of something, but he couldn't remember what at that particular moment. He parked the car and grabbed the envelope laying on the passenger seat. He looked up at the beautiful Georgian styled mansion house in front of him a magnificent building and he wondered about the things that must have happened there when Joshua had been in residence.

He rang the front door bell and waited to see who would open the door. Would it be Max he wondered as he normally did so at home, but it was not, it was Gideon.

'Blake, I wasn't expecting you,' said Gideon looking surprised, 'Do come in the children would love to see you. I'm not sure where they are at the moment but…'

Blake interrupted, 'No I'm not staying, I've just brought this around, it's rightfully yours and you deserve it for everything you have suffered over the years.'

Gideon looked a little perplexed, 'What is it?' he asked with a measure of atrophied ambivalence.

'I am sure you will understand. Hopefully it will bring you what you seek.'

'Sounds very enigmatic,' replied Gideon, somewhat reluctantly holding his hand out to take the envelope, 'it's not a writ is it?'

'No it's not, it's a gift,' said Blake smiling, 'just a gift for your new life together, that's all.'

'So what do you mean by, "all I have suffered over the years", I wasn't aware that I had suffered anything,' asked Gideon curiously.

'Haven't you?' asked Blake sounding unrealistically surprised, 'I think you have endured a great deal, the loss of your wife, the death of your daughter, the theft of your book and probably a few other things along the way, and of course the ultimate loss of your soul. I think at some moment in your life you reached a point when there was nothing more to live for and then somebody made you proposition that was too good to be true, so what did you have to loose….? so you took it, but now maybe I think you regret that decision and you're looking for salvation. All this retribution has cost you far more than you anticipated.

Gideon's expression changed.

'I think you've got the wrong end of the stick old chap,' replied Gideon now resorting to a mildly condescending tone.

'You think so?' said Blake.

'Yes I do,' said Gideon firmly.

'Well that's your prerogative, maybe I am wrong and if so, I apologise, but enjoy the gift anyway. Did Catherine give you the other item I gave her to give to you?' enquired Blake casually.

'No, she hasn't given me anything yet, but it has been a bit hectic here today with the moving in as you can imagine so maybe…'

'Yes, maybe later, anyway,' replied Blake.

Gideon cautiously took the envelope. 'Thank you Blake.'

'No problem, speak soon, ' He turned and began to walk back down the steps and across to his car.

'Blake!' said Gideon, shouting after him, just as he reached his car.

Blake turned, 'Yes.'

'This other Gideon person you speak of, my namesake,'

'Yes,' said Blake quietly, he now knew for certain he was right, this was the moment he had waited for.

'Do you think he loved his wife?'

Blake stared at Gideon for a moment deliberating over the question and the many other questions buried deep within the words, and slowly walked back a few steps to stand at the bottom of the steps and look up at Gideon standing at the top.

'Of course he loved her, he loved her more than anything in the world, and they had a daughter and he loved her too, he loved them more than life itself.'

'Than why was he so bitter?'

'Because there is no going back, no matter what the deal was, he was never going to see his wife or daughter again. That's why he is bitter, probably why he spent his life taking revenge on…. '

'Can he be saved?' interrupted Gideon

'I don't know, only he knows that, only he knows the terms of the arrangement.'

'The arrangement?' asked Gideon, 'What was this arrangement?'

'A Sacrifice, A Sacrifice of Souls,' replied Blake, 'that's what I think it was.'

'Oh,' said Gideon, 'I see. 'Do you think he was a good person?'

'I don't know, I imagine he was once, he didn't appear to be an inherently bad person, it was just some terrible things happened to him, they changed him, made him different….

He smiled. 'Well thank you Blake.'

'No problem any time, bye.'

Gideon shut the door and Blake walked back to his car.

He sat looking at the house for a few minutes before driving back home. He had done all he could. He had read Prospect Road and The Sacrifice of Souls over and over and he was sure he was right, but only time would tell now.

Chapter 35

'Who was at the door darling,' asked Catherine standing in the kitchen making tea.

'Oddly, it was Blake.' Gideon was holding some documents in his hands.

'What did he want, not a problem was it?'

'No far from it, actually I'm a little confused.'

'Why?' asked Catherine.

'Well you're not going to believe this, but he appears to have transferred all the shares in Clanford and Fox Publishing over to me,' said Gideon, still reading through the documentation.

'What,' exclaimed Catherine, coming into the dining room carrying a tray with two cups of tea.

'All of them, every share.'

'To you! but that doesn't make any sense, I could possibly understand it if he had transferred them to us, but to you?' she placed one cup of tea on the table next to where Gideon was sitting and the other on the small table next to her chair.

'He has written me letter explaining why,' said Gideon.

'Read it out, I'm intrigued,' said Catherine, 'or more accurately totally confused.' She sat down and took a sip of the tea.

Dear Gideon and Catherine,

I apologise for what may appear to be my rather odd behaviour with regards to the share transfer, but I will endeavour to explain why.

Many years ago a Gideon Drew wrote a very successful book, which was subsequently stolen by the original owners of Clanford and Fox, they claimed they had written it not Gideon Drew and they stole all the royalties, which were quite considerable at the time, it was a very popular book. Not long after book was published, Gideon's daughter became very ill with tuberculosis and needed some expensive treatment in Switzerland to save her, but Gideon had no money and so he couldn't afford to send her and she eventually died. The death broke his and his wife's heart and not long after this his wife left him cursing him for being such a fool and she died of a broken heart two years later.

Gideon disappeared for a number of years before resurfacing once again now a rich and successful businessman.

Now I don't know how exactly, but Mr Anthony Theodore Clackle found out about this and wrote about it in his book, but then he found out something else.

He realised that somehow this Gideon Drew character never seemed to age, and then Anthony came up with this ridiculous theory, which was that Gideon had sold his soul in order to buy him sufficient time to get back, that which was stolen from him in the first place. That was the money that would have been rightfully been his had the book not been stolen. Anthony believed that returning the stolen book and the wealth that Clanford and Fox had falsely acquired, or in essence the company itself, would effectively partially complete the contract you made so that is what I have done because that is what I believe Anthony was trying to tell me, before he died.

Gideon, you now own Clanford and Fox Publishers and when Catherine gives you what I gave her you will once again be reinstated as the author of A Sacrifice of Souls and hopefully your trials will now be over. Your wife and daughter cannot be replaced, but I believe that is why you have taken Catherine, Claudia and Max.

I believe your contract has now been completed in full and you must now pay the price.

Kind regards
Blake Thornton

Gideon held up the documents,

'These are all the share certificates for the company,' said Gideon holding up the documents,' looking a little stunned.

Catherine jumped out of her chair and left the room. Gideon thought that maybe she was upset at Blake's actions, but when she came back a few minutes later holding a book, she displayed no sign of distress or annoyance, in fact just the opposite. She passed the book she was holding to Gideon and smiled. 'And that, I believe is your book,' she smiled, believing she had done something to please him. 'but I still don't quite understand the last part of Blake's letter, what does that mean?'

Gideon looked up at Catherine, a look of complete and absolute fear in his eyes. His hand slowly, inexorably snaked out towards the book, despite his attempts not to reach out. He appeared to have temporarily lost control of his body as his hand edged ever closer to the tome in Catherine's hand before eventually grasping it tightly with his right hand. At that very moment his eyes began to shine, much brighter than they had ever shone before, the colour slowing segueing from crystal blue to a terrifying flaming red. He stood up, his whole body now beginning to shake uncontrollably, his eyes now much larger and much brighter than before, and he slowly began to levitate a few inches from the floor, his whole body no longer under his control. Catherine could see he was visibly beginning to age and at just as this strange metamorphosis was taking place Max and Claudia came into the room and seeing what was happening before their eyes they ran over to Catherine screaming out 'what is happening to Uncle Gideon mummy?... what is happening.'

Chapter 36

Thursday.

There was a knock on the door at just after nine o'clock. Blake had only just got up, he'd had rather a lot to drink the night before and he was still feeling a bit hazy.

There were two policeman standing at the door, both looking very sombre.

'Mr Blake Thornton?' asked the first one.

'Yes,' replied Blake.

'I'm Inspector Charlton and this is Constable Wainwright.

'Can we come in for a moment sir?'

'Of course, come on through.' He made his way into the lounge and pointed at two chairs. 'Please sit down,'

'Would you like to sit down sir, we have a couple questions we need to ask,' said Inspector Charlton

'Oh right, OK,' Blake sat down.

'I understand you live here with your wife and two children?' asked the Inspector.

'I do, or should I say did, but she moved out, yesterday in fact, why?'

'Do you know where she moved to?' asked Wainwright referring to his notebook.

'Yes, just up the road Clanford House, the big place on…'

'Yes sir, we know where it is,' interrupted the Inspector.

'On her own?' asked Wainwright.'

'To live with another man if you must know.'

'Do you know who this man was?' asked wainwright.

'Look where is all this going?' said Blake, suddenly noticing the use of the past tense.

'There's been an accident.'

'An accident, what kind of accident, is somebody injured?'

'I'm afraid I have some bad news sir, you see there was a fire at Clanford House last night, everybody in the house died, nobody...' he hesitated a little longer on the word, then repeated it, '...nobody was rescued alive.' He was possibly overstating the situation, but in his experience it paid to be precise as it quickly disposed of any suggestion of doubt, ambiguity or misunderstanding with regards to the possibility of any survivors.

'Who exactly died,' asked Blake.,

'Four people, three of whom we believe to be your Wife, Catherine Thornton and your two children Max and Claudia Thornton and an as yet unidentified person who we believe may be Mr Gideon Drew.

Blake said nothing, stunned into disbelief. This wasn't how he had anticipated it would end, he thought Blake might die, that was always a possibility, but not Catherine, Max and Claudia, that shouldn't have happened, that can't have happened, that can't be possible. Had he got completely wrong... his mind started to whirl around utterly confused by what he was hearing.

'We obviously need to have them formally identified by you if possible, but there is little doubt that it is them. We can't seem to locate any relatives for Mr Drew, but then there is virtually nothing left to identify, except for a wedding ring. Mr Drew appears to have been at the epicentre of the fire, it looked almost as if he spontaneously burst into flames and that had quickly engulfed the whole house. There is no evidence of any accelerant being used so it seems to be an accident of some sort, but the fire office has no explanation at this stage as to how it started. We will have his full report in a few days.'

'I am very sorry to have to bring you this news, but...' Blake interrupted Inspector Charlton.

'I understand, what you have to do. When do you want me to come down and identify my family?'

'Tomorrow would be fine, I will send a car, say eleven o'clock is that OK?"

'Thank you.' replied Blake.

'Do you have anybody that could come round or I could arrange for somebody to come and stay with you for a ..'

'No, that won't be necessary,' replied Blake, 'I have a friend I can call, he'll come straight over.'

The two officers got up and Blake showed them out.

It was brief, it was explicit and yet it didn't sound quite right, there was something missing, but he didn't know what. He went over the drinks cabinet in the corner and poured himself a very large Jack Daniels and took a very large gulp, the impact was almost instantaneous. He poured another large glass, sat down and began to think back over everything that had happened, once again he came back to Prospect Road and all it had predicted, but it never mentioned this. But would it have made any difference if it had, would he have taken any notice he wondered. He would have to read it one more time, but then what good would that do now. Maybe he should burn it, that would stop it forever, yes that's what he would do, it had all started with that manuscript and now he needed to finish it. He would take it out the safe and burn it in the garden, that would finish everything, but then everything was finished anyway. He swallowed his drink, then got up and went over to the drinks cabinet and took out the bottle and sat back down again and poured himself another drink. He needed oblivion right now and this was the quickest route.

He took another gulp and his head began to spin slowly, and he almost immediately fell unconscious. This time when he woke it wasn't Catherine waking him from a bad dream, he was sitting at the bottom of some stone steps leading up to what looked like the main door to one of the lecture halls at his old university. Looking around he realised he must have just fallen down the steps so he struggled to his feet and looked around trying to familiarize himself as to exactly where he was.

In the distance, he could see something coming towards him out of the shimmering misty summer haze. It was very indistinct at first, but as the vision drew closer, he could see it was a girl on a bicycle peddling frantically towards him.

When she eventually pulled up with a squeal of brakes and a scattering of shingle in front of where Blake was standing, she smiled and dropped her bicycle on the ground.

'Are you OK, I saw you fall down the steps?

'Yes, yes I'm fine thank you, I just tripped. Do I know you?'

'Yes of course you do. You are a silly arse Thornton, we made love last night, have you forgotten already? Is this is the effect I have on you?' declared Catherine indignantly, 'then it's not very complimentary.'

'No, of course not,' replied Blake, 'I'm just a bit dazed.'

'Dazed or dazzled by my beauty?' asked Catherine playfully twirling around and around.

'Intoxicated by your resplendent intractability,' replied Blake, with a grin.

'I'm not sure what that actually means,' said Catherine.

'I'm in love with you Miss Gayle,' explained Blake, that is what it means.

'Oh, I see, right well are you coming to the lecture or are you sodding around here all day?

'I'm coming to the lecture,' replied Blake.

'Right, good,' said Catherine. She picked up her bicycle and began to cycle away. Looking back, she shouted...

'If you can catch me Thornton... you can have my body... later.' She turned back and continued riding away.

'Wait! Shouted Blake, 'wait for me... don't leave me behind Catherine... not this time... not ever again.' He hit the play button on his Sony Walkman clipped to his belt and Billy Joel's "It's All about Soul" started to play. He smiled, then he laughed and then he jumped onto his bike and peddled after her as fast as he could ride.

The End

Proof

Made in the USA
Charleston, SC
12 July 2015